Behind Lace Curtains

A Novel

"Thus he will come to see with his spiritual eyes a number of sparks shining through day by day and more and more and growing into such a great light that thereafter all things needful to him will be made known."

Gerhard Dorn, "*De Speculative Philosophia*," in Theatrum Chemicum .(Ursek, 1602), Vol. I, p. 275.

Cauchemar Media LLC

COPYRIGHT

Cauchemar Media LLC
P.O. Box 176
Eunice, Louisiana USA

BEHIND LACE CURTAINS

Of all things real
      or not,
of all things that hide
      behind brick walls,
or leer at us
      from behind lace curtains,

the soul is the ultimate hostage.

Walls of substance
      separate minds
condemning souls
      to screaming solitude,
entombed
      in prisons
          of flesh.

Dance.

Dance alone.

Part One

Initiation

Chapter 1

NEW YORK CITY LOOMED in shades of grey.

Across the street, shadow forms hidden under dark coats hustled along the sidewalk, back and forth, like phantoms in a carnival shooting gallery. Sometimes a colorful scarf or hat caught Jacoby Preston's eye, breaking the monochromatic display. But only for a moment. He kept his focus on their eyes, searched for a look of recognition just in case one of *them* had finally come for him.

It was time.

Trudging toward his favorite Chinese restaurant, he hid behind the coarse black wool of his turned-up collar. A bitter wind flashed down the street, scattered discarded handbills and empty cigarette packs. Jake tightened his grip on the envelope of photographs tucked under his arm.

A taxi rocketed around the corner, forcing a crescent of dirty water from a puddle. It lashed Jake's legs and coat, leaving behind a sooty trail. He frowned, kept his head down, and continued toward his meeting with Fred.

The neon glow from the sign above the China Flower Restaurant crept into Jake's line of vision and lured him into a haven of red and black. A blood-red smile painted across the ashen face of an Asian waitress greeted him. She bowed and led him to a black-lacquered table in a far corner of the dining room. Fred waited for him behind an undulating whisper of steam that snaked out of a pot of green tea.

"Jake, been playing in the street?" Fred forced a stilted laugh and poured two cups of tea.

Jake placed the envelope on the table and removed his coat. He shook some of the splatters of soot from his coat, then carefully

1

draped it over the back of his chair and sat. The two parallel lines between Fred's olive green eyes drew together as he pulled at his wiry mustache. Something was wrong. Jake held the hot cup of tea in his hands and savored its warmth.

"So, what's up, Fred? What do you have for me?" He tasted his tea.

"The job in Louisiana—the wildlife assignment. They still want you. Big bucks."

"The answer is still no."

"But they upped the ante again."

"Forget it. Just the thought of it gives me the creeps." He shuddered, finished his tea, and poured himself another cup. "Mud and swamps and snakes. I'd probably end up as alligator bait."

He heard a whisper of silk behind him. The waitress appeared, a long scarlet tassel hanging from her raven hair gently teased the side of her face and trickled down her neck. Meandering with every subtle movement of her head, the red silken streams mesmerized Jake.

"Jake!" Fred tore Jake's attention from the animated slash of red. "Let's order."

As they waited for their food, Fred examined the photos. "Great vision. Your work is better than ever."

"Thanks. So why the hell are we here on a day like this, anyway? I could have had the photos delivered."

Fred fussed with his silverware, scattering tinkling, metallic notes into the half-lit atmosphere.

"Okay. Spit it out," Jake said.

"What the hell is going on with you, Jake? The way you have been acting lately. No, since you came back from that trip upstate."

It was all Jake could do to draw a breath. Relax. Fred has no idea what happened upstate. Relax.

"Hey. I've been working my ass off," Jake said. "Are you trying to tell me I'm losing my edge or something?"

"Don't get me wrong, Jake. It's not your work. It's your attitude. You've become so remote. You're missing deadlines. You don't even answer your messages."

"I told you. I've been working my ass off. Isn't that good enough anymore?"

"I spend half my time doing damage control for your screw-ups. Damn it, Jake." Fred slammed his palm on the table, evoking jingle-jangle sounds from the silverware and glasses. He cast furtive glances at couples dining nearby. Two women at the next table stared at him. His face reddened. With a lowered voice he said, "You wouldn't even leave your darkroom to speak with me when I brought a client over last week. What's wrong?"

"Don't worry about it."

"What the hell do you mean? Your career is on the line here!"

Jake rubbed his eyes and sighed. "I'm sorry. I know I'm acting like a jerk. But there is nothing you can do. He fingered the envelope of photos. It's personal."

A waiter brought their orders. Jake tried to avoid conversation by focusing on his plate.

"Rachel?" Fred's voice softened. "Is it Rachel? I figured you had it made when she moved in. I thought, this time, you two would be able to make it. Is she—?"

"No. She's perfect. We never argue. She's always there for me, but...it's like there's something missing."

"But—"

Jake rubbed his forehead in despair. "Didn't you ever wake in the night, hungry, not to fill your stomach, but to feed your heart, or your brain...no, your soul?"

Fred stopped blotting his lips with his napkin and shrugged. "There's more."

"More? More what?" Fred threw down his napkin. "This is bullshit. You're forty years old. Did you ever stop to think that's all there is? That maybe it just doesn't get any better?"

"After what happened upstate, I know. It's—"

"How can I understand when you won't tell me what happened?"

How could he tell Fred about something he wanted to forget? He had to get Fred off that subject.

"It's my photography, too." Jake leaned forward and lowered his voice. "When I'm in the darkroom developing a print, I stand there and watch the images appear. I wait for something more than trees, birds, or people." Jake knew it was useless, but he would try to explain, one more time. "It's like the camera should be able to capture some sort of magic I can't quite see, something—"

"Everyone who sees your photography sees magic. Why can't you?" Fred sighed and shook his head.

"I don't know. It was always this way." He shrugged. "But it, the magic, is calling to me." Jake's voice went hoarse. "Right now. I can almost hear the whispers. I have to be free to go after the secret."

"It? Secret?" Fred stared at Jake as if he were trying to read his mind. "What are you going to do?"

"New York isn't cutting it for me anymore." He forced himself to sound firm, so Fred would know he was serious. "Maybe I'll go back to Alaska. I felt something there."

"Did you tell Rachel?"

Jake looked down at his empty cup. "I don't have to. She already knows. I can see it in her eyes."

"You're not thinking of leaving Rachel behind. Not again."

"I love her to death. But I have to figure this out alone. Besides, she deserves better than me. I'm only hurting her."

"You need to talk to her about all this. She loves you."

"There is nothing left to talk about."

The diminutive waitress placed a bowl of fortune cookies on the table. Fred reached for one, cracked it open. "I'm going to meet a mysterious stranger. That's a pretty safe bet." He tossed the strip of paper in an ashtray. "What's yours say?"

"I'll pass. I already know what has to happen tonight. I have to get things straight with Rachel."

They rose and grabbed their coats.

Fred placed his hand on Jake's shoulder. "I'm really sorry. Call if you need me."

Jake felt a tickling at the back of his neck. He looked over his shoulder to see the waitress smiling at him from across the room. Her tiny hand slowly waved good-by, fingers fanned wide apart and punctuated by long, red-lacquered nails. Jake turned away and pushed himself through the door.

Fred looked up at the sky, swore, and hurried down the street. Jake watched him fade into the darkness.

Falling snow sparkled in the air like scattered shards of broken mirrors. They looked alive. Trembling, they fell gently to the ground and left a clean, white shroud. The neon lights above Jake's head cast mottled patterns on the glimmering flakes that tumbled down from the sky. He reached to grab a few of the kaleidoscopic bits, but when he examined what he had captured, he closed his eyes and bowed his head. Instead of multicolored segments of broken butterflies, he held only melting winter.

He had to get it over with.

The walk home was long, but Jake did not mind. He was not ready to see Rachel yet. He sat on a bench at the bus stop across the street from his building and stared at the weathered brick structures that flanked his home. They grew straight up out of the sidewalk, dull, gray, like the winter sky had been that day, every day. His feet tingled with cold. His hair was wet. Pale flakes littered his lap.

It was time.

Jake rose from the bench and slowly wove his way across the street. He fumbled with the lock on the iron gate between the pavement and his private world. The key would not turn. He struggled until his fingers were numb, but the lock was jammed. He grabbed the black bars, rattled them. The gate squealed open and hit his chest. Jake stumbled backward.

It was not locked.

He turned the knob on the inner door. The second barrier opened effortlessly. He would have to warn Rachel again about locking up.

Jake climbed the flight of stairs to the landing, his soaked shoes exuding squishing sounds, his sodden coat slapping against his trembling legs. He turned the corner and contin- ued up the last of the stairs to his loft, then stopped outside his office. A frail keening sound called to him through the space under the door. He strained to hear it. What could make that sound?

He pushed on the door. It was not locked. It should have been. It swung slowly open into his office, the hinges imitating the wailing sound that trailed from within. His heart hitched between beats.

Why was it so dark?

Even if Rachel had gone to bed, she would have left a light on for him. Jake reached for the wall switch, hesitated, and let his hand fall, deciding on darkness, on silence. He was good in the dark. He could find his way past his darkrooms without bumping into anything. He was used to operating in the dark. Color printing had taught him that, but this was somehow different. He held his breath and shuffled down the ebony hall to the bedroom.

A screech escaped from under his right foot. He gasped and jerked. A damn dog toy. When his heart stopped jumping, he swore silently and resumed his furtive journey, following the muffled, hollow wailing until he could tell it was coming from the bathroom on the other side of the bedroom. A jagged slit of light crawled out from under the bathroom door along with the pathetic lamentation. He could put it off no longer. Sliding his hand along the wall, Jake searched for the light switch.

Click.

An automatic reflex slammed his eyes shut. On his inner lids he saw a repeating image, like a red Jackson Pollock fan. He blinked. There it was, on the wall over the headboard of his disheveled bed. The fan painting. No canvas. No frame. Just a red splatter design. The lustrous red paint trickled down the wall.

Jake hurled himself into the white-tiled bathroom. More scarlet fans adorned the walls. Nikki, Rachel's little Yorkshire Terrier huddled next to a crumpled form on the red and white floor. Her golden head thrown back, Nikki howled to the ceiling light.

"Rachel!"

Jake dropped to the floor and wrapped his arms around his lover. No heartbeat answered his as he held her against his chest.

Chapter 2

*J*AKE COMPOSED HIMSELF enough to call the police; then he stood in his office, with his face against the cold glass of the front window. He trembled in the darkness and waited for sirens to shriek up at him from the street, for flashing lights to send colored beacons cutting through the falling snow. He listened to the footsteps echo in the outer hall and cringed as flashlights raked lightning across his face. The officers found the light switch and drowned the room in reality.

Jake raised one arm and pointed to the back of his flat. A big man in a black coat ordered one of the uniformed men to stay with Jake as he led the other two toward the back of the apartment. No sooner had their footsteps stopped, when the sound of snarling and barking was followed by a baritone curse. Jake wiped tears from his face and tried to get to Nikki before she could be charged with assaulting an officer, but his guard kept him confined to his spot by the window. The big man in the black coat returned to the front office, holding Nikki by the scruff of her neck. He looked Jake up and down, his eyes lingering on the bloodstains that covered his jacket and said, "Is this yours?"

Jake nodded. The big man handed the dangling dog to him. Barely noticing the crimson flecks that infested her golden hair, Jake cuddled Nikki and sat down on the black leather couch by the door. "I'm sorry I forgot you, Nikki...I'm sorry."

Jake and Nikki sat quietly and waited as men in white wheeled a stretcher into the bathroom. The next hour was a blur of flashbulbs, phone calls, and guarded looks. When the action died down, the tall man returned. A wreath of frizzy black hair encircled his head. He patted his right coat pocket and let his hand linger on a rectangular object. Then he reached into his

7

left pocket and pulled out a crumpled handkerchief. He wiped beads of perspiration from his forehead, and then blew his bulbous nose.

"You Jacoby Preston?"

"Jake—Jake Preston.

"Whatever. I'm Detective Rosselli. I know you've been through a rough time here, but it would be a good idea if you would come to the station with me. We need to talk about what happened. Besides, my men have more work to do here. We'd only be in the way. But before we leave, my men are gonna need that coat you're wearing."

Jake looked down at the coat—it was embellished with blood. His stomach turned. It was covered with blood—Rachel's blood. He put Nikki down on the couch and removed his coat. The detective grabbed a long jacket from the tree stand next to the door and handed it to Jake. As he slipped on the clean jacket, an officer inserted the bloody coat into a bag, then bent to snip hairs off Nikki's muzzle and topknot.

"What the—"

Detective Rosselli held up a hand to Jake. "Just doing his job."

Rosselli led Jake down to the street. Once outside, Jake tucked Nikki beneath his jacket, ducked under the flashing lights, and stumbled into the waiting black-and-white.

* * *

The squad car fishtailed to a shaky stop in front of the police station. Jake slipped on the ice as he climbed the glazed steps leading up to the double doors that concealed the inner workings of that particular outpost of the New York City Police Department from the darkness of the city streets. Two uniformed men, who had followed in a second car, flung the doors open and stood aside as Rosselli ushered Jake into to the building.

A harsh flash of fluorescent light rebuked Jake as he crossed the threshold. He wiped away more tears and squinted until his eyes became accustomed to the invasive glare. Ringing phones, garbled voices, clacking heels, and the ever-present boom box melded together to form an aural tableau of New York City life, a jangling symphony of extremes.

Jake's eyes adjusted to the overexposed scenario just in time to see a shouting match between a Latin couple erupt into violence when the wife, or girlfriend, whacked her partner's head with her purse, sending the contents of the satchel clattering across the polished floor. Rosselli motioned for Jake to stay put and rushed across the room to join the efforts to separate the sparring couple.

Through the din, Jake became aware of muffled sobbing. He dried his eyes and turned toward the sound that echoed his own feelings. On a nearby wooden bench sat a young boy dressed in ragged, oversized clothing. In between sniffs, the child wiped his nose with the back of a tattered sleeve. His immense, brown eyes looked up at Jake. With a wiggle and a woof, Nikki woke and stuck her head out from her hiding place near Jake's heart. Instantly, the boy's expression brightened, and he giggled. Jake walked over to the boy and sat next to him.

Jake said, "Want to say hello to the puppy?"

The boy reached out a mittened hand and patted Nikki's head, flattening her already disheveled, red bow.

"Hey, kid, didn't your mama never tell you not to talk to strangers?"

Jake turned toward the source of the wisecrack. Smiling at him from a corner of the room, sat a garishly made-up woman in a mini skirt and black fishnet stockings. As she swung her crossed leg lazily, a hole in the netting over her knee opened and closed like a sleepy eye. Before Jake could counter her remark, Detective Rosselli motioned for him to follow. As he left the room, Jake glanced back at the woman. She licked her ruby lips and winked at him. Jake shivered.

Jake followed Rosselli to the end of a long hallway lined with closed doors that muffled mumbles, yells, and laughter. The detective opened the door to his office, stood aside, and motioned for Jake to enter. Rosselli followed Jake into the dark room and pulled a cord attached to a hanging light. The bulb flashed on and swung back and forth, sending beams of light to search out every corner of the small, dreary room. The detective sat behind his desk and lit a cigarette.

Jake sat on a wooden chair in front of the desk and placed Nikki on the chair next to him. Before he could unbutton his jacket, Nikki jumped the gap between the two chairs and plopped onto Jake's lap, then shivered until he took her into his arms.

"So, J—Mr. Preston, why don't you tell me what happened at your place tonight. How you got all that blood on you."

Rosselli took a long drag on his cigarette and slowly blew the smoke straight in Jake's direction. Jake waited for the grey mist to clear before he answered.

"Aren't you supposed to read me my rights?"

"Mr. Preston, you're confused. That's only if we're taking information that might be used against someone. Right now, I'm just trying to get a picture of what happened. You're not a suspect or anything." He took another long drag. Letting the smoke escape in spurts as he spoke, Rosselli continued. "You don't have anything to hide, do you?"

"No! Of course not." Jake pulled his coat tighter around Nikki—around himself.

"So, what happened?"

"How should I know? I wasn't there—I spent the evening dining with my agent, Fred Adams. Then I went home and found...I saw just what you saw. I—I held her for a while. That's how the blood—"

"What time did you get home?"

"I don't know."

"What do you mean you don't know?"

"I don't know—that's all! Time was the last thing on my mind when I got home!" As Jake's voice rose with anger, his body followed. He stood, leaning over Rosselli's desk and yelled, "I just found my girlfriend with her throat cut! What does time have to do with anything?"

Unruffled by Jake's loss of control, Rosselli took a drag from his cigarette and continued. "How long were you home before you decided to call us?"

"I don't know—a few minutes—I guess. I told you, I held her for a while." Jake returned to his chair, slouched down, and rubbed Nikki's ears. "Five or ten minutes."

"I see." Rosselli reached over his belly, picked up a pencil and scratched a few notes on a yellow pad. He looked back up at Jake. "How many people do you let use your bathroom? Clients? Strangers?"

"I don't see what—nobody. Myself, my assistant, Jerry. Fred, once in a while…and Rachel."

"If you think of anyone else who may have been in there, let me know."

"Why?"

"Make it easier for us to sort prints."

"Sure."

"And we'll need to print you."

"Sure. Of course. Whatever you need to catch—"

"Can you think of anyone who could've wanted to hurt Miss Foster?"

Jake's heart skipped a beat, then tried to make up for it by thumping a little harder for the next few seconds. He forced himself to speak. "No, nobody. She never hurt a fly. Never hurt a fly." Jake closed his eyes.

"Are you okay, Mr. Preston?" Rosselli scrutinized Jake. "You look a little—queasy."

"I'm fine."

"How were you two getting along, you and Miss Foster?"

"Fine…I thought you said I wasn't a suspect."

"Right." Rosselli groaned as he leaned down to pull a Manhattan directory out of a cardboard box on the floor. "Why don't you go across the hall and wait while I contact your agent, have him come in just to confirm your whereabouts this evening. After that," he shrugged, "you'll be free to go."

Rosselli led Jake across the hall to another small, colorless room with one rectangular table in the center of the scuffed tile floor and a large mirror on the wall.

"Mind if I send one of my men in to fingerprint you, just to speed things up?"

"Do what you have to do."

* * *

After the officer collected his print kit and left, Jake walked over to a smudged mirror and wondered what hid behind it. Was it backed by a blank wall, or a silent watcher who waited patiently for Jake to perform some act guaranteed to finger him as guilty of murder? Only his own reflection peered back at him from the filthy glass. His thick black hair was still wet and plastered to his head.

11

He wiped his tainted fingertips on his coat. Seeing no answers in his red-rimmed eyes, he turned away from the suspicious mirror and moved to stand in front of the room's only window.

The light escaping through the window barely illuminated the narrow, dead-end airshaft that loomed outside. He pressed his face against the glass and strained to see if he could spot any stars in the sky above, but the height of the shaft blocked any possible visions other than those of crumbling bricks and his own distorted reflections bouncing back from other windows. Not a single snowflake dared travel the long shaft on a quest to bring him a spark of color. His black-brown eyes seemed sunken, giving his likeness a skull-like appearance.

Nikki shuddered in Jake's arms. He looked down and cuddled her closer. As he smoothed her tangled hair, he realized the scarlet specks on the side of her golden head were blood. Rachel's blood. He dropped into a chair, leaned his head on the table and closed his eyes, tried to erase memories of Rachel in her favorite pink nightie—on the bathroom floor—blood everywhere.

* * *

Rosselli burst into the room, and Jake jerked awake. His face creased from resting on his arm, Jake turned to Rosselli.

"Mr. Preston, I'm a little confused here. Your agent says you left the restaurant at approximately nine o'clock. You called us at exactly eleven fifty-six. I seem to remember you saying you called us five or ten minutes after you got home."

"Right. Whatever you say," Jake said.

"Well, what went on in those almost three hours between when you left the restaurant—and when you called us?"

"Nothing. I walked home and sat outside on a bench for awhile."

"Explain to me why I should believe you walked home in this kind'a weather when you could've caught a cab?" Rosselli raised one bushy eyebrow. "And then, you sat on a bench. In the rain?"

"I don't have to explain anything to you. I'm not a suspect, remember?"

"Hey, it would be real good if you would cooperate here. I'm just doin' my job. Adams mentioned something about you and Miss Foster breaking up. Sound familiar to you?"

"I don't think I'll be answering any more questions tonight, at least not until I speak with my attorney."

"Okay, Mr. Preston. Have it your way, but I suggest you don't make any plans to leave the city without checking with me first."

"Can I go now?"

Rosselli nodded. Jake brushed past him and left the room.

"Preston!"

Halfway down the hall, Jake heard the detective call to him. "By the way, where did you learn to speak French?"

"French?" Jake turned in confusion. "What the hell are you talking about now? I don't know any French."

"Never mind," Rosselli said. Jake continued his determined departure without looking back.

* * *

When Jake left the station, he spotted Fred standing out front, trying to attract the attention of a cab. He walked up behind his friend and placed a hand on his shoulder.

"You know they never stop when it's raining or snowing." Fred whirled around.

"Jake, you're out. I thought they were keeping you." Fred wrapped Jake in his arms. They held each other tightly and wept.

"I'm so sorry about Rachel. I don't know what else to say. Besides, I'm afraid I've already said too much. They kept at me and—"

"It's okay."

"I didn't know what was going on. I thought something had happened to *you*. They didn't tell me about Rachel until I started freaking out."

"Fred, it's okay. I do not have anything to hide. I wouldn't ask you to lie for me anyway."

"Is there anything I can do?"

"No. I just want to go home."

"Jake, don't do that. Come stay at my place. I know Wendy would love it. You shouldn't be alone tonight."

"Don't worry. I won't be alone. I have Nikki. I need to go home. I'm beat. Besides, Nikki has to have her regular chow. Thanks anyway."

"Okay, Jake, but if you change your mind, or need anything, just call or come over. We'll be there."

"Thanks, Fred. But I really need to be alone. I have some things I need to work out."

A cab stopped in front of them. Fred opened the door and climbed in. "Jake, c'mon, get in. Come with me."

"No, I'll walk over to the corner and flag another. After all, we *are* going in different directions."

Fred shook his head and slammed the door as his cab splashed off into the night.

Jake waded through the slush as he made his way to the corner where he was lucky to flag down a cab. It was late and traffic was sparse, so the ride to his loft was far too quick. He dreaded the thought of going home, but he had to find out. The police wouldn't know what to look for. They wouldn't know about *them*—wouldn't believe if he told them. Nobody who hadn't experienced what he did, upstate, right after Keith's death, could possibly understand. Jake paid the driver and started to climb out. With his hands still on the door handle, he noticed the yellow plastic ribbon draped across his iron gate—the yellow ribbon that announced, "POLICE LINE DO NOT CROSS." A policeman stood nearby, shivering in the cold.

"Hey, Rockefeller," the cabby shouted, "you gonna close the fuck'n door? We gotta pay to heat this thing."

Jake climbed back into the cab. "Take me to a hotel."

"Which one?"

"Any one. The closest one."

"Okay, I don't give a shit. It's your money."

The cab pulled away from the curb and splashed back into traffic.

"She never hurt a fly," Jake whispered.

Chapter 3

As JAKE SIGNED THE REGISTER, the concierge eyed him. "And your luggage, sir?"

"Uh—my things will be arriving presently."

"Yes, sir. Is there anything else we can do for you?"

"As a matter of fact, how about a newspaper?"

"Of course, the *Times*, the *Journal*, what's your pleasure?"

"It doesn't matter. She can't read."

The man behind the desk glowered at Nikki, wrinkled his nose, and handed Jake a well-read edition of the *Wall Street Journal*. "I'm told it's extremely absorbent, sir."

"Thanks," Jake said. He tucked the paper under his arm and looked for the elevator.

* * *

Jake locked the door to his room and went straight to the bathroom to lay the paper out on the floor for Nikki, then crawled onto the center of the bed and closed his eyes. Within a few minutes, he felt Nikki leap onto the mattress. She crept over to his side and shoved her nose under his hand.

"I guess this means it's time for room service." Jake rolled over and reached for the phone. "This is room 312. Could you please send me up some...some boiled chicken? Mix it with some rice and a carrot. Yeah. You heard right. And a bottle of wine. White Zinfandel. No. Make that two bottles of wine. Can you put a rush on it? Thanks."

After Nikki finished picking the chicken out of her dinner, she jumped up onto the bed and went to sleep on Jake's stomach. Just before dawn, after he finished the last of the wine, Rachel's favorite, Jake also fell asleep—

15

She pulled him back onto the bed. It was easy. He did not put up much of a fight. In the commotion, he knocked the lamp off the bedside table. When it crashed against the wall, Jake awoke.

Jake bolted out of the bed before he could fully open his eyes. The teal and mauve draperies reminded him he was not home. The lamp on his bedside stood untouched, and the only female in the room was Nikki. She lay watching from a far corner of the bed. The dark window scene told Jake he had slept around the clock. It was night again.

On numb legs, he went into the bathroom to wash the guilt from his face. He stood in front of the mirror and stared at his reflection. How could he have dreamt of another woman? How could the faceless, dark-haired woman enter his dream without his permission? She should have been blonde, should have been Rachel.

"It doesn't matter anymore," he murmured to the Jake in the mirror. "It's not your fault. She's gone. That's what you wanted, isn't it? It's not your fault."

Having left home with no personal possessions, he had only tap water to splash on his hair, to tame his defiant curls. When his hair was finally under control, and his dreams erased, he found his way to the hotel dining room. While Jake waited to be seated, he wondered whether it was hunger or guilt that clawed at his stomach.

"Sir, will you be dining alone tonight?"

"Yes—I'm alone."

The waitress led Jake to a small table near the bar. Sitting with his back to the wall, he ordered steak and vodka. He sliced his steak with intricate care, setting the last few chunks aside for Nikki, shaking the juice off each bit, one at a time, and placing them on a white linen napkin. A wine-colored stain encircled each slice as it drained onto the bleached fabric. Carefully, he bundled up the offering and hid it in the pocket of his jacket, then signed his tab and headed back to his room.

"Sir!" The waitress caught him on his way out. "You seem to have gotten some steak sauce, or something, on your shirt. Perhaps you should attend to it before the stain sets in."

16

Jake looked down and saw the reddish-brown stain on his white shirt, the stain that had already been given a day to set in. He rushed for the elevator without acknowledging the woman's comment. The trip to the third floor seemed to take hours. He held his jacket crossed across his chest, careful to keep his secret from the other passengers as his heart beat against the stain of blood.

* * *

As Nikki wolfed down her steak dinner, Jake stood in front of the sink again, in the accusing silence, using cold water and hand soap to scrub the stigmata from his shirt.

"It's not your fault," he said to the Jake in the mirror.

* * *

The cab sped away from the curb. "Take me someplace noisy. Someplace with loud music," Jake said.

"Okay, boss," said the cabby.

The colored lights of New York whizzed by. Jake shoved his cold hands into his pockets, and in order to avoid the accusing stares of penetrating illuminations intent on invading his privacy, he focused his gaze on the floor of the cab until it hit the curb and bounced to a stop. Jake's teeth clacked together with the impact.

"We're here. Great blues club. And loud. You'll love it. Lotsa' women." The cabby winked.

Jake stuffed his fare into the chute and ignored the driver's inquisitive expression, then dashed through the freezing rain and slipped into the sanctuary of the back-street nightclub. The interior of the blues club was even darker than the streets outside. As promised, the music was loud. It was a small establishment with only a few tables to separate the dance floor from the bar. Although the club was crowded, only two women interpreted the music together, holding each other close, shuffling in the dim light. Jake headed for the bar and ordered vodka. Before he finished the drink, a woman slid into the empty space next to Jake. He could feel her presence, smell her perfume.

"Hi. I'm Kerry. I don't remember seeing you around here before. And a great looker like you, I'd remember."

Jake turned toward her. Her dark hair startled him at first, brought back bad memories of the past, or perhaps, of unwanted dreams. He motioned to the bartender.

"Another vodka please, and whatever the lady is having."

She smiled. "Thanks. What's your name?"

Jake ignored her questions. Only a few comments uttered in the gaps between music and laughter managed to reach their destination. It did not matter. Words did not matter. Only the alcohol and distraction were of any consequence.

"Hey, let's dance."

"Sorry, I don't dance."

"Please, just once."

"I *never* dance." Jake clutched his glass. "It's just not me."

"Then what do you do?"

Jake downed his drink in one gulp.

* * *

The cab ride back to the hotel was quite different from the last. This time, Jake kept his hands warmed on the soft flesh that hid under Kerry's sweater. He had indulged in enough vodka to forget the eyes reflected in the rear-view mirror and the lights blinking by from the rain-soaked streets.

* * *

As they approached room 312, Jake fished in his pocket for the key. With Kerry hanging on his left arm, he slipped the key into the lock. A tiny wail reverberated inside his room. Jake hesitated and leaned his head against the door.

"I'm sorry, but you'd better go. Here." Jake handed Kerry a few crumpled bills. "Take this for a cab."

"But, why? I don't want to go home yet."

"I told you earlier. I don't dance."

"But, I thought—"

"I told you—I don't dance—that's all. I'm sorry."

Jake slipped into his room without regard for the furious woman who stuck out her tongue at him and hustled down the hall toward the elevator. Once inside his teal and mauve hideout, he sat on the bed. Nikki rushed over to his lap and licked his hand. "Nikki, this isn't working. Let's go home."

* * *

"Fuck you Rosselli." Jake tore the yellow, plastic ribbon off his iron gate, relieved that the police detail no longer guarded his loft. He slammed the black metal barrier and climbed the stairs

18

to his loft. He twisted the knob on his front door. It was not locked. This time, when he entered, his first move was to flick on the lights. All of them. Even the ones in both darkrooms.

He paused at the doorway to his bedroom, with his hand shivering on the light switch that could reveal the scarlet works of art.

Click!

There they were, still on display, undamaged by policemen, coroners, or whoever. It was obvious the drawers had been rifled, everything disturbed, inspected. Only the ruby splatters on the wall over the bed appeared untouched.

Jake moved toward the bathroom and pushed on the door until the brass doorknob hit the wall. He jumped at the knocking sound. After a deep breath, he reached into the black room and turned it to red and white with one flip of a switch.

He put Nikki on the bed, told her to stay, and strode over to the closet where he kept his chemicals. There it was, the chlorine disinfectant. He dragged it and the mop bucket out of the darkness. He filled the bucket with scalding water and added the harsh chemical until his eyes teared. Starting with the stains on the wall over his bed, Jake began the task of removing the traces of red from his memory.

The rite of purification was almost over. Jake removed his clothes and tossed them into the trash. To complete the ritual, he padded into the now black-and-white bathroom and closed the door. As he adjusted the water temperature for his shower, he felt his skin crawl. It was as though someone was watching him from behind. Slowly, he turned.

Jake lurched backwards and almost fell into the tub. In the full-length mirror on the back of the door, he could hardly see the reflection of his unshielded body through the splashes of red, through the message hastily written by a finger dipped in Rachel's blood.

"Le coquin qui vole aun autre, le diable en ris." Even though he could not read French, he was sure he knew what it meant. Jake closed his eyes to the truth.

Chapter 4

*J*AKE WOKE AS THE SUN WAS SETTING. Sleeping on the couch in his front office for the last few days had left him stiff and unrested. He went back into his apartment only long enough to feed Nikki and dress. Before leaving, he called Detective Rosselli.

"This is Jake Preston. What did you find out so far? Yeah, I want to talk to you, too. I'll be right over." Jake slammed the phone down and rushed out into the frigid night. The cold rain, or snow, or whatever it was that fell from the black starless sky plastered his hair flat against his head. He shivered as he opened the door to Rosselli's office.

"Mr. Preston. Nice to see you. Nasty weather out there. Have a seat."

"So, what do you have?"

The detective shuffled some papers around on his desk and lit a cigarette. "Well, I wasn't at liberty to tell you this before, but we found a set of fingerprints in your bathroom, a set we couldn't account for. We couldn't identify them at first. Could've belonged to anybody. Some bimbo you had on the side. Some other guy, when you weren't around. You know how women."

"There *was* no other guy."

"You can never be sure."

"I'm sure." Jake clenched his right hand into a fist.

"Well." Rosselli sighed. "As I said before, we couldn't find a match for the prints. Probably never would have, except for a fluke. You see, these guys in Jersey ran across this stiff out in the woods." Rosselli paused to blow smoke through his nostrils. He dropped the cigarette into a half-filled Styrofoam cup and lit another.

"And, while trying to identify the body, bingo, his prints matched up with the ones at your place. Might not have caught it on our own." He shook his head. "Boy, those computers sure are pissers—"

"So, who is he—was he?"

"His name was Robert Henry. Ring a bell?"

"No."

"You sure?"

"Absolutely!"

"Was Miss Foster ever in New Orleans?"

"No. And I am sure. Why?"

"That's where this kid came from. It accounts for the writing on the mirror. They say he spoke French, some kind of Louisiana French."

"So, what did he have to do with Rachel?"

"Why don't *you* tell *me*?"

"I told you before, Rosselli. I never heard of him. What was he doing around here anyway?"

"According to his parents, he turned up missing a few weeks ago." Rosselli lit a cigarette and filled his lungs with smoke. "One day, he just didn't come home from school for the weekend."

"School?" Jake asked, "How old was he?"

"Oh, about twenty-two, I think." Looking for his notes, through smoke that backed into his eyes, Rosselli dug into the heap of papers and crumpled fast-food wrappers that littered his desk. He shrugged and went on. "He was a student at Tulane."

A college student just like Rachel's brother. Jake's blood pressure spiked. He felt heat blast his face.

"W-what happened to him? How did he die?"

"Good question. We don't know. He was just dead. No signs of foul play, or drugs, or anything. Just dead."

Just dead—just like the others. Jake felt his chest tighten as if great fingers clutched his ribs, squeezing the breath from him. He fought a wave of vertigo. "Am I free to go now?" It took all Jake's strength to force out words. "I have to take Rachel back to where she belongs—upstate."

"Sure, Jake. We got lucky, you know. If we didn't find that kid, I'd still be looking at you, especially when you pulled that boner washing your floors like that."

"Yeah," Jake mumbled. "*We* got real lucky. And I'll wash *my* fucking floors whenever I want." He turned away from Rosselli and somehow found his way to the street and plunged into an onslaught of freezing rain.

He sloshed through sleet-covered streets, beads of perspiration mixing with cold drops flung down from the sky. Jake's breath came ragged and uneven as he lumbered toward his apartment. His heart slamming, he stopped to rest with his back against a wall, his eyes to the sky, hoping the rain would wash away the truth. "It wasn't my fault," he gasped to the turbulent sky.

The first thing Jake did when he entered his loft was run his shivering fingers through his Rolodex. He dialed a long-distance number and waited for an answer.

"Hello."

"Betty, this is Jake."

"Jake, I'm so sorry. I read about Rachel in the paper."

"Yeah, I'm sorry, too. Whatever happened to the Devereux house? You know what I mean."

"I kept an eye on the place. She never turned up. One day I saw a couple moving vans outside, loading everything. I had to be cool. You know. So I kept my distance. All I know is the trucks had Louisiana plates."

"That's what I needed to know. Thanks."

"Wait. What do you mean?"

"No—Betty—I love you—but I have to go—now." He hung up.

Jake dropped his rain-soaked clothing and shivered back toward the bathroom. He turned on the faucets and stepped under the flood of steaming hot water. Looking up into the stinging spray, with arms held straight ahead and hands pressed against the wall, Jake's words echoed in the white tiled room.

"Who the hell am I to think I could get away with murder?"

As the water pelted his closed eyes, the past washed over him in torrents, and he remembered how it all started. A year ago. With a phone call from Rachel.

Chapter 5

HE RED BULB EMITTED JUST ENOUGH LIGHT for Jake to watch ghost-like images materialize and take possession of a sheet of photographic paper that floated in a bath of developer. When the timer buzzed, he lifted the sheet from the enamel pan and placed it in the stop bath. Now, the possession would be permanent. Although he had spent most of his life in a darkroom, he never lost his awe for the magic of paper and chemicals and light. Other photographers found a way to become mechanical about their darkroom work; they had timers in their heads. Jake's head was a whirlpool of images. He needed the timer to keep him from becoming lost in the mystery of a smile or spellbound by the hint of a soul peeking out from beneath the sweep of an eyelash. Jake needed a timer to drag him back into the real world.

The phone rang without regard for the miracles taking place in the darkroom. Because the answering machine would sub for him, Jake could stay where he belonged, safe in his womb of red-orange lights, where the images were black and white, and he had ultimate control.

It had been hours since his last cigarette, so the siren song of a Camel had no problem seducing him. He walked across the length of his loft to the bedroom located at the back of the building, away from the street noises of New York City. He flopped down on his bed and lit the last cigarette of his first pack of the day. As he rested with one arm under his head, he exhaled and watched the bluish phantom escape his lungs and rise to the ceiling. He would have to quit smoking some day. . . but not today.

A tiny light, flashing to the left, reminded him of the phone calls he had ignored. He held the cigarette between his lips,

23

pushed the play button, then took another long drag and waited for the messages to roll.

"Fred here. I need the proof sets for the Wall Street shots. Pronto. Call me." Beep.

"This is Gloria. Don't forget, we're doing supper at my place tonight. I found the most luscious lamb chops you ever saw. See ya later. I can't wait." Beep.

"Jake—this is Rachel. I know it has been a long time, but I thought you should know—Keith is gone. I mean, he's—we buried him this morning. I thought you would want to know. I'm sorry I bothered you. Bye." Beep.

As the machine rewound the message tape, Jake remained still, unable to breathe. The voice from the past immobilized him. Keith was only twenty, maybe twenty-one. When the cigarette burned down to a short ember, it singed Jake's fingers, snapping him back to reality. He sat up and squashed the butt into an ashtray.

He picked up the phone and pushed the auto dial button that linked him with his travel agent.

"Hi, this is Jake. Get me on the first plane to Utica. No. Today. Now. I don't care what class. Just get me there, now. Non-smoking only? Okay, just have the ticket waiting at the gate. Yeah. Another emergency assignment. Thanks, Jenny."

Jake pulled a suitcase out of his closet, tossed a few things into it, grabbed his camera case, and headed down to the street. As he climbed into a taxi, he remembered the black-and-white prints he left swimming around in the rinse bath and wondered how long they could tread water.

* * *

Kennedy was crowded. The world hustled around Jake, but he ignored the distractions. He stood in front of the window near Gate 267 and reveled in the mellow glow of the autumn sun. There was time for one more smoke before he would have to board the plane, before he would have to face the past.

The stewardess broke the golden spell when she announced it was time to begin boarding. Jake lined up with the other *non-smokers* and shuffled toward the turnstile. The smiling attendant, with Scotty on her nametag, wished him a pleasant journey. He grinned back at her and quipped, "Scotty, beam me home." She rolled her eyes and pretended to be amused.

* * *

Jenny was on the ball, as usual. Jake arrived at the Oneida County Airport to find a rent-a-car had already been arranged for him. He loaded his luggage into the trunk of the sedan and began the short drive to Rachel's house. As he passed the Greek restaurant, he remembered Gloria's luscious lamb chops and guessed they ought to be right crisp by then. He would find a way to explain, but excuses would have to wait.

As he drove down Oriskany Boulevard, he saw his favorite homemade ice cream shop had closed, but otherwise, little had changed in three years. He turned right on Main Street and completed the last mile of his journey to Rachel's house. The house looked the same except new wind chimes replaced the pig family chimes Rachel had won at the firemen's field day. Instead of the dull clanking of ceramic pigs, the oriental resonance of metal tubes greeted him.

Jake stood on the porch for a few minutes before he raised his hand to knock. He still carried the house key Rachel had given him many years before, but he knew he had long since lost his right to use it.

Rachel greeted him, her eyes wide with amazement. Nikki greeted Jake by biting him on the ankle. Good ol' Nikki, bite first and bark later. Jake remembered how much he still loved Rachel and how much he still hated her rotten, little dog.

Rachel took Jake's hand, pulled him into her parlor, and locked the door.

"Jake, what are you doing here? You should have called."

"I knew if I called, you would've told me not to come. Why didn't you let me know sooner?"

"I didn't want you to think I was trying to ask you for anything, any favors or—I don't know what else. I don't know." She looked down and scrutinized her palms as if the road-map lines would offer an answer. "I guess it was bad enough dealing with all this. I didn't think I could handle seeing you, too."

Jake slid his arms around Rachel and whispered into the golden hair that spilled over her ear. "I'm sorry. I loved him too. You should have called me sooner."

Rachel pulled away from Jake's embrace. With a visible effort to regain control of her emotions she said, "Can I get you something to eat? I have tons of food. The neighbors brought so much stuff over, I don't know what I'll do with it all."

"Sure. That would be nice."

"Jake," Rachel said, as she wrinkled her nose. "You still smell like an ashtray. How many packs a day are you doing now?"

Some things never change, Jake thought, as he inhaled the odor of roses emanating from her alabaster skin. After Rachel left the room, Jake sat on the couch and pulled his sock down to check for damages. A small bruise was materializing where Nikki had bitten him. Luckily, her teeth had not broken his skin. They never did. When he looked up after thoroughly inspecting his ankle, his eyes met Nikki's gaze. She was sitting on a satin pillow, surrounded by her army of squeak toys, like the devil and her imps. She yawned and licked her lips. Jake stared into her eyes and whispered, "Slut!" One of her eyelids fluttered. Was she winking at him?

Rachel returned with a bottle of wine and a glass. "Here, Jake, I think you'll need this. A little something to kill the pain." She bit her upper lip and quickly retreated to the kitchen.

Jake was sure, in the privacy of her kitchen, Rachel was laughing. He looked back at the dog and wondered if dogs could laugh, too.

As he sipped White Zinfandel, Jake inspected the parlor. It was still decorated with crayon sketches and tempera paintings created by Rachel's special students. Pictures of smiling suns and happy faces lined up along with images of twisted landscapes and stick figures adorned with haunted eyes.

Sun-catchers and prisms defended the windows and waited patiently for daylight to arrive so they could resume their contest to see which could cast the most enthralling patches of light across the room. Jake's favorites had always been the long, pointed prisms hung on nooses of fishing line. A gentle twist could send their projections dashing around the room until the air became filled with bits of shattered rainbows and broken butterflies.

Armed with the wine bottle and glass, he tiptoed past the sleeping Yorkie and escaped into the kitchen where Rachel was busy fussing with home-cooked offerings lovingly prepared by family and friends.

"Is there anything I can do to help?"

"No. Supper is just about ready."

"I didn't mean kitchen duty. Is there anything I can do to help you get through this?"

"No. Besides, it's all over. Sit down." She motioned him toward the chair she had always saved for him before he moved to New York. She once told him she did it because placing his back to the window would help keep his attention aimed in her direction, help keep him from daydreaming. They sat in silence. Jake picked at his meal and Rachel used her fork to push food around on her plate.

"How did it happen? Was he sick?"

"No. He wasn't sick. They decided on—natural causes."

"What does that mean, natural causes? If he wasn't sick, how could he die from natural causes?"

Rachel shrugged her shoulders and looked down at her plate.

"Twenty-one-year-old kids don't die naturally! Answer me, Rachel. I have to know." When she continued to ignore his question, Jake tossed his napkin aside, left his chair, and knelt before her. He touched her chin and forced her to look at him. "Rachel, talk to me. I have to know. Was it something I could have prevented if I hadn't left?"

"They said his heart just stopped."

"Ridiculous! His heart was fine. He was always such a healthy kid. Was it drugs?"

"No!" Rachel jumped to her feet, grabbed the bowl of overnight salad, and threw it against the wall. "Keith never even tried drugs! Why is that so hard for everybody to believe? If one more person dares bring it up again, I'll punch the shit out of them! So shut up and finish eating." After a moment of silence, she sheepishly added, "You'll stay here, won't you? I don't want to be alone tonight."

* * *

Rachel started the dishes, and together they cleaned the kitchen. While Rachel finished washing the peas and bacon bits off the wall, Jake located a phone book and canceled his reservations at the Mohawk Inn. "Rachel, I'm going outside to get my stuff."

"Yeah, sure. Try to limit it to a half a pack. Okay?"

Knowing Rachel was on to him, Jake saluted and took the most direct path to the front door. As he left, Nikki danced around the parlor and barked good-bye, or perhaps, good riddance. Jake closed the door between them and sat down on the cold cement steps. When he finished the first cigarette, he flicked it across the front lawn. It sailed away in a graceful arch, like a jet-propelled firefly.

A subtle breeze tinkled through the wind chimes. The hair on the back of Jake's neck rose. Something felt different about Main Street. He sat quietly and tried to shake the feeling. Stopping short of finishing his third cigarette, Jake moved his luggage to the front porch. As he closed the door to the autumn mysteries, he heard Rachel speak from behind him.

There's only Keith's room, but...he'd want you there."

Jake smiled, opened the door, and dragged in his suitcases. "I'm way ahead of you."

Rachel grabbed one of his suitcases and led Jake to Keith's room.

"Rachel, I won't push you any further tonight, but I'm not leaving here until I know what happened. I never meant to lose touch with him. I meant to be there for him. I really did, but somehow—life got complicated." Before Rachel could revive the old argument, Jake switched gears.

"Try to get some sleep." He kissed her forehead and turned toward Keith's room.

Jake sat on Keith's bed. Pictures they had taken of tumbling waterfalls and gentle deer still hung on the walls. Keith's textbooks were haphazardly stacked on his desk along with a pair of scruffy sneakers. Memories of their times together flooded his mind with a sadness so sweet he could taste it. Jake threw his clothes on the floor, turned out the light, and tried to make himself comfortable on the foreign landscape of Keith's narrow bed. Just before sleep took him, he noticed a night-light glowing in the corner. Its unseemly light visited his dreams along with visions of Keith and the feeling that something was wrong with Main Street.

Chapter 6

*J*AKE WOKE BEFORE THE SUN ROSE. He went into the kitchen, started coffee, and searched the refrigerator for something to cook for breakfast, something that would please Rachel. Before he found a chance to clean up the eggs he had dropped on the floor, Rachel shuffled into the kitchen.

"Hey, chef Boy-are-Jake, I see you can still juggle eggs with the best of them."

He looked up to see Rachel standing beside him, bundled in a white terry cloth bathrobe. Her hair was tangled and her eyes edged with red. Jake could tell she had not slept. He poured Rachel a cup of coffee. As they sat across from each other, the kitchen warmed with an invasion of the morning sun. It spilled through the window and splashed onto the floor.

With the self-indulgent instincts of a total hedonist, Nikki arrived as soon as the floor had warmed enough to deserve her presence. She placed her bottom on the heated spot and drifted off to sleep while still sitting upright. Whenever her head started to droop with sleep, she jerked it back up and pretended a serious attempt at remaining awake. The little, red bow in her top knot was twisted sideways, and her hair stuck out in all directions.

"Rachel, tell me now. What happened?"

"I told you yesterday; I don't know. I don't want to talk about it." Hysteria building in her voice, Rachel continued. "I don't care if you feel guilty. You didn't have to leave. It was your choice."

Jake's fingers tightened around his cup.

"You know why I left this place!" Jake almost knocked his chair over as he hastily stood and paced over to where the second pot of coffee dripped. The metered drip, drip, calmed him enough to continue his defense. "You know I would have gone nuts if I had to take another wedding picture. You know I couldn't bear to spend one more minute in a darkroom trying to transform the evil stepmother into Marilyn Monroe in eight-by-ten. I asked you to come with me. No, I begged you to come with me—"

"Jake, if you will remember, I had a career too. I couldn't just pick up and leave."

"You could've kept right on teaching, but in the city. New York has plenty of handicapped children just praying for someone like you to care about them. You could've moved to the city. I was dying here. You knew that."

Every second of silence that followed placed one more brick on the wall time had built between them. Rachel launched the next attack.

"Jake, we both know it was more than that. There was always something lacking for you. There was always something more you needed. Whatever it was, I just didn't have it. Utica didn't have it. Even when you seemed to be looking straight into my eyes, you were seeing right through me, searching for something more. Something just beyond your reach. Something I couldn't give you."

His voice admitting resignation and defeat, Jake said, "I didn't come here to fight this fight again. We've done it a hundred times before. A thousand times. I'm going out for a while." He headed for the front door.

"Wait!" Rachel grabbed Jake's arm. "I'm sorry—I'm sorry. I didn't mean anything I said. It's just I can't accept what happened. I still don't understand it—I'm scared." Losing control of her facade of strength, still clutching Jake's arm, Rachel whispered. "Keith was scared, too. He wouldn't sleep in the dark anymore." Rachel's voice broke. "Jake, he was afraid of something, and I don't know what it was."

Jake took her into his arms, and they held each other until the spell was broken by the sound of the mailbox lid slamming.

"Will you be okay if I go out for a while?"

Rachel nodded.

Jake examined her expression to be sure she was telling the truth, then said, "Try to get some sleep. I'm going to check out a few things, okay? How about I bring home a pizza. I've got that same ol' pepperoni craving again."

30

Rachel smiled back at him, picked up the dog sitting on the hem of her bathrobe, and slowly headed up the stairs to her bedroom. Before she turned the corner, she called down to Jake, "How about you make half the pizza plain, for me?"

* * *

Jake stood on the porch and watched cars go by. Like exhaust from the passing vehicles, his breath made swirling patterns in the cold October air. He rushed into the shelter of the waiting rent-a-car, turned on the heat, lit a Camel, and headed toward the hospital.

* * *

Nurses and attendants with leaden eyelids wandered around the emergency room. It would soon be time for the day shift to put an end to their long night on duty. Jake walked up to a nurse who carried a pile of blankets in her arms.

"Is Arnie Hoffman on duty today?" She nodded. Ignoring her half-hearted protests, Jake advanced towards the room where he knew Arnie would be. He opened the door carefully, tiptoed over to the disheveled bed that stood in the corner of the small office, lifted a corner of the blanket, and growled, "This is the bed police. You got anybody in there with you?"

Dr. Hoffman snapped to a sitting position and pulled off the blanket that covered his head like a child's ghost costume. His glasses were askew, and he was fully clothed. He blinked his eyes as if to focus in the light that crept in through the half-opened door, he answered. "Jake, you bastard. What are you doing here? If I knew you were coming, I would have planned a ménage à trois. What's up?" A handshake closed the gap of time that stood between the two friends.

"I need you to help me find out what happened to Keith Foster, Rachel's brother. Do you know anything about it?"

"Yeah. No. I was on duty that night." Arnie removed his glasses and rubbed his face as if to erase the last remnants of sleep. "But I'll bet I don't know any more about it than you do. I was right here, sleeping, when I got beeped. I went straight out there, but there was nothing I could do. He was dead—no breathing—no heartbeat—no pulse—no nothing. He was just dead. We checked for drugs, everything we could think of, but nothing showed up. It was the same with the other two."

"What? What other two?"

"Two other kids were brought in here. All of them the same, dead without apparent cause. All within a couple months of each other. A full-fledged investigation didn't find Jack shit. That's why the powers-that-be decided it must have been some freaky kind of designer drug thing. The other two kids were not local, so their bodies were shipped out. I don't know about them, but I knew Keith for a long time, and I never figured him to be the kind to mess around with drugs. But you never know these days." Arnie stood and searched through his rumpled blankets. When he located his glasses, he put them back on and said, "But what do I know?"

"Arnie, can you give me the names of the other kids? I'd like to see if I can figure this out."

"Sure, just give me time to pull myself together. But remember, you didn't hear anything from me."

Chapter 7

*J*AKE SAT IN THE RUMBLING RENTAL CAR and read Arnie's list of names. All three were males about the same age and students at the same college. He put out his cigarette and drove to Wingate University, his alma mater.

* * *

Memories of the meetings concerning his apparent lack of effort gave Jake a chill as he walked through the administration building. Once in the registrar's office, he scanned the room and chose his mark—the shy-looking girl sitting at a desk in the corner reading a romance novel. He planned his scam as he walked over to her.

"Hello. My name is Randy Ketchum," Jake said. "I'm with the health department. Could you give me some information about three of your students?"

"I'm sorry, sir, but I would have to clear it with Mrs. Leary, and she's at a meeting."

"Isn't there anything you *can* tell me?"

"No, sir, that's the rule."

"Well, this puts me in a real bind." Jake leaned closer to the secretary and, taking the novel from her hand, spoke softly. "My boss has been on my case for weeks now. If I come back empty-handed, I will be in deep trouble. Could you tell me anything, like what programs they were enrolled in?"

She blushed and looked around the room, then smiled at Jake and whispered, "Who are they?"

He handed her the slip of paper with three names and social security numbers. Her fingers trembled as they pecked at her keyboard. "They were all matriculated into the Philosophy program."

Philosophy? No. Impossible. Keith had always teased Jake about his degree in philosophy, said it was useless.

"No, that can't be right. Are you sure Keith Foster isn't listed as an accounting major?"

She checked again.

"No, Randy, it shows here," she pointed to the computer screen, inviting Jake to lean closer again, "he changed his program at the beginning of last semester."

Jake thanked the secretary and left, pretending he did not notice the disappointed look on her face. He decided to try to find his favorite philosophy professor and hoped she would remember him, but only a little bit.

Dr. Betty Higgins opened her office door, looked up at Jake from under a disheveled wad of silver hair, and groaned. "Oh, no! You're back." The elfin woman placed a hand over her heart. "You finally remembered where you put your term paper!" She held up her other hand like a crossing guard. "It better be good. I take off major points for work over ten years late."

"Gee, Dr. Higgins," Jake said with the most innocent expression he could muster as he tried to guess if she had fixed her hair since he'd seen her last. "I think you must have me mixed up with someone else."

"No, Jacoby—"

"Jake."

"Mr. Preston, I never forget students who have to struggle to keep from staring out into space in a room that doesn't have any windows. Did you ever find that answer you were looking for?"

Jake shrugged.

Like a nosey dog, she sniffed Jake. "Smells like you still smoke." Hanging an out-to-lunch sign on her door, she closed it and carefully tucked a rug along the space at the bottom of the threshold. After opening a window, just enough to let out the fumes, they both lit up and sat peacefully until Jake handed Dr. Higgins the paper with three names.

"What do you know about these kids?"

She read the names and regarded Jake appraisingly. "I don't really know a whole hell of a lot. They are all dead, but I guess you already figured that out." She gazed out the window for a moment. "All I know is they were seriously involved in their stud-ies, all three of them. Like you were once, sort of. And they were not the only ones—I never saw anything like it. I have been here for twenty-seven years, and I never found a way to fire kids up like that. Then this new guy drops in from who knows where, and the students are following him around like he was a rock star."

"What new guy?"

"His name is Claude Devereux. His credentials are impec-cable. The department head took one look at his curriculum vitae and gave him a chance to teach a class. Bam! He was a hit. I never saw such a response to a class on the Pre-Socratic School. Then he started a club for students interested in Pythagorean philosophy." She shook her head. "The kids just ate it up. They gave him a full load this semester, and every class filled within a few days."

"What kind of person is he?"

"He's a lovely gentleman." Her face colored slightly, giving her a strangely girlish aura. "He invited us all over to his house for dinner a number of times. He and his daughter are both extremely charming. They live in that big old house down at the end of Main Street."

"Keith meant a lot to me." Jake leaned close to Dr. Higgins and touched her hand. "I'm serious about trying to find out what happened to him. Is there anything you can think of that can give me a lead?"

Dr. Higgins shook her head. Jake rubbed his cigarette until the small ember died and left it in the overfilled ashtray. "Thanks, Dr. Higgins. Can I call you if I have any other questions?"

"Sure, kiddo." She scribbled on a yellow note pad. "Here's my home number. By the way, if you ever find your term paper, I'd love to see it." When Jake left, Betty Higgins was busy fan-ning the smoke out of her office by flapping the rug towards the window.

* * *

After a few wrong turns, Jake found the way back to his favorite pizza parlor and ordered the perfect feast he had been dreaming about for the past three years. He rushed back to Rachel's with his prize, whisked into the house, and put the pizza

35

on the coffee table in the parlor. He lifted the corner of the cardboard treasure chest and inhaled the aroma of ecstasy. As he dashed toward the kitchen to find Rachel and a bottle of wine, he almost tripped over Nikki who was asleep on her pillow. He stopped and looked back. She was still asleep.

After filling his hands with all the supplies necessary to enjoy the pizza, Jake ushered Rachel into the parlor and sat beside her on the couch. With a flourish, he opened the box and reached for a slice with pepperoni. "I can't believe it! They screwed up my order, just like always. Damn! I was sure I smelled pepperoni! I know I did—I can't believe this shit!" He leaned back and covered his eyes.

"Don't cry little boy, mommy will get you another one, tomorrow." Rachel patted him on his head, turned on the television, and poured him a glass of wine. With something less than the full enthusiasm he had planned, Jake ate his imperfect pizza. It was not long before Rachel fell asleep with her head resting against his shoulder, pinning him down in a position that forced him to stare at the empty pizza box.

Nikki, who had not been around for dinner, jumped up on the couch and made herself comfortable on Jake's lap. He looked down into her little Yorkie eyes and considered the possibility that maybe she was not so bad after all. Just as that traitorous thought entered his mind, Nikki burped in his face. The unmistakable scent of pepperoni breath was damning. What Jake had mistaken for an attempt at peacemaking, on Nikki's part, was actually a sadistic act of torture. The little bitch wanted to make sure he knew exactly what happened to the pepperoni that had once graced his side of the pizza. If Rachel had not been so desperately in need of sleep, he would have throttled the little dog, right then and there. As Rachel slept on his shoulder, and Nikki slept on his lap, Jake contemplated the numerous ways little dogs could meet deadly ends.

* * *

After the girls woke and the daylight finally faded away, Jake excused himself and stepped out onto Main Street for a smoke. As he walked toward the big house at the end of the street, he wished he had taken Nikki with him. He smiled and pondered the possibility that her leash could have slipped out of his hand just as an eighteen-wheeler passed.

The autumn air, crisp and biting, pushed through the trees, spawning murmurs like the whispering of mourners waiting for a mass of lamentation to begin. As Jake stood across the street from the old mansion, wrinkled, brown leaves that had lost their hold on the trees of summer and fallen from the congregation above, swirled around on the cement as if they were lost souls enchanted by tiny tornadoes spawned of October wind. The little storms blew along the sidewalk toward the old house, then dissipated when they fell over the curb.

Jake lit another cigarette and started to wander back toward Rachel's place, wondering what it was he found so disconcerting about the house at the end of Main Street. He stopped and looked back. It took a few minutes to figure out what it was that needled him. The tangle of overhead wires that ran the length of Main Street, linking each house with the rest of the world, suddenly ended without attempting to cross the street to the Devereux property. There were no telephone or electric wires leading to the house. Jake decided he would pay a visit to the popular professor and his daughter, first thing in the morning.

Chapter 8

ON THE WAY HOME, Jake was so lost in his thoughts he almost wandered past Rachel's house, but the golden glow emanating from her front windows captured his attention and called him home. As he climbed the porch steps, the suncatchers carried out their mischief in reverse. They magnified the warm glow from within and sent beacons of light reaching out with gentle fingers into the darkness of night. This time, he used his key to let himself in.

Nikki trotted over to Jake and let out one woof before wheeling around and returning to her pillow. Rachel smiled as Jake entered her parlor. "Hi, I thought I locked the door."

"You did." He held up the key and watched Rachel's eyes widen with realization. "I still have mine."

Rachel blushed. "How was your walk?"

"Just fine, ma'am. How was your rest? You look a lot better."

Rachel answered with mock insult in her voice. "Are you trying to make a point here? Something to do with my appearance?"

"Not me. Not when you have your attack dog on duty."

"Jake, c'mon now. Nikki never means to do anything bad. She's just—protective. Loyalty is sometimes considered a positive attribute."

Rachel's last comment stung. Jake turned and pretended to look out the window.

"Hey, I was just kidding," Rachel murmured. "I didn't mean anything. Let's change the subject."

Jake turned back to face Rachel. "Would it be okay with you if I go through Keith's things? Maybe I can find something that can shed some light on what happened."

"Sure. It's okay, but I don't think I have the guts to help you. Besides, I was just planning on a long, hot bath. You go ahead. Maybe I'll join you later." Before he could thank her, Rachel disappeared into the back of the house.

Jake entered Keith's room and wondered where to start. How to start. The night-light flickered as though it could not decide whether to cling to life, or not. He snapped on the overhead light, exorcizing lingering shadows.

Jake began by systematically searching through the dresser drawers, from the top down. Socks, keys, and candy bars lay helplessly as he pushed them around. He found nothing amiss in the dresser, so he turned his attention to the closet.

After he let go of the pull chain, the bulb it controlled swung back and forth illuminating opposite ends of the closet, left then right, until it finally came to rest in the center. One at a time, Jake slid the shirts and jackets to the left side of the rod. One at a time, he searched through the pockets of each garment.

The boxes on the closet floor were the next sanctuaries to be desecrated. Jake systematically opened each vault, in order, and found nothing but shoes, baseball cards, and the usual odds and ends that had no place of their own.

The desk was the last region to attract Jake's attention. As he pulled on the handle of the top drawer, Rachel and Nikki entered the room. Like a criminal caught in the act, he dropped his arms to his sides. Rachel put her hand on his shoulder.

"Need some help?"

Rachel sat down on the floor next to Jake and pulled one of the desk drawers out onto her lap. Together, they sifted through the contents of each drawer.

"Why did Keith switch from accounting to philosophy?"

"I don't really know. We did a lot of fighting about it. He was doing so well with accounting until he signed up for that required philosophy course. I don't know—he just loved it. He talked about how much he'd been missing in life by spending so much time on absolute ideas." She thought for a moment. "Yeah, that's the term he used. Absolute ideas. It was all so strange, especially considering how he used to make fun of you and your day dreaming."

"Did he mention joining some sort of philosophy group? Did he mention going to the house at the end of Main Street?"

"Yes. He tried to tell me about it a few times, but I was so pissed at him I wouldn't listen." She clasped her left hand with her right and used her thumb to follow the lines life had traced on her left palm. "I guess I sort of lost touch with him, too—and I was right here with him."

Jake spoke, his voice gentle. "Yesterday, you mentioned Keith was afraid of something. Do you have any idea what it could have been?"

"I don't know. He wouldn't say. Actually, he said I wouldn't believe him. It started after one of his friends died."

"Keith was close to the other two?"

Rachel nodded.

"There was such a distance between us then." Rachel rubbed her palms together. "It's hard to know what was going on with him."

Jake took Rachel's hands. Shocked by how marble cold they felt, he placed one palm against each side of his face and held them until they were warm again.

On the floor, next to the desk, stood a stack of books. When Jake released her hands, Rachel grabbed the first book on the pile, held it up in the air, and flipped through it so any papers tucked between the pages would fall out. None did. Rachel repeated the same process with a few more books until her efforts were rewarded. Like birds shot in flight, folded sheets of paper fluttered to the ground.

The wing-like flurry caught Jake's attention. "Anything interesting?"

She retrieved the wayward scraps and skimmed their contents. "No. Philosophy stuff, I think. This one is a class schedule. This one looks like class notes." She read part of the final item. "This is a list of facts about Pythagoras. Hey, Pythagoras must have been some guy. Wow! Check this out. Did you know he believed there were eight planets, hundreds and hundreds of years before they invented the telescope? I wonder how he figured that out. This one's highlighted. It says Pythagoras believed the soul could exist apart from the body."

Rachel hummed a few bars of the theme to *The Twilight Zone.* "I guess that's how he found out about the planets." She laughed, crushed the papers into a ball, and tossed it into the trashcan next to the bed.

Jake tried to intercept the shot, but missed. He retrieved the paper ball and smoothed it out." He pointed at the list and read carefully. "I wonder why Keith chose to highlight this particular part of the list. It's so stupid, compared to the rest." He turned over the first of the two sheets and read a list printed on the back. "Oh, boy—this is a list of instructions on," Jake winked, "teaching your soul to travel. Is this the bogus kind of stuff they teach in school now?"

"This is really starting to get to me." Rachel's voice trailed off to a whisper.

Jake balled the paper and threw it into the can. "Hey, don't worry about this shit. It's nothing."

"Anyway, I'm very tired, and I don't think there is anything here for us to find. I really need to go to bed. See you in the morning." Rachel collected her already sleeping dog and left.

As soon as Rachel was gone, Jake rescued the stapled copies from the trashcan and placed the wad on the bedside table. Since it was only ten o'clock, he went into the parlor and picked up the phone. He pushed raven curls from his forehead as he waited for his assistant to answer his call. "Hi, Jerry. Yes, I know. There was a death in the family. I'm in Utica. If you need to reach me, the phone number is in the card file under the name Rachel. Can you get the Wall Street shots over to Fred? Yeah, they're all done. You know where to find them. Hey, did you take the black and white prints out of the rinse? That bad? Shiiiit! Go through the mail, open the business correspondence, and do whatever you can to cover for me. Just let the personal stuff pile up. I'll dig in as soon as I get back. Thanks, you're a lifesaver. Bye."

When Jake ventured out of the parlor, he found the rest of the house dark and quiet. He went into the kitchen to see if there was any beer in the refrigerator. There it was, one bottle of Saranac, cozying up to the lettuce. He removed the cap and relished the flavor he so missed when he traveled too far from Utica. Then, he decided to go back into the bedroom to commit an unforgivable crime. Smoke in Rachel's house. Just one. Just one would not hurt anything.

Since Rachel had no ashtrays, he snagged an empty can out of the recycling bin and returned to Keith's room. The night did not seem quite so dark, so lonely, after he made himself comfortable with the beer by his side and a cigarette in his hand. He flicked the ashes into his makeshift ashtray and sipped the beer until he felt sleep creeping up on him. He remembered Keith's list of instructions for soul travel. Should he take it seriously? A philosophy club connected all the kids. He opened the wad and, for a second time, read the promo sheet that proclaimed the marvels of the philosopher Pythagoras. His attention wandered to the instructions listed on the back of the first page. Step one: get into a comfortable position, never on your left side. Two: Relax. Okay, he thought. I'm one ahead of the game here. Step three: enter a state bordering on sleep. No problem again. Four: shift body awareness outside body. He read the rest of the list as he finished his beer. After tossing the empty bottle into the trash can, he turned off the light and closed his eyes. Somehow, the glow of the night-light was company. Sneaking another cigarette was out of the question, so he made believe, visualized clouds of blue smoke entering and leaving his lungs. Over and over. It reminded him of step four. Shift your body awareness outside the body. Try it, he thought. It's only a joke, so why not. He kept imagining the smoke, imagining his essence traveling away with the illusory smoke.

Jake slipped toward sleep, the list forgotten. He listened to what he guessed was the hum of the refrigerator kicking on, all the way from the kitchen. It relaxed him. Strange. The kitchen was so far away. Or was it a whispering? No, the humming came from within him. And he felt so heavy, so cold. Soon, the peculiar sinking feeling he sometimes noticed just before sleep took him came again. It was then he remembered he had forgotten to make sure his cigarette was completely dead and disposed of before Rachel could sniff it out in the morning.

Jake struggled to raise himself up, just far enough to reach the cigarette, but found he could not move. His mind remained awake, but the paralysis of sleep held his body prisoner. Confused, he strained to reach the can on the desk. Finally, feeling a bit lightheaded, he managed to sit up and reached toward the can.

The night-light flickered, off-and-on, off-and-on, as if threatening to die. Its erratic behavior urged Jake to look back in the direction of the firefly-like flickering, back toward the head of the bed.

There, only visible during the flashes of light, sleeping on his pillow, was a face sequined with perspiration. He squinted. He recognized the head resting on the pillow as his. It was his. Jake felt his face, the one sitting up, tingling as if he had been out in the cold too long. The tingling spread over his whole body and morphed into a flash of heat. Then he blacked out.

Jake awoke to find himself in the same position he had taken when he had first fallen asleep. As soon as he stopped shaking, he leapt out of bed, switched on the light, emptied the contents of the makeshift ashtray into his sweating palm, and returned the aluminum can to the recycling bin. Then he ran into the bathroom and quickly flushed the cigarette, desperate to bury the remains of his sin. As he watched the ashes swirl around and disappear in the whirlpool, he knew he would not sleep again that night.

Chapter 9

THE NEXT MORNING, JAKE SAT ON THE PORCH, shivering in the brittle air. A sudden, dissonant sound of clanging chimes railed. Jake flinched and dropped his cigarette. He twisted around and saw Rachel standing with her hand on the chime. To counter her attack, he blew his last puff of smoke at her.

"Well, good morning to you, too, Mr. Preston," Rachel said, sounding satisfied. "Today, you're the one who looks like shit."

What could he tell her? "Yeah, I had this really weird sort of dream last night, so I decided to stay up and finish going through the rest of Keith's room."

"Find anything?"

"No. I guess real life isn't always quite like it is in detective movies."

"Come on back inside. You look like you need some coffee." Rachel took Jake's arm and led him into the kitchen. The hot coffee banished the last remains of the morning chill that had doggedly followed them back into the house.

All through breakfast, Jake kept his eyes on Nikki. The little troublemaker paid an inordinate amount of attention to the bin that housed the empty cans waiting to be sent away for transformation into their next life form. She sniffed and scratched at the bin. Could she smell the ashes?

Jake, in an effort to bribe the would-be snitch, broke his Nikki embargo and offered her a piece of bacon from his plate. She wolfed down the bacon and immediately returned to her snooping post. Jake was sure she knew about his nicotine-driven crime and was most likely planning a way to pin it on him.

Rachel interrupted Jake's surveillance of the unfolding drama. "I forgot to tell you. Ellen called me. She wants me and Nikki to spend today with her. You won't mind if we leave you alone, will you?"

"You *and* Nikki? Sounds great to me. You could use a change of scenery. So could Nikki. Besides, I'm planning on paying a surprise visit to Keith's philosophy professor."

A cacophony set off by the box of empty cans being over-turned startled the trio. Nikki squealed and tore out of the room with her stump of a tail tucked away for safekeeping and Jake's laughter chasing after her.

* * *

Jake admired the striking Victorian charm of the professor's house. It was decorated with gaudy gingerbread ornamentation. A railing, supported by perfectly even, white balusters, walled the front porch from the yard. White wicker furniture sat artfully placed in small groups on each end of the porch. Two large windows posted on each side of the front door were partially veiled by white lace curtains. Jake used the brass knocker to announce his arrival.

He was about to knock a second time when the door opened. Jake's eyes focused on the petite woman who answered his call. Glossy black hair veiled a face illuminated by sapphire blue eyes that sparkled with good nature. She smiled and motioned Jake into the front hall without asking who he was or what he wanted.

"Good morning, I'm Jake Preston. I came to speak with Professor Devereux. Would you be his daughter?"

"Yes, I am Madeleine. Please, come into our morning room, and make yourself comfortable while I fetch my father." She gestured toward a cozy area of the room. "Help yourself to tea or fruit." She left him alone in a world that was a shimmering ghost of the past.

A fire crackling from behind an ornate needlepoint fire screen warmed the room. The lighting came from sinumbra lamps with cut-glass shades. A silver tray arranged with a bowl of fruit and a china tea service sat on rosewood Louis XV table. Jake sat down on a chair upholstered with red velvet cushions, just as Madeleine led her father into the room. Jake stood up and offered his hand to the professor.

"I'm so glad you have come to visit us." Professor Devereux seemed to purr as he spoke. "What can we do for you?"

Jake dropped his hand and followed his host's lead and recaptured his seat, then began the speech he had hastily prepared during the short walk down Main Street. "I am, or was, Keith Foster's friend. I lost touch with him a number of years ago and need to know what sort of person he became. I guess I need to feel closer to him, to reminisce. I heard he had a great deal of respect for you. Perhaps you can tell me something about him?"

Devereux shook his head with apparent sympathy. "Keith was a fine young man, an exemplary student. Madeleine and I thought very highly of him. We were desperately saddened by his passing. Even so, I do not think there is much we can tell you. Our relationship was one limited to an educational setting."

"Wasn't Keith a member of a group that sometimes held meetings here?"

"Yes, he was. However, you must understand, the Pythagorean Society is just a little ruse I use to get students interested in philosophy, to stimulate their desire to learn. It is an extension of my course offerings. You see, the study of philosophy has so much to offer young people. Unfortunately, for the most part, they just are not interested. Even so, I find Pythagoras has something to fascinate most students. I build on that interest and use the advantage to sneak in all sorts of educational opportunities. You know what I mean. Make learning fun. I know it's sort of underhanded, but the results are so strikingly positive."

"Yes, I understand what you mean. I must admit I didn't do right with my study of philosophy either." Jake scrambled for a way to get Devereux to keep talking. "In fact, I barely remembered who Pythagoras was until I ran across some of the information Keith left behind." Jake's memories of the previous night crept into his mind. He shook off the spell, regained his composure, and continued. "Most of it's rather amazing, but what about that soul travel stuff? Do your students actually buy into such garbage?"

Professor Devereux laughed. "Yes, as a matter of fact, it's one of my best attention getters. They love it. It's much more fun than Charades."

"Please, Professor, you don't mean to try to convince me it really works, do you?" A chill ran down Jake's back.

"Oh—I don't know. The verdict is not in yet. Some experts say that it is just a perceptual jump, a mental trick. Some think much more of it." Devereux leaned closer to Jake. "But—whatever—it's great fun."

"I can't buy it." The vision of a cigarette whirling into oblivion whispered into Jake's mind. He willed it away.

"You certainly are not alone in your skepticism, but why is it so hard for you to accept? First of all, I do fudge a bit. We use the word soul, but we really mean the mind or awareness. They say it's the mind or essence that travels." Devereux poured himself a cup of tea. "The human brain is ninety-nine percent air, and the mind isn't material, so why would you insist that a nonmaterial substance must be contained in an almost material place like the body?" After waiting for an answer that did not come, Devereux laughed. "Well, Mr. Preston, I can see you won't be joining our little group. Would you like to join us for breakfast, instead?"

"No, Professor Devereux. I have already had breakfast. Besides, I have a number of errands to run."

Professor Devereux rose and offered Jake his hand. Jake pretended not to notice.

"Please come back and visit us again. Next time, come when you can stay a while. We do so enjoy visitors." Madeleine rose and followed them to the door.

"Professor, may I ask where you and Madeleine are from? You have such an interesting accent, but I can't quite place it."

"Everyone asks us the same question. Madeleine and I have lived in many different locations. We seem to have picked up characteristics of various areas. We're from no place in particular, except from here, of course."

Jake walked down the long driveway, back toward the street, agonizing over the fact that he had just reached another dead end. By the time he arrived at Rachel's house, he was totally beat. Since he knew he would be alone for a while, he decided to use the opportunity to catch up on his sleep. He took off his shoes and stretched out on Keith's bed. The conversation with the charming foreigners played over and over in Jake's head. Thoughts of the bizarre dream from the night before, again, began to inch their way into his mind. A fine mist of perspiration spread across his skin. After re-reading the instructions Keith left behind, he decided to give it a real try. He had to know. Dream or not?

Keith's bed had become so very familiar to Jake. He knew exactly which areas fit him best. He snuggled down into a comfortable position and carefully repeated the numbered steps as he had done the night before. His thoughts began to dim.

* * *

When the phone rang, it took Jake a while to reorganize his mind. He teetered into the parlor fighting the fog in his mind, lifted the receiver and mumbled, "Hello."

"Sorry—wrong number," said a cool, male voice, followed by a click. Jake noticed the clock on the answering machine and realized he had been sleeping for almost an hour. Still groggy, he shuffled back to bed. Before long, he again drifted off to sleep.

There it was again, the machine-whirring noise. As he concentrated on the hypnotic sound, the sinking feeling returned. He knew he was still in bed, but he felt like he had dropped through the mattress and was on his way through the floor below. His whole body began to vibrate. Even though his eyes were closed, every aspect of the room about him was clearly visible, illuminated by a strange light. He was awake inside his sleeping body. A rush of panic scalded his face, while his body grew cold.

He counted his breaths hoping calmness would steady him. This time, there was no cigarette to reach for, no sin in need of a cover-up. A throwing off of shackles was his only excuse. This time, he made a conscious decision to explore. He had to know.

The instructions claimed it was all only a matter of willpower, so he willed himself to stand. At first, nothing happened, so he strained to raise one arm as he had done the night before. It worked. He could see a fluid-like version of his arm slowly separate from its body-double. His mind told him he should have been afraid, but he was not. He did not take time to wonder why. Mesmerized by his newfound power, he forced his other arm to follow suit. Then, with less effort than expected, he managed to bend one immaterial leg at the knee, separating it from its original as he had done with his arms. Soon, the rest of Jake's second body followed orders and began to shift. A shot of electricity shot through his torso as his shadow form lifted away from his body. The pain was momentary.

Jake found himself standing beside his bed, looking down at his sleeping form. A sense of absolute freedom intoxicated him. He had not expected that. It was like a drug. He was no longer afraidof—anything. He decided to test his mobility by walking, or whatever, into the next room.

The afternoon sun filled the parlor with faceted rainbows as it filtered itself through the sun-catchers and prisms. The splinters of color wavered in the air, tempting him to become part of their light show, luring him into their spectral dance.

Without a conscious decision, his phantom-self stumbled from the floor and tumbled in the air like one more butterfly among others born of the transformed sunlight. Gooseflesh spread over Jake's Main Street skin. His lips pulled back from his teeth in a wide grin. The small room limited his joy, so he decided to see if he could make his way outside. He tried to twist the doorknob, to no avail. His hand simply passed through it.

The front door was not closed all the way. A narrow sliver of light wedged its way through the length of the doorway, slicing the room in half. Perhaps, he could follow the light outside. He pressed himself against the doorway— remembered—will power, and slipped through the crack with little more effort than the sun had spent on a similar task.

Once outside, Jake was unsure of what his next move should be, so he lingered on the porch and marveled at how bright the world looked, admired the radiant colors of his newfound perspective of Main Street. The mailman trotted onto the porch, popped a letter in the mailbox, and left without noticing Jake's presence. Jake tried to coax music out of the wind chimes. Again, his hand failed to make contact with a material object.

Doubts began to tickle Jake's mind. Should he end the experiment? Was it time to return to his haven of flesh? How would he return? He felt like a caged bird, recently escaped from its gilded prison, afraid to fly to freedom, afraid of the unknown.

No, he decided on just one little flight. Fear could no longer hold him down. Addiction. Lifting off the ground was effortless.

With total abandon, he rose and tumbled in the air, laughing down at the passing cars. If they only knew, those souls imprisoned in their metal shells. He approached the power lines that ran the length of Main Street. His skin tingled. His hair stood on end. The feeling was not unpleasant, so he moved closer to the source of the new stimulation. As he drew nearer to the wires, he felt a force pull at him. In less than an instant, his cloud-like form became intimately joined to the power lines.

Static electricity buzzed and crackled in the air like a miniature storm. Will or no, he could not yank himself free. AS if he were a bit of lint adhering to a wool suit, the force held him captive. Every spark burned through him like a spike being nailed through flesh. He writhed as a prisoner tied to a whipping post.

As if in response to Jake's electrical dilemma, a wind blew in from the south, dragging clouds before the sun, tugging at trees, rattling leaves and plucking them from their moorings.

A few yards ahead stood a telephone pole and its crossbars. Perhaps, if he could get to the pole, he could anchor himself to it and pull himself free. Or maybe, he prayed, the pull of the electricity would be less powerful there. Hand over hand, he grabbed the wire, slowly and painstakingly dragging himself along its length. As he continued his torturous journey, sparks shot off the wires and disappeared into the air like psychotic fireflies. And the wind grew stronger. Trees bent over and leaves swirled into the growing darkness.

Jake looked ahead to see a squirrel barreling toward him, effortlessly running along the lines like a tiny locomotive, its cheeks packed full of the bounty of the day. Just before it would have run into Jake, the squirrel slammed on its brakes and spasmodically whipped its tail back and forth while staring in Jake's direction. It dumped its cheeks-full of sunflower seeds, changed directions, and ran as if the devil was chasing it.

Jake continued his snail-pace journey. He neared the pole, but the power of the electricity had not waned. He struggled to move one hand in front of the other and failed. Burdened by total exhaustion, Jake stopped fighting. He hugged the line and trembled in place. The wind whipped trees in rhythmic waves. Limbs bowed toward Jake, reached out as if they wished to touch him with soothing fingers. Closer. Closer. One limb laid its weight across the wires, shorting the line. Jake's new world of freedom flashed black except for occasional flares of lightning like those imprisoned behind tightly closed eyelids.

When he awoke, he was back where he belonged, back in the safety of Keith's bed. It took a long while before he felt steady enough to stand. When he grew strong enough to rise, his first impulse was to test if he could touch something without sailing right through it, so he picked up one of Keith's books, delighting at the feel of its weight.

Step two consisted of racing to the kitchen for a shot of vodka. The burning in his throat assured him his normal feelings had returned, indeed, if he had ever lost them. A smoke on the front porch would finalize his efforts to prove he was exactly where he belonged.

The frigid air tore through his jacket like a tiger's claws. As soon as he stopped trembling, he left the porch and walked down the street, looking up at the wires that had held him captive in his waking nightmare. He retraced his imaginary trip along the lines. As he approached the spot where he had met the hell-bent squirrel, something crunched under his heel. He bent down to scrape the bottom of his shoe and found what was crushed into the grooves of his heel. A squirrel-sized cheek full of sunflower seeds.

Jake dropped his cigarette and ran into the house. He slammed the door, making sure it was closed all the way. The tumult of his passing rattled the wind chimes. They clanged an unpleasant tune that continued to play itself out well after he locked the door.

* * *

Later that evening, Rachel and Nikki returned home, invigorated by their day away. Unfortunately, Jake could not claim the same benefits from his journey. As soon as she placed Nikki on the floor, Jake took Rachel into his arms and pressed her against himself.

"What's wrong?"

"Rachel, you don't know how good it feels to know you can see me."

"You been smoking something funny today?" Rachel pinched Jake's cheek. "I knew you'd pick up bad habits in the big city." She picked up the bag she had left standing next to the door. "How about some soup? Ellen sent us home with a care package, as if we need more stuff to eat. There's soup and cookies for us and steak for Nikki." She kissed his cheek and whispered, "Are you okay?"

"I'll tell you about it later. Let's eat first."

After they filled themselves with the contents of Ellen's care package, they repeated their long-practiced nighttime routine. Rachel took a book and a glass of wine into the bathroom for her bubble bath, and Jake headed outside for his last cigarettes of the day.

Before long, Jake found himself striding purposefully toward the end of the street. He could have walked in the other direction and stopped to watch the hardiest of the local kids playing basketball on the frostbitten playground. However, something, maybe the wind, pulled him in the other direction. The October moon cast a forbidding light on the house. The structure that sheltered the professor and his daughter no longer looked like a Victorian gingerbread house. The two front windows, glowing with candlelight, took on the appearance of menacing eyes peering out from behind drooping lids of white lace. The vertical slats of the porch railing mimicked perfectly spaced, well-sharpened teeth.

Chapter 10

*J*AKE TURNED HIS BACK on THE JACK-O-LANTERN APPARITION and hurried back to the warmth of his little family. He knew he would probably regret it, but he decided to tell Rachel everything that happened.

Jake found Rachel asleep on the couch, her knees pulled up, with Nikki curled in the angle formed by her sleeping mistress's legs. Rachel slept through Jake's entrance, but Nikki woke just long enough to reposition herself with her butt facing his direction. He lifted a crocheted afghan from the back of the rocking chair and placed it over Rachel. Nikki lay silently under the cover. For one moment, Jake considered the unlikely possibility that the dog would suffocate under the loosely woven material. His hopeful smile crumbled when he saw a little, black nose find its way to the edge of the cover.

Jake turned out the light, went into the next room, and prepared to try for a good night's sleep. As he lay on Keith's bed, he made a mental note to fix the night-light that flickered hesitantly in the outlet by the door. He had grown to rely on the small spark for company, and knew he would be devastated if it decided to resign its post.

While drifting off to sleep, he was careful to refrain from thinking about any of the steps that had led him into the nightmare realm he visited earlier. The need to forget, a need to deny, replaced his need to know. Instead, he concentrated on the stack of work he knew would be waiting to pounce on him when he returned to the city.

It started, again.

He knew his eyes were closed, but he was acutely aware of his surroundings. Damn, this was not supposed to happen. A chill slowly slipped into the room. Jake's hair stood at attention. He became aware of a presence standing in the room with him. He could not see what it was, but he knew something was there. He could feel its breath swirling in the air. He could almost hear its heart beat.

It had to be a dream—yes—only a frigid dream. Maybe, it was a draft from the window. To be sure, he tried to turn in the direction of the presence, but failed. He was paralyzed again. It had to be a dream. He did not plan this. He did not follow the list of directions.

With each tick of the clock on Keith's end table, another drop of perspiration joined the others that glistened on Jake's flesh. His heart beat so loudly, he was sure it would wake him, sooner— or later.

Whatever or whoever stood by his bed, remained. Watching. Jake still could not see it, but somehow he knew. His face burned with fear. Move. If he could just make himself move, he knew he would wake. His limbs ignored his frantic orders. He tried to force his lips and throat into a scream. He felt sure if he could just make a sound he would wake. His mind raced in an effort to find a way to end the nightmare. With all the force terror can give birth to, he directed his will power toward forcing out the pathetic groan that finally roused him. His eyes snapped open.

Jake leapt off the bed and lost his balance. Supporting himself by holding onto the headboard, he scanned the room for the silent watcher. He was alone, so he rushed into the parlor and turned on the overhead light. Rachel slept, exactly where he had left her, destroying his desperate hope that she had come into his room to be sure he had returned from his walk, that *she* had been the silent watcher.

"Jake, you scared me," Rachel mumbled, still half asleep. "I didn't expect to see you here. What time is it?" She blinked and squinted at the clock.

Jake checked the time and realized he had only been sleeping for two hours. It felt longer. He shook it off and went into the living room. "Rachel. It's midnight, maybe you better get yourself upstairs."

Rachel nodded and headed for the stairs. Before she started up to the second floor she said, "Jake, are you okay?"

Jake followed Rachel to the stairway. He touched her face. "No, I'm not okay. Let's talk about it in the morning. I really need to tell you about it, but it can wait until tomorrow. We're both too tired to get anything right tonight."

"But—"

"See you tomorrow." He kissed her forehead and watched as she climbed the stairs to her room.

Jake passed through the parlor on his way back to bed and noticed Nikki still asleep on the couch, oblivious to the fact that she had been forgotten. He crept over to the couch and sat down next to the dog. Gently, he scratched her belly. She stretched, yawned, slowly blinked her eyes, and did a double take when she spotted Jake. She jumped to her feet and frantically spun around in a disorganized effort, no doubt, to find Rachel. Jake scooped the bewildered dog up into his arms and carried her to the top of the stairs. When he placed her on the second floor landing, her legs were already in motion. She disappeared into the darkness. Jake smiled at his little prank as he headed down the stairs. It was not often he got the chance to outsmart Nikki.

Sleep claimed Jake in an instant, leaving no time to recite lists or deny reality. He simply flickered out like a faulty nightlight. In his dream, he was back in New York, in his darkroom. Someone called to him, urged him to leave his lightless sanctuary. Even though he was afraid to answer the call of the mysterious voice, even though he tried to resist, his arm reached out to open the dream-door. As his hand slowly turned the knob, he awoke to the realization that he still rested in Keith's bed, to the realization that someone or something was in the room with him, again. Just like before, even though his eyes were closed, he could see the room with sparkling clarity. He could see everything except the silent watcher who hovered even closer than before. He could feel its frigid breath fingering his face. A dream, he told himself. This is just another dream. Ignore it and it will go away, like before.

It was impossible to ignore what came next. Without any effort on Jake's part, without his consent, a separation began to occur. He felt his hidden self slowly lose hold of its protected position. He felt the two Jakes separate, a little at a time.

Stop! He screamed to himself. No! He used all his will to stay put, all his strength to stay together. To fight the vacuum that sucked his essence away. Wake! That's it! Wake up! He strained to force himself to wake. Move. Anything! He screamed in paralytic silence. If he could just move a finger—he could wake himself—he just knew it. Finally, whether by luck, or due to his frantic efforts, his eyes flashed open, and he was once again a member of the real world.

Jake sprang out of bed and snapped on a light. He knew he would be alone if the lights were on. Once he found his way into the parlor, he switched on the television and searched for a news channel. There it was, proof that the world was still where it belonged. He watched a film report of a tornado in the South, then an analysis of the floundering economy, and it went on and on until he was sure he had been properly reinitiated into the fraternity of the everyday man. He kept his eyes and thoughts glued to the screen until Rachel descended the stairs and kissed him good morning.

* * *

Telling Rachel his story was the most agonizing aspect of all that had happened in the last few days. Once, she tried to leave the kitchen, but Jake motioned her back to her chair. He felt like a total fool. Their breakfast of eggs and ham cooled without benefit of fork and knife. Throughout the whole ordeal, Rachel stared at Jake in apparent disbelief.

"Jake, I don't know what to say. We've been through some hard times. We've known each other for a long time. You've done a lot of things to make me cry, to break my heart, to make me wish I could force myself to hate you. But, the one thing you never did was lie to me. Part of me wants to laugh in your face. Another part tells me to believe you. I just don't know what to say. It's all so bizarre."

Rachel rose and removed the rejected morning meal from the table. Jake made no attempt to help her. He simply sat and waited for what would come next. He simply sat and waited to be accepted, or be branded a lunatic.

"Jake. I need to get away from here for a while. I have to get away to think. First Keith—now this. I don't know what to say. Please, forgive me." Rachel dried her hands and tossed the towel aside. "I'm going out for a drive. Maybe I'll go see Ellen."

Rachel left the dishes in the sink and dashed from the kitchen, leaving Jake sitting in front of the barren table. Since the sun remained hidden behind storm clouds, he sat without even the usual ray of sunlight for company.

Jake shuffled into the parlor. Rachel's coat was gone from its hook by the front door. Her reassuring presence had left him as quickly as had his silent watcher of the night before. There, on her satin pillow, sat Nikki. Rachel had left him alone with his archenemy, and Nikki was wide awake. Ready to take advantage of the situation.

Jake found himself a spot on the couch and spoke to his only current link to the flesh-and-blood world. "Nikki, we're stuck here with each other for a little while. How about a cease-fire? How about we form a temporary alliance until Rachel comes back?" He waited for a reply.

Nikki took only a moment to formulate her response. She hopped off her pillow, inspected the ranks of her squeaky imps, and chose a huge, especially worn, orange tarantula squeak toy. Then she trotted over to a spot right in front of Jake, growled, and shook the life out of the rubber spider. After rattling it to death, she tossed the spider down onto the floor at Jake's feet, went back to her pillow, and closed her eyes.

Jake glanced down at the spider and saw that its stomach had been chewed out. He looked back at Nikki and acknowledged her rejection. "Nothing like pissing on a guy's white flag."

Nikki refused to honor his statement with as much as a flick of an ear. Having had enough rejection for the day, Jake gave up the fight and returned to Keith's bed. It was broad daylight. It was Tuesday on Main Street. Nothing could happen to him now. Tuesday was real. He slammed Keith's pillows into the proper shape and pushed his face into the softness of the ruffled feathers. Sleep was not far away. Sleep was no farther away than a spider from its web.

Chapter 11

DREAMS OF KEITH AND RACHEL filled Jake's sleep. He relived his final departure for New York. Without warning, the dreamscape changed. Instead of standing at gate twenty-seven, waving to those left behind, he was there in Keith's damned bed again, there with his eyes closed, there alone with the silent watcher. The room was alive with morning mist and the flickering of the failing night-light.

Jake was so tired. Not just tired from the lack of sleep, but tired from the fight, tired from fighting—alone.

There it was again, the call of a force stronger than he could ever be, a force that wanted him, and him alone. Again, Jake felt his essence letting go of its hold on flesh, little by little. First at his toes, then his knees, then his hips. His hands and arms became light in contrast to the heaviness of his cold flesh. His shadow abandoned him at his solar plexus, this time, without pain. His head followed, lolling like that of a rag doll. The usual paralysis controlled his body, but his being rose to the silent call. His body, he could not tell which one, felt as it was being wrung like a wet towel, squeezing his spirit out, drop by drop.

He begged his body to wake. Cry out—yes—lips—cry out! Body, wake me! Make a noise, move, anything! Just stop the escape! It worked before. This time, all the will he could muster was not enough to stop the division of the two Jakes. His astral body deserted its Main Street form and rose towards the ceiling. His mind hovered along with his spectral form and betrayed the Main Street Jake, betrayed the New York City, hot-shit Jake. The see-through, all-by-himself Jake hit the ceiling and looked down at the sleeping Jake, with no power of will, with no control. He began to slide towards the doorway, towards the call of the silent watcher. His spectral fingers grabbed onto the metal slats that held the ceiling panels. No purchase could be found. His alternate self continued toward the bedroom door and became fluid enough to mold itself around the shape of the transom, then slithered across it like a molten serpent and across the parlor ceiling. Still, he could find no purchase. He could find no way to stop the unwilling exodus, no way to stop the abduction.

As Jake slipped away, he spotted Nikki asleep on the couch. She lay, belly up, with her head dangling over the edge of the cushion, her tongue lolling. He called to her with a silent scream, a last ditch effort. He called and begged her to wake him.

Nikki's ears twitched. She snapped her head up, lost her balance, and fell to the floor with a thud. She jumped up, shook her head, and looked around. When she cocked her head and searched the ceiling, Jake knew he had made contact.

Nikki tried to leap high enough to reach Jake. A few luckless attempts made plain the impossibility of her goal. She raced around the room sniffing and leaping. She barked and growled, then ran out of the parlor leaving him alone with his terror. Jake continued to use his smoke-like fingernails as claws, trying to slow the forces that pulled him toward the outside. There was no time for tears, no time to wave good-bye. There was only time to long for union with the colored shards cast by sun-catchers as he slid toward the doorway. Just as he was about to be drawn through the gap between the door and its frame, he heard a clap of thunder. As if in the clutches of the twister he had seen on the news, Jake whirled back into his corporeal body. The force of the spiraling return rattled the bedsprings. His body shook with electric energy, and he woke with the full-body gasp of a drowning man devouring his last breath. He opened his eyes and realized the cause of his sudden return to Main Street. Nikki stood on his physical chest, frantically licking his face. He sat up and hugged her without hesitation. It was all he could do to keep himself from crushing her in gratitude. She was real. She was warm. She had called him back to Main Street. Jake thanked God for dog breath.

Chapter 12

ACHEL AND JAKE WOKE to Nikki's frantic barking. She alerted them to the fact that the postman was filling Rachel's mailbox with more real-world clutter. They heard the lid of the mailbox close, his footsteps leaving the porch.

Jake warmed to Rachel's presence. He slid his right arm over her, minimizing the narrow distance between them. Her presence told him all he needed to know of her decision.

"Rachel. I have more to tell you."

"I kind of figured. You and Nikki, together? Now, *this* is hard to believe. When I got home, here you were, on Keith's bed, sleeping peacefully with Nikki, belly-up, on your chest. What a vision. Even though I can't comprehend anything you told me, I know it's right to trust you. You never lied. That's all that matters."

"Rachel, you ain't heard nothin' yet." Jake sat up and held his hands over his eyes. When he found he could shut out the sight of Keith's room at will, his heart beat slowly and calmly again.

I'm going out for a smoke, or two, or a pack and a half. When I get back, we need to put this all together."

"Rachel, do you ever get a creepy feeling when you pass that house on the end of the street?"

She shook her head.

Jake zipped on his jacket and stuffed his Camels into the pocket. "Those people seem so nice, but something bugs me about them. They know something. I can feel it. I need to talk with Professor Devereux again."

"But it's almost—?"

"I won't be long." He brushed against the wind chimes as he left the porch, forcing the metal pipes to repeat their well-practiced song.

Jake shivered in the damp air. There was little evidence that the sun had risen, and it looked like more rain. Dark, angry clouds jostled each other in the turbid sky.

He knew that it was time to trust his own feelings. There was no other choice. Main Street was becoming too confusing. He reached the Devereux house before he finished his third cigarette.

Jake's heart pounded as he slammed the brass knocker against the wooden door. Overhead, gray storm clouds moved in great groups, like a crowd of restless watchers bumping each other as they pushed toward their destination.

He knocked again. Madeleine opened the door. This time, she offered no smile of welcome. Instead, darting eyes and pursed lips betrayed an impatience she tried vainly to hide.

"Is your father at home?"

"I'm sorry, Mr. Preston." She shook her head.

"I'd like to speak with him."

"He's not here at this time. Perhaps, you could come back tomorrow." She pushed on the door, but Jake held it open.

"What time will he be back?"

"I couldn't say." She pushed the door again. "Try tomorrow."

"Thank you." Jake let go of the door. Before his mouth closed, the door slammed shut. He knew she had lied. He clenched his fingers into a fist and pulled his arm back with every intention of punching the door, but stopped when, as if in response to his indignation, the sky mirrored his emotions with a crack of thunder and a flash of brilliance.

The sky split, and rain crashed down on Jake. The freezing raindrops hit his face as if they had been shot from millions of well-aimed guns hidden in the sky. It was only afternoon, but the sky looked about to go dark. He dashed under one of the small trees that huddled alongside the Devereux porch. Rain beat down on the dying autumn leaves, evoking smashing sounds against their shriveled flesh, sounding like thousands of Lilliputian tents being hit by hail. Jake lit a cigarette and leaned against the house. The leaves and the overhang of the roof offered minimal protection from the attack of pelting raindrops.

As he hid from the stinging bullets, he tried to banish the anger, to gain control. The rainfall created a monotonous, white

61

sound, lulling him. He closed his eyes and leaned against the house. He felt the vibrations of the house as if it were a living thing. Two people were inside the house. He could feel them. Why were they avoiding him?

Jake threw down his cigarette and climbed the porch steps. Somehow, he knew they would be at the window. He wanted them to know he was there, to know he recognized Madeleine's lie. He walked toward the door with the intent of knocking, but when he glanced through the side window, the view thinly veiled by white lace stunned him. His raised fist froze.

Devereux and Madeleine were there, as he knew they would be, but they were not daintily sipping tea, or reading the paper.

Devereux stood in the morning room, facing the window, his eyes closed. Madeleine slowly unbuttoned his shirt and left a trail of passionate kisses down his unveiled chest. The leisured removal of Devereux's shirt revealed a fantastic tattoo of a dancing man, blue, with long, matted hair swirling around his head, locks reaching out to the universe like arms. Jake recognized the blue man. Siva—Siva the destroyer of worlds, of illusions, of ignorance. Siva—the lord of dance, poised, posturing, dancing the dance of creation, snakes writhing around his neck. An eye in the center of Siva's forehead opened, starred at Jake. Was the eye always opened? Or—

A few seconds of voyeurism was all Jake could handle. He spun and ran headlong through the torrents of rain. The lightning cracking around him only served to speed his journey.

Chapter 13

*J*AKE BURST INTO RACHEL'S HOUSE. His first instinct was to search for her, to make sure she was safe. He found her in the kitchen listening to a tape of Tosca, her favorite opera. She hummed while she peeled vegetables to add to chicken soup that would soon be bubbling on the stove.

When she spotted Jake, Rachel stopped her work and turned off the music, her eyes wide with apprehension. Before she could voice her concern, Jake spoke.

"Not now, Hon'. Did you see a small slip of yellow paper with a phone number on it?" Without waiting for an answer, he rushed into Keith's room and sorted the contents of his camera bag until he spotted the phone numbers Dr. Higgins had given him.

Jake dialed the first number and held his breath. No answer. He tried the other number.

"Hello, Betty Higgins here."

Jake exhaled. It was a real voice, not an answering machine.

"Doc, this is Jake Preston. I need to see you right away. It's very important. Is there someplace we can meet, someplace that allows dogs?"

"Jake, you sound awful. What's wrong?"

"I can't tell you over the phone." Jake paused to catch his breath. "You might hang up on me."

"Okay. Why don't you come over here." She gave him directions.

Jake hung up the phone and returned to the kitchen. "Rachel, I'm really sorry to mess up your cooking plans, but I have to go somewhere, right now, and I don't want to leave you here alone."

"What's wrong?"

"Don't worry. I'll clue you in on the way to Betty's."

"Betty?"

Jake took Rachel's hand and led her into the parlor. After helping her with her coat, he took Nikki's leash off the hook, slipped it around the little dog's neck, and they left the house. The drive to Betty's apartment was short and punctuated by vicious shots of thunder.

"So who is this—Betty? Old girl friend?"

"Silly. She was one of my favorite professors—philosophy. I would not have finished school without her help—patience. Everybody loved her. After Mom died, I got sort of attached to her."

"Sounds like my kind of teacher." Rachel patted Jake's shoulder.

Betty Higgins answered Jake's knock and ushered her guests into her tiny, jumbled apartment. Books of every color and size imaginable the walls, tables, and chairs. On top of every other stack of books sat a half-filled ash-tray. The air was heavy with the exhalation of uncountable cigarettes.

"So that's the dog," Betty said, when Nikki pranced into her home. "I'm glad it's a little one." She sniffed the air. "I just hate dog smell, but this one won't be too bad. Have a seat." She gestured toward the couch. "Can I get you anything?" Jake and Rachel found an open spot on the couch and sat. Nikki curled up on the floor at their feet.

Jake told Betty everything that had happened since his return, with minimal time wasted on breathing.

* * *

"Wow, that's some story!" Betty sounded like a child, amazed by a scary campfire story. "I've never heard one quite like it, not in person. I have heard about something quite similar a number of years ago. From what you have told me, your experiences sound like an example of astral projection. At least that is what some people call it. I never really paid much attention to the details. I always kinda' figured it was bullshit.

64

"Doctor Higgins—".

"Jake. Call me Betty." She nodded to Rachel. "You too. I used to know this fellow, Henry, when I studied in Chicago. He was a physicist—spent a lot of time looking into this sort of thing. He was always yakking about it to me. Maybe he could help us, if he's still speaking to me." She rolled her eyes and moaned, then lit another cigarette and watched the cloud of smoke dissipate. "Come to think of it, the Pythagoreans believed in the transmigration of souls, the immortality of the psyche. Jake," she pointed to her ex-student. "You should remember; it's Philosophy 101 stuff. He taught that the psyche is a splinter of the heavenly fire that is drawn down to the earth and becomes imprisoned in a mortal body. Pythagoras called the imprisoning body a tomb. Yeah. And all his followers were dedicated to evolving enough to release their souls from the tomb of flesh." As Betty became more excited, her words came almost too quickly to understand.

"Supposedly, after a body dies, the soul rides a beam of light, like a shooting star, back up to the world-soul. Bang!" she clapped her hands once. "The soul can stay there or choose to cross through a plane of oblivion and across a river of forgetfulness and be reassigned a new body. That is how the Pythagoreans explained the beginning of life. Supposedly, life began in an area of mud and water that had been pierced by a beam of sunlight. Oh yeah, I'm gettin' off the point here." She lit another cigarette.

"Back to your problem, Jake. Pythagoras, himself, is said to have preached that sleep is an irrational, even an evil state to be avoided as much as possible. It's a common belief among many cultures, including Gnostics. But, then again, many of his contemporaries considered him to be a phony, a con artist. We will never really know. It is all hearsay. Now I see where you get the connection with your experiences and Professor Devereux. Pythagoras' descriptions of transmigration and astral projection do seem to have a lot in common."

"Then you don't think I'm crazy?" Jake said.

"No, of course not. It is actually a common belief among ancients and primitive peoples. The Egyptians professed that human thoughts had physical properties. Some believe astral projection began in Egypt, that priests used the technique to help build the pyramids. As a matter of fact, Pythagoras spent ten years studying Hermetics in Egypt before he attracted a following in Greece—"

"But, what do *you* think?"

"Jake, if anyone would be susceptible to this sort of phenomenon, it would be you. I could never tell where your thoughts were when you were in my class. Maybe, your mind just wandered a little too far this time. Some people have an innate capacity to alter their states of consciousness, to block out the real world—or to open themselves to something else. They are often very creative people, like you. I'll call Henry and see what he has to say." She lightened her tone and tried to sound cheerful. "But in any case, I'm sure you're not in any danger—I don't see how you could be."

"Then what about Keith and the other two?" Jake said.

"I don't know what to say about that, but I will get right on this. I'm sure Henry will be able to help us figure this out."

"I have a feeling I'll be finding out more than I want to." Jake rose and offered Rachel his hand. "Thanks for listening. I don't know who else would have."

"Let's make sure we keep in touch," Betty said. She moved as if to put a hand on his shoulder, but pulled back. "I'll try to get back to you as soon as I reach Henry. Call me if you need me for anything. Really, anything."

"Right." It took Jake all the strength he could muster to keep from reaching out to hug Betty Higgins. However, Jake knew that proper Main Street people do not touch, at least not when the lights are on. "Thanks for believing me."

* * *

The ride home was an improvement over the trip to the Higgins apartment. The rain had stopped, and the angry clouds were gone. The air was still. Even though the sun would soon be setting, leaving a darkened sky, it was good to know the air was clear, and the stars would shine down on them while they slept.

Rachel and Nikki headed for the kitchen as soon as they returned home—they had chickens and vegetables to convert into a healing brew. Jake leaned against the door to the kitchen, with his hands in his pockets, watching the ritual. Rachel sliced and peeled, and Nikki waited for tidbits to fall to the floor. Each of the three had a special part in the ritual.

Rachel cooked, Nikki guarded, and Jake watched from the other side of the room.

After they devoured their dinner of soup and bread, the trio spent the rest of the evening in front of the television. Rachel watched, and Jake made believe. Nikki's only contribution was an occasional change in the tone of her snore. The evening slipped through their fingers, as did numerous attempts at communication.

"Rachel, will you stay down here with me tonight? I don't want to sleep alone. I—"

"No, Jake; I can't."

"Just sleep. I really mean just sleep."

"No, that won't work. You know better. I need to keep my distance. You will be gone soon, so I have to protect myself. That is just the way it has to be. Here, sleep with Nikki." She handed the yawning dog to Jake and kissed them both goodnight. "She won't miss you when you're gone."

* * *

Jake woke when he heard the wind chimes calling. The flesh writhing next to him was warm and smooth. Her silken legs were intertwined with his, like the snakes around Siva's neck. With movements slow and hypnotic, her agile fingers touched his face, his back. They caressed the nape of his neck, causing his hair to stand on end. Slowly she pulled away as if to leave. He clutched at her arm, but took hold for only an instant. When he tried to tighten his grip, his fingers slipped through the silken substance of her diaphanous flesh. He rose to follow her as she drifted toward the ceiling. With indolent sensuality, they continued their mystery dance as they rolled and tumbled in the air. Jake looked down at his solid double, the wall of flesh that usually held his inner being prisoner, keeping him from this singular form of communion, forcing his soul to dance alone. Momentarily, he felt only resentment toward the Main Street Jake form. Jake and his lover rolled and touched in total harmony. The wind chimes sang as Jake's psyche ventured into his partner's world of rays of light, of falling stars, of spirits starving for the mortal sensations only flesh can offer.

It was Madeleine's world.

The atmosphere chilled as the silent watcher entered the room. When Jake realized his partner was not Rachel, he forgot his quest for gratification. He pushed aside pleasure and forced fear into the empty place left behind. He struggled to return to his body, but Madeleine's shadow held him. The watcher's smoky image drew near and hovered over Jake's sleeping form.

Nikki woke, then stood and aimed a muffled growl at the mist-like intruder. Before Nikki could locate the invader, it formed a spiral, like the funnel cloud of a tornado, and through Jake's parted lips, whirled into his hollow, sleeping form and snaked down his throat.

Jake tried to pull away from Madeleine, but she held tight.

Jake's solid body moved without orders from its rightful owner. The silent watcher, now within the lifeless Jake form, tried out its new Jake-body. It jerked and twitched, then sat up with the graceless moves of a ventriloquist's dummy. Nikki barked and snapped at the trespasser. A Jake arm clumsily swung at her and knocked her to the floor. She hit the ground running. The Jake face screwed itself into a crooked smile as it watched the frightened dog retreat to safer territory.

Jake's traitorous form returned to its original place on the empty bed. As soon as the head hit the pillow, its mouth opened, and the silent watcher exited as easily as exhaled smoke leaves the lungs of a dedicated smoker. Madeleine let go of her hold on Jake, and all went black.

Suddenly, the two Jakes were one, again, alone. Jake's eyes opened to the racket of chimes and the pain of his heart smashing against the ribs that held it captive.

Jake waited for his heart to calm, then dressed and went into the kitchen to search for aspirins. He shook two white tablets onto his vibrating palm, tossed them into his mouth, and followed with a glass of water.

Jake felt a tug at the hem of his jeans and gave a start. There, at his feet, sat Nikki. She looked up at him as if trying to discern the identity of the form towering above her. Jake bent down and scratched her head.

"Thanks for trying to help. You're a tough little stinker." She cuddled closer and luxuriated in the feeling of Jake's soothing fingers.

"Excuse me, girl, I'm going out front for a while." Nikki followed Jake to the front door and watched him leave.

The early morning air was still and clear. Jake stood on the porch and watched cars whizz by. The drivers inside the metal forms made no notice of him. Their lack of acknowledgment made him feel invisible. He reached into his pocket for a cigarette, lit it, and filled his lungs with smoke. He exhaled slowly. The sight of the swirling blue cloud leaving his mouth sent chills down his back. He pressed his lips together, as if to keep his soul where it belonged. He yanked the cigarette from his mouth, threw it to the ground, and squashed it into oblivion with the heel of his shoe, then he whipped the pack onto the street. With equal determination, he strode toward the house at the end of the street.

Chapter 14

PROFESSOR DEVEREUX OPENED HIS FRONT DOOR before Jake had a chance to knock. Without a word, he ushered Jake into the morning room. Jake sat on a red velvet chair, his feet planted solidly on the floor.

"So, Mr. Preston, we meet again. You look a bit worn." He sipped from a tiny long-stemmed glass. "Been having trouble sleeping?" He smirked at Jake. "How about a little libation?" He made a sweeping gesture that emphasized a sideboard lined with crystal bottles filled with colorful liquors.

Jake sat, jaw clenched, staring into the professor's eyes.

Devereux smiled, tilted his head. "Cat got your tongue? Or, perhaps, was it that shitty, little dog?"

The Professor had dropped his mask. Jake knew there would be no more need to play games or worry about appearances.

"Jake, I can call you by your first name, can't I? After all, we have become rather close of late. You might even call our relationship." He took another sip. "Intimate."

Madeleine's musical laughter stung Jake from a far corner of the room.

"Now, Madeleine, we must show respect to our honored guest." Devereux opened a silver box, took out two gnarled, black cigars, and offered one to Jake.

Jake remained silent, motionless.

Professor Devereux shrugged his shoulders and lit his cigar. "Well, so, what is it you want from us?"

"No," Jake said. "What is it *you* want from *me*?" He jacked up the volume on his voice. "I don't know what you did to Keith and the others. And I'm not sure what you're trying to do to me, but it stops here! Now!"

Devereux leaned on the mantle and rested his chin on his hand. "What are you going to do to stop us? Will you set your killer guard dog on us? You know that will not work anymore. We've gone far beyond that point." He sighed and puffed at his cigar.

"I'll call the police."

Laughter bubbled up from somewhere deep inside Devereux. "What a novel idea." Devereux reached into his pocket, retrieved a silver object, and tossed Jake a quarter. "Be my guest. There is a phone booth down at the corner. If I had a phone, I'd let you use it." Devereux took a few puffs on his cigar. "Just be sure to let me know how many officers will be arriving so we can prepare enough tea and cookies." He flashed Jake a Jack-o-Lantern smile.

"What, do you think you have some sort of immunity or something?" Jake curled his hands into fists and leaned toward Devereux. "You can't just slither into town and destroy lives and get away with it!"

"Jake, but you are so very, very wrong. We can do just that. We do it all the time. You see, we do have immunity." He walked over to the front window. "That," Devereux pointed to the street scene, "is our shield. Our immunity. Reality. The common man's pathetic, fanatical will to hold onto *his* reality. His need to control the boundary between what he thinks is real and what he prays is not. Everyone out there. Well almost everyone," he winked, "believes there is a great big, solid brick wall between their real world and what they don't want to see. They think creatures such as I and everything else they're afraid or too stupid to see or feel are safely barred from their world by that phenomenal, brick fortification." His voice fell almost to a whisper. "But what they refuse to see is the fact that there *is* no brick wall. Never was. It is really quite sad, because the only secret Main Street people actually manage to wall themselves away from is—the magic. The magic of the eons. The magic their souls crave for survival." The magic their souls search for, in secret, while they sleep.

Devereux grabbed a handful of the curtain hanging by his side. "The only barricade between them and us, between light and shadow, is no more solid than this lace curtain." He slipped behind the curtain, and with sensuous languor blew a cloud of cigar smoke through the open-weave fabric. The blue seraph filtered through the curtain and slowly dissipated into the unclean atmosphere of the dimly lit room. "You see, Jake." Devereux flashed the sordid smile of an obscene bride and continued to speak from behind the lace veil draped over his face. "The border between our world and yours is no darker than a pane of glass, no more solid than this man-made cobweb." Devereux caressed the curtain, stroked it with the side of his face, as would a sensual feline. "We can reach out to you with no more effort than it takes for smoke to pass through this, oh-so-less-than-brick wall. *You* know that. And all it takes for us to turn what is sacred to the profane is—a touch of flesh."

Laughter edged its way between Devereux's words. "All they have to do to see us, to see the magic, is *really* open their eyes, dare to crawl close enough to peek through the holes in the curtain. But they won't! They never will!" They are asleep, drunk on dreams. Devereux giggled. "*That*, dear Jake, makes us invincible. *That*, is our magic shield, our mask. And there is nothing you can do to stop us. There is nothing you can do to end our rapturous masquerade.

"The only real walls are made of living flesh, and you know what they say—the grass is always greener on the other side. Some spirits crave spiritual union. Some crave the pleasures only flesh can offer. And some of us—want it all." Devereux winked at Jake. "Do you know which kind you are? Think about it, Jake. Think very hard—Try to remember. Which kind are you? On which side of the curtain do you belong? Do you even have the guts to crawl close enough to peek at what's on the other side?" Devereux giggled again.

With clenched teeth and sweating palms, Jake rose from the scarlet velvet chair and strode to where Professor Devereux stood. Then, without hesitating, he slammed his right fist into the professor's face. Madeleine screamed and leapt from her chair. She rushed to her so-called father's side, making hurried attempts to stop the flow of blood from his broken nose.

As Devereux stared in gaping amazement, Jake murmured. "Too bad about that lace curtain—looks like traffic travels in both directions. Tell *that* to the police."

Jake turned and found his own way to the front hall. All he could think of as he slammed the door was how proud Nikki would have been of him.

Chapter 15

*J*AKE SLAMMED THE DOOR after he entered Rachel's parlor. He threw down his jacket and went straight over to a phone to call Betty Higgins.

"Did you get in touch with your friend, Henry?"

"Yes, he just got back to me. He had lots to say. Let's get together as soon as possible."

"Absolutely! I've got lots to tell you too. Can you come over here, this time? I'll get pizza and beer."

"Okay. I have classes until three. I'll zip over right after I'm finished."

"Great. Doc, be careful." Jake hung up the phone and looked for Rachel. He found her in the kitchen, staring into a cup of coffee.

"Jake, where did you go?"

"Good question. I'm not real sure. Maybe the Twilight Zone. I just spoke to Betty and invited her over. She'll be here sometime after three. You don't mind, do you?"

"Of course not; what's wrong"

"I'm not exactly sure about what's up. Maybe Betty can help me put it together." Jake sat on his chair. "But, there is one thing I do know. I know Devereux had something to do with Keith's death, and no matter what, sooner or later, I'm going to figure it out."

"But, Jake—"

"Let's wait to worry about it until Betty tells us what her friend Henry had to say. Do you want to go out for breakfast? I'd really like to get away from here for a while."

Rachel brushed morning hair from her face. "Can I have a few minutes to pull myself together?"

Jake pushed up his sleeve and examined his watch, "Okay, five minutes—starting, now!"

Rachel laughed and ran toward the bathroom. Jake realized Nikki was nowhere to be seen. He quietly called her name as he searched. She was not on the ground floor, so he rushed upstairs and into Rachel's bedroom. There, on the bed, tightly curled into a shivering ball, lay Nikki. She jerked to life when she felt the touch of Jake's hand. He took her into his arms and hugged her. "I'm sorry, girl. I didn't mean to get you into any trouble. I didn't know you could get caught up in my dreams—my nightmares."

Jake checked to see she hadn't been injured the night before. Seeming none the worse for the wear, at least not physically, she wiggled and kissed him in return for his concern. When he left to meet Rachel, Nikki trotted down the stairs after him. Rachel met them as they passed through the dining room.

"Hey, sleepy-head." She bent down and patted her tiny partner. "I thought you'd never wake up today."

Nikki, freshly inspired by the attention of her human admirers, danced around their legs and trotted into the kitchen to check out the treasures that waited in her breakfast bowl.

* * *

Jake and Rachel had just finished preparing the parlor for Betty's arrival when they heard the wind chimes rail with anger. They looked at each other with startled apprehension. Nikki ran to the door and barked.

Jake motioned for Rachel to remain still. He steadied himself, then went to the door and held the knob for a moment before he turned it. He opened the door and, with relief, said, "It's okay." He stepped aside.

Betty stood framed by the rectangular, open space with the failing sun backlighting her tiny form. She held a bottle of wine in one hand and a cigarette in the other. "Hey, gang, nice bells. I know you don't mind my smoke." With her less than intuitive remark, she barged into the room, leaving a flurry of blue smoke trailing behind her. Slamming the door, she guillotined the blue trail, then pounded the wine bottle on to the coffee table, and plopped herself down on the rocking chair. "Okay, kids, you're going to flip when you hear what I have to tell you. All that

Pythagoras stuff ties in perfectly with what Henry told me. He is just as intrigued by it as I am. Yeah!"

Rachel and Jake found themselves comfortable places on the couch.

"Jake, remember what you told us about your experience with the power lines? Well, get this. You see, on power lines, the electricity is not inside the wires, it swirls around the wires—on the outside. That is why one touch from a tree limb, or anything grounded shorts them out. It turns out that many who practice astral projection avoid power lines because they have had experiences similar to yours. Henry says it has something to do with polarity. He says human bodies, all cells, harbor electric charges inside them. Those charges bind the astral being or psyche to the flesh. Electrical forces, like power lines, act as sort of false bodies. They bind the astral form to the source of the electricity and sort of give form to the psyche. That is why you were stuck. That is why you felt physical. It is why the squirrel saw you. At the very least, electricity hampers control, causes disorientation. Your psyche is safe while it is inside a body, but vulnerable while it is on the loose.

"Henry says many of the astral projectors he interviewed never plan trips when they know an electrical storm is brewing. Electricity is like kryptonite to some astral travelers. That ties in with the Pythagorean theory about psyches riding beams of light on a journey to the stars. Lightning. What if lightning can pull a psyche back up to the world soul? Makes sense."

Jake and Rachel stared at the chattering form rocking furiously in the chair before them. Betty appeared to notice that they were spellbound. "Yeah, you're right. I'd better calm down." She glanced around the room, looking worried, then shrugged and flicked her ashes on a paper napkin decorated with a grinning jack-o-lantern. "Nice accouterments,"

Rachel watched in apparent horror as Betty scattered ashes all over the table while complimenting the makeshift ashtray. Holding her temper, Rachel rose from her place next to Jake.

"Excuse me; I'll go into the kitchen to heat up the pizza." She turned to Betty. "Would you like wine or beer?"

Betty handed Rachel the bottle of wine and winked. As soon as Rachel left the room, Jake recounted his experience of the night before. Betty accepted the tale without the anxiety Rachel had registered after hearing the very same story that morning during breakfast.

Betty lit another cigarette. "Jake, there's something about Pythagorean lore I neglected to tell you. Actually, I didn't think of it until today." She blew a swirl of smoke into the air. "The legend of soul transmigration has a dark side to it. The Pythagoreans also called the body an evil enchantment, not just a tomb. They believed you are not alone out there when you travel, that some of the inhabitants of the universe are darker than others—that they are possessed by malevolent passions that could compel them to injure astral travelers. I used to think it was just poetic baloney. Now," she shrugged, "it's starting to seem like something we should be wary of. This part of the legend makes me think of Devereux—makes me afraid to think of what he wants from you. Henry said he did not think anything very bad could happen to you. But I don't know—I'm starting to get a little worried."

Rachel interrupted Betty's monologue by handing the wizened magpie a glass of wine. "The pizza will be ready any time now."

"Betty," Jake said. "What do you think Devereux wants from me, wanted from Keith and the others?"

"I don't know. There is so much we don't know, so much we have forgotten."

"I'm losing control, little by little. Hell, what am I saying? I totally lost control last night! I'm afraid to relax. Afraid to stop concentrating on Main Street. Most of all, I'm afraid to go to sleep!"

Betty cringed. "I wish I could offer you a magic solution, but I'm not prepared for this. Henry says sleep is not really the problem; it is that in-between time, that time when you are not quite asleep and not quite awake. That twilight time. That's when your brain produces just the right sort of waves that make you prone to out-of-body experiences, prone to suggestion."

Rachel entered with their lunch, pepperoni and all. They continued the discussion as they ate. Jake flipped a tiny pepperoni Frisbee to Nikki. She caught it on the fly and buried it beneath the folds of her satin ottoman.

"Why doesn't it happen to me?" Rachel said. "Why doesn't it happen to all of us?"

"All people aren't open to the experience," Betty said. "Down-to-earth, matter-of-fact, skeptical people unconsciously resist the possibility. They wall themselves off. Maybe that description fits you. It sure as hell does me. Jake is different. He has a mind, or imagination, that will not be held down by realities of the herd. It is as if they are more alive. I used to envy people like that. Now—"

"What about when Madeleine pulled at me?" Jake said. "I couldn't even touch an empty tin can without going through it. I couldn't make the wind chimes move. Explain that."

"Right, the way I understand it, it just takes practice. Because novice projectors do not realize their full potentials, they fail at simple kinetic tasks. It is somewhat like—you cannot do what you do not think you can do. A self-fulfilling prophesy."

Betty leaned closer. "What's your first thought? What do you want to do? Don't think; just say it. Jake." She rose from the rocker and stood in front of him. "I said, don't think. Just say it. What do you want to do?" She poked his shoulder with her pointer finger.

"Stop Devereux. I want to stop Devereux; I want to shove my fist through his damn lace curtain. I want his heart to 'just stop' like Keith's did. I want to sleep alone again."

"Okay, now that we have a goal, we need a plan. Let us figure out if we can do it. Like it or not, Jake, you're the real expert here." She poured herself another glass of wine and returned to her chair, rocking it like the ticking of a clock on an afternoon game show. Betty and Rachel watched Jake expectantly.

"Okay, we're civilized people. We can't really do anything to hurt him, but we can scare him. We can let him know we have the guts to fight back, that we can see through brick walls! Just scare him enough to make him go away. I guess that's actually all we can hope to do."

"How?" Rachel said.

Jake paced around the room. He pushed wayward curls away from his forehead as he looked out the front window. "I know he'll be back for me again. Soon. Tonight, if I let my guard down. My experiences are becoming more intense. Everything seems to be speeding up. They'll be back tonight, so we'll have to be ready for them." Jake stared at the street scene framed by the white painted window molding.

"Electricity!" Jake focused on the fence-like power lines. "What if the Devereuxs are just as afraid of it as other travelers?" He snapped his fingers. "That's why there's no electricity on their property! They need to be free to come and go as they please."

Jake returned to Rachel's side. He sat back with his eyes closed and let his mind replay his last visit from the Devereuxs. "What if we could think of a way to keep Devereux from getting back home the next time he visits me? Maybe it would only be for a short time, but just long enough to make him wonder what else we might think up in the future. We have electricity here. Betty, you said electricity can trap a psyche, just like a body can, right?"

Betty nodded.

"Why can he move around in Rachel's house without getting trapped?"

Betty wrinkled her forehead. "Most people who project have some amount of electricity in their house. It must just be the electromagnetic fields are placed in a way to limit their effect, or not strong enough. I am not sure. Maybe it just takes practice. Hell, maybe that's why those kids didn't survive. Not enough practice."

"I wish I knew more about this technical stuff," Jake said. "We have to find a way to mess with electricity, to surround him with an electric field close enough or strong enough to keep him here till we decide to let him go."

Rachel got up and ran toward the stairway. Jake began to follow her, but she waved him off and disappeared up the stairs. Within a few minutes, she returned with a large, over-stuffed trash bag.

"Here, I've been saving this even though I don't use it any-more." She undid the twist-tie that held the bag closed and dumped out a lavender electric blanket. "A few months ago, every time I turned on the news there was a report about the health risks of electromagnetic fields produced by these things, and hair dryers, and even alarm clocks. I got afraid to use it. What do you think?"

Jake took the blanket from Rachel's hands, unfolded it, and wrapped it around himself. "Gee, it's been years since I hid under one of these. I should have thought of this myself. All you have to do to keep the bogeyman away is hide under the covers."

"What are we going to do, throw a blanket over something we can't see?" Betty said.

"Good question," Jake said. "You can see me. Throw it over my body while Devereux is inside me. He'll be trapped—maybe."

"Jake, you'll be trapped too," Betty said. "You'll be locked away from yourself. I do not know how long a soul can be separated from its body before something bad happens. Henry didn't tell me anything about that." Betty poured out the last of the wine, eliciting a jangling sound as the bottle hit the glass. "Besides, how will we know when Devereux is in and you're out?"

"I'll have to find a way to signal you—Rachel, do you still have that crystal wind chime we bought in San Francisco?"

"Yes, it's packed away for the season. It's too delicate to survive fall winds."

"Hang it up in the far corner of the parlor. I'll have to learn how to make it ring, if Madeleine doesn't figure out what's happening, if she doesn't stop me. You'll know I'm out when you hear the signal. The minute you hear the chimes, throw the blanket over me, and wrap it around, tightly. Make sure it's plugged in and turned on first. You had better hide in Keith's closet, then leap out and make sure I'm surrounded by the blanket."

"Jake, you said Devereux made you move. What if he simply throws the blanket off while he's safe in your body?"

"I didn't think of that. Okay—you'll just have to tie me up to make sure I can't move. Then cover me up with a regular blanket and hope they don't notice until it's too late."

"How long do we leave you like that? I'm afraid!" Rachel grabbed Jake's hand.

"Well, you'll just have to be quick."

"What do you mean quick, quick at what?" Rachel's voice quavered.

"You'll only have to leave me like that until you get back."

"Get back from where?" Rachel clutched the arm of the couch, her eyes wide.

"Until you get back from moving Devereux's body so he can't find it when he tries to return. That will really piss him off. Betty, do you have an electric blanket?"

Betty nodded, mesmerized.

"Great," Jake said. "The two of you will go to the Devereux house, carry him to your car, and drive him to your apartment. Betty, your entrance is at the back of the building. It will be dark. Nobody will see you carry him into your place. Get him inside and wrap him up in your blanket. As soon as you're done, signal me with two separate rings on the phone. Then get right back here to uncover me. He'll probably rush right out. I wish I could see his face when he gets home. Wait—I will see his face. We'll go back to unwrap him together. I'll take off the blanket. We'll sit there and wait for him to find himself, and I'll be face to face with him when he wakes up. I can't wait!"

"What about Madeleine?" Rachel said.

"I'll take care of Madeleine. I'll keep her here with me. As long as she's here, she won't be able to interrupt your part of the scheme."

Betty rechecked the wine bottle to be sure it was empty. "I don't know. This isn't just some college prank. It sounds a lot like kidnapping to me."

Rachel turned toward Betty and answered, hands on her hips, her voice sharp. "What about what happened to Keith and those other kids? What does that sound like to you? You know Devereux had something to do with it. What happens to Jake if we *don't* do this? I'm in! I'm the biggest wimp in the state—but I'm in. What is Devereux going to do? Will he call the police and tell them two lady teachers dragged him out of his house while he was not at home? Remember what Jake said about the way Devereux uses our preconceived beliefs against us as a shield. Let's hit him over the head with his own damn shield!"

Betty rose. "Where's your bathroom?"

Rachel pointed her in the proper direction.

When Betty was safely out of earshot, Jake hugged Rachel.

"You never used to be so gutsy in the good-old-days. What happened?"

"Maybe I grew up—or maybe I'm finally pissed off enough to fight for something I want."

"Whatever it is, I like it. You're starting to sound like a New York City woman."

"Jake, cut it out. You know how I feel about that." Before Rachel could complete her response, Betty returned to the parlor.

"Okay, I give in," Betty said. "I'm in. I am still not sure we are doing the right thing, but I know you will go ahead with or without me. I cannot bring myself to abandon you now. You need me to make sure you do not screw up. Older, wiser head and all. Besides, I can pick a lock better than a repo-man."

Jake and Rachel looked at each other then back at Betty.

"So I lose my keys a lot. Anybody got good credit?"

The three confidants joined in a three-way hug. Jake broke the silence. "Let's get our plans nailed down. Rachel, how about some paper and a pen?"

Chapter 16

*T*HE SUN COMPLIED WITH ITS PART OF THE PLOT and set on schedule. After leaving Nikki in the safety of Ellen's care, the conspirators prepared Betty's apartment. They plugged in the electric blanket, turned it on, and spread it across the spot where they would place Devereux. Later, while they were clearing out the floor of Keith's closet, Rachel interrupted their careful preparations.

"What if Devereux wakes up when we try to move him?"

"We won't know until it happens, but I'm very sure that once he's busy with me, or locked in, nothing will be able to wake his body."

A gust of wind twisted a branch off an oak tree and slammed it against the side of the house. The trio started, then looked at each other, wide-eyed.

They turned on the blanket and folded it so it could be quickly deployed, like a parachute. It was time for the final step, time to prepare Jake for what they hoped would be his final test.

Jake held his hands behind his back where Rachel tied his wrists with a scarlet, silk scarf. He twisted his wrists to see that the scarf would hold, then sat on the edge of Keith's bed as Rachel tied his ankles together. Jake rolled down onto the bed and curled up on his right side as Rachel covered him with a light blanket. She kissed his cheek and retreated to her post in the closet.

Betty, in defiance of Main Street convention, followed Rachel's lead. She patted Jake's shoulder and nervously placed her own kiss over Rachel's, then joined Rachel in the closet. The clock ticked as they waited for the evening to unfold.

* * *

Darkness surrounded them as they huddled in their respective starting places—the two in the closet with eyelids stretched open and Jake with his eyes tightly shut. Jake followed Keith's instructions as he had the first time he slipped away. Relax. Control. Let go. Control. How could he make himself sleep, this time, when he most needed control? He decided to stop trying and let his thoughts wander to his darkroom. He lost himself in his own world of making. He withdrew to a world where *he* was the dancing creator, where he could look into the void and call up images at will. The wind, which rustled leaves on the almost-winter ground, seemed to forego the freedom of the outside to swirl around in the limited space held by Jake's mind.

Relax, he thought. Go with it. Do not try. The machine noise returned and was soon followed by the sinking feeling. He knew he was still on his bed, but it felt as though he had fallen into the cellar.

His mind raced. Go with it. Enjoy it. Wait for the silent seductress. Wait to feel that silken touch. Eternity.

No—do not wait. Take control. This time, play the seducer. He pulled himself free from the silken bounds. With little effort, he lifted himself away from Jake, leaving him there, curled and bound. At that moment, the front porch chimes rang the alarm, announcing the arrival of the Devereuxs.

This time, when Madeleine arrived, Jake was waiting for her. This time, Jake led the shadow dance. It was Jake who touched and teased. He led Madeleine's supple specter closer to the bedroom door. Just as he was about to lure her through the open doorway, the chill of Devereux passed through them.

The final test was at hand. Control Madeleine. Get just close enough to control, but not to confess. Keep her there with him until Rachel and Betty had enough time to complete their task.

The Devereux cloud slowly formed itself into the funnel that would soon invade Jake's solid form. Jake watched from the parlor as the trespasser silently entered his physical trap. The body under the blanket moved slightly.

It was time. Jake's ethereal hand stretched toward the delicate rectangles of glass that hung motionless in the parlor, but he could not quite reach. He tightened the grip on his spectral lover and rolled their intermingled forms until he neared the glass chimes. Concentrate. He centered all his will power into his foot as he kicked a desperate alarm.

The jingle-jangle sound brought instant action from the closet. Jake's hold on Madeleine transformed from that of a lover to the steel-trap jaws of an alligator. His only responsibility was to keep Madeleine there, keep her from rushing home and interrupting their plans.

* * *

Rachel and Betty jumped to the bed in unison, pulled off the covers, and threw the electric blanket over the Jake form. They rolled it over to make sure it was covered from all sides. The Jake body struggled against its bonds. When the stranger was completely wrapped, Rachel tied the bundle with a rope still damp from her musty cellar.

Without a word, without stopping for their coats, Jake's assistants left the twitching parcel alone on the bed and rushed out of the house and into Betty's car.

* * *

"So far so good," Betty whispered. Rachel did not reply. Her teeth were clenched and her muscles taut.

The drive to the Devereux house took five minutes. Betty ran the red light at the end of Main Street, then parked her car next to the Devereuxs' side entrance, the entrance that could not be seen from the street. They leapt from the car and flew up the three steps to the door.

Betty slid Rachel's credit card along the length of the doorway. Their breath created smoke visions in the moonlight as they shivered from the cold. She repeated passes across the bolt with no results. One more pass. The credit card broke off, leaving Betty with only a tiny, white stub in her hand.

"Oh, no! I can't believe this," Betty gasped. "What do we do now?"

Rachel moaned through the hand she held over her mouth and scanned the area with frantic eyes. She picked up a large branch that lay at their feet and smashed it through the door window. Shards of glass fell, jangled, to the ground.

"Darn, that wind, looks like it broke the window. Betty said."

Without hesitation, Rachel thrust her arm through the jagged, crystalline mouth. She turned the knob from the inside and pulled the door open. They slipped inside. Together, they hushed from room to room, velvet to satin, gas lights to crystal stem ware, trying, all the while, to be as silent as possible. Last to be searched on the first floor was a long, dark hallway.

Holding hands like frightened children, Rachel and Betty tiptoed down the passageway leading to the back of the house. Betty's sneakers squeaked with every step. Rachel placed a hand on the doorknob, turned it, and pushed the door open to reveal a red, gold, and mahogany bedroom. Devereux and Madeleine were there, together, asleep, naked.

"I can't believe it. We never thought of this," Rachel whispered.

"Stop griping," Betty hissed. "His clothes are right here. Move it!" She yanked Devereux's clothes from a chair by the window and piled them on the floor at Rachel's feet. "Undies first."

They hesitated—repelled—afraid to touch Devereux's multi-colored form. The dancing tattoo moved with the rise and fall of his chest. The twisted serpents writhed with rhythmic grace, as if they had lives of their own. Silently, so as not to wake Madeleine who slept next to her so-called father, they began the task of dressing the narcoleptic professor. Getting his shoes on took the longest. The argyle socks went on smoothly, but his limp feet resisted the confines of the shiny, black leather wingtips. Their hands trembled as they continued their Burke and Hare performance.

* * *

Betty and Rachel finished dressing Devereux. Each took two of his limbs and pulled him to the floor. One of Devereux's shoes slipped out of Rachel's hand, hitting the floor with a thump. The pseudo grave robbers each drew an expectant breath as they watched their victims for any signs of waking.

There were none.

Careful not to bruise his tattooed flesh, they dragged Devereux toward the side door. The highly polished wooden floors aided their journey down halls and around corners. Betty dropped the arm she clutched and peered out through the door to check for observers.

"The coast is clear," Betty whispered. They resumed their ghoulish odyssey. "Wait!" Betty stopped their progress again. "Grab that coat from the hook. He wouldn't leave without a coat. Not today."

"Right." Rachel threw the coat over the body, and each taking one of his arms, they continued their laborious journey down the steps of the tiny side porch. Devereux's heels thudded as they flopped down each step. Struggling against his weight, they sat Devereux in the back seat and snapped the safety belt over him. His head flopped forward. Rachel pushed his head back against the couch and jammed his coat under his chin, propping it in place. In the autumn frost, they were no longer cold. Perspiration soaked their clothes and glistened like tiny stars on their faces.

* * *

On the other end of Main Street, the games were over for Jake and Madeleine. They had become so close that Madeleine heard Jake's plans banging around in his disembodied mind, and he saw visions of alligators in hers. Instead of a silken embrace, Jake kept her locked in an unyielding grasp and concentrated on control. *He* was an alligator. He focused on teeth and claws, on holding. He sunk his astral fangs into her writhing, gossamer form and used his fingers, like claws, to hold her prisoner. Their desperate efforts, hers to escape, his to control, gave their forms an almost physical aspect. As their battle raged on, they tumbled and rolled, crashing into candles, lamps, and flower arrangements, upsetting everything in their path. The drawings taped to Rachel's walls flapped in the draft caused by the melee. Nothing could disturb the opponents' concentration—they were totally absorbed in a mutual death grip.

* * *

The drive to Betty's home took forever. They could not afford to run a red light with an unconscious passenger in the back seat. They dragged Devereux into the living room and heaved him onto the couch. Working together, they wrapped the blanket around him and tucked in the edges. The light on the blanket control switch was not on. Betty grabbed it and flipped the switch off and on a few times. The light stayed off.

Rachel yanked the control away from Betty and rapped the switch against her palm a few times. The light flickered on. Both women sighed and relaxed for a moment.

"Oh my God," Rachel said. "Do you have any rope? We forgot! We have to tie him up!"

"Shit! No. Wait!" Betty paused, her hands over her eyes. "If he can't get into his body, he can't make it move. We don't need to tie him—I hope. Besides, we don't need rope marks on his flesh to weaken the edges of our magic shield."

"Right. I'll give Jake the signal." She dialed her phone number and let it ring once. She re-dialed and let it ring once, again. "Let's get back!"

They ran to the car. Betty's hand shook the wheel as she steered. The wind become increasingly violent with each passing minute. It surrounded the car, rattling it like a child's toy.

* * *

Jake and Madeleine were so weakened by their struggle, they simply held each other like sleeping children. When Jake heard the phone signal, he let go of his hold on the Madeleine mist. It slowly filtered through the wall and was gone. Jake's essence sank to the floor

* * *

Rachel turned the key and she and Betty blew into the house and headed straight to Keith's bed. They pulled the rope off the Jake body and rolled him out of the blanket.

Rachel turned Jake's face toward her and bent down to check for signs of life. His mouth suddenly gaped open, and a blue cloud screamed out of it. Betty and Rachel covered their ears as the frigid, blue, Devereux fog swirled around them like a rational tornado. The beads of sweat that decorated their faces transformed into ice crystals.

As violently as it had surrounded them, the fog tore away and rushed out into the roiling night air. Betty and Rachel huddled together and watched Jake's motionless form. Suddenly, a rise and fall of breath. Rachel reached out and gently shook the sleeping form.

"Jake, are you in there? Are you Okay? Wake up. C'mon, Jake. Don't leave me again."

Jake's psyche felt Rachel's call. The body longed for the mind, and the mind longed to return to its private haven. The Jake, who had recently shown the strength of steel jaws, could only crawl in numb exhaustion, passing through Rachel as he climbed back onto the bed.

Rachel shivered.

"I feel him," she whispered. "He's going to be okay. Jake, open your eyes."

The Jake body let out a gasp as the two Jakes became one. His eyes flickered open to return Rachel's gaze.

"Jake, are you all right?" Rachel held his face in her trembling hands.

He smiled up at her, too weak to answer. Outside, the erratic winds stirred up a violent downpour. As the three partners waited in silence, rain pelted the roof of the house, soothing them with its static hum. Suddenly, a flash of lightning followed by a blast of thunder rattled the house, breaking the hypnotic spell of the rain. The night-light flickered with finality, and its tiny heart stopped, condemning Keith's room to total darkness.

Chapter 17

*I*T TOOK JAKE OVER TEN MINUTES to gather enough strength to sit up and call his equilibrium back.

"We better get to your place, Betty. We have to finish this right away."

They dressed for the weather and began the final step of their machinations. Rain and thunder punctuated the trip to Betty's apartment. Jake took the key from Betty's fingers and unlocked the entrance to her apartment. He slowly opened the door and scanned the scene before him. There, on the couch, sat the shrouded form of Professor Devereux.

Jake locked the door, energized by the prospect of his chance at revenge. Betty and Rachel watched, motionless, as Jake anxiously pulled the blanket off their victim's form. Devereux's head was tilted to one side. A trail of saliva trickled from the lower corner of his mouth. Jake lifted the professor's body so Betty could pull the blanket out from underneath his weight.

Jake shook Devereux's shoulders. There was no response. "I guess we'll have to wait a while. Maybe he hasn't figured this out yet."

Betty folded the blanket and hid it in the hall closet. The three conspirators sat and waited for Devereux to find himself and open his eyes. A half hour later, they were still waiting.

Betty rose, timidly took the Professor's wrist into her hand and felt for signs of life. "I can't find his pulse!" She moved her fingers to his jugular vein. "There's nothing here either!" Betty shook Devereux's shoulder, causing his head to flop loose like that of a broken doll. When she let go, he leaned forward and tumbled to the floor. "Guys!" Betty's voice shook. "I think he's dead."

Jake dove to the floor next to Devereux. He repeated Betty's futile attempts to find a pulse, then held his ear over Devereux's lips and listened for an escape of air. None. He pinched Devereux's nose and administered CPR until he was too weak to continue.

"Devereux, wake up!" Jake shook his prostrate enemy. "Where are you—you bastard?"

Rachel gasped. "What went wrong?" Her lips quivered and she began to cry.

"Probably the same thing that went wrong for Keith," Jake said. "Maybe it was just too much for him. Maybe it was the trip through the storm, the lightning. I don't know. The lightning. Yes. That's probably it." He sat on the floor with his eyes turned away from the ashen face he had planned to ridicule.

"You know," Betty said. "Certain primitive civilizations hold the belief that it's dangerous to move someone who is asleep, because if their soul is traveling at the time, it might not be able to find its way home—ever."

"What do we do now?" Rachel sat next to Jake. He took her into his arms and rubbed her back.

"I guess we'll have to call the police, after all. I'm so sorry I got you two involved in this. I never thought anything like this could happen. Maybe I should move him back home. I could set it up to look like I was alone with him. I got us into this, so I should take all the blame. Betty, where's your phone? I'll—I—."

"No, Jake, I'll make the call, Devereux style." Betty pulled a phone out from behind a pile of books, then cleared her throat and dialed. "Hello, this is Dr. Elizabeth Higgins. One of my guests has just had some sort of attack. I do not know. He was telling us a wonderful story, and he just keeled over. Please send an ambulance—immediately—nobody here knows CPR."

* * *

As they waited for the real world to arrive with stretchers and oxygen, Jake stared into the face of his fallen enemy. Devereux's last words rang in Jake's ears. "On which side of the curtain do you belong?"

Jake whispered to Devereux. "Which side of the curtain are you on now?"

* * *

A few days later, a newspaper article announced that a prestigious professor employed at a local college had died of natural causes while visiting friends. The article had been withheld while the police tried, unsuccessfully, to locate any relatives in need of notification. It appeared that the learned professor's daughter was away.

A couple times a day, Rachel and Jake would walk Nikki down Main Street. The house at the end of the street was an empty shell. A pumpkin, well carved out, it emitted no signs of life, not even a candle glow.

* * *

The candles in the center of Rachel's dining room table flickered, sent golden shadows scrambling across the faces of the trio of confederates. Rachel offered her glass of wine in a toast.

"To Keith, just in case he's listening."

"After what happened here, I doubt there's any question whether Keith could be near us or not. We have learned a lesson few people ever realize. There's more to life—and death—than we know," Jake said. "Betty, will you keep in touch with Rachel when I'm gone?"

"Oh, Jake, of course I will. You should know better than to ask. Do you have to leave right away?"

"I really have to get back to work, tomorrow. My assistant is starting to fall apart. I have a big mess to clean up in New York. The last couple of days gave me the chance to catch up on some sleep. And things are settled here, now."

"I still can't believe the police bought our story so easily," Rachel said. "They simply believed everything we said without batting an eye."

"It's just like Devereux told me," Jake said. "They saw what they wanted to see. They saw what Main Street told them to see. It is really frightening. I wonder what else goes on, unseen."

"I can't help feeling guilty," Rachel said.

"Stop that," Betty said. "We had no idea how our plan would work. We were just trying to save Jake. And that was a worthy cause. A necessary action. We had no choice. If we didn't do anything, Jake could have ended up like the others—dead—and we would be toasting *him* instead. In any case, let's make a pact. We never mention any of this again. Not even between ourselves. It is over. It never happened."

Three glasses jangled together in a promise.

* * *

The next morning, Jake loaded his luggage into the rent-a-car that stood encased in a crystalline layer of morning frost. "Rachel, are you going to be okay when I'm gone?"

"Jake, I can take care of myself. You know that."

"Remember, they still have kids in New York. They can still use you down there."

"I've been thinking about that. We have a teachers' conference planned for next month. It's only a few blocks away from your place." She looked down and traced the lifeline on her palm. "I might just decide to attend. You never know what might happen in the future."

"Don't forget to bring your watch-beast." Jake bent down and scratched Nikki's ears. "She'll love New York."

"We'll see."

They stood in the open doorway and exchanged farewells until the frigid air from Main Street filled the parlor. Jake tickled the wind chimes as he left the porch. While he warmed up his car, he pictured his loft in New York and told himself, "I'll have to make sure my place is dog proof. He shifted the car into reverse. Can't have Nikki licking chemical bottles. That damn dog gets into everything. Maybe I need a bigger place."

* * *

When the spray stabbing at Jake from the showerhead began to cool, he shook himself back to New York, back into the present, a year after Devereux's death, only days after Rachel's death. He stepped out of the tub, leaving the water still running.

In the steam-filled atmosphere, through the red splatters that still blazed across the mirror, Jake stood and stared at his reflection. The air, heavy with moisture, had reconstituted the once-dried blood. It beaded on the glass and began to run down the foggy reflection of Jake's naked form, giving the appearance of animated war paint. And Jake knew why he had not washed away the blood.

Slowly, with unblinking eyes, Jake stepped closer to his tattooed image. Reaching across the empty space between himself and the mirror, he used the palms of his hands to smear the haunting words into a meaningless blur of red, then he used his own scarlet-stained fingers to transfer the message onto his flesh, to transfer the truth of blood onto his own soul. He continued the ritual until his torso was painted with the crimson stain, and finalized the ceremony by covering his face with a glistening mask of red.

Without stopping to turn off the still-running water, Jake left the bathroom, picked up the phone next to his bed, and dialed.

"Fred, this is Jake. No, I don't know what time it is. I'm fine. Wait, just listen! I want that assignment in Louisiana. Set it up right away, first thing in the morning."

Jake hung up the phone and fell onto his bed. Covered only by a blanket of crimson tattoos, he was asleep in seconds.

Part Two

Vortex

Chapter 18

*J*AKE TURNED THE CORNER to the sound of crackling snow and ice. His last impression of Nikki consisted of a coal-black nose passionately pressed against a windowpane surrounded by the carefully starched lace that hung over Ellen's parlor window. Nikki had run from window to window, pushing curtains aside, clinging to couch cushions and standing on tables to peer down at his departure.

Jake guided his car along the New York State Thruway and scanned the roadside scenery in a desperate effort to erase the frenzied images of Nikki etched into his memory, but he couldn't wash away the vision of those tiny, black eyes frantically search-ing for a glimpse of him.

Jake knew he did the right thing. He knew he could not take Nikki with him. It might not be safe for her. New Orleans might not be safe for "shitty little dogs."

Six hours on the New York State Thruway were torture. Ice-cold rain fell in a fine mist, spawning patches of black ice, invisible to the human eye, lurking, poised to hurl an unwary driver into a death spin. Barren, black tree branches traced map-like pat-terns of river systems across the ashen palm of the sky. Endless, randomly scattered potholes seemed determined to slow Jake's journey. Like the silver sphere in a pinball game, he carefully dodged the diabolical traps.

After nine, maybe thirteen hours, he had lost count, Jake's eyes began to transmit erroneous information. Patches of swirling fog morphed into ghost-like images of unrecognizable, writhing creatures. He had drained his thermos of coffee over a hun-dred miles before, and the resulting caffeine deficiency weakened his ability to stay at attention. When he braked for one of the phantom images, Jake knew it was time to take a breather from his white-knuckled journey. From the incessant sound of rain knocking on the roof of his car. From the thunder that echoed through the mountains like a runaway locomotive.

Jake whipped into the parking lot of the One-Stop Truck stop. Eighteen-wheelers of all colors lined up in endless rows, like horses tied to hitching posts outside a western saloon on Saturday night. Jake parked close to the entrance, but not close enough to prevent getting soaked as he dashed across the blacktop, leaping puddles glistening with multicolor swirls of oil and reflections of neon light.

Jake rushed into the truck stop-Laundromat-shower room-restaurant-auto part sales center-gift shop where damp warm air enveloped him. The smell of laundry suds and chicken soup filled the building with the clean, homey scent of mothers going about their household chores. Haphazardly planted wire trees blooming with displays of jewel-like representations of unicorns and angels embossed on mirrors along with sentimental attempts at poetry or quotes from the Bible lined the isle that led to the dining area. Jake could not resist spinning the display trees as he passed. Their motion created an optical effect that reminded him of the extra long, pointed, crystal prism that once danced against Rachel's front window. The very same prism wrapped in a silk scarf nestled safely on the bottom of his camera bag.

A long, snake-like counter cut a zigzag path, creating uneven islands that dominated the restaurant area. Jake slipped onto a stool alongside the only unpopulated island on the counter, but he was not alone. Since Rachel's death, his guilt and passion for revenge accompanied him everywhere, standing alongside him like alternate shadows.

Jake perused the laminated menu for something that would sit well in his caffeine-jumbled stomach. The aroma of chicken soup soothed him and he thought of Rachel. He ordered.

Jake sipped his chicken soup and stared at the bottom of the bowl like a tealeaf reader searching for answers. When the soup was gone, he clutched the sides of the bowl and fought the wish to climb into the talisman of the past.

The sound of mournful country music oozing from wall speakers faded into the background, drowned by the monotone chanting of washing machines and the serpentine hissing of showerheads. Perfumed steam escaped the laundry room and banished the ghostly aroma of soup. Jake drifted toward a semi-sleep, and his thoughts focused on the New Orleans woman who had hired him to do her swamp shoots—Camille Patin. What would she be like? Would she wear a shroud of raven hair? Would she have musical laughter and sapphire eyes?

Would Madeleine's smile fade as he placed his hands around *her* throat? When the bowl cracked, Jake let go, momentarily satisfied.

* * *

Jake stood at the checkout with a newly filled thermos under his arm and inspected a display of guaranteed-for-life sunglasses. They were packed in boxes and neatly stacked, brick-like, between him and the attendant who was writing an expense-record receipt. Jake picked up the pair of sunglasses that hung on display. He chuckled as he slid a fingertip over the jagged fracture that shot across the right lens of the guaranteed sunglasses, a fracture like a bolt of lightning shooting across the sky.

"So much for promises," Jake whispered.

The dash across the parking lot cleared Jake's head. He was once again wide-awake, anxious to continue his journey, to fulfill his mission.

When the bullets of rain tired of pummeling Jake's car, they mutated into a fine mist and clung to him like an exhausted lover. The temperature that seemed to climb higher each mile had long since persuaded Jake to remove his sweater. He drove with the windows down and luxuriated in the damp warmth that crept into his space, keeping him company, stroking him with velvet fingers.

* * *

In Mississippi, the heat became oppressive. Occasionally, the sun would peer between banks of pregnant clouds, chasing away the fog, only to have it slink back when least expected. The sun and fog played cat and mouse all the way to Louisiana, to the Lake Pontchartrain Causeway, where the sun managed to over-power the fog, sending it into exile.

Shafts of solar brilliance shot down onto the rippling water, only to be repelled by the swaying, sequin-strewn waves. The sparks ricocheted into the air, obliterating the line of demarcation that should have been there to mark the boundary between water and sky, giving tacit approval for an unnatural union of opposing forces. Jake squinted through the blinding luminescence as he drove into the vortex. Eyes focused on the yellow line blinking before him, he drove, concentrating on the road, the only link to reality, as he entered what appeared to be the eye of a burgeoning storm.

* * *

There is was, New Orleans. Jake rolled down his windows for a better look. The heat rushed in and fogged his windshield so heavily that he almost drove off the road. The steam reminded him of the windows in Rachel's kitchen when she was cooking up a storm. He relished the odor of chicken soup again, but only in his mind. He rolled up his windows and turned on the air conditioner. The cold air nipped at the fog on his windshield, eradicating it bit by bit, clearing Jake's vision and his memory.

The view that emerged through the scattering fog was not unlike New York, at least not unlike some of its out-lying districts. Jake followed the map his new client had faxed to Fred.

Suddenly, as if under the spell of a crazed magician, the venue transformed. Horse-drawn carriages edged out neon-orange taxicabs. Sidewalks turned to cobblestone. Buildings, no longer utilitarian office structures, grew in close-knit rows, like flowers in a garden, some orange, red, blue, even violet. Stopped for a red light, Jake looked back over his shoulder to see two-story brick facades with intricately wrought iron porch rails cowering in the shadow of high-rise business centers.

Horses and sightseers, oblivious to the fact that they crossed streets in front of oncoming traffic, stalled Jake's passage through the French Quarter, or old section of town. A symphony of neighing, buzz saws, jackhammers, and strains of live jazz dethroned the mélange of omnipresent honks and shouts that tyrannize New York streets. Jake took another glance at the map and realized he was only one turn away from the hotel where he would be staying, again, arranged by his new client, whoever she was.

Jake turned onto the street that was supposed to harbor his hotel and hunted for his destination. He inched along the narrow street, searching for numbers, a sign, anything that would give evidence of a hotel called The Enclave. He found no electric sign or formal facade, no hint of any hotel at all. Rising impatience drew bands around his chest, making it hard to breathe. "Calm down. Calm down." He took a few deep breaths.

"Excuse me," Jake called to a passing mail carrier. "Do you know where number 1301 is? *The Enclave?*"

"Sure do. Right there." He pointed to an unmarked opening that gaped from the brick wall across the street. A metal roll-down door hung a quarter of the way up like a lazy eye lid.

"If it was a snake, it would have jumped up and bit me," Jake said. The mailman smiled and went on his way.

Jake looked into his rearview mirror and saw himself dripping with perspiration, his hair plastered down. He tugged at his shirt to separate it from his chest and drove into the parking garage. An attendant rushed over.

"Good afternoon, sir. Do you have a reservation?"

"Yes, it would be under the name Preston, or perhaps, Patin."

"Of course, we've been expecting you. I'm Brian. Let me take care of your car. I'll see that your luggage is delivered to your room." He grabbed the handle on Jake's door and pulled.

Just before he pushed on the door to the hotel, Jake turned and rushed back to his car. "Wait a minute, Brian." Jake reached into his car and grabbed his camera bag. "I'll take this one." He handed Brian a tip and turned back to the entrance.

Jake opened the door and faced an explosion of light and color. "Nikki. I have a feeling we're not in Kansas anymore," Jake whispered. He abandoned the cool darkness of the garage and passed into a court-yard filled with trees and immense tropical flowers of every color.

In the center of the garden, a three-tier fountain towered. Rivulets trickled from marble basins high above, then showered down over winged statues, finally bubbling into a reflecting pool that sparkled with pennies, dimes, and other coins that flooded the bottom of the pond. A toy sailboat bobbed and spun on the surface, entranced by the gentle current. Jake, lulled by the hyp-notic sounds of the marble brook, entered the hotel lobby.

The lobby, small by New York standards, was dark and cool. Above a jungle of potted, green plants hung slow-moving fans haphazardly perched on the ceiling like giant butterflies lounging in a summer garden, waving languid wings, flaunting seductive colors to their lovers. A few couches and chairs huddled in small, private groups. And behind the front desk stood a rotund fellow with a waxed handlebar moustache.

"Sir, may I help you? He looked Jake up and down, his stare oozing disapproval."

"Yes." Jake swallowed hard. "I'm Jake Preston. I believe you have a room for me."

The man behind the counter caught his breath and stepped forward.

"Of course." His eyes and mouth opened wide with unguarded excitement. "Please." He gestured toward large black book. "Please, sign our guest register. I will be honored to show you to your room—myself. Everything has been arranged for you." He turned the guest book toward Jake, and with sausage fingers held out a gold pen. Jake signed his name and followed the concierge into a waiting elevator.

"We're a rather small...organization, but I'm sure you'll enjoy your stay with us. Our service is first class, of course." He pressed the button for the second floor. Jake barely had time to read the name on his escort's badge when the elevator doors opened and they continued to his room.

"Our loveliest room," Matthew said. "It's on the corner, so you get to choose whichever view suits your frame of mind." He unlocked the door and placed a key in Jake's hand.

"Enjoy." He grinned and backed away.

Jake reached into his pocket for a tip, but Matthew, looking insulted, shook his head and departed, leaving Jake alone in the hall.

"Curious," Jake whispered as he watched his guide waddle back to the elevator.

Room twenty-two was indeed lovely. Delft blue, terra cotta, and gold blended masterfully to create a cool, relaxing atmosphere. The eleven-foot ceiling, striped with evenly placed beams, was sure to draw heat up into its clutches, sparing flesh below.

Next to the desk stood a small refrigerator. Jake peeked inside and found it packed with tiny bottles of liqueur, drink mixers, and beer.

Two doors to the outside, one on each outer wall, tempted Jake, but he was too tired for further explorations. He entered the bathroom on shaky legs, his first thought to look behind the door, check for a full-length mirror. Jake sucked in a deep breath and placed his hand on the knob.

The back of the bathroom door was barren except for a couple hooks for towels. Jake dropped his clothes to the floor and turned brass handles that blasted a spray of silver bubbles into his bath. The warm water caressed Jake as he reclined in the rose-colored tub. He rested his head against the pink and white tile wall and fell asleep.

* * *

Jake slipped and slid back under the cold water, gasping, inhaling deeply. Darkness filled the windowless room. He scrambled to locate the border between sleep and reality. Shivering from ice-cold water and a black, dreamless sleep, he panicked until he realized where he was, then he caught hold of the edge of the tub, poured himself over the side, and tumbled to the tile floor. Disoriented, doubled over on all fours, he coughed until he cleared his lungs. When he could stand, he found his way into the bedroom and ran a hand along the wall until he found a light switch. He snapped it on and leaned against the wall, face first. Sensing movement behind him, he whirled around to face a silent attacker, a slowly rotating fan hung over his bed. Warmth. He needed to shake the chill that still clung from his frigid bath.

Without stopping to dry himself, Jake wrestled jeans and a tee shirt over his damp limbs and rushed out into the night, seeking warmth. The street outside the parking entrance was dark and empty, but Jake could hear signs of life teasing him from around the corner, a few yards away. He joined the milling crowd and made his way down Bourbon Street along with the rest of the tourists. Moisture still clinging from his bath turned to steam in the evening heat, making his clothes feel soggy, hindering his movement as they had one night in New York, not so long ago.

Jake stopped to read a menu hanging on the front window of a small restaurant and realized he had not eaten all day. While the window framed a picture of happy couples inside, drinking, eating, laughing, it simultaneously reflected images of people in the street as they wandered aimlessly in the sweltering, liquid night. A female figure with long, black hair moved in the collage of opposing images. Madeleine? Already? Jake felt his face flush with heat. When he determined which world claimed her reflection, he raced across the street after her.

Jake cut through the lethargic crowd, bumping past all who stood in his way as his quarry disappeared and reappeared with the whim of the masses. Jake caught up with her and grabbed her wrist. She struggled to wrench away from his grasp, but he held fast. When she whirled around to fight back, her soft brown eyes wide with fear, it only took one disappointing glance to see she was not Madeleine.

"I'm sorry, really," Jake stammered. "I thought you were someone I've been searching for."

She twisted away from Jake's inappropriate grasp and raced off into the darkness. Panting, shivering in the heat, Jake leaned against a wall. Finding himself alone, encircled by accusing stares and muffled comments, Jake rushed into the nearest shop and distracted himself by studying rows of industrial-sized blenders. Like tiny cement mixers, they constantly stirred frozen cocktails of all colors. Like snow cones. That was what he needed. Ice to cool him. With a trembling hand, he pointed at a mixer churning up a red concoction and handed the bartender payment. The frozen daiquiri cooled Jake's throat as he wandered aimlessly, following the flow of the crowd.

* * *

Shop after shop displayed cheap, feathered masks, jester dolls, and Mardi Gras posters. He stepped into a shop and examined a wild-looking mask of peacock feathers and sequins.

"Go ahead. Try it on."

Jake started and whipped around to see a green-eyed, plump woman who smiled at him. He scrutinized her eyes and noticed that the green-colored contact lens over her right orb had slipped off center, revealing a dark-brown iris. Jake replaced the mask on its wall hook and backed out of the shop, fascinated by the tiny, green masks floating on the plump woman's eyes.

Just ahead, out in front of a corner establishment, a well-groomed black man, elegantly dressed in a black tuxedo, danced to music he alone could hear. He whirled and pranced, waving his arms. When Jake moved close enough to make eye contact, the dancer, using a hooked finger, beckoned Jake to follow him through the black-lacquered door.

"C'mon in—beautiful girls—unmentionable love acts. Audience par-ti-ci-pation. Live music. C'mon in and give us a try. There's nothing else like it in the Quarter." He grinned widely at Jake, exposing twin rows of perfectly placed, gleaming white teeth.

The pictures plastered on the outside of the building offered graphic evidence of the love inside, black socks and all. Naked bodies piled in heaps, men and women with blacked-out faces all engaged in anonymous *love*.

"Sorry, not tonight," Jake said.

The daiquiri hit Jake's empty stomach like an earthquake. It was all he could do to find his way back to his room, to fall back on his bed and drift off to sleep with the rhythmic motions of the fan repeating above his closed eyes and the roll of thunder off in the distance.

Chapter 19

*J*AKE WOKE TO FIND HIS ROOM flooded with morning light, overrun by a galaxy of dust motes that wheeled in the swirling air. The time! Damn! He leapt out of bed and grabbed his alarm clock from the night table. "That's the last time I drink on an empty stomach. His heart raced as his eyes focused on the dial. He could not miss his appointment with Madeleine—Camille Patin.

Eleven O'clock. Just enough time to pull himself together and get to his noon meeting at La Faim Restaurant. He rushed into the bathroom and jittered in front of the mirror. Just as he thought, his hair was acting up. Damn humidity. His curls were taking over again.

"Control yourself," he whispered. "Control. You can't let on you know." He plastered his curls down and turned away from the other Jake, the one who hid in the mirror. A city map clutched in his hand, he left the hotel and started toward Saint Charles Avenue.

The temperature seemed higher than the day before. Though La Faim was only a few blocks away, he arrived soaked with perspiration. Since he was early, Jake stood in the shadows across the narrow street, to watch the restaurant door for a while, maybe to catch a glance of a familiar face. While he concentrated on the window, his hands worried the map, rolled it into a tube, then slowly twisted until it split in two.

Unlike the night before, in the bright afternoon sun the front window of La Faim offered no clue of what went on inside. Like dark water at night, it reflected only a warped view of the outside world. Couples and groups entered, only to be swallowed up at the door, leaving behind no evidence of their former existence.

It was time. Time to join the ranks of those who had gone before him. Jake dropped the shredded map and crossed the street. He pushed the door open and marched straight over to the maitre d'.

"Could you please show me to Camille Patin's table?"

"Absolutely." Looking bored, the maitre d' gestured for a waiter to take his place and turned toward the back of the room.

Jake followed the short, red-haired man by instinct. Instead of paying attention to his guide, Jake's eyes scanned the room in search of his quarry. Jake's guide stopped beside a table where a lone gentleman studied a newspaper.

"Your table, sir," said the Maitre d'. He nodded and left without giving Jake a chance to contradict him.

The reading man put his paper aside and looked up, expressionless. "Can I be of some help?"

"No! Excuse me." Jake backed away. "I asked the waiter to take me to a woman's table. I guess he didn't understand. I'm sorry to have disturbed you." Jake turned toward the front door.

"No! Wait! This is where you belong—with me."

Jake looked back at the stranger. "But there must be some mistake. My appointment is with a woman."

Laughter sparkling in his black-brown eyes, the tall, blond gentlemen stood and offered his hand to Jake.

"I'm Camille. In these parts, Camille is a man's name as well as a woman's. Come to think of it, I seem to remember a spaniel of the same name, also." He squeezed Jake's hand. "In any case, welcome to the Big Sleazy."

A rush of heat passed over Jake. He teetered momentarily.

"Mr. Preston," Camille said. "You seem so disillusioned. Never fear, New Orleans is full of ladies, ladies of...all sorts. I'm sure you won't be disappointed." He nodded toward the chair opposite his. "Please, join me. I have already ordered for both of us. A little sampling of all the best our cuisine has to offer. All divinely evil. Butter. Cream. Deep-fried everything, all guaranteed to stop your heart if given half a chance. I'm sure you'll discover something new and tantalizing to add to your list of most-dreaded temptations."

Jake's hand shook as he slid a chair away from the large, round table. He bent to pull away the long, pink tablecloth that clung to the seat of his chair. The room spun around him in repeating, kaleidoscopic pattern of sparkling crystal, long-stemmed roses, and chandeliers dancing jingle jangle in the breeze that escaped air conditioning vents.

Camille poured delicate pink wine into an intricately cut glass that flashed sparks of light.

"Mr. Preston, please remember to close your mouth when you try this wine. You would not want it to run down your chin. It's very precious." He held the glass at arm's length.

Tiny searchlights of reflected light crawled over Jake's face. He winced as they passed over his eyes, then shook off the spell. Jake realized how ridiculous his gaping expression must have appeared and laughed.

"Jake. Call me Jake." He reached out and accepted the glass.

Camille wore a light blue suit, set off by a golden silk tie that matched his long, honey-colored hair tied back in a ponytail. He looked at Jake with black, emotionless eyes. Jake searched the black-brown orbs, scrutinized them for a hint of recognition—he saw none.

Jake sipped the wine. He was surprised when it burned a path down his throat. Pink. The hue had betrayed the true essence of the wine.

Disregarding the resignation that colored his voice, Jake said, "So, tell me about my assignment; why am I here?"

"As my correspondence already explained, we were extremely impressed by your shots of Alaska."

"That's very complimentary, but there are tons of good shooters around, experts on wildlife. Why me?"

"You see, we don't just want pretty pictures. And you are right; anybody can do that. You are different from all the others. Your shots have magic. That is what we need. *Magic*. Our purpose is not to entertain. We need photos that will convince the public to buy into our beliefs. Your Alaskan series exposed the soul of Alaska. Those birds shrouded by coats of oil, never to fly again." He shook his head. "You showed us the pain in the heart of the land, pain caused by man's selfish conceit. Here, in Louisiana, we may not have had something as dramatic as a major oil spill like the one in Alaska, but we have something much harder to sell. We have a quiet, surreptitious, systematic destruction of the land taking place. It has been going on unnoticed for so very long that nobody realizes what is happening. It's right there, out in the open, and nobody sees it because they do not want to. Every year, we lose at least thirty-five, maybe as many as fifty square miles of Louisiana and everything that lives in or on it."

"I'm not sure I understand." Jake drained his glass and Camille refilled it.

"Well, I believe the best way to explain the problem is to show you." Camille poured each of them another glass of wine. "Do you have any plans for tomorrow?"

Jake shook his head.

"Fine. I will make arrangements for a little field trip. We will drive down to Bayou Landing and behave like tourists. I know a gentleman who owns a tour boat. I'm sure he'll be happy to take us off the beaten path to where every grain of sand has to decide whether to become solid, part of the terra firma, or float out into the ocean only to become lost in the waves."

From somewhere behind Jake came the rattling of off-balance wheels. A waiter arrived, guiding a cart stacked with food. Camille looked up at the nervous youth and spoke with derision.

"Do something about those wheels. They distract."

The waiter nodded anxiously as he leaned over the table and set down a silver tray piled high with blood-red crabs, golden corn on the cob, and steaming, brown potatoes. With shaking hands, he placed a number of covered, silver tureens on the table and clattered away to disappear around the corner.

A harsh cracking snapped Jake's attention from the departing waiter. Jake looked back to see Camille smash the claw of a crab, using something that resembled a nutcracker.

Camille smiled at Jake's alarmed expression. "I know; it's so barbaric. Mother Nature spends eons designing this wonderful shell to protect Mr. Crab from predators and, voila, man comes along and the rules of the game change."

Jake ignored Camille's warning to save room for dessert. He passed on his share of crabs, but enjoyed the etouffee, gumbo, and a bit of everything else that warmed in silver tureens perched over flickering candles.

"Jake, I don't care how over-stuffed you may be; it's time for coffee and a beignet. A prerequisite in New Orleans."

"I guess I can squeeze in a little bit more." Jake raised one of the delicacies to his mouth. "But, I'll order tea instead of coffee." He bit into the beignet and a landslide of powdered sugar tumbled down the front of his jacket.

"Sorry. No way. In New Orleans, one drinks coffee." Into Jake's cup, Camille poured the thick, dark brown liquid that exuded the aroma of chicory. "You'll soon become addicted."

Before Jake downed his coffee, he tossed in a couple spoons of sugar and added cream until the liquid in his cup turned almost as pale as the bone-colored china and counted the minutes as he longed to run away and lick his wounds, to forget his failure, his stupidity. He had not found Madeleine.

* * *

The late afternoon heat was more oppressive than it had been earlier that day. After walking a couple blocks away from the restaurant, Jake tried to catch the attention of one of the neon-orange cabs that crept down the busy New Orleans avenue, but they passed by as though he were invisible. Hoping it would be cooler by the water, Jake followed the sound of hooting river-boats. He sat on a bench facing the river and turned his meeting with Camille over in his mind. When he thought of the black eyes that showed no sign of knowing him, his stomach knotted. It was all a mistake. All a mistake. Camille was not Madeleine. Jake sat brooding until just before dusk, then headed back toward his room. As always, gawking sightseers clogged the streets, still oblivious to the danger of oncoming traffic, oblivious to Jake's presence.

Jake was soaked by the time he found himself back in the neighborhood of his hotel. He stopped to rest in the shade of a building and watched a policeman standing on the corner, absent-mindedly twirling his night stick and whis-tling.

"I can't believe all these people wandering around in the middle of the street," Jake said. "If this were New York, the cabbies would have them rolled out flat as paper in minutes."

The policeman nodded without looking at Jake, still whistling as he scanned the area. He stopped spinning his nightstick, crossed the street, and hurried down the uneven sidewalk. Jake forgot the heat and followed the officer at a safe distance, anxious to witness some excitement, angry he had left his room without his camera.

The officer stopped in front of a girlie bar, his attention focused on a woman standing out front with a champagne glass in her left hand and her right hand on her hip. She wore a skirt short enough to expose lace at the top of her black fishnet stockings. The policeman appeared to be berating the woman for some sort of misbehavior. What crime she had committed? Perhaps she had strayed too far away from the door to the bar. Perhaps, the policeman was ordering her back into her dimly lit world of dark secrets.

The officer emphasized his angry words by pointing his nightstick at the woman, waggling it up and down. After a few minutes of enduring the tirade, the lady grabbed the nightstick with her free hand and pulled it toward her. The officer pulled back. The rhythmic, back and forth play continued until a broad smile spread across the policeman's face, and he began to lean toward the door of the nightclub, oblivious to the rest of the world. The officer began to lose ground. Inch by inch, the temptress pulled him further toward her world. Jake remembered Madeleine and turned away. It was all he could do to draw in one breath after another.

* * *

The wet air failed to mop Jake's face of sweat, to steam the wrinkles from his disheveled jacket. When he finally reached the Enclave, he was a mess. He slammed his body against the push bar on the front door and propelled himself into the air-conditioned lobby like the baseball he hit through Mrs. Bailey's picture window when he was ten. Instead of Mrs. Bailey's long, pointy finger and toothless scowl, Jake was greeted by a grin of welcome from a tall, skeletal, elegant black man in a navy blue suit that Jake believed tagged him as part of the hotel staff. Jake trudged over to him. "Damn, is it always this hot in the winter?"

"No, sir, the weather man on TV just said the all time record was eighty-five degrees on Mardi Gras Eve in 1972. But, we're topping that this year. And the humidity. It must be at least one-hundred percent."

"No way," Jake scoffed. "We'd be under water if the humidity was one-hundred percent."

"Welcome to Louisiana." The man laughed and pointed at Jake's wet suit. It appears you've been treading water for quite some time."

Jake looked down at his wrinkled suit. "Right, thanks for reminding me. Could you send a valet up to my room to see to my laundry? I can't use this suit again till it's cleaned."

"Excuse me?"

"You do have a valet service, don't you? The guy at the desk told me this is a first class joint."

"I wouldn't know. I only checked in a while ago, and I am still waiting for the bellman to bring up my luggage. I'd say the service is a bit lacking."

Jake felt as if the flame of a blowtorch passed over his face and knew his face turned every color that involved a touch of red. The tall man smiled at Jake's embarrassment.

"Oh, man. I'm so sorry," Jake sputtered. "I didn't mean. It's the suit. It looks like. No. It's a really nice suit. I just didn't—"

"Don't worry about it." The tall man held out a long-fingered hand. "I'm Tony."

Jake took his hand. The gold rings on Tony's slender fingers made his hand feel unexpectedly heavy.

"I'm Jake." He added, as if it was some sort of excuse or alibi, "I'm from New York."

"MMMMMM, then you're in for a big surprise, lots of surprises. This is not New York. It's New Orleans, Lou-i-si-ana." He said Louisiana in a hushed voice, as if it was a secret.

The bellboy appeared with a cart loaded with luggage tattooed by air tags from just about every location imaginable. Tony grabbed one of the cases.

"I'm sorry, but I really must go. I have to work." He held up the case as if it were proof that would convince Jake he was not a valet, after all. "My frottoir. I'm a musician."

"Your what?"

"I'm a musician."

"No. In the case."

"Oh, my frottoir." Tony winked. "Stop by the Creole Festival tonight. It's time you learned to dance the Zydeco." He pointed at Jake and, in a voice just above a whisper, said, "Mardi Gras is just around the corner. You'd better be ready."

Jake shook his head. "I don't dance."

"Don't dance? Shaaaame on you; to the universe belongs the dancer." Tony waved and dashed into the street.

Jake blinked away imaginary images of a dancing god with snakes writhing around his neck.

* * *

Jake locked himself in his room. He picked up his phone and dialed "911" for his suit. After the valet left, his arms piled with laundry, Jake poured a dose of vodka into one of the glasses alongside the tiny fridge. He shuffled through bottles of mixers, looking for ginger ale. When he found none, he twisted the cap off a bottle of something orange and poured it over the vodka.

Camille was not Madeleine. He was not even a woman. New Orleans was a mistake. All this way for nothing.

Disgusted with his failure, Jake downed the noxious potion. Surprisingly numb, he unlocked one of the doors to the curved balcony and entered the aqueous night. Jake was dazzled by the transformation that had occurred while he was anesthetizing his disillusioned mind. The sun was gone, no doubt embarrassed by the brazen display of colored lights.

He shuffled over to the black wrought-iron railing and leaned out for a better view. A spell of vertigo spun the mass of lights and milling tourists into a whirlpool of colors and limbs all seeming to reach up to him, all straining to pull him down into the maelstrom. Jake shoved himself back away from the rail. He crashed into iron furniture and grabbed a porch support to steady himself. Why the hell was he so drunk after only one drink? Was old age making him a lightweight?

When his balance returned, he shuffled the length of the porch, following its curved path as it wrapped itself around the side of the building a few more yards. The view from the other side of the building dropped Jake's jaw.

Nowhere to be found were the lights and limbs of the other street. Below was only a black, empty street, the windows blank, the doors locked. Only the garbled strains of music that managed to find its way around the curve marked this street as remotely related to the other.

Somehow, the empty blackness disturbed Jake more than the maelstrom of colors had. The black aloneness crushed Jake with the weight of his loss, his quest, his failed mission. Nauseous, he stumbled into the bathroom and prayed some supernatural power would purge the memories from his tortured mind as nature purged his twisted insides.

Chapter 20

*J*AKE SHOWERED, dressed, and stole out onto the street. The one filled with gyrating amnesia. There he became just another nameless set of sweating limbs among others that spilled out of open-air bars and danced on the sidewalks and streets—the perfect place to forget. Above his head, a set of oversized woman's legs formed from papier-mache' and properly decked out in black high-heeled shoes, thrust in and out through the wall of a strip joint. In and out. In and out. As if in mock celebration of the pantomime played out by the policeman and the dancer earlier that day.

Sweat drizzled down his forehead and stung his eyes. Again, swirling daiquiri machines that hummed in a row along a wall, like a psychedelic string of multicolored beads, lured into an open-air shop.

"Choose your poison," a bar tender said.

"Purple," Jake said. He did not care what it would taste like; purple just seemed the least similar to the orange deluge he had encountered not so long ago. Jake watched the parade of humanity pass by as he waited for his order. Gawking tourists clutched shopping bags and cameras in sweaty hands. A barely-dressed blond woman stood just outside, sucking up the last of her daiquiri. As a man walked by holding hands with his wife, he slipped his free hand around behind his back so he could sneak a hasty wave to the blonde.

Jake paid for his drink and continued along the sidewalk. The icy mixture slid down his throat and cooled him on the inside. A few blocks later, he passed a sign that read Creole Festival. He knew he should remember that name for some reason, but he could not place it, so he kept walking and drinking. Then it hit him. Tony. The musician from the lobby. That's the place Tony mentioned. He turned back.

When he entered the nightclub, Jake was assailed by a rhythm he had never before experienced. It was like the blues, but with an ironic touch of joy. Tables and chairs were pushed back against the walls; nobody was sitting. Everyone was dancing. Even the waiters delivered drinks in time with the music, whirling, trays held high. Jake moved closer to the stage and peered through the swirling smog of cigarette smoke and spotted Tony at the right end of the stage, a head taller than the rest of his fellow band members. Dressed in red suits, except for Tony, they stood in a single row and moved together like the Rockettes, except for Tony. He did not seem to fit in. He was a lone pine in a row of bushes; bending, turning, twisting in the wind, a part, but apart, calmly hiding behind his instrument, a slab of corrugated silver metal with extensions that fit over his shoulders, securing it to his lithe body like a protective shell or suit of armor.

He rubbed a feverish rhythm from his shell with metal strikers that looked like bent spoons. The other musicians focused on the crowd, or each other, but Tony stared up at the dark, smokey ceiling. He bent over his rub-board, wearing what appeared to be a mask of anger stretched across his face, and clawed at his shell as if in an effort to free himself by scratching it off.

The others danced, but Tony remained still except for his flailing arms. The others stood straight, Tony bent low. Still, he was an integral part of the action. The only pine in a forest of shrubbery, he was tall enough to catch messages whistling in the wind, messages only a pine can hear.

Jake stood in front of the stage, the only person standing still, except for Tony. Song after song, Tony kept the rhythm, but at the same time, kept apart. Jake watched, mesmerized.

The accordion player jumped down from the stage. The rest of the band followed, even Tony. They led a parade that embraced and seduced everyone in the building, everyone except Jake. The gyrating procession snaked around the room a few times, then danced toward the street.

Jake waited for Tony to pass so he could catch his eye, anxious to wave another apology. Jake froze when Tony passed, because he showed no sign of having recognized him. But at the last moment, Tony looked at Jake and mouthed two words—*Get ready.*

The snake-like line of humanity slithered away, leaving Jake stunned and alone in the empty nightclub; empty except for a few dim lights and the cloying blue smoke that caressed him as if in an effort to make him feel wanted.

Somehow, Jake found his way back to his room without getting lost. He flopped on his bed and fell asleep to the rhythmic beating of the fan whirling over his head. "Do the damn shoot and blow town." He closed his eyes and repeated the mantra. "Make a few bucks and blow out of New Orleans. You failed."

Chapter 21

*J*AKE STARED UP AT THE CEILING FAN, trying to figure out if it was he or the fan that spun in slowly repeating circles. It was eight o'clock in the morning. He grabbed the shirt he had hastily discarded the night before and threw it up at the fan. At the high point of its journey, the fan captured the shirt and held it prisoner. Arms flailing, the hapless shirt took a few trips around on the whirling blade. Suddenly, it lost hold, or was set loose. It cartwheeled across the room only to crumple against the wall and slide down to the floor.

It was Jake's turn. He sat up, a little too fast, and felt like he too was caught on the fan. He slapped both feet on the floor and hung his head between his knees. "Damn daiquiris," he mumbled to his toes as they clung desperately to the delft blue carpet.

* * *

Jake could hardly recognize his face in the mirror. It wore the mask of someone out of control. He would have to fix it, take control. Damn. What kind of shit do they put in those snow cones? What kind of place is this? I never acted like this before.

Into the bathroom. One hour later, when he checked the mirror again, his reflection satisfied him. He was once again the New York City, totally in control, hot-shit Jake. Even his hair was following the rules.

"I'm here to shoot swamp shots, that's all. The rest was only an illusion. Give it up. It was all just a big fat coincidence: Louisiana, Camille, Madeleine, Rachel. All an illusion. I'm here to shoot the swamp—that's all."

For the first time since Rachel's death, Jake felt alone. His hunger for revenge had kept him company, like a lonely child's secret friend. Together, they had spent every waking hour since

116

that night, plotting, visualizing Madeleine's eyes still, glazed, unseeing like those of a cheap doll. His hunger for revenge had kept him filled. Now he was empty, empty and alone.

* * *

Jake stuffed himself with a helping of each of the items on the hotel's breakfast buffet while he waited for Camille to arrive. As he poured cream into his third cup of coffee, Jake heard someone chuckling from behind.

"Told you so." Camille winked and sat next to Jake. "A few more days in New Orleans and you'll need to have your clothes let out." He reached for a cup. "And coffee too?" Camille's capricious grin revealed perfect, evenly spaced, white teeth.

Jake confessed with a shrug and swallowed another mouthful of beignet. He was surprised to see that Camille was not dressed-down, as he had expected. Instead, Camille wore a suit and tie.

"Hey," Jake said. "Am I okay dressed like this?"

"Of course. You are perfect just the way you are. I have a car waiting outside. Let's go. We'll finish our coffee on the way."

"Okay, but I have to sign for breakfast first."

Camille, already up and walking away, cup in hand, said, "No. Don't worry about it. I have you covered. Just grab your cup and we're off."

Jake followed Camille through the lobby. When they passed through the garden courtyard, the relentless heat slammed Jake like a blast from a furnace. In the dark, cool, cave-like entrance, a black limousine purred. They slid into the limo's air-conditioned interior and sank into the black velvet upholstery.

Jake watched through heavily tinted windows as the driver slowly nosed the limo down New Orleans streets not yet filled with tourists. Hitched to ornate, black carriages, horses wearing flower-covered straw hats stood idly twitching flies off their rumps while they awaited the first fare of the day.

Once outside the city, the limo sailed smoothly down the highway. Too much for breakfast, the vehicle's dark comfort, and the engines even hum threatened to lull Jake to sleep. He fought the will of his heavy eyelids and finished his coffee.

"How long will it take us to get where we're going?"

"It depends on traffic."

* * *

The limo skidded to a stop on the loose gravel driveway, stirring up a fine haze of dust in the sticky, morning air. After hovering over the limo for a few moments, the powder fell to rest on the polished black metal surface, partially hiding it from the glare of the sun. Jake checked his case to make sure he had remembered to pack extra film and slipped his camera's carrying strap over his head.

"You won't need a camera today," Camille said. "Today's trip is just to get you in tune with our message."

"I know, but you never know what might happen. Can't take the chance of missing a once-in-a-lifetime shot." He added, tongue in cheek, "Besides, I can't see without a lens to look through."

"I guess you could be right," Camille said, peering at Jake with an exaggerated squinting expression. "Some of us do see better than others. Let's go inside and wait for Captain Bill to get here with the small boat. I've arranged a private tour."

The heat of the grey stones radiated though the soles of Jake's sneakers as they side slipped on the uneven surface of the parking lot. He followed Camille into the restaurant office that doubled as a gift shop. A plump, grey-haired woman smiled at them from behind a cash register. The counter that separated her from the public was covered with baskets filled with alligator teeth and other swamp souvenirs. Reptile skeletons bleached ghost white hung on the walls. Gaping, white, alligator and snake skulls yawned at Jake as he followed Camille's lead through the office into the restaurant.

"Here." Camille put his hand on the back of a chair. "Have a seat and I'll see when Bill will be ready. Order yourself a cold drink if you like." He left Jake at a table near a bay window at the back of the dining room.

Outside, two children in knee-high rubber boots laughed and played at the edge of vacillating water that lapped the poles holding up the back of the building. Splashing through the shimmering surface, they busily tried to catch tiny, minnow-like fish that swam in schools and darted away whenever the children dipped their rusty coffee cans into the water. Between the rough floorboards under his feet, Jake saw brilliant hints of water, rippling as boats passed.

Jake reached down to remove the lens cap from his camera and caught a glimpse of furtive motion under a table near the kitchen. Because he did not want to give the impression he was ogling nearby diners as they cracked crabs and took long draws from icy beers, Jake pretended to fuss with his camera as he watched the floor. There it was again. A surreptitious shadow scuttled from under one red-and-white plaid tablecloth only to scramble under another. The graceless perambulations reminded Jake of grade-Z horror movies he had loved as a child, movies of disembodied hands that scampered along rows of piano keys or clutched the throats of the unwary. Jake held his breath as the half-drunken diners pushed away from their table and ambled out of sight. When the room was empty, he put down his camera and crept over to the table under which the tiny apparition had last been seen.

Jake lifted the tablecloth, allowing daylight to race ahead of him. He peeked underneath. The little creature backed away and clattered along the wall, heading for another hiding place. Jake followed until it backed into a corner. There, the runaway crab held up its only claw as if to shield its eyes from the light, as if to blind itself to the fact it might soon become lunch.

"I wish Nikki were here to see you," Jake whispered to his daring companion. "You sure got guts."

Jake nabbed a spoon from a nearby table and tapped the single, upheld claw. The crab grabbed the spoon, startling Jake. They dropped the spoon in unison, letting it jangle to the floor. The crab held its ground, brandishing the lone claw as if it were a high-tech space weapon. Its rear end backed against the wall and black bead eyes trained on Jake, the crab slowly fingered its way over the wooden floor, bumping along the back door, unaware it was a possible avenue of escape. Jake's shadow fell over the crab as he reached over to turn the doorknob. When the wall fell away behind it, the crab backed out toward freedom, its attention still fixed on Jake.

"Hey. I'm on your side," Jake said as his shadow pushed the crab outside. "I'm helping you bust out."

"C'mon," Jake said. He followed the crab along the board-walk. "Jump off. Pick a side, any side, but jump off."

The crab ignored Jake's dare and stood poised for battle. Squatting down next to the little, grey and blue warrior, Jake tried to grab him from behind, but the crab eluded Jake's grasp. It spun around, perched high on its nimble legs. Jake snapped his hand toward the crab, hoping to grab it from behind. The crab whirled and clamped his claw shut on Jake's finger.

"Shit!" Jake's body rose with his voice. He tried to shake the crab loose, but it held fast. "Damn!" He shook the crab until it whipped free. It cart skipped over the water, landed with a splash, and disappeared into a cloud of swirling sand. Jake inspected his finger. Two rows of tiny puncture wounds remained to give evidence of his good deed.

"See what you get for trying to be a hero?" Camille stood leaning against the side of the building with his arms crossed and a crooked smile on his lips.

"Yeah! Nothing like biting the hand that frees you," Jake said. He bent to rinse his throbbing finger in the water, but pulled back from the murky liquid. He could not see beneath the glittering surface where anything could be hiding.

Chapter 22

"BILL IS HERE AND READY TO GO." Camille handed Jake a can of beer, and they retraced their steps to the parking lot and followed the shoreline.

Captain Bill's sun-baked skin cracked into a smile as he waved them onto the dock. They followed the path of uneven, knothole-riddled planks and climbed onto the waiting boat. Jake was glad for its canopy of red and white striped canvas. Though the sun hid behind gathering clouds, its power penetrated the grey barricade and clawed at their skin. They sat silently in the relative shade as Bill slowly guided his boat along a narrow channel of chocolate water. The waterway widened, so the captain turned up the speed until the boat bucked over the water like a wild horse fighting to dislodge an unwanted rider. Jake gripped the sides of the bench seat, his knuckles white.

Jake sighted a stand of gaunt, ashen trees. He motioned to the captain and pointed. Bill slowed the boat and guided it toward the area Jake had indicated. Within moments, they were surrounded by a conclave of frighteningly barren trees, rising straight up through the water, standing tall and mute, clad in garments of battered lacy moss, like ancient skeletons of wise men who had taken their secrets to the grave.

"Cypress trees," Bill said.

Jake leaned over the water and focused his lens on the uneven, tangled threads that hung from the trees.

His voice just above a whisper, Camille said, "Jake, it's okay to touch."

Jake reached out and pulled shreds of the silver-grey-green lace from a branch.

121

"That's Spanish moss. It lives on water and sunlight—never has to touch the earth," Bill said. "It's some kind of relative to the pineapple family."

Jake said, "It's not dead?"

"No. When it's dead, it turns black."

Like a child hanging silver icicles at Christmas, Jake reverently returned the moss to the tree.

Bill pointed. "That's Lake Polourde up ahead." He headed them onto the immense area of open water. As they crossed the lake, silver streaks leapt and glistened without benefit of direct sunlight, then splashed back into the water.

"Fresh water mullet. Good eating fish," Bill yelled over the roar of the motor. Suddenly, he cut left and headed straight toward a huge, white bird that bobbed peacefully on the surface of the water. It flapped its wings, barely lifting off in time to avoid a collision with the boat. Bill laughed and gunned the motor, still trying to catch the bird. Jake glanced over at Camille. He was smiling.

* * *

They entered a channel that cut its way through a heavily wooded area. Small, green plants began to gather in their path, bobbing in the boat's wake. Bill slowed the boat to a crawl.

"Those are cabbage plants, or duck weed," Bill said.

Jake leaned over the side of the boat and focused on one of the green floaters. Just as he was about to release the shutter, one of the spastic, silver fish leapt up from beneath the fragile carpet of plants and crashed against Jake's lens. Jake jumped back, almost dropping his camera into the water.

"Guess he didn't want you spying on him," Bill said, in between guffaws.

Jake dried his lens with his shirt and tried to ignore the raucous laughter. "Could you pull up to the edge over there? I'd like to walk out into the woods and get some light readings, see if I can get a shot at that owl."

Bill leaned over, fished a tree branch out of the water, and tossed it into the wooded area. It crashed through the green carpet, causing it to waver and separate for a few moments. Slowly, the green veil returned to its original, solid appearance.

When Jake realized what he had taken as terra firma was actually only a transitory veil of fragile, green plants, he decided to sit back in his seat and keep his mouth shut.

The floating plants grew more dense until they completely covered the channel with an undulating, green, lacy barrier. The boat cut a path through the plants, but as soon as it passed, the green covering healed itself and closed back over the water. Jake noticed a sweet, mint-like smell in the air, but he did not comment, afraid Captain Bill would whip out a pack of peppermint gum and laugh.

Camille, who had kept silent so far, held up a hand to Bill. Following the unspoken command, Bill turned off the motor.

"Listen to the life," Camille whispered.

They sat silent as the birds, or whatever, chirped and whistled a well-practiced symphony. Every now and then one bird would call out in opposition to the harmony, screeching out its song as if to argue that the swamp was undirected, indeed, wild after all. Jake wondered how the animal life could be so lively in such searing heat. He leaned over and watched the not-quite-still foliage. Every few seconds the plants would waver in the wake of action from beneath the brown, opaque water, that protected the things that lurked just below the surface, on the other side of the intertwined green vegetation. As the boat slowly drifted, secret shapes, members of a hidden world, darted away from their approach, unseen but for sudden ripples on the water.

Jake reached down with both hands, but using only his fingertips, gingerly drew the floaters apart, exposing a mirror-like section of black water. His reflection had only a moment to glance back at him before underwater turmoil disturbed the water, warping the image beyond recognition, like a fun-house mirror. Chilled, Jake pulled back to the safety of his place in the boat.

A snake rose from the water, hooked its head over, and glared at the boat and its occupants.

"Water Moccasin," Bill said.

He started the motor and edged away from the serpent's territory. "You usually don't see them this time of year. Too cold. But now, damn heat has them all confused. Usually don't see the big gators either. They know better. But yesterday, I saw a real whopper. They must think it's summer."

As they continued, Bill pointed out blue herons, nutria, and more pelicans. The swamp was filled with life—on both sides of the surface.

"There. Look on that platform!" Bill turned their attention toward a wooden structure, a remnant of some oil producing activity. On the platform lounged an immense reptile with a long, serpentine tail, its eyes half closed in a look of ecstasy. "Look at the size of that one," Bill said, awe edging into his voice.

"What's he doing there, out in the open?" Jake said as he looked through his viewfinder.

"They like to bask in the light cause it burns the parasites and algae off their skin. Turtles too," Bill said.

Before Jake could get set for a shot, the alligator slid off the platform and made a bee-line for a brown, beaver-like creature that swam a few hundred feet away.

"Oh, oh," Bill said. "Look out, Mr. Nutria."

Without breaking stride, the gator grabbed the hapless rodent and disappeared beneath the green lace curtain that hides the mysteries of the swamp from the eyes of those who do not belong.

With his eyes fixed on the spot where the alligator had dived below the surface, Jake said, "Can the little guy get away?"

"No way," Bill said. "The gator will roll him a few times then, bye-bye."

A cool shadow crept over Jake. He turned and saw Camille standing behind him, his legs placed wide so as to steady himself in the gently rocking boat.

"Jake, how do I begin. The game is so much larger than we are. We are only pawns, grains of sand. This, here around us, is a microcosm of the universe, the ebb and flow. Water from all over the country travels down to this delta universe, carrying with it silt, grains of sand, each particle, rolling and tumbling all the way, all the way fretting over its grand decision—to go—or stay—to Become solid, a part of the real flesh and blood world—or to roll out into the ocean only to be extinguished in the suffocating waves. It used to be a free choice; the grains could stay, Become part of something solid, palpable, and not waste its Being as a part of some fluid, insensate mass. Most grains, of course, chose solid. That is what made this place. That's what makes a delta."

Then, man came along. Man, so worried about *things* that he started building walls, levees to keep the water away from his things, levees everywhere, levees that prevent the grains from making a free choice, from choosing solid, levees that allow the ocean to whittle away at the shore line, levees that—look around you, Jake. Listen to the sounds of life reveling in sensations. Sounds. Smells. Slithers. Bubblings. Screechings. Flesh, furred, scaled, feathered, all losing their hold on this reality because man can't leave the flow of the universe, alone."

That is what our movement is all about. Solid. Choice. Letting nature choose its own course. We want to preserve all of this." He raised his arms. His eyes blazed with sensation, passion. He looked up into the sun and wrapped his arms around himself in a solo embrace. "Jake—join us. Help us reveal *our* truth, convince the others to see it *our* way, to choose solid, the way of the flesh, of Being. Nobody could do it as well as you. Only you can save all of this."

Jake chilled in the heat, chilled by Camille's words. "I'm only a photographer," Jake whispered to the swamp.

A roaring engine turned their heads just in time to see a boat full of whooping fisherman speed by, leaving a powerful wake in its path. Churning waves pummeled the side of Bill's boat. It rocked furiously, unceremoniously plunking Camille back down onto his seat, stunned, his mouth open.

"Mr. Patin," Bill said. "I think Mr. New York has had enough. He looks as if he's about to melt." Bill winked and nodded. As they roared back to the landing, Jake clutched a rail to steady himself, his eyes closed, thankful for the cooling passage of air, trying to banish the memory of his reflection floating on the water, his image, a fun house mask warped by the motion from underneath the surface of the undulating waves.

* * *

The long, hot tour of the swamp had taken its toll on Jake. He was exhausted. It was all he could do to keep his head upright. Each heavy droop of his eyelids lasted longer than the one before.

Through the fog of sleep, Jake heard Camille croon, "It's okay, Jake. Let go. You are not used to the heat yet. Some sleep will do you good. Sleep and forget."

The last thing Jake saw before he closed his eyes was Camille's friendly smile. It echoed through his dreams of green lace curtains and comforted him as yellow eyes peered at him from just above the surface of chocolate water.

"Jake." Camille's gentle voice stole past the barriers of Jake's unconscious mind, waking him.

Jake rubbed his eyes and yawned. When he realized the limo was parked in the entrance to the hotel, he sat upright and said, "I'm sorry. I can't believe I slept all the way back. You must think I'm a total jerk—I didn't snore, did I?"

"No. I do not think you are a jerk. And yes, you snore. But don't worry about it. I am glad you were comfortable. You are my guest. It takes some time to get used to the kind of heat we have down here.

Come to think of it, why don't you stop by my art gallery? Tonight. We are getting ready for a new show. I will introduce you to some of my friends. It's right around the corner from my restaurant."

"Your restaurant?"

"Yes, La Faim. Remember? We met there yesterday."

"Right," Jake said. "What time?"

"We'll be there all evening. Stop by any time. My gallery is called Les Deux Visages."

"Sure." As Jake yawned and walked away from the glossy black limousine, he thought that if it were not for the television and bar, the vehicle could have doubled for a hearse.

Chapter 23

*T*HE EMPTY FEELING GRIPPED JAKE again as soon as he closed the door to his room. His breakfast binge had not eased the hollow feeling, so he decided dinner would be a waste of time. Instead of ordering food, he grabbed a beer from the fridge, went out onto the shady side of his porch, and sat on an iron chair that still radiated heat stored when the sun had beaten down on it. Jake closed his eyes and listened to the rhythmic clop-clop of horses hooves on the pavement below and wondered how the sun-baked street would feel under bare feet. And he wondered, worried over Camille's intentions. What is he up to?

Jake held the beer can against his forehead, but could not prevent errant beads of perspiration from breaking out and trickling down his face. It was time to end the sweating contest he was having with his beer can, so he went inside. The late afternoon was far too hot for porch sitting. Once back in his room, Jake realized he was far too restless for bed sitting. He poured out the unfinished beer. Was it was daiquiri time again? Daiquiri time and forgetting time.

Jake dressed, slipped his camera around his neck, and soon found himself drawn into his favorite daiquiri shop, pointing at the green mixer. Ordering the large size offered the advantage of a free shot of anything on top. "Vodka," Jake said to the shopkeeper. What the heck, he thought; he had time to kill before he had to be at the art gallery.

Armed with a jumbo, green treat, Jake roamed the streets in search of distraction, in search of a vision worth capturing on film. He raised the viewfinder to his eye again and again, but always disappointed by what he saw, he ended up replacing his lens cap without letting light reach the film. The thought of standing still gave him jitters, so he kept walking. Killing time. Purposefully, he walked away from the crowds, away from happy and not so happy couples walking hand-in-hand. He walked away from reminders of what he had lost, or never had.

Too stubborn to admit he was lost, he kept wandering without asking for directions. For the first time since he had discovered photography, he realized how unbearable the weight of a camera could be.

When he had just about run out of energy or determination, he was elated to see a street he recognized, St. Charles. He knew that, one way or another—St. Charles would lead him to Camille's restaurant, to the art gallery, to something and someone familiar.

Left or right—Jake chose right. A few blocks down St. Charles, he stopped. Something tickled the back of his mind, told him to turn around, to head back in the other direction. At last he felt he knew where he was going. In ten minutes, he found himself standing in front of Les Deux Visages, Camille's art gallery. A hand painted sign over the door said, "Coming soon, Form VS. Function." Displayed in the window was a pair of the ubiquitous theatrical masks of comedy and tragedy. Jake moaned in disappointment and went in.

Jake made his way around stacks of boxes and packing cases of all sizes, through forests of sculptures, or whatever, all veiled by white sheets. He caught a flicker of light in the semi-lit lobby and turned quickly to find himself facing a video monitor. At the same time, a figure flickering on the monitor turned and looked straight at Jake, straight into his eyes. Jake's hair stood on end. He shook his head to rid himself of an unpleasant sensation. He checked the screen again. It was blank.

Okay, Jake thought, Camille was looking into the lens of a camera, not at me.

Jake followed the heavy black cable that snaked from the monitor, down a short hall, into a large, brightly lit room that vibrated with activity. He heard Camille's voice on the other side of a portable room divider.

"Let's try again. First, focus on the white card. Make sure it fills the viewfinder. Press the white balance button. When the light stops flashing, we're set. Okay?"

"Got it."

Jake peered around the screen to see Camille standing a few yards in front of a video camera. He held a large, white square of cardboard and wore an irritated expression. When he spotted Jake, he smiled and waved.

"Hi, I'm really glad you decided to stop by. Let me show you around." Camille dropped the white square and rushed over to Jake. "It isn't exactly New York, but you'll be surprised by the quality of our exhibits. Come, let me show you around."

Jake followed his excited guide and noticed for the first time that Camille was not dressed like a proper business person. Instead, he wore jeans and a loose-fitting silk shirt that accentuated his graceful gestures. A small gold earring glistened on his left ear.

"You probably saw the sign out front. Right?" Camille said. "Well, our theme plays off the old form versus function debate. Some of it is just for fun, but some—is for real. We plan to prove, no matter what the form, all art has a function even if it is only to give sensory pleasure. Let me introduce a few of our more popular artists." Camille pointed and named names Jake did not recognize, names he knew he would not remember for more than ten minutes. It was all so boring, so pointless.

Overcome by fits of yawning, Jake said, "I'm really sorry, but I'm getting tired all of a sudden. I guess all that fresh air and water is finally hitting me. And I walked all the way over here, too. I need to grab something to eat, and crash."

"We'll be done here any minute." Camille's excitement spread into his voice. "Afterwards, we're going over to La Faim for supper. You are welcome to join us. Please, stay."

"Thanks, but I'd really rather take something back to my room. I don't think I'd be very good company tonight."

"Of course," Camille said, his voice lowered in obvious disappointment. "I understand. However, before you leave, I would like you to meet one of our most interesting talents. We set up his display in a separate room. You see, he needs lots of wall space." Camille opened a door and ushered Jake into a room adjacent to the main gallery.

"Now this is something you won't see very often, not even in New York."

Camille held up one arm and struck a pose as if in imitation of a magician's assistant. Jake half-expected Camille to say, voila, or to hear a drum roll. Partly to cover his grin of amusement, Jake lifted his camera to his face and captured Camille on film.

* * *

The display that enchanted the walls of the dimly lit room was magical. Across the stone-grey walls ran herds of wild beasts reminiscent of Paleolithic cave paintings like those in Lascaux: horses, bison, deer, all near life-sized, all exuding spirited strength, brute force, base animalism. Barely able to take his eyes off the leaping, running forms, Jake was startled by Camille's voice, hardly above a whisper.

"Jake, I'd like you to meet—Simone."

Jake focused his attention on the small, red-haired man who faced the wall, oblivious to, or ignoring the intrusion of modern man.

"Simone." Camille put his hand on the artist's shoulder. Slowly, Simone turned away from the wall. He appeared to recognize Jake and smiled. The corners of Simone's mouth turned up and a thick, black paste oozed out from between his lips, then ran down his chin. He held out a dirty, freckled hand to Jake.

"Hello, remember me?" More of the nauseating, black offal crept out of his mouth as he spoke. "I'm the maitre d' at La Faim."

Jake nodded and stared back at the man. He looked like a freckle-faced child who had just eaten a mud pie. The black paste welled up in rivers between Simon's teeth and along his gum line. Matching eyes, so dark as to appear black, joined the blacked-out teeth, all suspended under a canopy of orange hair, giving him a jack-o-lantern appearance.

"Simone's contribution to our exhibit is without comparison."

Jake started when Camille interrupted his appraisal of Simone.

"It's the quintessential example of the power of art. It is from an ancient time when art was life. When there was no line of demarcation between the imagination and reality. When art was—survival." Camille's movements and voice were electric. "You see, the hunters, artists, would mix charcoal or ocher with water and saliva to make paint—from their souls. When they spit the 'paint' on the walls and the animal they created became their other self. Their inner self. The artist became the animal itself. Thus, he could control the beast. Control of prey meant control of life. Art became life." He turned back to Simone. "Show him."

Simone bowed over a table littered with chunks of charcoal and mud-red ocher and fingered the assortment until he found a piece that suited him. He popped the charcoal into his mouth, chewed it, then sipped from a dirty glass of water and swished the mixture around in his mouth like a wine taster trying to extract total pleasure from a new vintage. He concentrated on the wall for a moment then spat infinitely controlled blasts of the black paste in a curved line along the wall. Soon, the graceful line began to take the form of a buffalo, including intricate shadings that emphasized the muscular strength of the leaping bison.

Camille stood watching with rapt attention like a proud parent at his child's first recital. Jake bit his lips to wall back impending laughter.

* * *

Jake closed the gallery door after himself, rushed around the nearby corner, ducked into a doorway next to an iron-gated alley, and laughed until tears ran down his face.

"Spit art," Jake said. "I can't wait to tell them about this one in New York."

When Jake's fit of laughter played itself out, he sensed motion nearby. From his dark hiding place, he could see three shadows across the street, arguing. Heavy accents and raging anger distorted their words, making the subject of their conversation indiscernible. One reached out and shoved another against a wall. He retaliated by punching his attacker. Wordlessly, the three scuffled. Then, one broke away from the other two. He reached inside his jacket and pulled something out from a hiding place against his body. It flashed twice, echoing down the avenue like thunder. The two combatants, who still fought, slumped to the pavement and lay motionless. The gun dropped next to them with a metallic crack.

The last of the trio squatted and riffled through his fallen partners' clothing, removing the contents of their pockets. He stood, and without looking around, ran toward Jake.

Chapter 24

*J*AKE SLAMMED HIMSELF BACK AGAINST THE DOOR in his small hiding cove, grieving at the sound of his pulse throbbing against the glass pane. He held his breath and prayed the runner would not hear him. Without appearing to notice Jake's presence, the killer disappeared around the corner. As the sounds of escaping footsteps faded, Jake gasped up all the air he could fit into his starving lungs.

Shaking, Jake peered out from his sanctuary. He saw no one in the street, no one except for the heap of motionless flesh. Without considering whether he should question the condition of the victims, Jake ran off into the dark street. In a direction opposite the one taken by the murderer, off in a direction he knew would lead him away from his hotel, away from what little he thought he knew.

With every leap, his legs took to lead him to safety, his camera pounded against his chest in opposition to the rhythm of his heartbeat, reminding him of the way a priest had once taught him to pound his fist against his chest in admittance of guilt, just before confession. Well away from the scene of the murder, he doubled back in the direction of his hotel.

Whenever Jake heard voices, or felt the presence of others, he slowed to an innocent stroll. With sweat springing from his flesh as if it was being pumped out by his frantic heart, Jake tried to look relaxed. He waved at passers-by or sometimes pretended to snap a photo.

Everyone Jake passed seemed to scrutinize his appearance, examine him for evidence of guilt, so he stopped to check himself in the reflection from an antique mirror on display just on the other side of a showroom window. Jake peered at his image, an image framed by a fantastic display of Mardi Gras masks. The masks, like none he had ever seen before, were of all shapes and sizes, some almost large enough to cover a bed. Peach. Green. Purple. Red. Black. Some with streamers of feathers that trailed to the floor. Some of satin and thousands of sequins. Some of leather.

Jake wore a stark white mask. Its eyes were wide and staring with bloodshot lightning patterns. Instead of feathers, the Jake mask was festooned with disheveled, black curls that hung heavy with perspiration. Jake's mask, his fright wig, sent shivers down his spine. He felt as if he had become a part of the display.

He stayed in the shadows and put one foot in front of another until he was once again on a deserted street and ran his hand along an iron fence as he walked, his fingers making flapping sounds like a limp, worn-out baseball card clipped to the fork of a bicycle, relentlessly slapping the spokes of the wheel. When his fingers became sore from strumming the iron harp, he stopped to rest against the fence. Loose paint chips, barely keeping hold of the iron fence, cut into Jake's forehead. He moved back to sweep the crumbs from his face and focused on a figure that stood motionless on the other side of the fence. The larger-than-life figure stood with arms outstretched, in a posture of supplication, its huge, feathered wings casting shadows across nearby graves, defending them from the glow of a street lamp.

Jake ran down the street until he located the entrance to the cemetery. The gate hung open, only secured by one twisted hinge, so Jake slipped through the gap and searched for a place to rest, a place to hide until he could pull himself together. He stumbled down paths between concrete graves set up aboveground, above the water level. Some, with tall gravestones, looked almost like beds. When he reached the giant angel he had seen from the street, he slumped down at its feet and rested his back against the cool limestone, the lens cap firmly clamped over the eye of his camera. He sat quietly in the angel's protective shadow, motionless, and waited for his fluttering heart to slow. He closed his eyes to the night, pressed his lids down tightly and watched the light show on his inner lids until sleep slipped over him as gently as the whisper touch of silken feathers.

* * *

A low murmuring tugged at Jake's consciousness. It dragged him out of the infinite darkness of dreamless sleep into the graveyard darkness of faraway street lamps, overhead starlight, stone-still shadows, and the not-so-still shadows of two forms that flitted from grave to grave. Were they the murmurers, or was it they who giggled and squealed as they touched and chased? With his back still pressed safely against his angel, safely hidden in its shadow, Jake studied the erratic movements of his two new neighbors. One wore a diaphanous, flowing, white dress. A man and a woman?

They ambled toward Jake's general direction. His muscles tensed and his hands pressed against the base of the angel, ready to push him off at full speed if necessary. Down the path that led to Jake, the one in the long, white dress turned ghostly pirouettes, again and again, around and around, her loosely sleeved arms outstretched. She wrapped her arms around herself and rolled onto the grave right across from Jake. Her cohort fell on top of her, and gone were the giggles and squeals. Only murmuring and moans were left to tumble in the air along with the gentle, midnight breeze.

For the second time in as many hours, Jake was again forced to play the voyeur. The tuxedoed, black street-dancer's words echoed in Jake's memory, over and over. *C'mon in, beautiful girls, unmentionable love acts. Audience par-ti-ci-pation.* Jake drew his breath silently, careful not to disturb the show, careful not to be heard over the murmurs and moans.

When the performance was over, the man rolled away from the dancer and stood by the grave, looking down at his partner. She sat up and pushed herself back against the headstone. Slowly, the grave dancer's lover reached into his shirt and removed something.

"No!" Jake yelled. Taut muscles pushed Jake off his resting place, thrusting him toward the couple. The dancer screamed, leapt off the grave, and ran toward the gate. Her partner dropped whatever it was he held and stumbled after her, tripping over and leaping across graves on his way.

134

When they disappeared into the darkness, Jake crept over to the location of the lovers' tryst. In the dim light of twinkling stars, Jake saw what was left on the makeshift bed. It was a crumpled, brown paper bag, not a gun. Jake pinched the bottom of the bag, lifted it off the stone surface, and emptied its contents into the moonlight. Out clattered a syringe, candles, a spoon, and a plastic bag of something white.

Jake realized that even though he was alone, he could still hear restless, garbled murmurs tumbling in the air. He turned and followed the path toward the gate as quickly as he could, with the whispers and sighs whirling in the darkness behind him.

* * *

The rest of the trip back to his room was uneventful. The few individuals still on the streets looked as bad as Jake. Only the most dedicated partiers would be out at that time of the night. Ashen faces and staggering steps appeared to be the height of fashion for New Orleans street wear just before dawn.

Jake slipped into the hotel. The deskman was asleep with an opened newspaper draped over his head, like a ghost costume. The only sign of life came from the overhead fans. They flapped around in their half-lit hiding places, like butterflies no more. The slow-moving fans, like somnambulant bats hanging from the ceiling, gently flapping their wings in dreams of night-cloaked flight, cast menacing shadows across Jake's face as he stole across the lobby on the way to his room.

Jake locked the door behind himself. His room was as he had left it. Lights on and the fan circling. He turned to the wall and flipped the fan control off. The fan ignored his orders. He flipped the fan switch off and on quickly. Still, nothing happened.

Jake fell onto his bed, face down. He slammed a pillow over his head and fell asleep wishing he was alone, listening to the whooshings produced by the wings of the fan slicing through the oppressive morning air.

Chapter 25

THE WATER WAS AS COLD AS A STAINLESS STEEL TABLE in the morgue. Jake jerked awake. He reached for the sides of the tub, but they were not there. His arms flailed, frantically, trying to grab for anything that could keep him from sinking under the water. He tried to tread water, dog paddle, anything, but it did not work. The vines wound around his legs, slowly pulled him under. Every time he gasped for breath, his mouth filled with duckweed. He spat them out, only to gasp up more. He fought against the pull of the vines until he had no strength left. Finally, he gave up, stopped fighting, and felt his face slip beneath the green lace curtain but did not bother to snatch a last breath. He simply closed his eyes and smiled as the secret things under the mire caressed him on his way down to the bottom of the swamp.

* * *

The racket of a jackhammer stabbing the street dragged Jake out of the swamp, back into the nightmare world of grave dancers flirting with death and freshly stilled lives heaped on the sidewalk. Refusing to open his eyes, Jake felt for a pillow to use as a sound baffle. A light shield. He could not locate a pillow, so he eased his lids open. The fan above still practiced its lazy, solo dance—flap—flap—flap. His bed was barren except for a bottom sheet that barely clung to its duty. One corner of the sheet wrapped around Jake's shoe, the rest trailed to the floor, lifeless. His heart thrashing for oxygen, his stomach screaming for food, Jake sat up with deliberate care, and pulled off his shoes without untying the laces. It was the first time Jake had dreamt since he left New York.

Too burned-out to show his face in the hotel restaurant, Jake called room service and ordered breakfast.

136

After he wolfed down everything the waiter had delivered, he picked up the phone and dialed Camille's number. Three rings disrupted the silence of the empty line, then Jake punched the receiver button before he could make a connection, before he had a chance to confide, to confess. He did not know why. Instead of hanging up the phone, he held the receiver to the side of his neck, his head bowed, his pulse ringing against the earpiece. Jake opened his eyes, dialed another number, and raised the phone to his ear.

"Ellen—I'm okay. How is Nikki? I knew she would be okay. She's the toughest ball of flesh in the world—Oh, no! You cannot let her keep biting people. She'll be arrested. No, it is not cute. Ellen, can you send me a picture of her? Overnight, or something like that? Just a snapshot? Nothing special. I'm starting to forget what she looks like. Great. Thanks. I miss you both. Tell Nikki I'll be seeing her soon enough."

* * *

When the maid arrived to straighten up his room, Jake went out onto the porch for the rest of the day, switching from chair to chair, moving along the porch's length only to escape the shadow left deserted by the retreating sun. Like a parasite-ridden alligator, he sat in the sauna heat and sunlight, hoping to burn the night from his flesh. Late in the evening, having avoided the mirror all day, he ordered more food and fell asleep before the few scraps left on his plate turned cold.

* * *

Jake awoke the next afternoon. Was he really awake? A noise? He gathered his courage and checked the room to be sure he was alone. He tried to remember his dreams, but could not—and he was glad. While he knelt down before his refrigerator, checking to see if the maid had restocked it, he felt someone outside the door. He was sure this time, so he held his breath and waited for a knock. None came. Instead, his vigilance was rewarded by a flash of white worming into his room at the base of the door. Could it be the picture of Nikki, already?

Leaving his refrigerator open, he crept over to the white square and sat on the floor as he opened the envelope. It was an invitation to the opening of Camille's art gallery at nine o'clock that evening.

At the bottom of the white square of embossed paper, was a hand-written postscript from Camille, "Don't bring your camera; I want you to have fun."

Jake knew he had to attend. And he knew that at nine o'clock it would be dark outside. But he would have a chance to nail Camille down to a date for the shoot. He grabbed a beer and shuffled into the bathroom, adjusted the shower until it was hot, just below the point of scalding, and stood under the waterfall, keeping time by methodically sipping his beer.

As the empty beer can swirled around over the drain of the tub, trapped in the whirlpool of escaping water, Jake prepared to hit the streets in search of food, enough to hold him over until the party.

* * *

For the first time since his late-night adventure, Jake was once again out in the streets of New Orleans. Sounds of a band tuning up lured him into an open-air restaurant. He found himself a stool at the bar. While he waited for a bartender to notice him, Jake studied the daily menu hastily scribbled in colored chalk on a blackboard that hung over the cash register.

"Wha' da ya want?" The barman scowled at Jake.

"Hey, are you from New York?" Jake asked.

"Okay. Sorry. I get you. I'm just in a bad mood. My wife's been driving me crazy lately. Four stitches." He pointed to a bandage on his head and exhaled slowly.

Jake laughed. "Been there."

"Oh, no you haven't. You see, her mother died a couple weeks ago. That part was okay. She was real old. But then, the last few days, my wife starts seeing her. *Seeing* her mother. Not just dreaming about her. *Seeing* her. She, my wife that is, keeps me up every night with her carrying on. So, I told her to go see a nut doctor. So then, she really flips out and whacks me with a frying pan. Why don't you try the chicken and sausage gumbo? It's great today, and my wife didn't cook it. It'll go with the Cajun band."

"Okay, gumbo sounds fine," Jake said. While he waited for his gumbo, Jake spun his stool around so he could watch the band members preparing their equipment. The dining area of the establishment was filling up with couples and families. They piled bags and cameras under and on tables or hung them over chairs. They laughed and clicked snapshots of each other with love or at least excitement in their eyes. The hum of conversations, or maybe it was the P.A. system, came to Jake as an indistinct whispering—a whispering not quite clear enough to understand.

On the wall, across from Jake, over the heads of the gathering crowd, hung a much-larger-than-life, green, papier-mâché' alligator who sat, pole in hand, happily fishing from a flat-bottomed, wooden boat. Under the boat swam a world inhabited by hundreds of miniature, blinking lights, all caught up in a fishing net. Jake watched the silent tableau and waited for one of the blinking beings to leap up over the imaginary water level and scare the smile off the dozing alligator's face. Visions of being pulled under the surface of swamp water crept back into Jake's mind. Jake flinched when the barman tapped him on the shoulder and spoke.

"The beer's on the house."

Jake considered refusing the *Abita*, but his thirst overrode his common sense. He took the beer and chugged half the bottle.

"Gee," the bartender said. "You look like *you* just saw a ghost."

"Yeah," Jake said. "Feels like it too."

"I'm Ralph, by the way." The bartender offered Jake his hand.

As Jake enjoyed the gumbo in the air-conditioned bar, the steam that rose from the bowl reminded him he would soon be back out in the sauna of New Orleans. Since he was sure he would not like Cajun music, Jake left just before the band began to play. He waved to Ralph as he crossed the invisible barrier between the cool inside air and the boiling atmosphere outside.

The crowd on the street seemed thicker, moved slower than usual. The feel of it was like one of those dreams where everything happens in slow motion. Jake sensed someone watching him, following as he lumbered back toward his room. Every time he turned to look behind himself, he was disappointed or relieved. No familiar face appeared.

When back safely on his bed, Jake called the desk and left a wake-up call so he would not miss Camille's reception that night.

He would get serious with Camille and insist on a date for the shoot. Before long, he fell asleep wondering how one dresses for a New Orleans spit-art show—and he fell asleep wondering if the sidewalk around the corner from the gallery would have Jackson Pollock, red-splatter works of art still on display, or if someone had come along to wash away the earthy-red-ocher-colored stains.

Chapter 26

THE DARK NIGHT SURROUNDED JAKE. As he walked toward the gallery, he slowed when he neared the corner—the corner where he had run to hide only two nights ago. In slow motion, he turned the corner, one hand gripping the brick building for support. There, camouflaged by inky shadows, was a form bent over the spot where the bodies had once been piled. Against his will, the sight of the hunched form drew him like a vacuum. As he wavered closer, he could see it was a woman, rubbing her hands along the sidewalk and wiping them on her long, red hair. What the hell was she doing? Jake tried to resist, tried to back away, but he was drawn to her, drawn to see who she was, what she was doing.

She repeated the ritual over and over as he drew near. Jake stood before her and realized what he had taken as a shock of ruby-colored hair was actually a glossy, raven-black mane smeared with something red. Raven hair?—Madeleine? Her hands and lower arms glistened with cloak of sticky blood. She began to shake when Jake's shadow fell over her, and throwing her head back, her face a mask of red glee, she looked up at him and shrieked with laughter. Mask and all, it only took him one glance to recognize her.

Madeleine!

From faraway, he heard wind chimes calling to him.

* * *

A persistent ringing of a telephone crept into Jake's dream. He woke suddenly—he was safe on his bed—maybe.

"Matthew. Thanks for the wake-up call." Jake mumbled into the phone. "Could you have a taxi waiting for me in about an hour? Thanks."

Jake got up so he would not fall back into sleep by mistake. As he sat on the edge of his bed, holding his head in his hands, he wished he had not quit smoking and knew it was time to quit drinking.

* * *

Jake, feeling naked without his camera, did not look out the windows as the cab sped toward Les Deux Visages. When they arrived, he paid the driver and headed straight to the gallery door without looking right or left. No ghost-like shrouded figures greeted him when he entered the lobby. All the sheets had been removed from the displays. Overhead, bright lights danced on fine crystal chandeliers. Well-dressed strangers wandered around the room, sipping wine from crystal glasses as they ooohed and aaahed over paintings and sculpture. As Jake sampled the hors d'oeuvres, he let a waiter pour him a glass of champagne. It sparkled on the way down Jake's throat, reminding him of tiny blinking lights that twinkled under the papier-mâché' alligator. Another glass of champagne followed another until the past began to fade, or was hastily buried in a shallow grave of forgetfulness.

The artists were decked out in their finest, so to speak. Their finest ranged from a velvet suit to a chain-mail mini skirt, but all were obviously trying their best to play their parts. Even Simone smiled through a freshly laundered face. Jake examined the works that had been previously covered with sheets. Some were, as Camille had said, just for fun, but some were for real and showed a great deal of promise. When he finally spotted Camille in his black tuxedo, posing among the crowd, Jake went over to him.

"Camille, I have to hand it to you, this is a really great show. I am impressed. I wish I brought my camera."

Camille's face flushed. "Do you really think so? I was so hoping you would like it. I've been worrying about it for a long time. I am so relieved. Did you get enough to eat, drink?"

Jake nodded and smiled.

"Jake, before I forget, everyone, especially myself, would be honored to have you at our post-opening celebration. It will be a real special party, New Orleans style. You need to get wound up for Mardi Gras. Oh, please say you will come."

142

"Sure, Camille, I wouldn't miss it, Jake said as he remembered Tony's warning—better get ready. Will it be at La Faim, like the other night?"

"Oh, no. It's at Bete Noir."

"Where?"

"Bete Noir. It is what you might call a private club I open only for special occasions. Did you ever notice the alley with the black wrought-iron gate, right next to La Faim?"

Jake nodded and swallowed hard.

"Well, that's where it will be, right after the show closes. The gate will be open. Just go through it, but be sure it is closed after you. We would not want outsiders wandering in. Then, follow the alley around a corner and knock on the door. Someone will let you in."

Jake laughed, "Will I need a secret password?"

Camille put his hands on his hips and pursed his lips at Jake in mock disgust, "No Jake, no password. This isn't Captain Cody and the Space Rangers, silly." He spun around and left Jake laughing. The rest of the evening blazed past Jake in a flurry of pasty smiles and polished diamonds. As the crowd began to thin out, Jake decided to check Simone's finished work.

The door to the room that harbored Simone's spit creatures was open. Jake peered in to discover a display lit only by candles. The flickering flames cast uneven swarms of luminosity and quickening shadows across the walls. The dim, wavering light not only created a cave-like atmosphere, but it provided the appearance of motion to the herds of running, panting beasts. Jake walked to the center of the room and stood still. He held his breath and marveled at the reality racing and leaping around him. Though he stood motionless, the candles continued to flicker. Why? He glanced around the room, searching for the source of a draft. Not even a window. Then he looked up. Slowly circling on the ceiling, were the black wings of another damn fan. With a shiver, he turned and left the cave.

Jake found his way back to the main lobby and was shocked to find it empty. He could not have been in Simone's room that long. Or could he? The only sign of life was a clean-up crew. One of them unlocked the front door only long enough for Jake to leave.

He stood with his back to the gallery door. "Camille's club is only around the corner. Only around the corner," he whispered. He had not planned on being caught outside alone after dark, but calling a cab for a one-block trip was out of the question.

"Okay," he whispered to the street. "I can do this. I'm from New York. This place is cake, compared to The City."

He straightened his back and started off toward the Bete Noir. As he walked, the street seemed to whisper back to him.

He reached the corner. One hand on the building that blocked his view of the other street, he stepped around the turn. Without looking to the left, to the other side of the street, he plodded along using all his strength to pull oxygen in through his constricted throat, into his screaming lungs. Once past the nightmare corner, his speed increased until he reached the iron gate.

He stepped back to make sure it was the right gate. Yes. It was contiguous to La Faim. Gingerly, he pulled on the black gate. It opened on well-oiled hinges that refused to allow the escape of a single sound. He closed it behind himself and started down the alley. Someone whispered from behind. He whipped around to face whoever followed him. No one was there. The gate was still closed.

Jake shook his head to rid his ears of unwanted sounds and followed the alley until it ended with a heavy door of black wood. He knocked. Nobody answered. He searched for a knob or handle. There was none, so he knocked again. This time, his bruised knuckles drew a response. The door opened, and a giddy blond girl peeped through the opening.

She smiled. "Come in. We've been waiting for you." She opened the door all the way, grabbed Jake's arm and pulled him in, slamming the door behind him.

The Bete Noir was not what Jake had expected. It was not a building or even a room. It was nothing more than an open courtyard surrounded by two-story brick walls. Potted trees reached up toward a starless sky along with swirling plumes of smoke that rose from charcoal grills. A crew of cooks and waiters hustled to keep serving tables covered with delicacies.

The music was provided by a band that belonged in Soho, not New Orleans. The musicians, who appeared to be albinos,

144

danced in place as they spewed out pseudo-punk chords, their silver hair teased out like something left over from Saint Marks in the early eighties. The dance floor was packed with laughing guests, jerking to the music, drinks in hand. Jake was the only one there dressed in a suit, the only one who stood alone, motionless. Thoughts of Tony crept into his mind, thoughts of the lone pine and his warning that Jake should learn to dance.

Camille burst out of the crowd with a curly-haired girl in tow. "Jake, you made it. We thought that you'd decided to ignore us."

"Oh, no. I was carried away by your show. Time just flew by."

Camille glowed with pride.

The curly-haired girl grabbed Jake's arm. "Let's dance."

"No, thanks. I don't dance."

"Come on. You're kidding."

"Really. Honestly."

The girl let out a harumph and strutted away.

"Oh, oh. She's mad," Camille said. "She's been panting to meet you since she spotted you at the show. I promised I'd introduce you."

"Thanks for the help, but I'm not interested in women," Jake said.

Camille smiled, tilted his head and looked at Jake questioningly.

"No! Not that! It's just that I had a bad experience a while ago, and I need to hang loose for a while. Pull myself together, sort of."

"Oh," Camille said, obviously disappointed.

Jake noticed for the first time that both of Camille's ears were pierced. A waiter passed carrying a tray of glasses filled with champagne. Camille grabbed one for himself and one for Jake. As Jake took the glass from Camille's hand, he checked Camille's fingernails. They were freshly manicured and shone with clear polish. Yes, Jake thought to himself. Just like New York. He shrugged and took a sip of the champagne and shivered.

The crush of the crowd separated Jake and Camille. Champagne and garbled conversations filled the night air along with the hysterical music and spastic dancers.

From time to time, Jake would catch a glimpse of Camille who appeared to be spending an equal amount of time talking with men as dancing with women. Once, as Jake made his way through the crowd, he spotted Camille pressing a woman against the wall with the length of his body, his lips close to her ear. Jake was relieved.

A passing waiter slipped another glass of champagne into Jake's hand. One would not hurt, so he toasted Camille's validity, according to the world of Jake. He downed the champagne in a few gulps and reached over to return the glass to a passing waiter's tray, which appeared to split in two, to reproduce before his very eyes. There they were, double trays. Which one? He chose the one that appeared most solid. When he let go of the glass, it fell to the bricks below and smash into a thousand shards. Realizing how drunk he was, all he could do was lean back against a wall and watch the view spin before him like a crazy, live, incarnate kaleidoscope. How? He only drank one glass of champagne.

* * *

"Jake, are you okay?" Camille waved his hand in front of Jake's face. "Wow! You're really fried. Want me to call you a cab?"

Jake could not respond.

"Simone," Camille called over his shoulder. "Come here. Please."

Camille and Simone each took one of Jake's arms and led him to the back of the courtyard, behind the makeshift stage. Camille slipped a key into a barely visible door and pulled it open. They led Jake into a lavishly decorated apartment and tilted him onto a velvet couch.

Camille opened a quilt and spread it over Jake's prostrate form, then spoke loudly, as if talking to a deaf person. "Jake, you can sleep here. It's okay. You're too drunk to go out on the streets alone. I will check in on you later."

Jake was asleep, or blacked out, before Camille and Simone could reach the door.

* * *

Jake woke partially. He could not quite get himself to move. Could not quite open his eyes. He began to panic, began to pray it was alcohol that paralyzed him. Through a fog, he heard Camille's

146

voice crooning to a woman. At least she giggled like a woman. They stumbled around in the dark, then went into another room and closed the door behind themselves. The giggling continued for a while, but was soon replaced by murmurs and moans. Images of cemetery dancers flitted through Jake's mind. With only the sounds of faraway life to keep him company, Jake slipped back into unconsciousness, wondering if Tony was also sleeping alone.

Chapter 27

WHEN JAKE WOKE THE NEXT MORNING, his head hurt so badly he did not open his eyes. He knew daylight would only add to the pain, so he lay motionless, listening for the whir of the overhead fan, waiting to hear the familiar flapping sound as it chopped through the air.

The room was silent.

Where was his damn fan?

Where was he? He forced himself to open his eyes, a little at a time. The ceiling harbored no fan. In its place hung a crystal chandelier. With a wave of nausea, he remembered where he was. Jake grabbed the top of the couch and pulled himself into a sitting position, just in case he had to run for a bathroom.

Just as Jake was about to lower himself back down, a door opened and Camille, in a black satin robe, entered the room followed by the curly-haired girl. She stuck her tongue out at Jake and disappeared through another door. Camille walked over to Jake and smiled down at him.

"Champagne hangover. They're the worst. Mmmmmm. Could be fatal if not treated properly. How about some breakfast?"

Jake's answer was a moan. He flopped back down on the couch and pulled the quilt over his head.

"Okay," Camille said. "How about coffee instead?"

Jake slid one hand out from under the quilt and flashed Camille the okay sign.

* * *

The coffee went down better than Jake expected, and it only needed a small amount of cream to make it palatable. He managed to follow the coffee with a slice of toast.

148

"What the hell kind of champagne was that last night? I only drank one and," Jake shook his head. "I think I've had too much time on my hands lately. I want to get working, right away. Can you hook me up with a boat?" Jake held his head and moaned. "Something big enough not to rock too much."

"Not today. Please. You're in no shape to go out on the water. It's the heat, you know. Another day won't matter. I'll get something put together for tomorrow."

"I guess you're right about today. But, I want to start tomorrow. For sure. I have to keep my mind occupied on something concrete."

"Jake, if there's anything you need to talk about, feel free. I'm a good listener."

"No—it's okay. I just have to get myself on a regular schedule. Get some work done. That is, right after I go back to my room and sleep for a few more hours."

"Fine. I'll call you a taxi. You're in no shape to walk. In fact, you're in no shape to crawl."

* * *

Jake flicked the switch that controlled his overhead fan. Again, nothing happened, so Jake grabbed the phone and dialed the desk.

"This is Jake Preston. I have a problem here. No, the room is fine. No, it's clean. It's the freaking fan. I can't shut it off. The control is broke. I don't care if everybody else likes to keep the air moving. I like my air still. Stagnant. I'm from New York. I get high on exhaust fumes. Okay? Why can't you get it fixed today? Fine—whenever."

Jake slammed the receiver down, picked up the whole phone and threw it up at the fan. The cord was too short to allow a complete trip to the ceiling, so it jerked the phone back, bouncing and jingling across the bed.

Jake walked out onto the porch. He stayed a moment, then retreated to his room and opened the fridge. No. He did not want to drink. There were no answers for him in the bathroom either. He paced back and forth across his room, running his hands through his hair. Standing in front of the mirror, he spoke to his sickly reflection, to bloodshot eyes encircled by grey swellings. "What am I doing in this God-forsaken city? Madeleine is not here. Rachel is gone. I don't belong here. I don't belong anywhere."

The telephone, left off the hook for too long, buzzed Jake back to the real world. He turned to the bed, returned the phone to its place on the end table, and dropped onto his mattress. He pulled a pillow out from under the bed cover and held it close, resting his face against its cool surface.

* * *

Jake stroked Rachel's golden hair and held her close. Part of him knew he was dreaming, but he did not care. It felt too good. "When did you get back?" Jake whispered into her ear. She did not answer, but it did not matter. She was there, warm, soft. Tears trickled from Jake's eyes. "I'm sorry I didn't take good enough care of you. I'm so sorry. It was all my fault. Stay this time, please."

She pulled away.

"No! Please! Stay!"

Rachel did not answer. She slid off the bed and tumbled to the floor. Jake scrambled to the edge of the bed intending to grab her. Then he saw it—froze—used his cold, trembling hands to steady himself by clutching at the carpet—his fingers frozen into a claw-like position.

A large black dog, with red foam dripping from its mouth, had Rachel by the foot. Backing away from the bed, with golden eyes fixed on Jake, it pulled Rachel's body towards the porch.

Jake shook off his fear, grabbed Rachel's arms and tugged against the dog's strength. It growled and shook Rachel like a terrier snapping a rat's neck. The dog's vicious tactics ripped Rachel from Jake's grasp. Snarling, drooling, its hair standing on end, the roach-backed beast dragged her through the door and out onto the porch. Jake heard Rachel sob a last good-bye. He dropped to his knees and tried to crawl after her, grabbing fruitlessly for her hands. When the face, framed with blond hair, looked up at him, Jake froze. The face of the form being pulled over the black iron railing was not Rachel's—it was Camille's. Shaking off the shock of recognition, Jake ran over to the rail and gaped down at the street below. There, laughing up from the pavement, poised

150

on all fours, crouched Madeleine, her glossy, black hair reflecting the colors of the neon signs that flashed across the street.

* * *

Jake woke to the sound of laughter in the hall outside his room. He jumped up, staggered to the door, and peered through the peephole. Through the tiny lens, he saw the distorted image of an elderly couple strolling down the hall clutching jumbo daiquiris.

With shaking hands, Jake opened the refrigerator door and snatched out a beer. He crept out to the porch rail and looked down. The street was dark and empty. He took one long drink of beer. "Damn. This tastes like shit." He let the can drop to the street. When it slammed against the ground, the beer foamed out of the battered can and lathered across the sidewalk toward the street.

Where are these dreams coming from, he asked himself. I never drank before. Well, not like this.

Back in his room, Jake locked the porch door. He grabbed a Coke from the refrigerator, fumbled for the television remote, sat on the edge of his bed, and searched the channels for signs of real life. He found the ten o'clock news and turned up the sound.

A faceless voice-over said, "And now back to Leila and Frank for our final story of the day."

"So, what's our parting story today, Frank?" Leila smiled and looked over to her partner.

"Well, Leila, our source at the Crescent City police department reports that there have been numerous sightings recently."

"You mean UFO's?"

"Right, but not the kind you're thinking of. These sightings are all *unbelievable familial observances.*"

"Come again?"

"You heard me. The police switchboards have been lighting up with calls from hysterical citizens reporting sightings of recently deceased family members. It seems that New Orleans is haunted. Not only are we the murder capital of the country, but we can now boast more ghosts than any other city."

"Well, Frank, it makes sense to me. If you have the most murders, it follows that you should have the most ghosts too. Good night everybody, and remember, leave your lights on tonight."

Jake flicked the television off, grabbed his pillow, and sat in the chair by the door, hugging his pillow, planning to stay awake all night. It's not me. It's this city. There's something wrong with this city.

Chapter 28

A BELL RANG. Jake dropped his pillow and wobbled to his feet. He stumbled to his bed and grabbed the phone.

"Yes." Jake cleared his throat as he listened to Camille. "What do you mean; Bill's unavailable for a few days? Oh, a funeral. Isn't there anyone else on that whole basin who can take me out? Okay, it's your money. If you want me to wait for Bill, I will. Let me know as soon as you can set me up. I really need to get working. Fine."

Jake paced his room. The only thing that could salvage his trip to New Orleans would be work. If he did not get to work soon, he would go crazy.

Jake jumped at the sound of rapping, then crept over to his door. He squinted through the peephole. On the other side of the fisheye lens hovered a distorted version of Matthew, already distorted by years of overeating. He was tapping an envelope on the palm of his hand and looking left and right as if to make sure Jake would get a chance to admire his most photogenic side.

Jake opened the door.

Matthew held up the envelope and said, "Special delivery, sir." With a sharp nod, he handed the envelope to Jake and left.

Warily, Jake searched for the return address. "Yes!" Jake's yell echoed down the hall. He rushed back into his room and, his back against the door, ripped the envelope apart. Packed between two pieces of cardboard, was a picture of Nikki. Her hair perfectly coifed, she sat beaming at him, one paw on her tarantula squeaky. Jake grinned back at the snapshot and memorized every inch of it.

It was noon. Careful not to mar the photo with fingerprints, Jake leaned it against a lamp on the nightstand. He rolled down onto his bed and tried, again, to sleep in the relative safety of the afternoon sun. He closed his eyes and lay still, but his mind would not cooperate. It kept telling him he needed to be somewhere, that there was something he should be doing. He grabbed handfuls of his hair and pulled, as if he could rip the messages from his mind. He gave up the fight with his rebellious, confused thoughts and went out onto the porch.

It was already at least ninety degrees on the street, but Jake did not mind. He was getting used to it. Through the honking and neighing came the sounds of the damn whispering, again. Jake stepped over to the edge of the porch and looked down at the street. The people there paid no attention to him, and certainly were not whispering up to him. To be sure his porch neighbors were not playing games with him, he walked the length of the balcony and stood listening at each end.

"I must be going fucking nuts," he mumbled. "Schizoid."

He returned to his room, grabbed his camera and his picture of Nikki, and walked out onto the street, still dressed in yesterday's clothes. He shuffled down the street, slowly reading every sign, every menu, window-shopping. When he finished his vodka, he tossed the glass into a trashcan and bought a daiquiri, a number of daiquiris, all red, in hopes of drowning the whispers in oblivion. But, he could still hear them, just barely.

Out of a corner bar came the sounds of a guitar being tuned, a blues guitar. "Noise," Jake said to the whispers. He entered the bar, slipped onto a chair by the only empty table, and waited for the music to start, to overwhelm the whispers. Jake's table was in a good location—in front of an open door—so he could see outside and still watch the band set up, and the dance floor. The heat remained outside on the street where it belonged, leaving it cool and dark inside.

A warm breeze passed Jake as it cut through the bar on its voyage from one street to the next. In a corner of the lounge, gambling machines winked in the dim light. Hundreds of dollar bills plastered the redbrick walls. Jake was surprised to see that the clock peeking out from behind the glued-on currency read six forty-five. Why was it was so late?

A waitress sauntered over to Jake. "What ya drinking?"

No thanks. I'm not—.

"Oh yes you are. Can't waste a table on A. A. rejects. You drink or you walk, dude."

"Okay. Vodka and cranberry."

While he waited for his drink, Jake watched the Technicolor street show. As if it was a humongous, vertical, large-screen television, the doorway framed New Orleans life. Tourists passed by, directing their courses with dead eyes. Cabs and horse-drawn carriages inched down the street clogged by growing crowds.

One of the carriages stopped in front of the door, held up by the glut of tourists. Its occupants, laughing and kissing, threw empty drink cups to the street, scattering ice cubes across the sidewalk. The jettisoned cubes tumbled erratically, like crystal dice, only to be crushed under the weight of the crowd. When the waitress returned with Jake's drink, she plopped it down in front of him, making the table wobble as if it were drunk, sloshing vodka onto its glossy black surface.

Across the street from Jake stood a gift shop, its exterior built of an intricately woven pattern of red bricks, its windows filled with novelty tee shirts. Cats Suck," read one with a cartoon depicting a dog and cat engaged in oral sex. Above the shop hung the obligatory balcony with an intricate, wrought-iron rail. A row of multicolor foil strips hung along it, fluttering in the wind, reflecting the light, like tangled hair. Tall French doors with ten panes lined the wall. Jake counted them and wondered why so many New Orleans shutters and doors were painted blue. His eyes again followed the beautiful brick pattern. Slowly, one of the second-floor, blue-framed doors opened as if a ghost were passing through—no one stood in the open space. Jake held his breath while he waited for the occupant of the apartment to appear. Around the end of the fluttering foil, tiptoed a black and white cat. It waddled to the edge of the porch, plopped his rear end down, and yawned, then flopped down on the hot patio to roll in the sun. As it rolled, it knocked a beer can off the edge. The can clanked to the street below, empty. The cat continued his show long enough for Jake to catch him on film.

The uneven clip-clop of another oncoming horse dragged Jake's attention back to street level. He tried to count the color layers of the paint that peeled from the doorframe of the bar. Everything was peeling, shedding skin. Black. Green. White. Blue. The horse still clopped, but did not pass Jake's door-stage. The erratic clicking began to sound like a horse on acid. Leaving his drink to hold his place, Jake wobbled away from his table and peered out onto the street. There were no horses on the street, but a crowd had formed a circle around something, someone. Jake made his way through the crowd to see what was going on. There, in the center of the circle, were two black boys. One boy stood aside, waving his arms and pointing to a low-cut cardboard box that lay on the street before him. The box was littered with dollar bills. The second boy, dressed in a dirty football jersey and long, nylon pants, furiously tap danced in the crushing heat of the afternoon sun. Somehow, he had affixed taps to the bottoms of ratty sneakers. As he danced and twirled, sweat beads sprang out on his face and ran down his neck. The ecstasy in his eyes fascinated Jake.

Jake switched on his power winder and snapped a series of pictures. When the crowd began to whistle and cheer, a breeze rushed past, blowing the dollars out of the box. The tapper continued, unconcerned, while his partner scrambled to catch the money as it fluttered down the street. Jake, disturbed by the scene of the boy crawling after the money, returned inside to his place by the teetering table. "And what am I crawling after?"

While Jake was out watching the tapper, the band members had finished their preparations. They lined up on the small stage with the red brick wall behind them and rows of black fans above, slowly and meticulously slicing the light that poured from red bulbs. The guitar player led the first number, drowning out the tapping from the street and the hum of air conditioners. Jake could barely see the band through the dim light and heavy smoke. The guitar player began to sing, and the band joined his lead. His long, black ponytail swung back and forth over his shoulders as he turned to harmonize with the harmonica player. Jake tried to decipher the tattoo that peeked out of the singer's Harley shirt, but the light was too dim, and dancers had packed the cramped dance floor. Clinging to their partners, couples shuffled around the floor, bumping into each other like plastic ducks in the carnival race booth. Jake sat alone, apart, and not a part, unlike Tony, unlike the lone pine in the forest.

The fans whirled overhead, and the dancers turned below. Out from the tightly packed crowd danced a lone figure, not tall like Tony. She was small, dressed in torn jeans and a white tank top. Sandals, barely held by golden straps, covered the bottoms of her feet. Long, red, curly hair stuck to the sweat that shone on her bare flesh. She turned and twisted with the music, one with the lyrics. With black, intense eyes, the singer watched her every move as he moaned into the microphone, their disparate relationship growing more entangled with each note. She sometimes touched herself, ran her fingers along her arms as if she was trying to be sure she was real. Did she also have nightmares? Jake felt drawn to her.

Because a gathering audience blocked his view, Jake stood and moved toward the dance floor, stopping under the brick arch, afraid to disturb the unconventional duet. The song ended and couples wandered off to their tables. The solo-dancer walked straight toward Jake, not appearing to notice him. She tried to pass. Without thinking, he moved in front of her, forcing her to look up at him, perturbed. She tried to back away. Surprising himself, Jake grabbed her wrist and held her there. She looked up into his eyes, at first disturbed by his presence. For moments that passed like lives, she returned his gaze, reversing the situation, holding Jake prisoner with the power of her piercing scrutiny. Jake felt as though she was sucking every thought from his mind without offering any in exchange. They circled each other, still locked in eye contact, like sparring animals, alone in the forest, sizing up an aggressor.

Suddenly, her pupils dilated, and a profound expression of recognition spread across her face. Her mouth fell open, and she sucked in a deep breath as if to speak.

"Sara! No!" A greasy-looking, thin man with a long, drooping moustache and stringy, black hair yelled and grabbed her by the hand and yanked her way from Jake. Together, they ran down the street, hand-in-hand, pushing others aside. Jake followed, crashing and bumping into anything in his path until he lost sight of them. They were nowhere to be found.

Jake leaned back against a building. His heart slammed against his chest. Perspiration tickled down his back. He slid down to the street and sat with his head hanging down, catching his breath.

What if she was Madeleine?

From his shirt pocket, Jake retrieved the picture of Nikki. He stared at it, longingly, wishing he could crawl into the picture, wishing he could hold Nikki close enough to feel her tiny heart flutter against his. He rested, panting. Someone walked by and tossed a quarter at his feet. It jangled and danced as it hit the cement, waking Jake from his daze. "I'm not a beggar." He kicked the coin away. Humiliated, he pulled himself upright and returned to the blues bar.

It was break time. The singer pressed up against the bar. Jake slid next to him. "Hey, you know that red-haired woman who was dancing alone?"

"Yeah, the one—"

"Who is she?"

"I don't know. Never saw her before."

"You just said you knew her."

"No I didn't."

"But I have to find her. It looked like you were singing to her. Are you sure you don't know who she is?"

"Are you sure you don't want me to put your fucking lights out? I said I never saw her before. The world is full of bitches like that. Go find another one." He grabbed his beer and returned to the stage.

Jake questioned all the waitresses and bartenders—nobody knew her. He left the bar and noticed the clock still read six forty-five.

By the time Jake harassed every bar tender, wait person, and passer-by on the street who would listen to his frantic queries, he was stone-cold sober. His last stop was the place where he had gotten the chicken and sausage gumbo. Ralph, the bartender, remembered him.

"Hey, New York. How you doin'?"

"How's things with your wife?"

"She's still freaking out on me. I'm ready to kick her ass out."

"Whoa, isn't that kind of harsh?" Jake said.

"Yeah, I'm only kidding."

"Ralph, have you seen a little woman with real long, curly red hair?"

"Thousands. Why, you looking for one?"

"Yes. Please, if you see anyone like that, try to keep her here and call me." Jake grabbed a pen from next to the cash register and scribbled the hotel number on a napkin. "It's real important to me."

"Why?"

"I don't know. I think maybe I know her from somewhere, from New York."

"Hey, New York, you been hanging around with my wife?"

"No. Please, just try to remember."

"Okay. Okay. Want a beer?"

"No, thanks. It's getting dark. I think I'll go to my room and crash."

Jake wandered back toward his room, scanning the crowd, watching reflections in store windows, still searching. When he peered in through the mask shop window, the owner's eyes were violet. He did not go in to question her.

* * *

The first thing Jake did when he got to his room was check the fan. The switch was still broken. He grabbed his phone and dialed. "Matthew. I thought someone was coming over to fix my fan switch today. I don't care if it's a busy time for electricians. Never mind. I'll fix it myself."

Jake slammed the phone down and jumped onto his bed without removing his sneakers. He leapt up and grabbed a fan blade. Using his weight for leverage, he ripped the fan out of the housing that held it captive and dragged it down, leaving behind a trail of torn wires. He threw the fan blade assembly against the wall where it leaned for a moment before tumbling down into the deep, blue carpet. After tucking Nikki's picture behind the frame of the mirror on his dresser, Jake went out onto his porch and pulled a chair over to the edge. There, he sat and watched every movement on the street below until nobody was left for him to scrutinize—until he was sure Sara was not around.

When the streets emptied, Jake went to bed. A breeze that blew in through his open porch door generated the only movement of air. He wished he had thought to snap a picture of Sara as she danced alone. Sara—Madeleine—she had to be.

Chapter 29

*J*AKE DIALED PROFESSOR BETTY HIGGINS when he woke the
next day.

"Betty. This is Jake."

"Where are you? I've been trying to call you," Betty said.

"Why?"

"What do you mean why? I was concerned about how you
were doing. You were a mess at the funeral."

"I'm okay. I'm in New Orleans. I'm staying at a hotel, The
Enclave."

"I don't like the sound of your voice—Jake, are you still there?
What are you doing in New Orleans?"

"Searching—I think—I think I found Madeleine. Maybe."

"Think? Maybe?"

"Yeah. I met this weird woman yesterday."

"What do you mean, weird?"

"I don't know. She was dancing alone. But, that's not it.
She recognized me. Really recognized me. I shocked her. I think
it's her."

"Madeleine?"

"Betty, she didn't look anything like Madeleine, but she knew
me, and I never saw her before. I am positive I never saw her
before, and I'm *positive* she knew me. Who could she be if not
Madeleine?"

"Jake. Get real. She probably saw your picture in a magazine or something like that. Maybe you just reminded her of
someone."

"No. She knew me. The real me. Why couldn't Madeleine be
in someone else's body?"

"For how long?"

"I don't know. I guess I don't know much of anything."

"Jake. What's done is done. Go home. Start your life again. Put the past behind you. Give up this hopeless quest."

"No. I can't. I won't." He stopped to gather himself. "You didn't see Rachel on the bathroom floor. You didn't see her blood on the mirror. I can't go home until I finish this. Until I find Madeleine. I know she killed Rachel—I know."

"You'd better be careful," Betty said. "This woman might just be some innocent nut. Maybe you just thought she recognized you. Jake, you are a beautiful man. Maybe she was just stunned by your appearance. Be careful. She could be totally innocent. So could Madeleine. You do not *know* if she had anything to do with what happened to Rachel. Don't do anything you'll be sorry for."

"Don't do anything I'll be sorry for?" Jake's voice rose with self-recrimination. "It's a little late for that. Sorry is all I have left. I guess I'll just have to handle this for myself."

"No, Jake. Hold on. What is it you need me to do?"

"See if you can find out for me. About a new body. Could Madeleine have a new body?"

"Jake. This is crazy."

"Please."

Jake hung up the phone and remembered the promise they had made at their last supper together, a promise never to speak of the Devereuxs again.

* * *

Jake was out on the street before the crowd. He began to search for Sara immediately. The street outside his hotel was empty except for a lone man with a heavy beard and thick, long brown hair that hung out from under a black beret tilted to one side. His wildly piercing, black-brown eyes returned Jake's stare, then he stepped out of a doorway and walked away.

Jake planned to question someone from each bar, daiquiri shop, restaurant, or whatever, all along Bourbon Street before the crowds could steal the employees' attention away from him. His search was futile. He repeated the process one street over, the next, and next, until he was too tired to walk any more.

He found himself in Jackson Square, hungry, so he crossed the street and found an empty table at a coffee shop. He ordered coffee and beignet and questioned his waiter. He questioned every waiter who passed. He attacked street vendors next, with no luck.

"Mister, do you know how many people come through here every day? Every hour? Get a life." The man at the cash register of a bookstore snorted and went back to his girlie magazine.

Shaking his head in dismay, Jake went over to the curb, sat down, and removed one of his sneakers so he could pull up his sock. He massaged the back of his heel where the bunched-up sock had rubbed a raw spot. Dreading the need to slip his tender foot back into the shoe, he bowed his head and killed time by examining the debris that lay squashed along the curb. Out of the collage of deserted items, he retrieved a crumpled cigarette pack. He stuck a finger through the small tear at the top and searched the inner darkness out of long practiced habit. His finger felt a familiar, slim object, hooked around it, and pulled out an abandoned cigarette, perhaps overlooked by an avid smoker anxious to start a new pack. He straightened out the bent cigarette, held it under his nose, and inhaled deeply, smiling. Jake considered bumming a light and smoking the mangled cigarette until a slow-moving cab edged through the crowd, leaving behind a curling trail of dirty blue smoke. Jake remembered his soul, like blue smoke, leaving his body. He shivered, crushed the cigarette, and leapt off the curb. Then he hopped, one-shoed, after the cab and caught it before it inched around the corner.

Though he slouched low in the cab's back seat, the sounds and smells of Bourbon Street warned him he was near his hotel. He sat up and leaned over the front seat, "Let me off here. This is close enough."

* * *

Jake stood on a corner near a bar. For the first time, he realized how ugly New Orleans, or at least his area, smelled. It reeked of urine and filth, like a massive shelter for scores of homeless, unwashed street people, people who have given up their quest. Maybe it was his turn. Listen to Betty. Put your job first. Protect your professional reputation if you plan to go on with your life. Enough. At least, move to a better side of town.

Jake hobbled the rest of the way to his hotel, no longer searching every face for a flash of green eyes, every hat for the escape of a red curl. He walked with his eyes to the street only observing enough to keep himself from crashing into another lost daydreamer. Sneakers, shoes, and sandals passed by without a misstep until a pair of worn cowboy boots shuffled up and stopped in front of him, blocking his path.

"New York."

Jake moved his center of vision up the male figure, stopping at its ashen face. It was Ralph, staring at Jake through blood-shot, red-rimmed eyes.

"Jake—I saw her."

"You did?" Jake grabbed Ralph's shoulders. "Where? Where is she? How do I find her?"

"What?"

"Sara—the red head."

"Who?"

"You just said—"

"No—not her." Ralph's voice lowered to a hoarse whisper. "My wife's mother. I saw my wife's mother. Her fucking dead mother. Sitting on the couch in front of the television. Like she was waiting for it to come on. Just sitting there with her hands on her lap, waiting." Ralph shuddered and used the back of his hand to wipe away a tear that etched its way down his face. "Now I'm fucking nuts too." He twisted his shoulders free of Jake's grasp and continued on his way to work, worrying his wrinkled brown paper lunch bag in his sweating hands. From over his shoulder, Jake watched Ralph's hunched form disappear into the crowd as thunder cracked over his head. When Jake carelessly turned to continue the trip to his room, he crashed into a longhaired man with wild, black eyes. Apologizing, Jake stepped around the man and headed to his room wondering why the hairy man seemed so familiar. Had he seen him before?

* * *

The hotel restaurant was cool and dark. Jake chose a stool at the bar and ordered dinner with his vodka. Above the line of bottles, Frank and Leila, the local newscasters, flashed silently across a television screen.

"Excuse me," Jake said to the bartender, "could you turn up the sound? I like those goofs."

"You're the only one." The bartender reached under the bar and handed a remote control to Jake.

"Well, Frank, any more UFO reports today?"

"Yes. Tons. It seems New Orleans is still having a spook convention."

"I hate to do this to you," Leila said. "But I can top your UFO report."

"No way."

"Yes way." Leila adapted the demeanor of an obnoxious child. "From our affiliate station in Baton Rouge comes a report that the Northern Lights have moved to a location somewhere over the Atchafalaya Basin."

"Somewhere, where?"

"The location is uncertain. It seems the phosphorescent lights move around, only flash now and then."

"I guess it's true about that national trend to relocate to the South. Should we start calling them the Southern Lights?"

"Okay, Frank. It's time to let Bill Beauregard tell us about the weather."

Jake listened to statistics on the record-breaking heat, predictions of heat lightning, and hopes for a rainstorm and lower humidity. The bartender snatched the remote control away and switched the station.

"I can't take them another minute. Here," he mixed Jake another vodka, "have this instead." Jake shivered and pushed the drink away.

* * *

Thoughts of his nightmares haunted Jakes' thoughts. He flailed around on his bed for hours before calling off the quest for sleep. He had to relax, so he grabbed a beer and opened the door to the porch. Outside, the night was quiet, the street unnaturally empty. Thunder called from the sky in answer to flashes of heat lightning. Jake went out on the porch to watch the show. With his feet on the iron rail, he pushed back on his chair, rocking it gently. Occasionally, from a dark doorway across the street, he would catch a flash of a glowing cigarette. Watching the repetitive motion as it waxed and waned with the smokers breath made Jake feel sleepy. Maybe it was the beer. Whatever, he returned to bed. Impossible.

* * *

Jake woke with sweat pouring over him. He tried to get up to close the porch door, to lock out the heat. Try was all he could do. He could not move—just like the times in Keith's bed.

No. No more. Please.

From a spot near Jake came the barely audible sounds of life. The faintest of heart beats. The tentative drawing of breath. Jake prayed in silence and begged. Oh, no. Not again. Please.

The specter drew closer, inch by inch, crawling across the bed until Jake could feel the heat of breath licking his face, until Jake could feel the feather-light touch of lips upon his. A sleek form slipped over him. Weightless. Silken limbs stroked his. Rapture. Arms wrapped around him. Shelter. Possessed, Jake tried to move, not away, but toward. Not toward physical gratification, but toward the inexplicable, yet unmistakable feeling of . . . home. Still, he was powerless, immobile. When after only a few precious minutes of ecstasy his covert lover began to retreat, Jake strained to follow, but failed, his heart racing to the bursting point. From somewhere near, came an inaudible calling, then from the porch, then from outside. When the sky drowned out the calling with a crash of thunder, Jake woke with one word on his lips, home. He ran to the door and looked out at the street.

The only sign of life was the faltering red glow of a cigarette being flicked into the street from its haven in the dark doorway. Jake watched the doorway fireworks until tears smeared the visions into an abstract work of art.

Chapter 30

*J*AKE WATCHED TELEVISION until the sun came back on duty, returned to its task of making the city safe, safer, by searching out every dark corner and exposing the dangers that lurk in every shadow. The rigid wooden chair Jake sat on guaranteed he would not fall asleep during the *Lassie* reruns. The chair had no arms, so the slightest lack of attention on Jake's part would have sent him tumbling to the floor with only the television remote to cling to. He would be safe from his world of nightmares—safe from the knowledge of other worlds.

Stretching and groaning off the oppression of the night, Jake hobbled to the porch, his legs numb, his heel still aching from his search of New Orleans. His eyes immediately focused on the corner doorway across the street. No silent smoker hid in the dubious shelter of the sun-drenched portal. Jake grabbed his shirt from its resting place against the wall, draped over a defeated fan blade, and guided his tingling legs to the lobby and onto the street. Jake searched the site of the late-night smoker's hideout. He squatted and examined the pattern of discarded cigarettes. They were all the same brand. It appeared one person had spent the entire night smoking in the doorway. Why?

"Here, buddy." A pack of cigarettes hit the sidewalk in front of Jake. "There's a few left in there."

Jake closed his eyes. Mistaken for a beggar again. He ignored the unsolicited donation and turned his attention toward the portal. He tested the doorknob. It would not turn. Upon closer scrutiny, he realized the seam where the door met the jamb had been sealed over with countless layers of paint, transforming the door into just another part of the wall. Jake stepped up into the concrete alcove and pressed his back against the door. He

167

closed his eyes trying to imagine why anyone would spend the night there. A drug dealer, perhaps.

Jake opened his eyes and the sun forced his lids back down, momentarily. His pupils overcame the sun's assault and answered Jake's question. His eyes revealed a clear view of his porch, both sides, and all the entrances to the Enclave. Jake realized the doorway was a perfect cover for someone bent on spying—on watching his every move.

Jake hesitated for a moment as he stepped over the half-empty cigarette pack that still lay on the sidewalk, but he resisted temptation and did not stop to retrieve it. Instead, he continued back to his room to regain control, to regain his New York City, hot-shit Jake image. He showered and promised never again to let himself be confused for a street beggar.

* * *

Jake tipped the garage tender for bringing his car around to the street. The organized, or more accurately, the lame Jake, had decided to search the streets for Sara from the comfort of his car. Thankful for the snail-like crawl of city traffic, Jake methodically scanned the crowds as he trolled each street in turn. In agreement with his disillusioned eyes, his guts told him he was wasting his time. His guts told him, whoever she was, he wouldn't find her unless she wanted to be found. As he edged past his cemetery, he rolled up his windows and turned on the air and the radio, afraid the murmurs still clinging to life from the night of the grave dancers might steal into his car and follow him home like a pack of hungry vampires.

* * *

The phone was ringing when Jake returned to his room. He scrambled across his bed to answer it.

"Jake?"

"Yes. Hi, Camille."

"How was your drive today? Did you go out to the swamp?"

"Swamp? No—how did—?"

"Oh, just ignore me. I was worried, you not knowing your way around and all. You need to be careful."

"I'm fine. I'm a big boy."

"I'm glad to hear that," Camille purred. "I have some potential clients due in at any second, so I'll let you go."

"Hey, wait a minute. How'd you know I went—?"

"Ooops. They're here. Au revoir."

"Camille. Wait!"

* * *

Jake listened to the buzz of the open line for a few minutes before he hung up the phone. Keeping close to the wall, he crept to the porch door offering the best view, and peered around the curtain. Standing in the shadows of the setting sun, stood the hairy man, still wearing the black beret, still smoking. Jake shoved his keys into his pocket and ran for the elevator. When the automatic door closed before him, he kicked it. He searched for an emergency exit.

Skipping steps, demonstrating about as much control as a rudderless raft buffeted by merciless currents, Jake surged down the stairwell, hardly easing up long enough to pull in breath. When he burst out onto the street, he zeroed in on the shadow-draped doorway.

Empty.

Jake slammed the door and lurched across the street as if a closer inspection would prove his eyes wrong. He leaned against the deserted alcove, his muscles in agony over a lack of oxygen. The only sign that gave evidence to the existence of the doorway watcher was a still-smoldering, half-smoked cigarette that exuded a snaking trail of fog. Jake crushed the ember with his heel as he began one more trip down Bourbon Street, one more search for the woman called Sara.

* * *

Jake kept his eyes averted from the attention of the fishing alligator that grinned from its place on the wall.

"Hi, is Ralph here today?"

A waitress Jake did not recognize answered, "Nah. I heard he called in sick today. I can help you if you want anything." She snapped her gum and grinned.

Thinking her Cheshire cat expression was a bit too similar to that of the papier-mâché' alligator, Jake left without answering. He crossed the street, diagonally, and for a while, stood outside the corner blues bar to gather the courage he would need to go inside, one more time, to be shot down, one more time.

169

Jake recognized the band. It was the same one that had played that night. His heart thumped out of control. He threaded through the crowd on the dance floor, searching. He shivered when he made momentary eye contact with the guitar player. Battered by the dancers, Jake jostled his way over to the door across from the tee-shirt shop. Leaning against the doorjamb, he looked up at the second story porch above the sidewalk rack of obscene shirts. He was relieved that at least the feline litterbug was still where it belonged. In the feeble light seeping from the about-to-set sun, Jake watched the black and white cat rub its sides against the porch rails as it made its way toward the blue-shuttered door. Before re-entering its hideout, the cat stopped to sharpen his claws on the carefully laid red bricks that had fascinated Jake the other day. The cat stood up like a little person in a hair costume and yanked away, digging its claws into the red wall. Suddenly, it yowled and leapt back as a section of the bricks peeled away from the building, revealing an undersurface of rotted wooden siding.

"Brick face," Jake said. "Only an illusion. Only another fucking illusion." He ran his hand along the black woodwork that surrounded the doorway. Chips of paint fluttered off, leaving fresh, multicolored wounds on the painted surface, scattering rainbow confetti to the ground at his feet.

Resolute, he strode back to his room and packed his bags.

Clutching Nikki's picture and a collection of swamp tour brochures, Jake sat on his porch all night, watching the mystery smoker's monotonous light show in the corner doorway, waiting for the sun to rise so he could decide on which direction to aim his car. He knew it would not be safe to close his eyes with secrets being whispered by the wind.

* * *

Without checking out, Jake called and asked to have his car brought around to the street.

"Will you be gone long?" The attendant said.

"Nope, just gonna take another spin around town." Jake held his camera up and said, "Just looking for some fun pics to shoot for my personal use."

"Good idea. There's lots to take pictures of around here."

170

Jake waved to the grinning attendant, pulled out of the garage, drove around the corner, and squeezed his car into a skimpy parking spot a block away. Jake re-entered the hotel and climbed the back stairway to his room. He snatched his luggage, and stole out the emergency entrance, glad to see the corner doorway empty. His belongings safely stashed in his trunk, he used a pay phone to call the art gallery. Camille was not there.

* * *

Just as instructed by Camille's secretary, Jake pulled on the iron gate that led to the Bete Noir. He did not have to knock on the wooden inner door; it was open. Traces of the Bete Noir were nowhere to be found. In its place was a staid, carefully laid out garden courtyard. Potted flowers and trees cast mottled shadows across white wrought-iron furniture. Glass-top tables were furnished with fresh flower arrangements. Jake knocked on the door to Camille's living quarters. Just as he was about to knock a second time, Camille opened the door.

"Jake, it's so good to see you. My secretary told me you called." Camille hooked his arm around Jake's, pulled him into his parlor and led him to the couch. "Would you like anything? A drink?"

"No, thanks. I just stopped by to talk. To check in. Any word from good old Captain Bill?"

"Not yet. But I'm sure he'll be back soon. Any day. Don't worry. I haven't forgotten you."

Camille slipped down next to Jake, sinking into the lush, red velvet upholstery like a fat cat. "How have you been?" Camille fixed his attention on Jake's eyes as he spoke.

"I—I've been having a sort of weird time. I don't think I like New Orleans as much as I'm supposed to."

"Oh, I'm sorry. I see I haven't been a proper host."

"No. Don't blame yourself. It's me—I think." Jake shook his head. "I think I should get out of the city until Bill is ready for me. Maybe check out another part of the swamp."

"Don't do that! Please. It's not a good idea for an outsider to go roaming around the countryside alone. You could—"

"You don't seem to understand, New Orleans isn't easy for an outsider to handle, either. And there is this woman."

"Tell me about her." His eyes opened wide, Camille placed his hand on Jake's knee. "I care about your welfare—really."

Jake looked down at the perfectly manicured hand that rested on his knee and felt a wave of nausea.

"Okay," Jake said. "I'll be okay until Bill is ready for me." He stood up quickly and headed for the door. A chill ran down Jake's back as he felt Camille's delicate hand slide along his leg as he rose. "This is a very nice place you have here." Jake cleared his throat. "How did you manage to get your hands on all these connected properties?" He flashed Camille a smiling mask.

"It's all been in the family for a long time."

"All?"

"Yes. You know." Camille appeared to assess Jake's demeanor and said, "The whole block."

"Niiiiiice. The only thing I inherited from my family is a birthmark." Leaving Camille with his mouth hanging open, Jake raced back to his car and guided it toward I-10 and tried to imagine the sunset view from the other side of the basin.

Chapter 31

I-10 ROSE OFF THE GROUND and reached over a body of water, or maybe the ground dropped down under the water and the road remained level. Jake could not figure it out. Whatever, the effect was disarming. Water surrounded him on both sides. Not silver, sparkling water like under the Lake Pontchartrain Causeway, but placid, black water that reflected only the vine-covered trees spearing up through its surface. The traffic slowed, then stopped, allowing Jake to get a good look at his surroundings, urging him to grab his camera and dessert his shelter. Young people donned in-line skates and whizzed between parked cars. Some tossed a football back and forth. Other waylaid travelers gathered in groups and passed around beers, making the best of their situation. It appeared that they had experienced similar traffic jams and were prepared to take advantage of them. Jake stood apart and watched through his viewfinder. One of the group broke away from his temporary comrades and strolled over to sit next to Jake on the guardrail.

"You must be from New York, eh?" He nodded toward Jake's license plate. "You on a vacation?"

"No way. I'm here to get a job done." Jake pointed to his camera and said, "Photographer. What's up with the traffic?"

"Probably they had a wreck; one of those eighteen-wheelers ran into somebody. It don't surprise me. They drive so fast we get a wreck every other week here. Them people are crazy."

"It's the same way in New York. Believe it or not."

"Where you going, to Lafayette?"

"Where?"

"Lafayette."

"Never heard of it. I'm on my way to find a tour guide who will take me out on the swamp. Any ideas?"

"Oh—mais yes—that's pretty easy. What you gonna do is, you gonna take that exit, eh, at the Henderson exit, and then you take a left. You pass under the bridge, and when you gonna get to that intersection, pass the gas station, and you take a left. Go all the way to the levee. Then, when you get to the levee, take a right. But don't go on top the levee. They got some sign. They just fixed the levee. They got a levee cop that patrols that. They don't want nobody riding on the top, and they see your license plates, they gonna want to give you a ticket, maybe. So, just stay on the bottom, and they got some landings over there. Go to the third landing, Fisherman's Landing. They got some swamp tours. They're the best, them."

Just as the stranded motorists gathered, trapped on the bridge, steel-grey storm clouds congregated above, erecting an ominous, grey canopy that walled the sky off from the earth, or allowed the sky to hide. Flanked by reinforcements of thunder, crooked spears of lightning pierced through the barrier of clouds and stabbed into the water. The bridge troops retreated to the safety of their portable bastions, abandoning beer cans and cigarettes. Jake watched them scrambling away from the oncoming attack like rabbits running for cover from the shadow of a circling hawk. Ozone filled the air, standing Jake's hair on end. In the sweating embrace of the heat, he shivered as a molasses fog crawled across the water, hiding all evidence of its existence. With the advancing fog came the return of the whispers. Jake clapped his hands over his ears without effect. When he felt the rumble of engines turning over and car horns calling to each other through the darkening air, Jake gave up his listening post and continued his painstaking trek to Fisherman's Landing.

A conglomeration of landing signs, standing in a tangled mass like a group of has-been actors fighting to upstage each other, alerted Jake that it was time to exit I-10, to veer away from the rest of the convoy and set out on his own. He squinted through the cloying fog as he edged past haphazardly placed roadside arrows.

At the end of the paved road, two gravel trails branched off into the swarming fog; one ran to the top of the levee, and the other alongside it. Jake chose the low road, as directed. Afraid he would lose control, or crash into an unseen vehicle, Jake barely toed the gas pedal while his fingers gripped the steering wheel and he peered through the quickening fog. The white mantle rolled toward him, tumbling across his path like phantom bears, wrestling, or mating. Jake cut through, effortlessly, leaving them to reconstitute their chimera shapes in the wake of his passing.

Eventually, a reddish square with a slash of blue across the bottom loomed ahead. Jake could not read the message on the sign, but anxious to escape the rolling mist that dripped down his opaque windows, he followed blue arrow that led up over the levee. His tires kicked off stones that clacked against the underside of his car as it crawled up the steep gravel incline leading to the top of the levee, like a roller coaster heading up toward the point where it would be dropped back to the earth.

The road finally lifted Jake above the earth-bound clouds. With teeth still clenched, Jake exhaled and tried to let go of the tension that clenched his neck and shoulders. His foot firmly pressed on the brake pedal, Jake scanned his surroundings for signs of life.

Sparsely planted trees thrust over the fog like the arms of drowning men reaching up for the last time. Yellow globs of light, like giant, unblinking fireflies or wary tigers' eyes, glowed from below. Holding his breath, he let up on the brake pedal just enough to allow his car to creep down toward the lights.

Edging over the precipice without permission, like a runaway roller coaster, Jake's car gathered speed as it skidded over loose stones, then slid crazily over wet grass. When his downward landslide finally ceased, his car spun around and came to rest with its nose facing back up the incline, as if in preparation for escape. Jake turned off the engine and gasped for breath in time with the ticking sound of his key chain rapping against the steering column. When both rhythms had slowed considerably, he put a shaking hand on his door handle and pushed his way out into the silent shroud.

Babbling voices echoed through the fog. Shaky, Jake gingerly stepped toward the sound of gossip, the squabbling sounds of life. Black and white shapes milled around, close to the ground, darting in and out of view. What were they? Moving closer, he saw his companions were ducks and geese scrambling for corn, nipping at each other, some dancing over the waves that licked the shoreline. He watched the dinner-time scuffle until the gathering was interrupted by two specter-like forms that sloshed up to the shore, appearing through the fog like space travelers reconstituting, one cell at a time. With unsteady footsteps, the tall, extremely thin figure using a twisted wooden walking stick, they marched up the bank, scattering the waterfowl, sending them squawking and flapping into the water. The two men trudged past Jake as if he was invisible. He followed their sloshing rubber-boot footsteps across the rocky, uneven landscape, up creaking, bowed-in-the-center, wooden steps, and through a swinging screen door that slammed shut after each entry.

The screen door slapped Jake on his back, urging him to step closer to the gaping mouth of a huge fish that loomed menacingly from the ceiling of a restaurant dining room. A menagerie of life-like, lifeless, taxidermied creatures crowded the vaulted ceiling and protruded from the polished wooden walls. Comatose alligators snarled silently, flashing rows of gleaming teeth. Petrified ducks flapped widespread wings, motionless, except for the strings of Mardi Gras beads that hung from their outstretched necks and shimmered in the breeze of overhead fans. The dining room was at least forty by sixty feet. The floor had been polished smooth by the soles of uncountable shoes. Outside the dining room stretched a porch where customers dined, perched out over the water. Walled off by a frosted glass barrier, was a barroom. Jake followed the wet rubber boot prints around to the other side of the glass.

It was easy to pick out the two Jake had followed from the shoreline. Puddles of water spread in murky circles around their feet as they waited for the bartender to finish a phone call. His arms folded over each other and his head tilted to press the phone against his shoulder, the dimple-cheeked bartender smiled as he listened to the caller. The man next to Jake noticed him and he said, "Yeah, that's a lover boy, that."

"I sort of guessed," Jake said.

The man reached out a hand to Jake. "Hi, I'm Chaoui."

Jake took Chaoui's hand and marveled at the red and blue tattooed flames that flickered their way up his arms, up under the sleeves of a black Harley tee shirt tucked into tattered jeans. From a black leather, silver-studded belt hung a black leather flail. A baseball cap, worn backwards, kept almost waist-length, stringy, black hair away from his face.

The other wet-footed man slapped the bar with the palm of his hand, raising the attention of the dimple-cheeked bar tender, turning his freckled face toward them. After whispering into the phone, he hung it up and said, "The usual?"

The bar tapper smoothed his long, red beard and nodded. The bar tender opened the top flap of a cooler. As he fished around inside, ice cubes cracked as they slid against each other and banged against the sides of their aluminum cell. He ripped the tab off an already sweating can of beer and placed it in front of the bearded man before the hissing escape of compressed air could dissipate. He looked back over his shoulder to Chaoui and pointed, "Shirley Temple?"

Chaoui nodded, placed his hand over his mid-section, and looking over to Jake, said, "Ulcers. Man, I got a bad stomach there. I got some damn ulcers. I hardly got a stomach left."

"Sorry about that," Jake said.

Chaoui shrugged, tossed coins on the bar, and reached out for the drink the bartender handed him. He plucked the cherry from his Shirley Temple and popped it into his mouth. With the stem hanging from the corner of his mouth, he said, "Man, I wish this was a J.D."

"So, I guess you're a regular here at Fisherman's Landing," Jake said.

"What? Fisherman's Landing? This is Alligator Landing."

"No, this has to be Fisherman's Landing," Jake countered.

"Oh, no, man. Phew! You passed that up three miles down the road over there. This is the wrong place. You gotta turn back."

"What? What do you mean, wrong place? But I didn't see any signs."

"Well, you know, everything's not always easy. Sometimes you gotta figure out something by yourself. Especially when you're way out here. There's no arrows to point out where you go. You just gotta become part of the land and use all your senses. That's just the way it is here. Sometimes signs are hard to see. Sometimes you just got to listen real hard."

Before Jake could question him further, Chaoui's voice rose from its slow, metered pace. Pointing with the top of his walking stick, he said, "Give my partner here a J.D."

"No, thanks," Jake said. "I don't like Jack—"

"Oh, come on. Why don't you drink one for me. And let me watch. Yeah?"

The bartender slid a shot glass in front of Jake. It was already filled with the golden-brown liquid. Chaoui bent over the offering, inhaled slowly through his nostrils, and nodded anxiously as Jake reached out for the glass.

Jake closed his eyes and shuddered as the Jack Daniel's burned down his throat. Chaoui sighed and turned back to his glass of ginger ale and cherry juice.

Jake placed his hand, momentarily, on Chaoui's shoulder as he passed behind him on his way to the row of windows that lined the back wall. The quickening fog pressed up against the windows and stared in at Jake, unblinking. Singular, black skeletal trees, their branches devoid of leaves, adorned only with shreds of rotten, black-lace moss, seeming to float in mid-air, stretched up from the water, pointing up to the sky, arms raised to heaven as if in supplication. Behind it all glowed a ball of lip-red fire that spread across the horizon like a river of molten rubies. Jake shuddered again and turned back toward the line of drinkers who stood bellies to the bar. Chaoui nodded to Jake, then leaning heavily on his walking stick, made his way to the exit and was swallowed up by the ravenous fog.

A jukebox came alive with screaming-wild heavy metal music. Jake jumped away from colored flashing lights as the music blared and bumped his head on the window. A man wearing a white kitchen apron hustled out from behind the bar. He dried his hands on his apron and yanked the jukebox away from the wall. The record skipped and screamed wildly. Reaching behind the conglomeration of vibrating speakers and flashing lights, he yelled, "I'll fix this fucker, once and for all." The racket died instantly and the man's voice kicked down a few notches. "We don't need this shit." He offered his hand to Jake. "Hi, I'm Delta. I'm the owner here."

Still shaking from the sudden start the jukebox had caused, Jake's voice wavered as he spoke. "I'm Jake Preston. I saw your sign about swamp tours. I need one right away."

Delta looked out the window, then with one eyebrow cocked, looked back at Jake. "Hey, it don't pay you to go out now. It's too foggy. Can't see nothing anyway. Besides, we're fixing to have a party. Look, why don't you hang around."

"But—"

"It's gonna be kicking ass around here in a few minutes. You're gonna have a good time. Don't worry about the tour, right now. I'll take you out later. My brother's got a great little band, and there'll be free food, so just stick around. I'll fix you up later. You just stay for the party and I'll take care of you." He quickly dismissed Jake by returning to the kitchen without another word.

Angered by the constant roadblocks that littered his Louisiana experience, Jake stomped into the dining room and sat down with a sigh. A woman of well over seventy smiled at Jake as she handed him a beer. "Ma Cher, Delta sent you a drink; so have a good time." Her face, worn by age and years in the sun and creased by worries only mothers know, crinkled in contrast to her glow-in-the-dark, blue eyes. She turned and bounced back toward the kitchen.

Just in front of the buffet table that lined the wall near the kitchen, was a man down on his knees, untangling heavy, black wires that snaked out of a beaten, wooden box. One by one, he plugged the wires into speakers that he had already arranged facing in Jake's direction. He looked up at Jake, and with the same laser-blue eyes, flashed a look of acknowledgment that radiated kindness the likes of which Jake had never seen before. Jake guessed that the man on the floor must be Delta's brother and the wizened waitress, their mother.

As the sun dropped below the vague horizon, it pulled in the red line of fire that spilled from it like a long, snake's tongue.

Singly, and in groups of two or three, an aggregation of mismatched people entered and joined the menagerie inside. Each was followed by a puff of fog that was quickly cut off and banished each time the door banged shut.

As the evening wore on, frustrated by being held a prisoner of the fog, Jake felt the need to withdraw from the sparkling eyes and guileless handshakes. He moved to a table far from the microphones and movement and sat with his back to the wall. Whenever the wiry waitress returned with another beer, Jake was careful to keep his gaze averted from her x-ray eyes, afraid she could read all his secrets. Instead, he concentrated on the grim determination so blatantly displayed on her fixed, stoic lips, her mouth, carefully trained by years of practice at hiding the pain and tribulations of life.

Jake sat, using his thumbnail to scrape the side of his beer can, wishing it was a bottle with a waterlogged label he could peel away at will. The rending sound of audio feedback whistling to him from the speakers snared his attention.

The room had filled with men in boots and jeans and with women surrounded by airy, full skirts. The screech of feedback played itself out, and the sound of laughter and conversation reached Jake's previously tuned-out ears. Fiddlers fussed with bows while guitar players repeatedly plunked off-key strings, trying to force them into compromise. A cacophonous symphony of opposing notes filled the air with the incongruous sound of disunion as the man who had set up the audio equipment bent to open a lacquered box. Out of the box, he removed an accordion— not the huge, unwieldy Lady of Spain type with rows of piano keys, but a small, compact version, brightly stained in green, purple, and brilliant gold.

He sat down on a wooden chair, and after gently placing the accordion on his lap, he unbuckled the leather strap that constrained the multicolored squeezebox in a closed position. He stretched the accordion open and pushed out a series of staccato notes that blasted the assemblage to attention. Beers were deserted, conversations truncated, and tuning-up sessions ended. Everyone, except Jake, moved to follow the lead of the insistent accordion notes. Partners, haphazardly chosen, rushed to the open space on the floor as if to demonstrate to Jake how the roughly hewn, wooden planks had become so perfectly smoothed so as to appear as one.

The dancers were young and old—some very old. Babies, held in the arms of dancing parents, squealed in delight, one with generations. Gone were the looks of determination, the lines that etched proof of many years of toil on the faces of the shuffling and hopping dancers. Grandmothers were, once again, beautiful young girls as they gracefully turned in the capable arms of their lovers of many years. The men, careful to steer their ladies out of harm's way, avoiding collisions on the crowded dance floor, were proud young bulls again, stomping the floor, showing off their strength and agility. Always in physical contact, the couples spun and twirled in intricate patterns, with entangled arms, and well-practiced maneuvers like those of long-time lovers who need communicate only by touches and sighs.

Like a sleepwalker, Jake left his beer and moved a few tables closer to the action, then sat with feet tapping in rhythm with the music. A broad grin spread across his face when the same waitress brought him another beer. This time, he realized how beautiful she was. She danced her way back to the bar, leaving Jake wishing he had known her in another time.

Delta had not forgotten his promise of free food. He arrived at Jake's table with a tray arranged with two plates of food and a heap of warm bread. As he stood holding the empty serving tray, about to speak to Jake, Delta noticed that his crew of bus boys and cooks were lined up in the dining room, just outside the kitchen door, arms on each other's shoulders, dancing like a disheveled row of Cajun, all-male Rockettes in work boots. Delta left Jake's side and rushed over to his dancing employees, and with the lightweight aluminum tray, he bonked the head of the boy at the end of the line of dancers, sending them scurrying back into the kitchen, doubled over with laughter.

Jake laughed and turned his attention to the plates of steaming food. Unlike the pretentious layout Camille had arranged in New Orleans, this food was down-home, solid. Glad he had plenty of beer to sooth the burn of the more highly spiced items, Jake ate every bit of his supper, even the bread pudding.

Jake was disappointed when the crowd began to disappear, and horrified when the last note was played out. He realized he liked Cajun music after all, and he realized he was too drunk to move . . . and he realized it was okay, because there was no other place else he'd rather be.

* * *

When the restaurant emptied, Delta walked over to Jake's side, "C'mon buddy." Gripping Jake's arm, he helped him onto his feet. "You can crash in my office." Delta led Jake past a beaten door, into a small, cluttered office. As he curled up on a three-quarter length leather couch, Jake fell asleep wishing he could press rewind and play the evening over.

Chapter 32

*J*AKE WOKE. His head pounded and his back ached from spending the night with his limbs bent to fit the couch. Even so, he was charged with a feeling of well-being—he had no lingering nightmares to haunt the coming day. His face broke into a smile when he heard good-natured laughter bubbling on the other side of the office door. He unfolded his limbs and stood bent over at the waist to ease the pain in his back. As he moved to open the door, he noticed the map of Louisiana hanging on the thumbtack-infested wall. Highlighted in green, was the Atchafalaya Basin area. Jake looked for the you-are-here dot. There was none. He raised his hand to the tattered map and traced the river patterns. Not knowing why, his finger stopped, and with a will of its own, clung to a water-covered spot in the center of the basin.

Jake shook his head to clear his mind and strode into the restaurant. Diagonally across the dining room, gathered around a black iron wood stove, sat a circle of men in heavy-duty work clothes. When Jake drew nearer, he realized the one in the rocking chair was Chaoui. Chaoui ceased his back and forth motion and turned toward Jake.

"Man, I hear you really got pooyied last night. That's a man. That's a man."

"Where's Delta? I need to get out on the water."

"Relax, man. You got lot of time." Chaoui pointed to an enamel coffee pot that warmed on top of an electric hot plate.

Jake poured himself a cup of coffee and said, "Isn't it hot for you guys to be sitting around a fire?"

"You people from New York must be crazy?" Delta said from behind. "They don't got no fire in that stove right now."

183

"But why—never mind. I need that tour. Can you hook me up, right now?"

"Sorry. I can't go right now. I got a bunch of stuff to do, but I'll tell you what. My brother is gonna take you on the first tour going out. They got a tour bus coming in at about eleven o'clock."

"I don't want to go with a bunch of tourists. I need to go— now. Alone."

"Delta, you want me to take him?" Chaoui said. He stood up and hobbled over to stand in front of Delta. "I'll take him."

Delta threw up his arms and let them drop to his sides like a bird that had changed its mind about flying away.

"It must be time," Chaoui said.

"Okay, have it your way."

Chaoui headed straight for the door. As he followed Chaoui through the parking lot, Jake stopped at his car.

"Chaoui, hold on a minute." Jake fished his keys out of his pocket, opened his car, and pulled out his camera. As he slid the strap over his head, Chaoui yelled to him.

"Ain't you sick of that fuckin' albatross around you neck yet?"

"What?—Albatross?—Hey, this is my camera. I'm a photographer."

"Yeah, right."

"Hey," Jake said.

"Hey, that's you." Chaoui tossed his walking stick into a boat, stepped over the side, and plopped himself down. "C'mon, photographer, get in."

Jake ran the rest of the way to the water, his camera thumping against his chest with every footfall.

* * *

A foot or so of fog still hovered over the surface of the dead-calm water. Chaoui eased the boat away from the dock, cutting a path through the white mist, leaving it to swirl back into place in the wake of their passing.

"Stop." Jake said.

"You want to hear the tourist stuff? You know, there's a tree, there's a 'gator, there's a duck shit stuff?"

"Shhhhh," Jake held up a hand. "What's that?"

"What?"

"That sound."

"I didn't hear nothin'. What it sounded like? My stomach's growling."

"No." Jake was afraid to utter his next words, afraid of ridicule. "It sounded like talking. Whispering."

Chaoui shrugged. "Sound carries a long way over the water."

"Oh, yeah. Right. I knew that. Oh, what about those lights I heard about on TV. Can we see them?"

"Feufollet," whispered Chaoui. "You can't go looking for them. They look for you. "

"But"

"But, nothing." Chaoui stated with a firmness with which Jake could not deny.

Except for the low, constant hum of the motor, they continued in total silence, broken only by the occasional slamming of the shutter in Jake's camera, which opened only long enough to let in the exact amount of light needed to record a perfectly framed, two-dimensional, rectangular view of reality.

Jake looked down at his camera to check the number of frames left. An electric tingle ran up his spine. It stopped just below his hairline, tickling the nape of his neck. He straightened up and rubbed the back of his neck, wondering how long it would take to recover from his night on the couch. As he was about to look back down at his camera, he heard the sound again. The whispering. He turned back toward Chaoui.

"Pardon? I didn't hear what you said."

"Said? Me? I didn't say nothing. And it wasn't my stomach either."

"But I distinctly—" The tingling came back—all along Jake's spine. "Shhhhhh." He held up his hand to silence Chaoui and strained to hear another sound. The whispers returned like a gentle breeze flitting across his ears. He turned his head in the direction of the murmurs and used his raised hand to point.

"That way. Chaoui—that way." Jake pointed to a stand of trees.

"Chaoui turned the boat and followed each direction Jake gave him, only veering off course long enough to avoid a floating tree branch or a bobbing, air-filled, plastic milk jug. The tingling spread over Jake's entire body.

"Stop."

Chaoui obeyed.

Jake closed one eye and began to raise his camera to his face.

"Put that damn thing down already." Chaoui reached out and pulled at the camera. Leaning in close to Jake, he whispered, "See for yourself. Put that picture in your head. It's time to stop hiding behind that thing." He took the camera and slipped it into a compartment at the back of the boat. "Just listen."

Jake sat in silence and listened. Without regard for Boy Scout boat safety rules, Jake slowly raised himself to a standing position, the fog swirling around his feet, filling the bottom of the motionless boat. They were surrounded by a stand of cypress trees that had not been desecrated. Heavy drapes of Spanish moss festooned the ancient trees. Survivors of countless hurricanes and woodsmen's blades, they surrounded Jake like a circle of ghostly angels with gossamer wings hanging low, their cover protecting Jake from the unholy eyes of early-morning tourists and earthbound fishermen. Jake felt as if the dayspring sun's rays were entering him, bouncing around inside, then bursting out as though he was the center of the universe. Then, suddenly, at the "V" formed by two trees, a yellow glow burst from the water, like a ghostly, flickering candle flame.

Jake raised his face to the sky and closed his eyes. He knew he had come to the right place after all, that eventually, all his questions would be answered. The whispers reached his ears, un-garbled by brick walls and lace curtains. The whispers called his name—his true name—and he felt loved. Over and over, the whispers called his name. Jake wrapped his arms around himself, feeling a love he never imagined possible.

* * *

Jake was still numb when he and Chaoui returned to shore, numb, but calm and strong. His mind, still somewhere out on the basin, he followed Chaoui up the bank, back toward the restaurant, thankful for the reassuring, clacking sound of the cypress walking stick as it struck the loose stones that tumbled out of their path.

The restaurant was inundated with a busload of flabby, white-skinned tourists. They milled around the dining room, gawking, fish eyed, at the lifeless animals that hung in suspended animation all around them, snapping pictures of each other as they stuck their arms or heads into the stone-dead alligator's mouths and pretended to be in pain. They pointed at pictures of old-timers and laughed, confident in their own superiority. Jake was relieved when they filed out the door like good little sheep, bleating about whether the tour would take too long. One of them, rushing for a quick last-minute trip to the bathroom, threw his newspaper to the floor in front of Jake. Jake rose above escalating feelings of resentment for the outsiders.

Jake moved to retrieve the newspaper.

Chaoui pinned the newspaper with his walking stick and shook his head. "No, Jake."

Jake peered into Chaoui's jet-black eyes. Seeing no explanation there, he put his hand on Chaoui's shoulder and gently pushed him away.

"Jake," Chaoui whispered without breaking eye contact. "Be careful, man. Mardi Gras is just around the corner." With a long sigh, he turned and left.

Jake bent down and picked up the paper. The *Lafayette Daily*. Sitting at the nearest table, he turned the pages, scanning each with intense interest. Images of unfamiliar politicians and chubby church ladies flipped past his mind, meaningless.

He opened the second section to more of the same until he saw it. A picture of two men. One of them, the greasy man with the long, drooping moustache. The man who pulled the red-haired woman away from him in New Orleans. Over the picture was a caption in white, bold print over a black background. ACADIANA'S MOST WANTED. And underneath: white male, 39 years old, height 5'7", 168 pounds, black hair, brown eyes. Wanted for carnal knowledge of an infant, hit-and-run driving, theft. Name— Michael Limon. Report tips by calling: 1-800-555-1212.

Jake ripped the page from the paper, folded it, careful not to crease the picture, then tucked it into his wallet. He hurried to his car and drove west toward Lafayette, not caring when he remembered the camera he had left stowed in the empty boat. His thoughts were focused on his destination, on the whispers growing ever louder and more clear.

Chapter 33

*J*AKE SPED TOWARD LAFAYETTE, his eyes hungry for the first sign offering a promise of leading to *Acadiana's Most Wanted*. He planned his strategy as he drove. Take the first exit to downtown Lafayette, and then check into the first hotel. Then, pull Randy Ketchum out of wraps—Randy Ketchum—private eye from New York City.

Lafayette was right off I-10. Though he knew he still had a few blocks to go, he flipped on his signal lights the minute he saw a sign for the Jackson Hotel. In his zeal to check in, he overshot the driveway and thumped over the yellow-painted curb, scraping the frame of his car. Without stopping to see if his car was damaged, he rushed to the front desk, breathless.

"Do you have a vacancy?"

"How many?" The frizzy-haired desk attendant peeked over her bifocals.

"I'm alone."

"Sure, we can fix you up."

Jake handed the woman his credit card. She held it almost against her nose for a close examination as he signed in.

"How do I find the county sheriff's office?"

She peeked over the rim of her glasses.

"County? Oh, you mean parish. He's downtown on Magnolia Street, right next to the jail."

"How do I? Never mind. I'll find it."

Jake only carried one outfit into his room. After donning his funeral suit, he locked his room and headed downtown, dressed like a television detective.

* * *

Street after street, Jake searched downtown Lafayette for an open parking spot. One-way streets lead him astray. Police

189

barricades placed across streets foiled his attempts to cross town to find the police station. When he passed a parking garage entrance, he screeched to a stop, then backed up and guided his car next to the tollbooth.

"Any spots open?" Jake said to the garage attendant.

"I believe so. Up on top."

"What's going on here, anyway?"

"It's Friday. Downtown Alive."

"What?"

"It's sort of a street party. They do it every Friday, well almost. They don't usually do it this time a year, but it's so damn hot, and everybody is so riled up—from the heat, or whatever."

A horn blared behind Jake.

"How much?"

Jake gave the man a dollar and followed the arrow-marked, spiral path. He nosed his car up, ramp after ramp, until he found an open spot on the top level. He checked his tie and searched for the elevator.

* * *

The street was filled with sweating partiers. Just like in New Orleans, they wandered the streets, drinks in hand, dressed for the heat. Jake was about the only one not wearing a hat to ward off the sun, the only one not carrying a beer. As always, he didn't fit in.

At the intersection of Jefferson and Vermillion, longhaired men put the finishing touches on a make-shift stage. Down the street, smoke rose from a charcoal grill. Jake could smell hamburgers sizzling. Unaffected by the heat, children ran and laughed in the middle of the blocked-off intersection, daring to play in a place of death. Jake continued across town, not asking directions, knowing he would find his destination soon enough. When he crossed Myrtle Street, he knew he should turn right. He wandered one more block and spotted the Parish Sheriff's Office. Jake prepared his speech on his way, fluffed up his Randy Ketchum demeanor. Ready for action, he burst through the door and marched up to the officer at the desk.

"Could you please direct me to the Sheriff's office?"

"It's upstairs. This is communications."

Jake nodded to the officer and waved thanks. The wood-paneled stairway that circled up to the sheriff's office looked like it belonged in a Southern home, not a police station. Pictures of past sheriffs lined the wall, displayed like long-lost relatives, haloed by matching wooden frames. Piercing eyes followed him all the way to the second floor.

The large, loud lobby Jake expected was not there. Instead, it looked like the reception area of a stockbroker's office. He considered turning back, going downstairs to ask for directions again.

"Can I help you?" Golden hair, carefully arranged over a calm expression, a woman sitting behind a polished walnut desk smiled at Jake. He moved closer to her cornflower-blue eyes.

"I was looking for the sheriff's office, but—"

"This is the right place."

"Are you his secretary?"

She smiled. "No, I'm Sergeant Broussard."

Jake searched for proof of her statement. She wore a neat, double-breasted, navy-blue suit embellished with gold buttons. There were fresh flowers on her desk. A silver-haired man lounged on a black leather couch across from her desk.

"I need to see the Sheriff about some information. Is he here?"

She nodded. "You need to turn around."

As soon as his eyes met those of the lounging man, the sheriff, Jake swallowed hard.

"Hello." Jake held out his hand. "I'm—J—Randy Ketchum."

The Sheriff did not move to accept Jake's hand. Without answering, his sun-worn face solemn, he patiently sat back and waited for Jake to keep talking—waited for Jake to hang himself.

"I'm a private detective from New York. I'm here looking for someone."

"Looking for someone? Why?" The Sheriff spoke without a trace of the accent Jake had expected.

"It's confidential. You know, client confidentiality."

The sheriff watched and waited.

Jake slipped out his wallet and unfolded the picture. "Here's the guy I need to find."

The sheriff glanced at the picture without any sign of recognition, then looked back at Jake.

"Well, Mr.—"

"Ketchum."

"Mr. Ketchum. May I see your license?"

"License?"

"Yes, license. Private detectives need them to operate in Louisiana. I am sure with all those laws you have in New York, that private detectives need licenses. I heard even your hot dog vendors need licenses."

"Right. You're right. I mean about the detective license. I don't know anything about hot dogs."

"Well, just show me your credentials and we can go into my office and talk."

"I didn't bring my license. You see, I was on vacation, sort of, then I saw this picture in the paper and—"

"I'm sorry, Mr. Ketchum, but I can't help you." The sheriff and his sergeant traded knowing glances.

"But—"

"I'm sorry."

"But—"

"I'm sorry," the sheriff said firmly.

The Sheriff's mouth, stern and set, his eyes boring into Jake's, unwavering, unblinking, ended the interview.

"Thanks, anyway," Jake said.

"Have a nice vacation," the Sheriff said. The pretty sergeant in the blue suit smiled good-bye.

*　*　*

Though the police station was air conditioned, Jake was sweating before he returned to the street. His heart pounded. His mind raced with his heart, wondering if posing as a private detective was illegal in Louisiana. All the movies he had ever seen about Southern jails played before his eyes in fast forward. Jake headed back toward the cold beer, toward the festival. Surely, in such a small town, somebody in the crowd would know Michael Limon.

*　*　*

The size of the crowd had increased exponentially. Hundreds of people stood at the crossroads, waiting for the band to finish setting up. As the musicians took their time, fussing with bows, banging drums, or counting into unresponsive microphones, a bank of dark storm clouds appeared on the horizon, also waiting, but far away in the cheap seats.

Jake pushed through the throng to get closer to the barbecue. The chef, probably the only person in the state crazy enough to stand next to the glow in such heat, flipped burgers, examining them thoroughly. When they were just right, he would flop them on a bun and cover them with sauce. They were instantly snapped up by a long line of famished partiers. Next to the grill was a black peanut roaster with a silver faceplate. It rolled batches of peanuts over and over until they spewed from the silver, pig-like face of the oven, steaming hot. Instead of getting something hot to eat, Jake decided on something cold, something to calm his nerves and wipe visions of men in striped suites chopping rocks at the side of the road.

The entrance to the bar that stood behind all the roasting and grilling was packed. Jake had to stand in line to enter. Once inside, he could almost feel that beer sliding down his throat. As he pushed his way toward the bar, a sign that announced *Hurricanes* turned him aside.

Yeah, he thought, a red drink. That is what I need.

* * *

Jake sucked up the drink so fast his straw collapsed. He pushed it aside and drank from the cup, hoping it would not give him a red moustache. By the time Jake jostled his way back out onto the street, his hurricane was half gone. Across the street, Jake spotted a parking lot jammed with Harleys. Bikers, who refused to disavow their black leather in defiance of the heat, stood in the shadow of a building, guarding their herd of chrome and steel horses.

Jake crossed the crowded street and made his way to the parking lot. That is when he saw it. The vertical mural covering the side of the building that walled off the parking lot and cast its shadow over the bikers. Painted over red bricks, was a haphazardly stacked pile of car parts. The stunning use of perspective made the heap look more like a sculpture than a two-dimensional painting.

Wherever chrome was a part of the mural, the artist had painted in reflections of musicians, dancers. At the bottom, a silver moon hubcap reflected a warped, fish-eye lens view of fiddlers with the swamp whirling behind them.

His eyes came to rest on the section of the mural where a long, shining bumper was painted with amazing depth of field. It seemed to protrude from the side of the building like a spear thrown down from the sky. Jake's balance faltered.

In order to regain his equilibrium, Jake dragged his gaze from the mural and focused his eyes on the crowd. But still mesmerized, his attention crept back to the glistening bumper. On it was painted a long line of horsemen, hooded, costumed horsemen. Jake's stomach flipped as his eyes followed them. Their reflection was painted following a line of perspective perpendicular to the line of the fender, creating an aberrant effect. The bumper did not reflect life that stood in front of it like the rest of the chrome objects. Instead, it mirrored images of another dimension, or perhaps, images of some magical past. The line of medieval phantoms disappeared into a distance somewhere on the other side of the building, into some alternate existence. Afraid if he stared any longer he would be sucked up into the picture, somehow become a part of the line of riders, he tore his attention from the warped reflection and pulled out his picture of Acadiana's Most Wanted.

Apart from the crowd stood an extremely tall biker, bearded, long-haired. Jake walked over to him. "Would you have any idea how I could find this guy?" He handed the picture to the giant.

"What is this? Because I'm a biker, you think I hang out with child molesters?"

"No, I just thought—"

"This is what we do to child molesters." The giant crumbled up the picture, popped it into his mouth, then chewed and swallowed. He followed the picture with a gulp of beer. The biker belched and turned away.

Jake shivered in the heat. How could he continue his search without the picture? A drum roll drew his attention. The band begin to play, so he followed the crowd back to the crossroads.

It was a Cajun band. The area before the elevated stage was crammed with dancers whirling in the heat. Jake positioned himself on the line of demarcation that separated the dancers from those who stood and watched.

Dancing or not, the crowd was possessed by the musicians. Like the Pied Piper, the accordion player called the tune. He turned the excitement up a notch with the start of every song, cranking up the audience as he continued. He was a master puppeteer, pulling all the strings, effortlessly. The bank of dark clouds lurking overhead drew closer as did the crowd below. Lightning began to crackle in the electrified air.

"Boy," yelled the man next to Jake, "I sure hope it rains soon. I don't want to see the party end, but this heat and damn humidity just keeps building. It's like we're all stuck in a pressure cooker, and somebody keeps turning up the heat. It's making everybody crazy."

"Yeah," Jake yelled back. "Some rain would feel real good right now."

Without missing a step, the accordion player kept his eyes on the rolling clouds. Trusting their leader to look out for them, the band members ignored the lightning. They followed him, instinctively, flawlessly keeping up with the constantly increasing intensity of the music. The clouds and lightning crawled closer with escalating speed and the dancers, whipped to a frenzy, screaming every time the music cranked them up another notch, became a unified, spinning mass.

When a shaft of lightning tore through the sky, only a few miles away, the accordion player stopped, mid-song. Still in unison, all the band members began to break down their equipment to the accompaniment of earth-shaking thunder. Silver microphones, standing like lightning rods, came down first.

The crowd, released from the spell, dissipated and ran for cover only to be disappointed. It was a false alarm. The rain never came. And as soon as the music dematerialized, so did the storm.

* * *

The clouds still lurking overhead called up an early sunset by completely blocking out the last of the evening sun. On the ground, the revelry continued, so Jake toured Jefferson Street. It was like a mini version of Bourbon Street, but without the tourists and the pornography. Every bar on the street offered live music. Every bar was filled with patrons who spilled out onto the street, laughing, drinking. Blaring music followed them to the street, giving rise to assorted groups and single couples who danced on the hot pavement. Jake stood inside one of the crowded bars, in front of a large window, with dancers behind him and more outside. On the wall across the street, the dark shadows of a dancing couple whirled. Like two intertwined sets of black fan blades, the specters whirled and whirled along the brick wall, always touching. Jake longed to be a part of the shadow show.

"Hey, don't look so sad," said a man. "It's okay. Everything will be okay." After squeezing Jake's shoulder with his hand, the man disappeared into the crowd. Not believing the forecast, Jake headed for his car. He had decided to give up his quest for Sara, for Madeleine, for revenge. Back to New Orleans.

* * *

Jake pulled out of his parking spot on the top floor and slowly followed the downward spiraling path out of the parking garage. Down and around, then back onto I-10. He did not need to check out of the hotel. He had never actually moved in. All his things were still safely locked in his trunk.

A scarlet fog settled over Lafayette. It reflected the glow of city lights, inexplicably appearing red like the sunset over the swamp in Henderson, its glow particularly unnatural since it was eleven o'clock and the sun had set hours before.

Jake tried to focus on New York, on heading back to a world where he could feel in control. However, over the hum of the road came the sound of the whispers, louder than before, from somewhere behind Jake, from somewhere in Lafayette. Jake renounced them. He turned up the radio and found a rock station. He left Lafayette far behind, but the whispers still followed, flittering into his thoughts, breaking through the wall of blaring music.

Up ahead, Jake spotted hints of flames off to the left of I-10. When he approached, he could see heaps of whatever, sporadically placed in an empty field, had been set on fire. From each pile, a tassel of the reddest of flames meandered far up into the sky. The red, like fresh streams of electric blood, burned wavering images onto Jake's retinas, causing the scarlet visions to repeat

196

long after they were out of view. Red visions like the silk tassel in the Chinese restaurant, in his bathroom in New York. A vision of Rachel's face hovered in his mind.

Jake slowed down at the next sign that warned against U-turns, and without checking for cross traffic, whipped his car around and headed back to Lafayette.

* * *

Jake could not sleep all night even though he was exhausted and hung-over. Praying the sheriff would be in his office on a Saturday morning, Jake drove downtown, still dressed in suit and tie, like Randy Ketchum, wrinkled detective. Jake, once again, passed the gauntlet of ex-parish Sheriffs as he climbed the black, stone steps to the current Sheriff's office. There was no pretty sergeant on duty. Instead, the Sheriff sat behind her desk, leaning back on her chair.

"Hi. I'm back."

"Thought you'd be."

"My name isn't really Randy Ketchum."

"Right, Mr. Preston. How they been treating you at the Jefferson?"

Jake sank down onto the black couch, his eyes searching the floor for his next words.

"I'm not really a detective. I'm a photographer." Jake pulled his gaze off the floor and looked straight into the sheriff's laser-beam eyes. "I'm only looking for the guy because there is this woman. He pulled her away from me in New Orleans. It's really her I need to find. But if I find him, I'm sure I can find her. I don't know how to explain but—"

"He's a real dangerous man, Jake. I believe you should just go back to New York and forget the whole thing."

"I can't. It's a personal thing. I can't go on with my life until I settle this."

"You may be too late. We have not seen hide or hair of him for a long time now. Child molesters don't always last too long around here. Sometimes—things happen to them."

"So I've heard."

As the Sheriff examined him, top to bottom, Jake waited patiently, like a small stray dog being circled by the leader of the pack. The sheriff broke the silence.

197

"The last place he was spotted was at an abandoned house down on Weevil Road. Get on ninety and pass through Scott. About three miles out, turn left. It's at the end of a long, overgrown driveway. It's only marked by an oak tree that was hit by lightning. You'll see it. It's split right in two. Be careful."

When the sheriff rose and took his hand, Jake could feel the evidence of many years of hard work on his calloused palm.

"Orgeron, the sheriff said, the name's Orgeron."

As he followed the stairway down to the street, Jake used his baby-soft palm to rub the sheriff's gaze off the back of his neck.

* * *

The driveway to the house on Weevil Road consisted of two tire tracks barely visible underneath the dry grass that grew from them. Jake slowly navigated his car over the rocks and ruts. The field of weeds and bushes that wrapped around the house had grown so tall the building was invisible from the main road. Jake's wheels bumped against something, slamming his chest against the steering wheel, knocking the breath out of his lungs with a woof.

Jake got out of his car and watched the house before approaching. A fallen tree was nestled in the weeds at the end of the driveway, jammed under Jake's tires.

The house was old, made of grey, worn, once whitewashed, wooden planks covered by a sloping, corrugated tin roof. It stood above the ground, perched on concrete piers shaped like miniature pyramids. Windows, tucked behind shutters, rose from the porch floor to the roof. Rows of corn stalks, dry and brittle, encircled the house like a long-forgotten platoon of decrepit soldiers. Jake followed a vague path to the house. As he drew close, he heard rustling, scurrying under the house. Quickly, he jumped on the porch, glad it did not collapse underneath him. He tried the front door; it was securely locked, as were the floor-to-ceiling windows. Jake rattled the shutters. They held firm. The slats that ran across the shutters lined up like sun-bleached ribs, some of them fractured.

No stairway remained, so Jake jumped off the porch. He walked around to the back of the house. Squirrels, sounding like storm troopers, raced after each other across the tin roof. There was no porch on the back of the house, and the back door was locked—boarded over. Jake could not reach the windows, and guessed they would firmly resist his entrance, also. He turned his back on another wall, this one old and brittle, but stronger than the will of an outsider. The rustling from under the house urged Jake to hasten his retreat.

* * *

On the way back to his hotel, Jake went grocery shopping. He bought himself a bottle of vodka and some ginger ale. Something to help him sleep. Even though he downed the prescribed amount, the vodka did not work. Jake sat on his bed, unable to lie back, unable to muster enough determination to remove his suit and tie.

One more day. He would stay and search, one more day.

Chapter 34

*J*AKE GOT UP to fix himself another drink, make another attempt at mixing up a sleeping potion. He poured the last of the vodka into the once sealed-for-his-protection glass and reached for the bottle of ginger ale. Just before the golden liquid could bubble into the vodka and evolve into a new element, he pulled back, screwed the cap back onto the soda, downed the vodka straight and slammed the empty bottle into the trash can. Grabbing his room key, he turned his back on the rumpled bed and headed toward the darkened streets of Lafayette.

The raucous revelries of the night before were no longer in evidence. There were no partiers in the streets, no graceful dancers, no whirling shadows caressing the sides of the buildings, none but the solitary specter caused by Jake's passing. He followed unfamiliar streets that led him in opposing directions until he was no longer sure where he was. The sense of being followed returned. He glanced around, trying to look nonchalant. Then the tickling returned at the back of his neck. He stopped to rest his forehead against the cool window of a darkened shop. The glass rang with the sound of his name, the sound of the calling. When he failed to will the sound away, he whirled to face the length of the moonlit street and screamed into the darkness. "Who are you?" His words echoed down the empty boulevard like the whistle of a locomotive. No answer to his question returned. Hands in his pockets, he continued his walk, not knowing if he was going toward or away from the night caller, no longer caring.

* * *

Feeling followed, he looked behind himself. There on the wall behind another parking lot stood another mural. Jake turned back and walked toward it. Spotlights glared across the painting, emphasizing the electric color of the turquoise blue butter-fly. Upon closer inspection, Jake realized that vivid symbols of Louisiana, such as dew-covered leaves, bugs, and frogs were trampling indistinct, painted photographs of Louisiana. Jake could almost hear Chaoui saying, "See for yourself. Put that picture in your head." The artist seemed to be repeating Chaoui's command. "See Louisiana for yourself, before it's too late." Above the mural was printed the title, "Louisiana Postcards," and the artist's name, Robert Dafford. Jake whispered to the iridescent butterfly, "How the hell did he get so smart? I'll have to wring that guy's neck. I'm a photographer." He turned and walked on.

The silence of the darkness was soon broken by murmurs of music that flitted past him with every gust of the gentle, evening breeze. Like a lost child, he followed the music as if it was the sound of his mother's voice. He rounded the next corner and noticed what appeared to be a small, purple warehouse. It was surrounded by randomly parked cars. Beams hurled down by the overhead street lamps glistened off windshields and chrome as he moved closer to the building.

The music grew louder as he approached its source and was accented by the sound of the laughter of locals who lounged on the porch that ran the length of the warehouse. In the small front yard, a lone man stood behind a barbecue grill. As he busied himself with the task of overseeing whatever it was that smelled so good, a cloud of smoke wrapped itself around him then headed up into the star-sequined sky. He looked up from his work, smiled, and slowly waved hello with a heavily gloved hand.

Music lured Jake toward the entrance. Weaving himself through the jovial crowd, he climbed the steps, passed through the doorway and entered an alcove. The volume of the music assaulted him, but it could not drown out the sound of his name being whispered, the sound that echoed through his soul.

Someone grabbed his arm. "Excuse me, but there's a ten dollar cover charge."

"Oh, sure." Jake reached into his pocket and peered through the darkness to locate a ten-dollar bill. He handed the cash to the gatekeeper and wandered closer to the source of the music.

Inside, the warehouse was one large open space with a stage on one end, and on the other, a bar that ran the length of the building. The room was packed with couples dancing belly-to-belly, bathing each other in sweat. There was no air conditioning. Instead, an attempt at dispelling the oppressive heat was accomplished by sporadically placed fans. Not graceful, slow moving fans like Jake had seen in New Orleans, but huge industrial-sized fans that spun like the wings of giant, angry bees. Big, black fans, some on stands, and some set in box-like frames, blasted the dancing couples lucky enough to have claimed the areas in front of them. The torrents of wind blew their hair into the air and pulled at their clothing.

Jake knew there was only one way to silence the calling, to bestow forgetfulness, so he bellied up the bar and waved a bartender over to where he stood.

"Vodka. No, tequila. Two." The bartender held up two fingers and tilted his head like the RCA dog straining to hear his master's voice. Jake nodded and yelled over the music. "Yeah, two!"

Jake dispatched the shots of tequila with haste, then turned and leaned against the bar so he could watch the dancers move to the music. The floor recoiled in rhythm with their gyrations. Sweat beads danced on Jake's forehead. When he felt a small river trickle down his spine and soak through where his back met the bar, he pulled his tie loose and unfastened the first few buttons of his shirt. The calling in his head became more profound as if turned up by the intensity of the fans. He rubbed the back of his neck in hopes of relieving the strain. The alcohol finally reached Jake's toes, a sure sign that he would soon be losing total contact with reality. "About time," he whispered back to the secret voice.

The band turned up the heat a few notches by concentrating its efforts on a hot blues tune. A harmonica called to the crowd, eloquently speaking of passion and sadness. Jake watched the dancers as they twirled and laughed, all the time never quite letting go of each other, separate, but still attached, if only by finger tips. The world seemed to move in time with the music. Even the air vibrated. Something pulled at him. Jake stood up straight and moved away from the bar, toward the stage, toward the source of the vibrations. As he moved closer to the speakers, he felt closer to the source of his misery. It was as though the epicenter of his discomfort was there, near him, somewhere in the room, touching his face with hungry lips. He stood in the middle of the dancing forms and turned 'round and 'round like the beam of a light house alone in a hurricane, straining to see through the clouds of smoke and the clinging darkness.

Off to a side of the room, in front of one of the hell-bent fans, he spotted a singular figure dancing alone with her long hair blowing away from the fan. As the lone dancer turned and twisted in the wind, her red hair sometimes caressed her, some-times appeared to be as serpentine fingers reaching out in Jake's direction. He awoke—became sober at once.

Afraid Sara would escape again, Jake pushed through the crowd as though the dancers were invisible to him, he could see only one moving form. A whirling elbow bashed his right temple, throwing him back a step, but Jake continued his journey until the way was barricaded by a long table. He moved along its edge only to find his way blocked by another. Without taking his eyes off Sara, he felt his way through the maze of barriers. She was no longer dancing when he stepped in front of her—she stood motionless, her head bowed. Jake moved closer until the ten-tacles of flying curls stroked him. Slowly, she lifted her head and looked into his face. The music stopped with a flourish of syncopated drumbeats. Jake took advantage of the comparative silence.

"Why do you dance alone?"

She smiled the smile of a patient teacher and said, "Everybody dances alone. They just don't know it."

"What? What are you?"

The music resumed and she reached one hand to his face, caressed his right cheek. After resting on his face for a moment, her hand slowly slid down along his jaw line, then down the side of his neck, pausing over the spot where his pulse raced with the drums. She moved to the sultry music, eyes closed and lips parted. Her other hand mirrored its partner and came to rest on the opposite side of his neck. Together, her hands slowly slid down the slender column and found their way under his collar. Jake's shirt parted as her fingers continued their downward journey. When her hands had exposed the flesh that waited, once hidden by the upper half of his shirt, she moved closer, still keeping time with the music, gently placing her lips on Jake's chest. He could feel her tongue on his flesh, tasting his salt as she kissed him. Jake gasped as her electric touch filled his body with tension. She turned her head and stroked his chest with the sides of her face until her cheeks were wet from his perspiration and her hair clung to her face.

Jake grabbed her wrists and shook her away, then peered angrily into her eyes, searching for Madeleine. She had to be. Without knowing why, he let go his hold and dropped his arms to his sides.

Wait for her to give herself away.

Sara's hands resumed their journey and slowly unbuttoned his shirt. When the last button was undone, still moving in time with the vibrations emanating from the speakers, she lifted her shirt, just high enough to expose the pale flesh of her belly. She moved against Jake with rhythmic deliberation. Lubricated by their perspiration, she rubbed herself back and forth across him. Jake, who had so far stood motionless, felt his body begin to move to the rhythm of the room. No longer caring who she was, he folded his arms around her gracefully undulating form, and holding Sara captive, began to move in unison with her. Even if she were Madeleine, it was too late for Jake to resist.

She responded by slowly sliding her arms around his shoulders and gently biting the tender curve where Jake's neck met his shoulder. They continued their mystery dance until the music ended.

She broke contact with Jake and gently fingered his willful curls from his forehead, then reached over to a nearby table and drank from a plastic cup. Pushing tangled hair away from her own face, she spoke. "Sweet, could you watch my drink for a minute, I've got to go and fix myself up a bit. I'll be right back." Jake's attempted response was overpowered by the reappearance of the blues. He took the drink from her hand and watched her back as she disappeared into the crowd, as she headed toward the ladies' room.

The band ripped into another tune and Jake stood holding her drink in his trembling hand with only the melting ice cubes to feel his heat. When the band stopped again, the harmonica player announced it was time for a break. The crowd cleared and rushed outside for the relief of the relatively cool night air, as if trained to act in tandem. Jake searched the dance hall for a sign of long, red tresses, but found none.

"No, not again," he muttered to the voice that no longer called. He made his way to the ladies' room and caught the attention of a woman who was on her way out.

"Excuse me, is there a woman with long, red hair in there?"

"Sorry, it's empty."

Jake threw the drink against the wall and rushed into the sanctuary of overheated ladies. He frantically searched for Sara, kicked open each stall door, angry that he had let her slip away, again. After his fruitless search, he ran out onto the porch, hoping she had just gone outside to cool off, but he was wrong. After a haphazard search of parked cars, Jake found himself in the center of the parking lot, desperately trying to slow the frenzied beating of his heart.

She was gone.

He closed his eyes and covered his ears with his hands, the nonexistent music still pounding in his mind, her sweat not yet dry on his chest. Glad he was sober, with his eyes closed, he slid his hands from his ears, moved them to his chest, and slowly rubbed their intermingled salts together. He continued by anointing his face in the same manner. When he opened his eyes and gazed up into the star-filled night, he saw the grey house with the tin roof. He saw the floor-to-ceiling windows and knew she would be there, knew she would be waiting. He reached into his pocket to retrieve his car keys and realized he was on foot.

Chapter 35

"**D**AMN!
Jake heard laughter from behind and turned to see a thin man in a cowboy hat, smiling.

"What's up—lock your keys in?"

"No, I don't have a car. I mean it's back at my hotel. Hey! Can you give me a ride to the Jackson Inn? I'll pay whatever you want."

"Sure," the cowboy said. "Jump in."

Jake ran around to the other side of the pick-up and took his place in the passenger seat. He tried to conceal his rage, but he lost control at the first stop light, red of course.

"Damn!" He pounded on the dashboard.

"Hey, calm down buddy," the cowboy said gently. "We'll get there in good time."

"You don't understand. I have to catch this woman before she gets away, forever."

"Woman? Hell, why didn't you say so." The driver slammed his foot on the gas pedal and ran the red light. They barreled down city streets, running every red light and stop sign, speeding around slower cars. When they screeched into the hotel parking lot, Jake turned to hand his accomplice payment for his assistance.

"No way. Just go and get her."

Jake slammed the truck door behind him and ran for his car. He backed out without looking in the mirror and sped toward the whitewashed house—toward Sara.

After what seemed like an endless drive, Jake turned down the dirt road where he knew she waited—his headlights pathetically inadequate in the heavy darkness intensified by a swirling mist. Like furtive fireflies, pairs of glowing eyes blinked at Jake from the tangled undergrowth. Sometimes they scurried across his path or jumped aside at his approach. His tires hit the log that marked the end of the road, causing Jake to lurch forward and slam against the steering wheel. Sparing himself only a moment to catch his breath, he left his car in the care of the blinking eyes that still glowed in the moonlight, even without collaboration from his headlights. Instead of taking time to find the narrow footpath that led to the lone house, he crashed through the weeds and bushes taking a direct route to his destination.

When he reached the porch, he could see in the silver moon-light that one of the windows was unlocked. The shutters were thrown back against the house, and the panes were open. When he finally stood in front of the portal, he could see her there, standing just inside the threshold, waiting for him in the flicker-ing light of a single oil lamp. They were only inches apart. As he moved to reach for her, a breeze swirled past, taking with it the tattered lace curtain that hung down from the open window. Its spider-web fabric fluttered between them, creating a tenuous, life-like barrier. Without letting go of the hold his eyes kept on those on the other side of the curtain, he reached up and pulled the barrier aside. The delicate fabric ran its fingers across his face as it passed, still animated by the night wind.

When the barrier was finally disposed of, Jake crossed the threshold and gently took hold of Sara's hair. He pulled her against him and whispered. "Who are you?"

Bending down, he touched her lips with his and again felt the tongue that had tasted him earlier that night. He felt the beat of her heart against his, both trembling like two musicians not quite in sync, trying to catch up to each other. He let go of his hold on her hair and grasped the hem of her shirt, pulled it up over her head and threw it on the floor. Their flesh met again. Just as before, they paid no heed to the eyes around them, to the blinking green and golden lights that watched from outside, from the other side of the rippling curtain. Sara looked up at him and fondled his rebellious curls. Jake could see the silver tracks of tears running down her face.

"I've missed you so," she whispered.

She ran the palms of her hands down his chest, loosened his belt, and bent to remove the rest of the barriers to Jake's flesh, leaving a trail of kisses and tears in her path. When all their clothing was added to the pile on the floor, they tumbled to the bed that stood against the wall facing the window. Jake could hear a blues harmonica echoing in his memory. They rolled in time with the music, legs entwined, fingers directing, tongues tasting, taking advantage of every sensation flesh had to offer in the moonlit night, in the gentle, eye-spangled night, as the breeze kept silent witness.

When Jake rolled on top of Sara, he gazed into her eyes and saw that she could hear his music. The palms of their hands met, and with interlaced fingers, he pulled her arms up over her head and pressed them down on the mattress. When he slid his legs in between those of his willing prisoner, he met with no resistance. He could feel her flesh calling to his, calling him to join with her. They began to move in unison, to dance to his music. The opposing tempos of hearts that beat against each other in the sigh-filled night finally came to terms with each other and caught up the same rhythm—Jake's rhythm. They continued to dance until the music ended, until there was no more need for motion, no more need for flesh.

For Jake, it was not enough—as always—but this time he knew he could have it all. Still joined, he pressed closer to Sara. He let go of her hands and slid his arms around her ribs, and pressing her closer, concentrated on her pounding heart, on the timing of their breaths. Holding her close, he rolled their inter-mingled forms back and forth until their heated flesh no longer kept them apart.

Their spirits rolled free from the flesh. Without walls of flesh to separate them, they continued to roll as one until they broke completely free from their earthly prisons. Together, they drifted into the winking night. Together, they passed through the filigree curtain and knew each other absolutely. There was no longer a need for tastes or touches. Such sensations were forgotten in the presence of the music of the spheres. As Jake rolled in ecstasy with his other half, he knew that they had always known each other, and he knew that on the face of his motionless, Main Street Jake-form, silver tears glistened.

Sometime during the night, when back in his corporal form, Jake woke and instinctively searched through the darkness for Sara's flesh. She was there beside him, sleeping silently. He grabbed a lock of her hair, wound it around his hand, and closed his fingers over it to assure himself that she could not escape him while he slept in the dew-filled morning. He drifted back into sleep with the scarlet ribbons firmly entwined in his fingers, clenched in his fist.

* * *

Jake awoke the next morning knowing he was alone. The breeze was gone and the lace curtain hung limp, blocking his view of the scene outside. He sat up and looked over at the spot where Sara had once rested. Only the indentation made by her body remained. In his palm lay a lock of red hair, neatly cut off where it once attached itself to Sara's crown. He closed his fingers around it and held his fist to his forehead. She was gone and he knew not where. His mind was empty, and no secret voice called his name. He crawled to where Sara had once lain and placed himself over the shadow left by her sleeping form, sure that she was not Madeleine, knowing it was she who had brought home to him that night in his room in New Orleans. Jake rose from the bed and smoothed the sheet that covered the mattress, careful to be sure no images of their forms remained.

Sunlight poured in through the window, illuminating what was once left unseen. The room was barren except for the bed, the oil lamp, and a pile of cold ashes that spilled from a crumbling stone fireplace. All was surrounded by walls hidden behind paper adorned with purple cabbage flowers. The purple-splattered paper peeled away from the walls in spots where water had seeped between thin layers of color. Yellow peeked out from under purple only to be pushed aside by layers of newsprint. Under it all, was the supporting layer of bone-grey wood.

Jake searched the house for any clue to the mysteries it concealed. Empty cans and broken crockery, all exposing jagged edges, littered the unswept floors. Jake exited, as he had entered, through the window. He grabbed the window sashes to close them behind himself, but the rusted metal latches affixed on opposite sides would not match up. As he lifted one window up so it would meet the other, a wad of paper fell out from under one of the hinges that loosely gripped the wall. Just a scrap of trash?—No— Something told him it was more. He bent to pick up the paper and unfolded the wad. It was the stub of a paycheck issued to a Sara Guidry, issued by a restaurant called La Mangez-Moi, in New Orleans, only a few weeks before.

With trembling fingers, Jake added the check stub to the pocket where he had safely hidden the red lock of hair and hurried back to pack his things, to return to New Orleans.

* * *

Once back at the Jackson, Jake asked the woman at the desk to arrange a hotel reservation for him in New Orleans. After he had finished packing, Jake returned to the front lobby.

"How'd you do with that reservation?"

"Sorry, Boo." The frizzy-haired woman shrugged and shook her head. "There isn't a room to be had in New Orleans. It's too close to Mardi Gras."

Jake thanked her and left, certain he knew where he could find a room.

Chapter 36

$\mathcal{T}$HE FOG RETURNED TO PLAY GAMES along I-10, as if to keep Jake from returning to New Orleans. It hung the heaviest right around Henderson, over the Atchafalaya Basin. Jake was tempted to pull off the road, to return to the electric-blue eyes, to retrieve his camera, but his craving for Sara kept him going. It guided him like radar as he inched through the fog.

Jake checked the contents of his pocket every few miles as if the tattered stub or lock of hair could crawl away while he was unaware. They were still there, his last clues to finding Sara, his last chance to go home, both carefully concealed along with the image of Nikki, his only family.

Jake approached New Orleans in traffic as bad as any he had ever experienced in New York. His hands went pale from the pressure of his grip on the steering wheel. Afraid to keep running the air conditioner in the stalled traffic, he shut it off and opened his windows. He was sweating in seconds.

Jake was amazed by the remarkable metamorphosis that had taken place since was last in the French Quarter. Out of the brown cobblestone and phony brick face cocoon had crawled a magnificent butterfly, all purple, green, and gold. A blizzard of brilliant tinsel, sequins, and feathers had fallen off the creature's magical wings, littering the city with its colors.

The crowd had also changed. As if caused by a snap change in the psychic weather, the crowds were livelier, faster, more tightly wound. Some were even wearing masks or multiple strings of cheap plastic beads that glittered with a thin layer of sparkling paint that would soon chip off, leaving the valueless, imitation pearls exposed to the glaring light of day.

Jake returned to The Enclave. Like a penitent runaway child, having learned his lesson, he shuffled over to the check-in desk and asked to be accepted back.

"Of course we have room for you," Matthew crooned. "You never checked out, silly boy. Your room is waiting for you just where you left it." He grinned, ear-to-ear, exposing well-polished, acrylic teeth.

"Thanks," Jake said as he checked to see his room key was still on his key chain.

Jake's room was as he had left it, except for one thing. The fan had returned to its place on the ceiling. However, it was not moving. Jake flipped the wall control on and the fan began to move, lazily. He flipped the switch off and the fan slowed to a crawl, then stopped. His new control gave his a sense of power.

Jake double-checked the address on the pay stub and rushed off in the direction of La Mangez-Moi. He was almost running when he turned the last corner approaching the restaurant. As soon as he reached his destination, he grabbed the door handle and pulled, then yanked.

It was locked.

He spun around and kicked the door. It rattled in place. As he was about to follow the kick with a punch, he noticed the sign: "Ready to serve you every day from 3 P.M. until 4 A.M." Feeling foolish for his impatience and relieved he had not reached another total dead end, Jake decided to go back to his room.

* * *

Stone sober, Jake rolled onto his bed and realized how tired he was. He fell asleep, face down, on a cool pillow, glad he had remembered to turn on the overhead fan. Funny, he thought, how his attitude about the fan had changed when he gained control over it.

* * *

He woke knowing someone was in the room with him. At first, he was excited. Maybe it was she. The silken lover. Sara. However, when the air chilled upon his visitor's approach—he knew better.

He tried to roll over, but could not. He could not move at all. Because he lay face down with a pillow rucked up around his eyes, he could not see. He broke out in a cold sweat, a sweat the fan could not dissipate.

He felt its weight move onto the bed—onto his back.

God. No! His mind screamed as the thing crawled onto his back, then straddled his waist and sat on him as one would a horse. It leaned forward and gripped Jake's shoulders with bony fingers. After breathing heavily for what seemed an eternity, it started to growl and shake Jake's torso with the grip it held on his shoulders. The shaking became more violent. Its growls turned into screams. Every time it ran out of breath, it quickly inhaled, then screamed again, louder, more shrilly, rattling Jake faster and harder in its death grip.

Though he was face down, blindfolded by pillows, Jake realized he could see all as if he were looking down from above. The screaming rider was sexless, gaunt as a skeleton, with a protruding rib cage that hung over a sunken-in belly. A shock of silver hair burst out of its head, the only covering on its naked, grey, ulcer-covered skin.

The phone rang.

Jake woke, too shaken to answer the jangling call. After the ringing ceased, the red message light on the corner of the phone began to blink.

So sleeping in broad daylight was not as safe as it should have been.

Jake regained his composure, stood, then scrambled to the refrigerator and mixed himself a drink. He pulled a blanket off the bed, wrapped it around himself, and sat huddled on the floor, clutching his shelter and the cold drink. Jake's trembling hand shook around the glass. The ice cubes in his vodka clanked against the tumbler, tinkling like a delicate, crystal wind chime.

When Jake had warmed up and calmed down, he glanced at the clock. It was after three o'clock. He threw off his cover and leapt to the mirror. After a few passes of a comb, his appearance miraculously passed inspection, so he headed straight for the street.

* * *

The door to La Mangez-Moi opened on the first try. Jake was greeted by a woman clad only in black fishnet pantyhose.

Trying to keep his gaze locked well above the oversized breasts that reached out to him across a tiny service bar, Jake asked for directions to the manager's office.

"He doesn't have an office, sir."

"Okay. Fine. Could you point him out to me? I need to speak with him."

"Perhaps...*I* could do something for you?"

"No, I really need to see him."

"Oh—I don't know. He's not in a real great mood today. Things aren't going so good. We're real short-handed. A bunch of the girls just quit."

"Okay. Just describe him to me. I'll find him for myself."

With only a sketchy description to follow, Jake scanned the dining room for a thick-haired, fat man in a plaid suit. Plaid Polyester. Jake spotted the owner, stepped in front of him, and held out his hand. The thick-haired man, whose hair turned out to be a cheap toupee that did not quite match the rest of the thatch, ignored Jake's offer of a handshake.

"I'm sorry to bother you, but—"

"So don't. I'm really busy." He began to walk away. Jake repositioned himself in front of him.

"I only need to ask you one question."

"So ask it already, then get the hell out of here."

"Sara Guidry. Do you know how I can reach her?"

"What, does the bitch owe you money or something? You a pusher?"

"No. I just need to find her. I'm a friend."

"Bull shit. She ain't got no friends. She's too fucking crazy for friends."

"What do you mean?"

The manager stared at Jake with eyes sharply focused. "I thought you said you knew her. You a cop?"

"Please, just tell me how I can find her."

"I don't know. The bitch cut out on me a few weeks ago. Left me high and dry. Not that she was such a great waitress."

"Please, do you have an address?"

"No, I said."

"Do you know where she was last? Do you know anyone who would know where she is?"

"Go to Charity Hospital. She ends up there every time she tries to snuff herself."

"What?"

"You know, snuff herself."

"You mean—"

"Yeah, she's tried it all, pills, drugs, even cut her wrists once. Some ass hole always gets there on time and saves her." He stopped and thought for a moment, then smiled. "Maybe that's why she didn't come back. Maybe she finally did something right for once. Why don't you check the cemetery?"

Jake resisted the urge to make the toupee the victim of a violent crime, but he left quickly, before he had a chance to change his mind.

Chapter 37

"ANOTHER DEAD END," Jake mumbled.

The man on the other side of the bar said, "What? We don't have that kind. Just read the signs and pick one out."

"Red," Jake said.

The bartender rolled his eyes back and clucked his tongue. He filled a plastic cup with a daiquiri from the first red mixer he reached. Instead of walking, drink-in-hand, Jake sat at a table in the daiquiri shop. With his attention glued to the see-through top on the cup, he sucked the frozen drink through a straw, stopping every few swallows to cough from the chill in his throat.

A shadow slipped over Jake's drink. Someone slid onto a chair at Jake's table. He saw her at the corner of his eye. Her short, spiky brown hair and thin, pointy-chinned face were of no interest to Jake. She sat quietly until he finally looked up at her and made eye contact.

"I heard you in the Eat Me," she said. "I was there picking up my check, not that it will make a dent in my debts."

"Why are you here?"

"I was wondering when you saw her last, Sara. If she was okay—since the last time. I called the hospital, but they said she ran away. I'm scared. What if she's dead?"

"I saw her last night. She was alive then."

"Great." She sighed in relief. "You know, she's really a super-nice person. Just screwed up."

"What do you mean, screwed up?"

"I used to live with her. She had this really mean bastard for a boyfriend. Crack head. He treated her like shit, but she loved him anyway. He'd beat her up then steal her money and clear out. A couple times, she'd try to, you know. And just when she'd start to pull herself together, bingo, he'd be back. I had to move out. Didn't want to. But he was always hitting on me when she wasn't looking."

She put her hands together, wove her fingers between each other, and rubbed her thumbs together. She looked down at her hands as if she was contemplating going into a *here's the church here's the steeple* routine, successfully avoiding further eye contact with Jake.

"I kind of feel guilty leaving her with him. You know—all she ever wanted was for someone to love her. That's not too much to ask for, is it?"

Jake waited until her last statement had time to dissipate before he spoke again.

"Can you give me her address—write it down so I won't forget?" He reached into his pocket, then handed her a pen and the check stub, face down. She stared up at Jake's face, her lids flitting over brown eyes.

"You aren't a cop, are you?"

"No."

"I didn't think so."

She gingerly reached a finger close to Jake's pen and rolled it over to herself. She grabbed the pen and wrote the address, slowly, carefully, as if she were in a penmanship class waiting for Jake to spot an error in her form.

"Can you tell her I miss her? That she should give me a call?"

"I'll do that."

She smiled and blushed. "My name's Heather. You kinda' act like you like her. You know, she really deserves a nice guy. You a nice guy?"

Jake swallowed hard.

She rose to leave, then hesitated.

"It's on the second floor, blue shutters. Blue for protection. She keeps a spare key under a loose floorboard at the end of the hall, under the front window. She was always losing hers. Well, we was both always losing them. Be careful. It's not a real great neighborhood." She shrugged. "It's all we could afford."

Thinking she was hinting for a donation, Jake reached for his wallet. She shook her head and left.

* * *

Jake caught a cab and read the address to the driver.

"Slumming, eh?"

"Just get me there. Quick."

The drive to Sara's place was short. To Jake, the neighborhood did not appear much different from the rest of the city. Even so, he wished there were more streetlights. It would soon be growing dark.

"There it is." The cabby pointed to a house across the street.

Jake pulled on the door handle and had to use his shoulder to push the dented cab door open.

"Hey! Hey! Hey! Where you going? You didn't pay yet."

"You didn't get me back to my hotel yet."

"I ain't waiting around here for you."

"Yes you are."

"I'll call the cops if you don't pay."

"Great. Do that. It would make me feel a lot safer."

* * *

Jake crossed the street, his eyes trained on the French door with blue shutters. He could still hear the cab driver swearing. The porch creaked under Jake's weight as he opened the moth-eaten screen door. The holes in the metallic fabric were so large a cat could jump through. Inside, sitting halfway up the stairs to the second floor, sat a little black girl of about six, with endless rows of skinny braids, each ending with a colored rubber band, standing out from her head like the spikes on a mace. She examined Jake with huge, liquid eyes, then checked to be sure her dress covered her knobby knees. She made no attempt to get out of Jake's way when he excused himself, so he carefully stepped around her on his way up.

The key was exactly where it was supposed to be. After knocking to be sure nobody was there, Jake unlocked the door to Sara's apartment. He let it swing open all the way, then scanned the room before he entered. The apartment consisted of a combination kitchen-living area, a bedroom, and a bathroom. All could be seen from the door.

Jake closed the door behind himself. Once inside, he wasn't sure what to do. The air was stale, stagnant. He could tell the apartment had been deserted for quite some time. Over the sink, a row of red clay flowerpots harbored skeletons of long-dead plants. Jake stuck his finger into one of the pots. The soil was dry, rock-hard. When he opened the refrigerator, the odor of long-forgotten food knocked him back a step. He closed it quickly and stepped over to the French doors that opened onto the iron-railed balcony. He slipped his hands behind the lace curtains and opened the doors to let in air from the outside, air that was not much better than what he had just encountered in the refrigerator. There was no breeze to give life to the curtains. They hung limp, refusing to caress him as had the ones in the grey wooden house near Lafayette.

He turned away from the window and headed down the short hall that led away from the living area. The tiny bedroom was only large enough for a bed and a small dresser. Jake picked up a brush from the dresser. It was festooned with tangles of long, red hair exactly like the streamers that were still safe in his pocket. He went through drawers, looked under the mattress, searched everywhere, but found no clue of Sara's whereabouts.

The bed was disheveled. Jake bent and ran his hand over the imprint left by whoever had last slept on the mattress. He longed to feel a connection to Sara.

* * *

Jake startled the driver when he returned to the rumbling cab. The cabbie's hand quickly slipped under an open newspaper tented over the passenger side of the front seat. When he recognized Jake, he grabbed the wheel and said, "Haul ass." Jake did. He jumped into the front seat, pushing the newspaper aside, revealing a glistening black pistol.

Chapter 38

WHEN JAKE FLOPPED BACK ON HIS BED, he remembered the red, flashing message light on his phone. He reached over and dialed the desk.

"Sir, you do have two messages. Both from Mr. Patin. Please return his calls. Thank you."

Jake dialed Camille.

"Jake, I was so worried about you," Camille said. "Three days without a word. I feared the worst."

"I'm sorry. I just needed to get away." Jake sighed and rubbed his face. "I'm back now."

"Please have supper with me at La Faim. Tell me all about it then. Captain Bill is back. We can plan your shoots."

"Okay. Great. I'll pull myself together and be right over."

"Wonderful."

Jake hung up the phone.

Great. Bill is back and my camera is in Henderson, at the bottom of a boat. Do I even give a shit? What the hell. I can use the money. Perhaps it might be the only way I can salvage anything from this bullshit trip.

Jake rolled off the bed and rummaged through his camera bag to check out his back-up camera. It was old, outdated, but had never let him down. As he pulled out old faithful, Rachel's prism, the long pointed one he had forgotten about, clattered out of its silk wrapping. It lay on the dresser, unbroken. Rachel. Jake caressed it, then took it over to the window and held it up to the last remnants of sun light. It managed to produce a single rainbow fan that it projected onto the wall over Jake's bed. He carefully re-wrapped the prism and returned it to the lightproof camera case.

* * *

Camille's eyes lit up when he saw Jake enter the restaurant. He leapt from his place and hugged Jake, then pulled out a chair for him. "Please, sit, you look tired. Here." He poured Jake a glass of wine. "This will make you feel better. What would you like for supper? Order anything you like. If we don't have it, we'll send out."

"Calm down, Camille. Everything is okay."

"But you look so dejected or—"

"Don't worry. I'm fine. I think I'll have a steak. A plain, old-fashioned, medium-rare hunk of red meat."

Camille waved for a waiter. The curly-haired girl, who had once stuck her tongue out at Jake, flitted over to the table, bag in hand, pursing her lips to even out a layer of freshly applied lipstick. She tossed her bag to the floor and sat next to Camille.

"Jake, you remember Nina, don't you?"

"Sure. Of course. I met her at your party."

"I'm so honored that you remember me." She stuck her tongue out again. Camille winked at Jake.

* * *

Jake's steak was wonderful, as was the salad, wine, and dessert. Everything always seemed so perfect, so under control, when Camille was around. Perhaps it was time to stop judging Camille, stop suspecting him of ridiculous plots.

"Jake. Tomorrow night, I'm having my first Mardi Gras party at the Bete Noir. Tell me you'll attend."

"*First* Mardi Gras party?"

"Oh, yes. I will have as many as I can squeeze in. Mardi Gras is my most favorite time of the year. I make it last as long as possible, start as early as I can. Then again, so does just about everyone in New Orleans, everyone else, except the police, that is. Outsiders think Mardi Gras is a one-day affair, but that is so wrong. Here, it is a season that starts twelve days after Christmas. It is not one parade—it is many. Then," he smiled and his eyes seemed to lose focus for a moment, "there's the private side of the season. We'll teach you all about that too."

Nina giggled.

"I don't know." Jake shook his head. "I'm not one for costumes and stuff."

"That's fine," Camille said, his eyes glowing. "You don't have to wear a costume. We like you just the way you are. Right, Nina?"

"Riiiiight."

"Okay. I'll be there—maybe."

Camille's shoulders fell when Jake added the "maybe" to his acceptance.

"What time?"

"Any time you wish. We'll start at dark and keep going until no one can keep going."

* * *

It was hotter than ever when Jake left La Faim. Anxious to postpone his return to the hotel, he decided to walk back. The heat insisted on a slow pace that fit in perfectly with Jake's intentions. Put off the inevitable. Put off admitting the truth; that he wouldn't find Sara unless she wanted to be found—that he wouldn't find Madeleine unless she wanted to be found—that they were probably both illusions, like everything else in the chimera they call New Orleans.

He felt an overwhelming restlessness spilling from the crowd, like perspiration, an agitated demeanor, an aggressiveness he hadn't experienced in New Orleans before, anywhere before. It frightened him. The strength he felt after his time in Henderson had bled away, leaving him feeling weaker than ever before. Maybe it was just the damn, never-ending, bone-melting heat. The humidity was so heavy he stopped walking to bend over and cough fluid from his lungs.

Jake felt the need to escape the hostile crowds, so he wandered in another direction until he saw the iron fence that barred the crowds from *his* cemetery. He could be alone there, safe under the protection of an angel. He crossed the street, unaware he was almost flattened by a cab until its blaring horn hit him. Slipping through the lopsided gate was easy, but once inside, he questioned his actions.

The restlessness he left on the streets was even stronger inside the cemetery. He considered backing out, but he remembered his angel. He turned to the right, and there it was, tall, ghostly, standing like a lone cypress tree with the street-lamp glowing over its shoulder, a mock sun. Jake headed toward his angel, ignoring the rustling in the bushes.

Stepping in front of the angel caused an eclipse of the street light. Jake sat in the shadow cast by the angel—wishing it would bend down and wrap its wings around him in protection—wishing it were a cypress tree that would whisper gentle answers to all his questions.

The moisture and the restlessness in the air were like a steamroller pressing the wind out of Jake's chest. While he sat wondering how he would be able to keep walking in such oppressive heat, a light flickered.

He turned and watched for it to happen again. It did, but far over on the other side of the cemetery. He did not notice soon enough to see it clearly. His chest tightened again, but not from the heat. His heart beat faster as he strained, wide-eyed, afraid to move. A few yards ahead of him, a phosphorescent glow emanated from one of the graves. It rose like the wavering, gossamer lights of the aurora borealis, its colors mutating as it drifted away. As thunder follows lightning, a long, mournful sigh followed the light. For what seemed like hours, Jake was afraid to move.

* * *

Jake decided it would be his last night in New Orleans, in Louisiana. It was over, time to lock away the past. He locked his door and went out onto the porch with a beer. It was too hot outside, so he went back in and drank the icy beer in one long series of gulps.

He turned off the lights and turned on the fan, then went back to the glass door to look out at the doorway across the street. The waxing and waning red glow flickered. There he was, the all-night smoker, standing in the shadows, invisible but for a glowing ember. Jake no longer cared who he was because it was his last night in New Orleans. It did not matter anymore. Nothing mattered any more. He drank another beer, crushed the can in his hands, and threw himself on his New Orleans bed for the last time.

"Fuck Camille's party. Fuck the job. Fuck Louisiana."

Chapter 39

AKE WOKE, his foot in excruciating pain. A black dog had him by the foot. Golden eyes glowing like campfires in the night, the dog let out a low warning growl each time it bit deeper into Jake, shaking him as if he were prey. Jake tried to pull away, but could not. He could not move.

The pain was not just in Jake's foot. It was everywhere. Trying to scream or kick out at the dog proved futile; he could not move. The dog, its black hair bristling like a porcupine's quills, whipped Jake's foot back and forth until he managed to pull the spiritual foot loose from the solid one. Then the dog whipped the limb it held, as a homemaker whips the wrinkles out of her laundry. After repeated efforts, the dog managed to whip the rest of Jake loose from his body.

Once free, Jake knew he could fight the dog. He kicked out and scrambled for something to hold onto as the raging dog dragged him toward the door. Jake's efforts were for naught until he remembered the alligator. He braced himself against the floor, arms outstretched, and rolled over, taking the dog with him, knocking it off balance. Once the dog lost hold of his grip on the floor, they floated free, up toward the ceiling. Kicking and snarling, they thrashed about the room until the dog found a foothold. With his feet firmly planted on the ceiling, the dog continued to drag Jake toward the door, upside down.

Jake saw his chance whirling ahead of him. The fan. The ceiling beams offered Jake an absolute advantage over the dog. Jake had fingers. Hand-over-hand, Jake pulled away from the dog, dragging it back toward the side of the room that harbored the bed and the spinning fan. Jake crawled, heart slamming, eyes popping, until his captor was next to the slicing blades. Jake knew one more roll would do it; so with all his strength, he rolled over one more time.

When the dog hit the fan, it shattered into a million whirling shards of glossy jet. The lustrous, black shards hit the floor, flashed, and disintegrated. Jake crashed into his corporal form, waking wide-eyed and gasping.

Fighting nauseating waves of vertigo, Jake stumbled from the bed and into the bathroom.

* * *

Jake showered and dressed for the trip home. Though it would be hours before the sun would rise, Jake stood in front of his mirror, combing his hair, angry over how long it had grown since he left New York. It was getting harder and harder to keep his curls from undermining his smooth exterior. The comb slipped out of his twitching fingers. It ricocheted off his dresser and flipped onto the carpet. Jake shuddered, hesitating to look down for fear of spotting an ebony shard.

He tried to place his hands on his dresser to steady himself, but his camera case got in the way. Jake pulled it open and shuffled lenses out of the way, searching for the silk-covered suncatcher. He unwrapped it with reverence, as if it were a holy relic, a fragment of the bone of a saint, a glimmer of times past. He pulled the cable release out of his case and yanked the jack and button off the ends, then threaded the wire through the eye at the end of the prism and tied the ends together. Bowing his head, he slipped the circle of wire around his neck and tucked the prism under his shirt. With the remains of yesterday's sunlight safely hidden against his flesh, he went out on the porch to wait for daylight, to wait until his nerves were steady enough to handle driving back up north.

* * *

The phone rang early in the morning. Jake did not answer it. It had to be Camille and he did not want to lie to him. A short time later, someone knocked on his door. The persistent rapping continued until Jake whipped the door open.

"Mr. Preston, I'm afraid we have some unfortunate news."

Jake eyed Matthew and the police officer standing next to him. Jake's jaw tightened.

"I'm very sorry to have to notify you that, last night, vandals broke into our garage and damaged a number of cars. Yours was one of them."

"What do you mean, damaged?"

Jake tried to remain calm, even though he felt ready to explode.

"Well, I don't know much about automobiles, but I understand certain parts of the engines were removed along with hubcaps and tires, whatever was stored in the trunks."

Jake began to tremble.

"I thought your parking area was secure, that you had a watchman."

"We do. Did. He seems to have come to work under the influence. They say he slept through the whole episode."

"Where is he? I'll wring his fucking neck." Jake tried to push past Matthew. "I'll kill him."

"Whoa, Mr. Preston." The officer moved to hold Jake back. They scuffled until Jake felt himself slammed against the wall.

"You better get a hold of yourself or I'll be arresting *you*."

"Mr. Preston," Matthew crooned. "We've already dismissed the watchman. Don't worry. We'll have your car as good as new, tomorrow. At no expense to you, of course."

"I want to see it." Jake pushed toward the garage.

* * *

Jake's car looked like the frog he had dissected in high school. Its hood was open, exposing gaps where valuable components had been cut away by inexperienced hands.

"What slobs," Jake said.

"Probably kids," the officer said. "We'll need you to come down to the station to sign a report, sometime soon."

"Bull shit; you sign it. I'm not going anywhere but out of this hell hole. Until my car is ready, I'll be down the street getting shit-faced. If you don't like it, punt. I'm the victim here. I don't *have* to do anything."

"Mr. Preston, calm down. You're losing it."

"The only thing I'm gonna lose is you. All of you!" Jake stomped toward Bourbon Street.

* * *

Jake sat at his table in the blues bar, the one where he had found Sara, lost Sara. He did not look outside or at the stage.

He was too angry to see anything, too worried that Sara was in trouble or in a hospital or...

* * *

By the time she sat down next to him, Jake was drunk.

"Hi, remember me? Nina?"

"Yeah. Sure."

"I saw you through the door as I was passing by. How you doing?"

"How does it look like I'm doing?"

"Fine. You look real fine."

"Bullshit."

"Really. I've always been attracted to you."

"I heard."

"That Camille is such a blabbermouth. What are ya drinking?"

"Vodka."

"Yuck! Let's do some tequila."

"No. I don't like it that much. I don't think I'll do it ever again. Bad memories."

"Oh, oh. A woman, eh?"

"Yeah."

"I'm a woman—and we're all the same in the dark."

"No—that's not true."

* * *

Nina kept ordering more shots. Jake kept downing them. He was not used to tequila. It left a fire in his belly, glowing, like the wood fire in a cast-iron stove. He kept stoking the fire. Nina stood close to the heat.

Nina reached into her oversized purse and pulled out a silver flask. She shook it in front of Jake's face.

"This is the really good stuff. We can take it back to your place."

Jake reached for the flask, but Nina snapped it out of his reach, giggling, her laughter like the tinkling of broken glass.

"No thanks. I told you in New York, I don't dance."

She giggled again. "What are you talking about? I've never been to New York."

Jake tried to focus. Why did he say that? Nina was nothing like Kelly. Must be the booze.

"Oh, right. I don't know why I said that. I'm fucked up."

"C'mon, Jake, some of this stuff will fix you up."

"I'm not broken."

"Yes you are. C'mon." Nina teased him with the flask. He reached out, cat-like, and grabbed the silver container away from her. Holding her prisoner with his gaze, he slipped the flask into a back pocket of his jeans. It was curved, so it fit his form perfectly. She reached around behind him, trying to retrieve the bottle. Jake grabbed Nina's wrists. Her arms continued their journey around him. One tiny hand fit itself into Jake's empty back pocket. The other found a home in a front pocket on the opposite side.

"C'mon," Nina whispered into Jake's ear, her tongue punctuating her request. "Let's go home."

There was that damn word, again. The word he had not said since that night, the word he never really understood until that night when, in a delft-blue hotel room, home had come to him.

Jake tried to choke off his words, but failed. "Okay," escaped his throat.

Nina pulled her hands out of his pockets and grabbed one of Jake's hands. She yanked him along the sidewalk. Jake stumbled after her, eyes closed tightly, lids walling back tears. They continued until someone crashed into Jake, or maybe it was Jake who did the crashing. As Jake struggled to hold his balance, he opened his eyes to catch a momentary glimpse of the impediment. She turned away just as his eyes focused, then ran off with red curls bouncing out from under a baseball cap. Dressed in a jogging suit, she loped off around the corner without regard for Jake's state of paralyzed shock.

"Sorry. Forget it." Ignoring her protests, Jake yanked his hand from Nina's grasp and ran after the red-haired jogger, losing his drinking partner in the crowd.

Jake kept running, sure that when he pulled off the baseball cap a river of red hair would spill from it like a setting sun. The alcohol in his blood screamed to his lungs and heart. His breath came ragged, but still he ran, block after block, into the grave-dark night. She stopped at a corner and bent to tie her shoelace. Seeing his prey within reach, he gave the last of his strength to his pursuit. She did not hear him behind her even though Jake was sure his gasping lungs should have been audible for at least a block.

Jake grabbed the brim of her hat and pulled it off. No sunset spread from her glowing red pate. The runner slapped her hand to her head in a reflexive move meant to catch the hat. Jake fell to his knees, grabbed her, and spun her around. A muffled scream escaped Jake's throat and his forehead came to rest on his knees as the red-haired boy ran away, sobbing. Breathing heavily, Jake crawled over to sit on the curb.

When he could stand, he felt his back pocket. The flask was still there. He moved into a shadow and let a sip of the tequila slide past his parched lips, down his burning throat. The world whirled, so he walked to prove he could. He had no idea where he was, but he kept putting one foot before another, anger building in his chest like the fire in his belly.

A gaggle of pre-Mardi Gras revelers, dressed in purple, green, and gold costumes of pirates and princesses, pranced down the street, sheltered from street-light glare by elaborate umbrellas twirling above their heads. They whooped and sang in an accompaniment for their mini-parade. One of the masked dancers bowed and tossed Jake a string of purple beads. The row of tiny, glistening spheres landed, draped over Jake's foot. He kicked the string away, sending it snaking over the curb, clattering into the gutter.

"It's all an illusion," Jake groaned to the darkness, anger continuing to build. He slipped into a dark doorway for a swig from the glittering flask, drained it, and sent it clattering after the beads. He leaned his forehead against the cool glass of the door to a shop filled with masks. More Mardi Gras masks. More illusions.

"She was only illusion—just another illusion." His hand clasped the prism that hung around his neck, hidden beneath his shirt. "Rachel was real. I should have held onto what was real, solid."

Letting go of Rachel's crystal, he formed his hands into knots of anger, and with his eyes trained on the Mardi Gras masks, he pounded his fists against the window. Jake gasped as a storm of shards blew against his face, hailed down on his head, stinging and cutting him. With bleeding hands, he swept the shards from his hair. They jangled to the ground around his feet and glistened like a freshly fallen layer of snow reflecting the light of a full moon. It took all the strength Jake had left to resist entering the shop to demolish every mask along with the secrets that hid behind them. Instead, with a red-stained hand, Jake caressed his shirt, over the spot where his own secret hid.

* * *

Jake staggered through the hotel lobby, his face and hands filthy with blood, his shirt a canvas splattered with red. Other guests surreptitiously whispered to each other, wide-eyed. They stepped aside as he entered the elevator, letting him ride to his floor alone. As Jake burst out of the lift, his toe caught on the gap between the elevator and hotel floor, sending him careening down the hallway toward his room, painting scarlet streaks on the walls as he passed, trying to regain his balance with hands dripping blood.

He stood before his door, trembling, like a tree battered by storm winds. Jake fumbled as he tried to slip his key into the door lock. It fell. He picked it up and dropped it again. "Fuck!"

What is that smell? A strange, metallic smell. It gagged him, sending a shiver along his body. He recognized the smell, but could not remember from where.

The lock clicked.

He turned the knob and pushed the door open into his room. He stood, just inside, with his hand on the doorframe. The lights were on. Jake held his breath when he saw his dresser drawers hanging open. Empty. Slamming the door after himself, he rushed over to the closet and looked in. Empty. Where were his things? What was that gut-retching smell? Then it came to him— where he had encountered that stench before.

"Rachel," he moaned into the dark, empty closet.

Trembling, he turned to face the other side of his room.

A small form huddled under the bedcovers. Who could it be? Small. A woman? Not moving. His stomach lurched. Jake stepped forward and pinched a corner of the spread, slowly pulled it back, and screamed.

"Wake up! I know if I scream, I can wake up. Please—wake me up!"

Frozen, Jake was forced to accept that the scene before him was not part of a dreamscape, that the little curly-haired girl who had once slipped her tiny, warm hands into his pockets was lying on his bed—her eyes and mouth gaping—her wrists and ankles tied to the bed posts—naked except for a peek-a-boo veil of red streaks and splatters on her flesh—her throat cut, ear to ear—the bedclothes flooded by a hurricane of blood.

Jake sucked in a gasp of oxygen and clung to consciousness, but the room began to fade to black. Where were his things? Staggering, he double-checked his drawers. Empty! The bathroom. Empty! His car keys. Gone!

"Fingerprints," he stammered. He grabbed a towel and began to polish the dresser top.

Stupid! This is your room. Your prints are everywhere. Wheezing like an asthmatic, he escaped the nightmare in his room and raced down the emergency stairs. He turned the corner to the first floor landing and tumbled down the last few stairs. Lying crumpled at the bottom of the stairs, he said, "Camille." There was no one else to turn to, nowhere else to go. And most of all, there were never any whispers when Camille was around.

* * *

Bourbon Street was filled with drunken dancers. One of them bumped into Jake. The inebriated man, ready to start a fight, had beer foam slathered across his moustache and beard, giving him a rabid-dog appearance. He edged closer, a fist raised, then backed away from Jake's hysterical eyes and blood-etched face.

Jake continued on his single-minded trip, a nightmare walking among the wide-awake. He staggered to the black iron gate that separated the Bete Noir from the world of the wide-awake, pulled it open, and threw himself into the vortex where all bad dreams belong.

Chapter 40

*L*IKE A RABBIT, recently engorged by a snake, Jake made his way along the serpentine alley that seemed to undulate as he passed, to waver as his reflection had on the rippling water that first day in the swamp. He knew he should be afraid, but he was not. He was numb. The alcohol had a way of making just about anything palatable. With fingers brushing the sides of the alley, the walls slippery with mildew now turned to slime by heavy moisture hanging in the stagnant air, he skated and slid his way along the narrow, dark passage until he found the final door. The door to Camille's Mardi Gras party. His knock brought an instant response from the other side.

"We are honored." Simone bowed and swung the door wide. Jake passed through the final barrier. The party was in full frenzy. Masks spun on faces unrecognizable behind walls of feathers and satin and sequins. Some, leather. Some black. Some with horns.

Jake felt naked.

His Main Street Jake face was open to the full view of secret eyes as they laughed and danced before him. For the first time in many years, Jake was a virgin, inexperienced, tender, afraid of what would happen next.

There he was, Camille Patin, dressed in a gown of the sheerest of fabrics, green purple gold. Threads of gold, woven through green and purple gossamer. Even though he was masked, Jake recognized him instantly. Camille's golden hair was no longer bound, but flowed freely, mimicking the fluid movements of the long, gold earrings that dangled from his ears. As Camille turned and danced, the silken fabric of his costume spun around his graceful form.

Jake felt drawn toward the crowd, drawn toward Camille's circle. It was their smiles—their thoughts. "Jake, we want you just the way you are. We love you. There's no more need to search—this is all there is—this is all there is."

Camille took Jake's hand and led him to the center of the whirling, mind-numbing colors. Without benefit of music, the dancers gyrated with only the rhythmic stomping of their feet to mark the beat.

"Jake, you've finally come to me," Camille purred. "You finally chose flesh." He offered Jake a silver goblet filled with something red. Though he knew he did not need more, Jake let Camille hold the sparkling vessel to his lips. He drank it all with choking gulps, allowing some to run out of the corners of his mouth. Camille wiped Jake's face with his bare hand, then licked the red off his sticky fingers.

As the congested courtyard spun with the freakish kaleidoscope of dancers, Jake's reeling mind took up the wordless chant of the crowd, "Stop searching—this is all there is—just now—that's all." Giving up the search was such a relief. A grand liberation.

Camille lifted a long strand of large, glowing, scarlet beads from his neck. Jake bowed his head so Camille could slip the glistening spheres around his neck. The crimson, serpentine strand, warm from the heat of Camille's flesh, molded itself to fit Jake's form, its color blending with the blood on Jake's clothes.

"Jaaaaaaaaaaaaaaake." Removing his mask, exposing his heavily made-up face, Camille drew closer and placed a gentle kiss on Jake's defeated lips.

Jake felt his flesh respond.

He was at first relieved.

Camille slowly replaced the gentle touch of his scarlet lips with the cold touch of his alabaster teeth, the tomb-cold touch of his death-cold teeth. Camille slipped his arms around Jake's shoulders, around his shivering, forlorn body, and Jake leaned into the vacillating abyss, his arms clinging to his anchor in the empty sea, his buoy, the only object in the churning brine capable of keeping him from sinking beneath the green lace curtain that keeps the secret things below the water hidden from the eyes of the uninitiated.

Camille was Jake's only hold on reality—any reality.

Jake's heart thumped in time with the beating feet of the reeling dancers. His blood raced after his heart.

Camille drew Jake out of the circle, away from the churning crowd. He followed without argument.

Too tired to fight the pull any longer. Too tired to care any longer.

Sick of the fight.

Too tired to fight any more.

Any arms to hold him safe—any.

As they were about to leave the garden through the black door that led to Camille's living quarters, a spell of vertigo caused Jake to swoon in his captor's arms. Jake's head fell back, and he looked up into the sky, up into the star filled night. A lone, falling star left a graceful tail of furtive fireflies scattered across the velvet-black, dead night, the night with a clear sky filled with blinking eyes like the green and golden eyes that kept silent watch during his night with Sara.

Far beneath galaxies of astral fireflies, Jake felt himself begin to slip beneath the green lace. When his gaze returned earth-ward and caught the lascivious look in Camille's eyes, Jake's Main Street body wretched with disgust. In a burst of passion, he pulled away from Camille like a drowning man with arms hys-terically flailing, fighting for survival, fighting the very person who had come to save him. The shuffling rhythm of the dancing feet accelerated.

Instantly, Camille knew the game was over. He crooned to Jake in a low, calm voice.

"Jake, why did you have to ruin it? We would have been so good together."

"No, this isn't right. It's not supposed to work this way!"

"What way?" Camille fluttered his eyelashes in mock inno-cence. "I don't understand. What way?"

"You know what I mean!"

Camille laughed and tore the front of his dank, flaccid gown open.

"You mean this?" He gracefully moved his unveiled, mascu-line torso back and forth in a languorous, sensual dance. "You mean this, Jake? You do not understand. This is all there is. The form does not matter.

Jake! Flesh is flesh! Form does not matter. It is the function that counts. This is not art. It is all the same. Flesh is flesh! That is all there is. Enjoy it while you have it! Taste it! Bite it! Love it! It is all there is. Jake, I have wanted you for so very long—for eons. It worked before."

"Worked before?" Jake shook his head in an effort to wake from the fog of lust and vodka and music and the swollen, star filled night. He shoved Camille back against the noxious wall, slamming his head against the bricks with a cracking sound. Camille groaned and examined the back of his head with trembling fingers.

Camille's seductive leer flashed into a grimace of hatred.

"You stupid man. You very stupid, stupid man. You fucked it up now. Flesh is all there is. You hurt my flesh you fucking bastard! You stupid bastard. You are so stupid.

All along, you thought it was Claude who wanted your flesh, you stupid bastard. It was I all the time, not Claude! Why couldn't you just go with the program? You stupid, stupid bastard. It is all over now. You fucked it up—again."

Camille, holding his throbbing head with both his hands, his face a mask of pain, said, "Le coquin qui vole aun autre, le diable en ris." Then he screamed to Simone, "Show him the trophy!"

Simone smiled and bowed with a flourish. Camille dipped a finger in a nearby ashtray, then drew an inverted cross on Simone's upturned forehead. Simone blessed himself, then out of his mouth, he removed what at first appeared to be a small, white wafer of some sort. He handed the mysterious square to Jake who squinted through the night to examine what turned out to be half of a broken credit card emblazoned with the name, Rachel Fo . . . the rest of the name, truncated by some frigid, mysterious force, the force of the cold October night when Professor Higgins used the card to attempt a surreptitious entry into the Devereux house.

Jake looked up into Camille's face, the face once adorned with sapphire eyes and shrouded with raven-black hair and accompanied by musical laughter.

"Madeleine."

Camille laughed at Jake's horror.

"Finally, you said something intelligent. Yes. Madeleine—Perry—Lucinda—Francis—whatever. It doesn't matter," leaning toward Jake until his lips gently brushed his ear, "flesh is flesh." He turned and growled to his henchmen, "Simone, take care of this piss ant!"

Simone bowed, reached over to a nearby banquet table and chose a knife that was swimming in a mire of Crawfish Etouffee. He licked the residue off the knife and handed it to his mentor. Without acknowledging Jake's horror, Camille reached over to Simone who had fallen to his knees and assumed the posture of a penitent waiting for communion, waiting for forgiveness.

Camille placed two fingers into Simone's open mouth and pulled out the unresisting tongue. With the glistening knife blade, he cut a lengthwise slash along the willing sacrifice, along Simone's willing tongue. Blood ran down the length of the knife-edge until it spilled over onto Camille's fingers. One at a time, Camille put each finger into his mouth and sucked them clean.

"You know, Jake, I'm still a thief," said Camille. "I stole from you once, no twice. I can steal from you, again. I can do it any time I want. Remember that, Jake! Remember how it felt!"

Like that time in Rosselli's office, in New York, Jake felt the massive fingers wrapping around his chest, squeezing him so tightly he could not breathe.

Simone closed his mouth and bowed his head, still playing the role of the supplicant, finally forgiven, one with his maker. Then, unlike the devote' he mocked, he began to spit out the blood that filled his mouth, the blood of his maker, in staccato blasts against the black mildew canvas that nature had stretched across the brick wall. Within seconds, the scarlet splatters mutated and took form, the form of a raptor in flight. When the picture was complete, the Simone form dropped to the floor like an empty body bag thrown aside by a careless undertaker.

Moments after the Simone form slithered to the floor, a wet, scarlet form wiggled out of his mouth, screaming with the pain of birth. The newly born bird shook like a wet dog and rose from the fallen Simone form. It fluttered with the spasmodic wings of a rabid bat. The frantic, red shadow attacked Jake's paralyzed form. It pecked at Jake's Main Street eyes, and its hysterical wings slapped against his face until he was awake enough to stagger to the exit, to tumble down the dew-filled alley, to make his way into the scarlet-green-gold-purple street with shrieking laughter and frantic wings chasing after him. Jake stumbled onto the ravenous street and fell into the arms of the wild-eyed, hairy man.

Part Three

Legion

Chapter 41

HE BLACKNESS WAS OVERWHELMING, RAVENOUS. Afraid the void would suck away his soul without bothering to taste its sweetness, Jake slammed his lids over his eyes and clenched them, creating flashes of light and color over his pupils. The pathetic bursts of color dancing across Jake's lids failed to provide enough light to search out the recesses of his desolate inner world, failed to reassure him his soul was still where it belonged. His arms folded over his heart and his knees pulled up to his chest, Jake's bone-weary form lay shivering in the heat, cradled by a heap of rags that reeked of oil and gasoline.

The universe rocked back and forth, lulling Jake into a semi consciousness. His heart beat in unison with the rhythmic slosh-ing-slapping sounds that rushed repeatedly against the edges of his world. His breaths came ragged and uneven as he wished he could remember how to pray.

The muffled voices of two men echoed over to Jake. Indiscernible dialogue drifted back and forth between French and English like the ebb and flow of waves washing the shore. Jake strained to catch the meaning of the garbled discourse. He strained to catch a glimmer of his fate. A popping followed by the sound of air hissing out of an aluminum can prefaced one full sentence in English.

"Man, I wish this was a J.D."

"Chaoui." Jake pulled himself into a tighter ball and allowed himself to float off into a deep, dreamless sleep.

* * *

A small door creaked open, allowing a square of searing light to blast into the darkness. Arms reached in through the open portal and stretched over to Jake. He backed away, too weak to fight. He whimpered as the wild-eyed, hairy man grabbed his wrists and pulled him out into the cauterizing sunlight and machine-whirring sounds. Jake fought against consciousness, fought against the knowledge as the hairy man lifted him off the deck of the small, weathered, wooden boat and carried him along a narrow plank onto a rocky, shoreline.

"Jake! Wake up! It's Chaoui here." Jake felt slaps on his face but refused to open his eyes, refused to allow light to burn images on his retinas.

"Keeyaw, he's still doped up," Chaoui said. "Let's haul ass."

Still cradling Jake in his arms, the hairy man followed Chaoui along a dusty, unpaved road that wove among dilapidated, metal buildings. Jake covered his eyes with his hand to protect himself from the agonizing sunlight that burned through his lids. A constant wind moaned around and through the buildings, whipping grains of sand into the air. The rabid grains stung Jake's face like a swarm of angry bees intent on rousing him from his drug, or fear-induced stupor. Jake allowed his lids to flutter long enough to let a few jumbled, stop-action images reach his brain.

Directly ahead, whirled a firestorm of dust. It spun in place like a confused tornado, unable to decide in which direction to carry out its mission of arbitrary destruction. The rag-tag procession continued in a collision course with the storm. When they reached the whirlwind, Chaoui planted the tip of his walking stick into the limestone dust and stood motionless as if waiting for the tempest to acknowledge his presence.

Jake spotted movement in the center of the tornado. Out of the cloud of flailing dust and sand, lumbered a form hidden inside the sort of suit Jake remembered seeing bounding across the surface of the moon. Ignoring Jake's efforts to blink the image away, the hulking form waddled closer, forcing itself into Jake's reality.

The square of glass on the front of the headpiece flashed reflections of the relentless sun at Jake as the shroud of dust dissipated and flittered to the ground. Leaning over, the spaceman examined Jake.

"Sure don't look like much, huh?" Chaoui said.

The space traveler reached a heavy gloved hand to his head and pulled the hood off his regalia. The unveiling revealed a face with finely chiseled, deeply tanned features accentuated by the grime that filled every crease. Black eyes flashed with raptor-like sharpness and intelligence. Blue-black, curly hair was pressed back by a red and white kerchief tied around the space walker's head, giving him the look of a pirate recently dragged from the past by the supernatural storm.

"You found us a place to hide, yeah?" Chaoui asked.

After slapping dust from his intricately patterned, Three Musketeers beard, the pirate turned and pointed to a red-and-white, iron boat that hung low in a finger of muddy, green-brown water. "Wave Dancer" was boldly painted across the prow of the boat. Chaoui nodded approval and the pirate flopped his hood back over his head and returned to his work. Within seconds, the firestorm reconstituted itself and surrounded him in a hail of whirling grains of sand.

Jake gave up the battle with his heavy lids and closed his eyes. Letting the sound of hammering, hissing, and machine-hummings lull him, he fell back to sleep, dreaming a stop-action video of a pirate in a space suit.

* * *

Jake woke covered with sweat. He opened his eyes and scanned the small, grey, iron room that surrounded him like a prison cell. Muted rays creeping in through the small, round window told him the sunlight was waning. He sat up on the narrow cot that supported his feeble body. It took a few minutes for the room to stop spinning. When the world finally settled, Jake stood and gingerly walked to the window. Squinting through grime, he could see he had not been taken far from the spot where the tornado had whirled. Turning his back on the worn, glass eye, Jake inspected his surroundings. Besides the cot, only a table and a single chair furnished the room. Jake lowered his creaking body onto the chair and yanked open the drawer that hung under the metal table.

When a screwdriver clattered toward him, Jake jerked back, startled. Underneath scraps of paper were a few girlie maga-zines. He thumbed through one of them. Repulsed by the lurid photographs, he shoved the rest of the publications aside and dis-covered a pair of wire-framed sunglasses. One of the lenses was cracked. Jake straightened out the bent wing on one side of the frame and fitted the heavily scratched lenses over his face.

"Guaranteed not to break," Jake whispered as he headed toward the door. He pushed on the door. It was not locked. He sighed in relief and stepped out onto the deck. The red and white paint told Jake he was on the Wave Dancer. A pitiless wind inundated him with the odor of rotten fish, and a wave of nausea washed over him. He grasped the metal rail that surrounded the boat, lowered himself to the deck, and sat facing the water, his legs dangling over the side of the boat.

Resting his forehead against the white rail, Jake studied the brackish water that lay in wait beneath him, motionless, so near his suspended feet. Every now and then, movement from beneath would disturb the placid, brown surface, causing concentric circles to form. Tiny insects swam across the opaque veneer, leaving trails like the wakes of Lilliputian motor boats. Some etched squiggly patterns like waltzing mice dancing crazy patterns across dirty ice. A curious, lime-green dragonfly flitted before Jake's face, drawing his attention to the foreign landscape that loomed on the other side of the water.

A jumble of metal buildings teetered at the edge of a forest of black, obelisk-like poles that reached hundreds of feet into the air. The poles were topped by sun-yellow, pointed caps. Among the black and yellow monoliths, towering, metal cranes took refuge. The machines stood mute, motionless, like the skeletons of prehistoric monsters caught in a nuclear blast so sudden it whipped the flesh from their bones with such speed that the astonished behemoths had forgotten to fall, leaving them doomed to remain forever suspended in confused agony. A chill fell over Jake. He shook it off like a wet dog.

A rhythmic tapping on the metal deck warned Jake of Chaoui's approach. He looked up to see Chaoui standing over him, his walking stick in one hand and two blue-speckled enamel cups hooked together by one long finger of the other.

"Where the fuck am I, Mars?"

"No. You in the Port of Iberia."

Chaoui groaned as he sat down next to Jake then handed him a cup of black coffee.

"So?" Jake chugged the coffee as he waited for Chaoui to answer.

"So, you must be hungry by now, yeah?"

"Chaoui. Cut the shit."

"What you mean?"

"Don't play dumb. I know better. Why am I here? How did I get here? What the hell is this all about?"

Chaoui slipped an arm around Jake. Jake stiffened and pushed Chaoui away.

"I want answers, now!" Embarrassed by his lack of control, Jake paused, then continued, his voice barely above a whisper. "Please—I'm lost. You have to tell me."

"Jake, don't push it. Sometimes you push and you end up where you're not supposed to be. You gotta learn to follow. You gotta get rid of that hard head of yours and let things happen when they're supposed to."

"Follow what? Let what happen?" Jake searched Chaoui's eyes for an unspoken answer, but saw in the glistening, black orbs only his own reflection, alone in a hail of colored specks. Overcome by another wave of vertigo, Jake closed his eyes to the kaleidoscope vision and clung to the rail for support.

"Man, you need some food. You didn't eat in two days, at least."

"No. I think I ate yesterday."

"Awwww, you were passed out in the bottom of Joey's boat yesterday."

"But—"

"But nothing. We at least a hundred miles from New Orleans. It took two days to get here. There's locks and bridges. And we had to stop a couple a times to put gas."

"We?"

"Yeah, me and Joey."

"Who?"

"You know, that fella that's been looking out for you in New Orleans."

"You mean the scary looking guy who never stops smoking?"

"Shhh. Don't talk about that. It gets him pissed off."

"What? That he's scary looking?"

"No. About that smoking thing. He's been trying to quit every day, but he can't. C'mon, let's go see what they got for supper. Joey's been cooking up something in the galley for hours."

Jake pulled his feet up away from the water and crouched on all fours until he felt steady enough to stand. He grabbed the handrail and staggered along behind Chaoui.

* * *

The galley was so poorly lit that Jake had to remove his sunglasses to find his way through a maze of pots and pans hanging from the ceiling. Joey, looking not nearly as wild-eyed as Jake remembered, rested his flat belly against a battered stove as he stirred the contents of a black iron pot. Steam swirled around him, blending with the cigarette smoke that spewed from his nostrils. A long, crooked snake of grey ash protruded from the cigarette that dangled from the corner of Joey's mouth, the cigarette's single, red eye, blinking with each draw. When it became too long to support its own weight, the ash broke free and dove into the black pot. Joey, unconcerned, kept stirring and puffing.

"How's it coming?" Chaoui leaned over the pot of bubbling whatever. Joey did not answer. Chaoui motioned to a rickety, wooden table and said, "Jake, have a seat. Man, you're gonna love this stuff."

Joey cranked a knob, shutting off the gas that had glowed blue underneath the iron pot. Then he lifted the pot from the stove and carried it over to the table, placing it down with a splat. After stirring the contents of the pot one more time, he lifted a heaping scoopful out and splashed it down on Jake's plate. A grain of rice leapt out of the multicolored mass and stuck to Jake's face. Wiping the errant grain from his cheek, Jake examined the offering on his plate. It was rice mixed with some sort of meat and colored bits of something else. Before he dared taste the mysterious conglomeration, Jake slipped his sunglasses back over his eyes, then ate in the sympathetic cloak of darkness. Then with a full belly, he returned to his grey cell and tumbled onto the bed.

* * *

"Jake. Wake up." Chaoui shook Jake until his eyes flicked open. "How you feeling, buddy?"

"Rough."

243

"You got to get up, partner. Them boys will be coming for you pretty soon."

"Boys?"

"Yeah. Delta and Tommy and Rene. You know, them guys from Alligator Landing."

"What do you mean, coming for me?" Panic chilled Jake's voice.

"They're gonna take you back to Henderson, to hide you."

"Hide me?"

"Yeah, man. You know."

A blood splattered vision of Nina flashed its way into Jake's consciousness. He shivered and shook it off.

"You mean—from the police?"

"No. Those guys couldn't find you if you had a shirt with your name on it. We took a crazy trip away from where we going so they would lose us. Anyway, they probably not even looking in Henderson. And they couldn't follow the back way we took you anyway. If you stay by the basin, you'll be alright."

"Then who—?"

"C'mon, get up. You gotta wake up and get rolling."

"What about you? Aren't you coming with me?"

"No. I got to bring Joey's boat back to Henderson cause he's gonna be sticking with you. I'll meet up with y'all later."

* * *

After two cups of coffee and a plate of leftovers, Jake stood alone at the bottom of a cement ramp that led from the water up to ground level. Lapping the shore, along with the ugly water, were hundreds of dead fish that floated on their sides, their silver skin refusing to cast reflections in the brilliant noontime sun. Above Jake, loomed a heap of immense chunks of cement. The smell of the rotting fish drove Jake up the ramp. After huffing up the incline, he sat on the heap of amorphous chunks, wondering what kind of structure had been torn down, only to become a jumbled monument lying crushed at the edge of a finger of murky water

Above the constant murmur of machines and compressors, came the atonal screeching and yowling of a catfight. The wail of each combatant trailed off into wobbling, pseudo-verbal vociferations. Their back and forth vocalizations rang in the air like the chantings of two sorcerers throwing curses at each other in a battle for supernatural supremacy. The clamor echoed off metal buildings and ricocheted in all directions, magnifying the sound, obscuring its source.

Jake searched but found no hint of its location. The only signs of conflict were scattered tornadoes whipped up by more heavily cloaked, anonymous men using explosions of sand to blast rust or whatever off heaps of odd metal artifacts.

Overhead, helicopters flailed the air. Dragonflies of electric blue and neon green danced around Jake, reflecting images in reverse perspective to their giant, metal brothers hovering overhead. Feeling like part of a team of archaeologists searching for clues to understanding the decayed remnants of a lost civilization, Jake wandered off into the sun-bleached, limestone-stung ruins.

Every tread of his feet kicked up a fine dust, revealing a litter of crushed paper cups, seashells, and corroded metal fragments of antiquated machinery. Who were those people who populated this place before the plague, or whatever, drove them into oblivion? Like the earthling settlers in the *Martian Chronicles*, Jake prayed for a vision of the magical, once-upon-a-time inhabitants of this barren, hostile place. Would they have answers for him?

Jake passed miles of pipes—green—rusted. Stacks of oxidized valves and tanks littered the bone yards. Clouds of other searchers, other archaeologists, blew in the wind as they blasted rust from the ancient ruins. Up on a metal, table-like structure, three or four stories high, a lone vision blasted the unclean surface, his identity obliterated by the obligatory spacesuit that protected him from the harsh, Mars-like environment. All was lulled by the constant hum of machinery and the hiss of rubber snakes that exuded a venom of blasting sand.

Then, Jake saw it, the metal structure, the one that looked so soft, so gentle, lying on its side, at least one-hundred feet long and fifty feet wide at its base, its surface, covered with a whitish layer of something that looked fur-like. Jake was drawn to it. He had no choice. He had to discover it.

Stumbling over chunks of cement with reinforcement rods protruding from their sides like Roman spears, Jake staggered to the alabaster monument lying on its side, defeated. The whitish covering that looked so soft, so gentle from afar, was actually the petrified bodies of hordes of undersea creatures, mollusks, barnacles, creatures that had once lived under the sea surface, protected by the green lace curtain. Unsuspecting sea creatures, lured by the promise of sanctuary, of home, carefully fitted their lives around the deceitful, metal structure. Were they frightened when the earthlings yanked their home from water, only to let their bodies bake in the yellow sun? Jake's mind reeled with the pain he felt emanating from their phantom cries as he used his thumb to crumble sharp-edged, petrified skeletons from the metal structure, from their once-upon-a-time home.

"You picked the wrong side," Jake mumbled to the skeletons. "You picked the wrong side." As Jake turned to rush away, brambles ripped at his legs, tore his flesh through his jeans, as if his flesh was exposed, uncovered, underneath the searing sun.

Trying to run as fast as his weakened limbs would carry him, Jake stumbled away from the omen. Staggering and leaping, he tumbled over something too wide to avoid and landed face down, giving birth to a grey cloud of dust. Trembling, he rolled over the limestone ground to examine whatever it was that had interrupted his escape. There it was, a snaking row of red bricks, lying tumbled on the ground. A wall that once was. "And the walls came tumbling down." As he beat the limestone dust from his clothes, Jake whispered the sacred words, not knowing why.

* * *

Jake found himself standing at the end of another finger of brackish, offal-tainted water. The finger of water, created by man, was held in place by casings of metal and wood that shored up the edges of the land. Jake looked straight down into the murky water. Nothing but the etchings of surface insects revealed themselves to him.

A thin shadow sidled up to him and Jake heard Chaoui say, "You keep looking down and you can't see where you're going. You gotta face the light sooner or later. C'mon Jake, do it. Let in the light."

Slowly, afraid of the sun's power, Jake did as ordered. There, upon the brackish, brown water, danced legions of sequins that appeared to have been scattered by giants in the sky. Sequins that flickered like immense fireflies, like the twinkling lights that hid under the papier-mâché' alligator's boat in New Orleans. Sequins that had found the courage to rise above the green lace curtain and dance in the sun. Jake held his breath, enthralled by the brilliant, animated beauty, each bit of light, a numinous flicker of intelligence.

* * *

"Jake," Chaoui whispered, "Them boys are here. You ready to go?"

"Yes." Jake's voice cracked through his parched throat.

Jake followed Chaoui's faltering steps over to a red pick-up truck. Sitting in the bed of the truck were two earthlings, separated by a metal tank with a pump protruding from the top. One was wearing a *Rocky the Flying Squirrel*, brown leather hood with earflaps and a pair of yellow goggles. The other wore a backward baseball cap and a sweatshirt with cut-off sleeves. Both men were tanned dark by long hours under the pitiless sun. Tommy, the dimple-cheeked bartender from Alligator Landing, leapt from the truck then vigorously shook hands with Chaoui. The other followed.

Chaoui pulled the leather cap and yellow goggles from the second man, revealing an incongruous, college boy face. Reverently, he pulled the leather cap over Jake's head and slid the yellow goggles over his eyes. "Now you look like you just spent the last fourteen days off-shore. Except for that vanilla ice cream skin."

They laughed and lifted Jake into the bed of the red truck. Tommy tossed Jake the sleeveless sweatshirt and entered the pick-up, taking a place next to Delta. The man sitting next to Jake tied a blue and white handkerchief around his head, donned dark glasses, and offered his hand to Jake. "I'm Rene. Pleased to meet you."

Jake took his hand. Rene's smile reached Jake through the barrier of yellow lenses.

Jake pulled the sweatshirt over his three-day-worn, *I Love New York* tee shirt as Joey roared past in a black jeep.

"Chaoui," Jake leaned over the side of the pick-up, grabbed Chaoui's shirt, and whispered, "I don't know how to follow. I don't know how to let things happen."

"Yeah, sure you do," Chaoui whispered back. "You found your way to Alligator Landing, eh?"

A grim smile twisted Jake's mouth. He rested his battered frame against the back of the red truck just as the sound of the revving motor drowned out the hissing, humming Martian sounds. As they rumbled over the ditch-riddled road, Rene reached into a small cooler and handed Jake a can of beer.

Chaoui stood shadowed by the hundred-foot-tall, metallic, prehistoric harbingers of doom, his arms outstretched, one hand gripping the top of his walking stick and the other waving good-bye, his black, stringy hair draping over his shoulders like Spanish moss. Chaoui's image wavered in the heat then gently faded as the red truck turned onto another well-worn road that ran between two thickly planted fields of neglected sugar cane. The wind whispered through the green fronds that looked exactly like the ones a priest would hand Jake every Palm Sunday. The green palms undulated like the ocean—they waved at Jake from both sides of the road as if they were clutched in the hands of a multitude of invisible believers, standing shoulder to shoulder, many rows deep, straining to catch a glimpse of a messiah. A shrill chorus of thousands of trilling cicadas rose and fell like the quavering ululation of a hoard of Arab women celebrating the heroism of victorious warriors, or perhaps . . . mourning their passing.

And Jake knew he was meant to be in Louisiana.

Chapter 42

Y THE TIME THE RED PICKUP SCRAMBLED over the top of the levee, Jake was battered and bruised. Each rock and pebble trampled under the thick-treaded tires sent a shock wave through every muscle in his body. When the truck careened to a stop next to the Alligator Landing restaurant, Jake slid his legs over the side of the truck and lowered himself to the ground. Walking like Frankenstein, Jake lurched up the steps to the restaurant porch. He almost sat on a wind-tossed, wooden rocker that ticked back and forth over the uneven floorboards, but instead, he chose a stationary perch and settled down on the wooden bench next to a stack of firewood. Alongside the rocker was an old-fashioned, wooden cradle. A hand-knitted blanket had been folded and tucked into the bottom of the tiny bed.

When Jake reached out and gently rocked the cradle, a giant roach ran out from underneath. Angry the insect had tainted the wholesome picture, Jake stomped the bug, leaving behind a sticky mess. He turned away, disgusted. Like a siren, a wave of screaming cicadas caught Jake's attention. He looked up and peered through a row of crawfish traps that hung from the porch roof. They floated in the breeze like diabolical, Chinese kites. Just on the other side of the dock, a mobile island of ducks swam a zigzag pattern. Following a few yards behind was a lone, black duck. Its head bobbed as it swam furiously, trying to keep up with the rest of the pack. They disappeared around the other side of a long finger of land that protected the small bay.

A smile flickered across Jake's lips. He closed his eyes and tried to memorize the picture, but it dissolved on his eyelids as a faint, crackling noise teased his ears.

Jake looked down toward the source of the snapping and found the floor of the porch overrun with activity. A squad of huge, shiny, black ants was tearing the crushed roach to pieces. It was already half gone, the shell that had once protected it, torn away, exposing the creature within. Jake gasped and a small moan of disgust escaped his lips.

The screen door of the restaurant slammed. Jake whipped his head around to see who was approaching. Toward him marched the woman who had served him beer at the party a few days ago. She was dressed in a royal-blue dress with an intricate tatted lace collar. This day, her stern lips wore a soft expression. In her arms nestled a tiny baby. She deftly stepped between Jake and the woodpile to lay the child in the cradle. Then, she touched its face with one finger, caressing its rosy cheek. The baby's turquoise-blue eyes glowed up at her. Grinning, the child waved its arms and kicked its legs as it cooed with excitement.

"Hey, remember me?" Her blue eyes glistened at Jake as she spoke. "I'm Delta's mama, Marie." Marie looked down at the child. "Cher, 'tit be be. That girl is fine, fine, fine. Don't she look beautiful just laying there in her baptism gown?" Marie looked up at Jake, her eyes exploding with pride.

Jake could not help grinning back at her. Marie kissed the baby and stepped back as if to admire the child from afar, from a different perspective, as one would a fine painting. Suddenly, her smile of adoration dissipated when she pursed her lips.

Marie reached down to the floor next to the rocker and grabbed a fly swatter. Jake flinched when she whipped the swatter through the air, killing a fly that dared wander too close to the cradle. Jake, remembering the half-eaten roach, looked down to where he had squashed it, next to the cradle. It was gone . . . totally. In its place, was scattered the legion of black ants. Looking dead, or at least drugged, they lay on the wooden floor, motionless. Jake shivered.

"Bugs. I hate them. No purpose for them."

"Mais, yes," Marie said. "Everybody and everything has a purpose. Sometimes they just don't know it."

"Marie." Jake waited for a response that did not come. However, he continued because he knew she was listening. "Do you have a purpose?"

"Mais, yeah!"

"What is it?"

Marie rocked for a while before she answered. "I guess it's the same as the rest of us." She leaned over the cradle, towards Jake, and whispered, "I'm here to help protect the secret."

"What secret?"

"You know. The one out there." With a sweeping arm motion, she gestured toward the water. "That's why we're all here."

"All?" Jake asked, "The whole world?"

"No." Marie began to show signs of frustration. "Us Cajuns."

"I thought you were here because you got kicked out of some-place in Canada."

"I guess you can look at it like that. Most folks do; but I'm a renegade." She lowered her voice. "I say we got called. We got called cause we were special. We believed in magic. And all that other stuff was like when a blacksmith hammers iron to make it stronger. We had to be strong enough to fight to keep the magic safe." Marie leaned over to Jake again. "You see, magic things have to be watched over or outsiders will pick them apart like bad boys that pull the wings off butterflies. That's why we stay here. We're tied to the land...to the magic. And if one of us tries to leave, they get called back. I told my son Jimmy that. He didn't want to listen to his mama, so he ran off to California like that was some kinda big deal. I told him, Jimmy, it's just like you see on the TV about them people who move ten million miles from home and when they get there, they leave the door open, and their cat sneaks out! Then, a couple years later, that cat turns up right back where it started. I told him, Jimmy, you gonna leave here, and your soul will come crawling back just like one of them cats, and then you're gonna have to come back looking for it. Well, see?" She gestured toward the baby. "Now he's back with his wife and baby. And she's gonna believe in magic too." Marie grinned at Jake.

Sara. Marie knew more about his situation than he did—that they all knew more. Did he dare ask her about Sara—about himself?

Marie, why am *I* here?"

Marie leaned down and fussed with the baby's gown.

"Marie, I know you know. Tell me, please."

"Jake, you're not ready for that."

"Look at that." Marie stomped a foot. "That's Retarded Chuck. Look at that. He belongs under the water. What's he doing out here?"

Across the lot, swaggering away from the water, toward the levee, was a fifteen-foot-long, green-black alligator. Standing high, perched over scaled legs, his body snaking with every step he took.

"Delta!" Marie yelled. "Mais, where's them damn Catahoulas when you need them?"

A moment later, the screen door slammed as Delta left the restaurant, drying his hands on his apron.

"Oh, no. What's this shit? Is that Chuck? He never did anything like this before." Delta ran down the stairs and disappeared under the porch.

Out from under the deck flashed a yelping, howling pack of speckled hounds. They raced over to the alligator and made raucous efforts to herd him back toward the water. The alligator stood as high as his legs could hold him. He arched his back, as if trying to look as large as possible. With a whip of his tail, he sent one of the hounds sprawling. Then, calmly, keeping his ego intact, the alligator snaked his way back down the bank into the water.

Chuck slid under the waves, scattering the island of ducks. In a panic, they waddled up across the shore, squawking. The little black duck, still following far behind, hobbled after the flock as swiftly as one foot and the stub of another could carry him. White geese, wanna-be-swans, honked back at the ducks as if to berate them for their cowardice.

Delta whistled and the dogs raced over to his side, circling him with pride. One of them jumped up against Delta, leaving paw prints on his white apron. Delta swore and swatted at the dog. A wave of cicadas screamed and Jake looked down to the floor for his pack of tiny, black hounds only to see that the ants were gone, as if they had never existed.

Delta returned the dogs to their pen and ran up the steps to Jake.

"Hey, partner. I'm gonna take care of you in a little while. I just gotta finish up with a few customers first."

* * *

A car rolled down the levee and parked. A smiling, blond woman left the car and ran to the porch. Marie handed her the baby and they began to leave. Before Marie started her descent down the wooden stairs, she turned back to Jake and opened her arms. Without hesitation, he rose and let Marie wrap her small, strong arms around him.

"Remember what I tell you, Jake. Stay out over the basin. You'll be safe there." She lowered her voice and looked around to see that nobody was close enough to hear. "You know, if you sleep out under them cypress trees, sometimes, they tell you their secrets." Marie patted Jake and went down the steps. As Jake watched her leave, he noticed that her shoes were mismatched. One was black, and the other was a dark navy. Jake almost called out to her, to let her know, but he didn't. "She's a renegade," he whispered as Marie entered the car.

* * *

"C'mon, Jake." Delta rushed out onto the porch. "Let's go."
Jake started. "Go?"
"Yeah, man. I'm gonna take you someplace safe."
Jake followed Delta down to the shoreline and into a small boat. The sun turning to a red ball behind their backs, they putted out into open water, out into a forest of dead-looking trees that floated over the water. For every tree, there were ten stumps to mark where others had been massacred. "Delta," Jake said, "what did it look like before all these trees got torn up?"
"I don't know. That was before my time. I guess you have to ask them," Delta said as he nodded toward a stand of untouched cypress trees. He turned on the engine and they were off.
Here and there, a houseboat was tethered to one of the trees. Some of the houseboats were occupied by smiling folks who waved and shouted greetings as they passed. Off in the distance to the North, Jake could hear the traffic whizzing by on I-10.

* * *

Delta tied his boat to a pole on the deck of a wooden house-boat anchored in the middle of the basin. The sight of the rope

253

slammed Jake's mind back to a picture of Nina, her wrists and ankles tied to a bed, mutilated like a butterfly.

"Jake, you alright?"

Jake shook off the vision and climbed onto the houseboat deck. Bolted to the front of the houseboat was a huge, patio-like deck with a roof that extended almost to the edge. Jake traveled all around the narrow walkway that circled the house. He peered into the windows but could not see inside.

"Jake. C'mon in." Delta said as he held the screen door open and flicked on a light.

The house was one large room with a kitchen and dining area in the front. To the left were two bunks. To the right was a couch.

"Jake. Check this out. Do we know how to live?" Delta ushered Jake into a small bathroom. Jake looked around and nodded approval.

"Over here." Delta showed Jake another small room next to the bathroom. "There's a generator and tools in here. We got whatever you need."

On the way back out onto the deck, Delta bent down and pulled two beers out of a small refrigerator and grinned at Jake. "And they call this a camp."

* * *

Delta and Jake sat on a bench in front of the steering shed and watched the sun set. It flowed red and gold, casting halos over the cypress trees that surrounded the boat, igniting the sky. Jake half expected a legion of Thomas Cole angels to flutter out of the sun's rays.

A gurgling, bellowing noise drew their attention aside. The first bellow was followed by another, then another.

"It's contagious." Delta said. "Funny, they usually only do that roaring stuff in the morning, and never in February. It's this heat, I guess. You can tell the males when they bellow, cause before you hear the roar, the water dances around them. It's cause of some kind of something-sonic thing we can't hear."

They walked over to the edge of the deck and surveyed the water. Slowly, a reptilian form rose up over the water, shrouded with moss that gave it a topiary-like appearance. Bubbles of water danced around it just before the alligator bellowed.

"See," Delta said. "That's a male."

The effect was mirrored by another alligator. "That's another male," Delta said. "Maybe we're gonna get to see a fight."

The two reptiles eased over to each other and took turns pressing each other with their chins, touching in a languid manner. Then one crawled on top of the other, and it became obvious what they were up to.

"Oh, oh," Delta said. "That ain't fighting, that. Can you believe? I ain't never seen anything like that. I don't know what's been going on around here lately. Things are getting real crazy. The other day, my buddy Tommy said one of his bulls tried to do his horse. Go figure."

They drank their beers and watched until the twisted love scene was played out.

"Delta. Where is Sara?"

Delta slapped Jake on the back. "Well, buddy, I've got to get going. My wife will be wondering where I am. You just stay here and you'll be safe."

"But—"

Delta waved, jumped into his boat and chugged off into the darkness. He passed the circle of cypress trees and disappeared. The black-shadow trees, half under and half over the water, surrounded Jake with an almost solid wall of protection. Between two of them, he caught a glimpse of the distant shoreline, a restaurant, or some sort of establishment, lit with strings of yellow lights. As people passed in front of the bulbs, momentarily blocking their glow, they appeared to blink like giant fireflies, like the golden eyes that watched from the bushes outside the white-washed house near Lafayette. The eyes that had watched Jake and Sara that night. Exhausted, Jake padded into the house, peeled off his sweat-soaked clothes, and flopped down on one of the bunks.

As Jake slept, the trees whispered to each other, and aurora borealis lights flashed and waved in the sky.

Chapter 43

SARA LOOKED DOWN AT JAKE. She smiled. Her green eyes glowed. She touched Jake and his flesh returned the glow. Red curls brushed against his face as she lowered herself onto him. She placed a warm cheek on his chest as if to listen to his heart. Jake felt the red sun glowing hot, safely hidden beneath his ribs. He lifted his arms to wrap them around her trembling form. Then he awoke.

The night was dark and suffocating. Only sweat graced his chest. Only beads of salt water listened to his racing heart. Jake remained motionless, his eyes pressed shut, wishing he could force himself back to sleep, to pick up the dream where he left off. He remained frozen in the heat until blades of sunlight sliced through the window blinds to burn stripes across Jake's chest. He deserted his bed and wobbled out onto the wooden porch.

The sun was an electric silver globe, teetering on the horizon, threatening to rise into the air like a burnished balloon. Jake's eyes could only bear to look upon it for a split second. It burned its radiant image onto his retinas, and haunted, long after he turned away. He felt its gaze on his naked back. He heard its solemn chant repeating in his heart—remember, remember, remember. With a will of its own, his right hand rose and clutched at the prism that still hung from his neck, dancing with the rhythm of his heart.

Jake's gaze rose to the roof of the deck. He searched until he found a nail jabbing out of a crossbeam. Jake reverently hung Rachel's prism on it, then stood stone still, his hand wrapped around the crystal spear. Staring at the planks under his feet, Jake counted his heartbeats and listened with intense concentration. As the sun rose to electrify the clouds, crowning them with silver halos that cast down sequins to dance upon the waves,

Jake opened his fingers and let the unbearable brilliance pass through the prism to be translated into a collage of colors that spread across the deck. A rainbow kneeled at his feet. He passed his hand under the beam and watched his flesh mutate from one color to another—like a chameleon.

Jake knelt and felt the emblazoned deck. It was warm. Like the lazy cat, he eased himself down and stretched out under the blanket of many colors and became part of the light show as the rainbow stripes coursed over him. He lay holding his breath, listening intently, listening for the secrets of the cypress angels. However, the only secret message whispered into the sultry air came from his own lips, "Sara."

* * *

Jake jerked awake when Delta's boat whacked the side of the houseboat.

"Hey, bro, put some clothes on. Company's coming."

"What?" Jake mumbled as he searched for a rainbow that had fled with the sun. It was already late afternoon.

"Get dressed."

"Company coming?"

"Yeah. We're gonna boil some crawfish."

"Here?"

"Yeah. Wake up. Ya gotta eat." Delta jumped on board.

"Crawfish?"

"Okay, Yankee. I brought you a sandwich to hold you over." Delta yanked a battered ice chest from his boat, then dragged it into the house. Jake followed. Delta tossed a sandwich into the air. It bounced off Jake's chest, and he caught it on the rebound. Blinking the sleep from his eyes, Jake picked at the cellophane wrapping until, frustrated by his failure to find an opening, he tore off the covering and devoured the sandwich inside. He washed it down with a root beer.

As Jake pulled on his jeans, he heard a whooping yell from outside. He peeked through the screen door and saw Delta's brother throwing a rope onto the houseboat deck. Delta grabbed the line and wrapped it around a post.

"Jake, you met my brother, Donnie, right? He played at our party last time you were here."

257

"Well, I sort of remember."

"And, this is his buddy, Tracy. He's in Donnie's band."

Tracy climbed onto the deck as Delta held the small boat steady. Donnie handed Tracy the box Jake recognized as the one that housed the purple-green-gold accordion. Next, a violin-shaped case and jugs of water were passed aboard and lined up at the far end of the deck.

Delta and Donnie pulled a large kettle and gas burner from the shed. With well-practiced movements, they assembled a makeshift cooking set up, then began to fill the kettle with water. Once the kettle was filled, Delta lit the gas burner. A blue flame roared and licked at the kettle.

By the time the water began to bubble, the deck was filled with partiers. All came with a contribution of food or drink. Some arrived with mesh bags filled with wiggling, brown crawfish. Whistles of appreciation accompanied their offerings.

Donnie and his fiddler sat on the bench and entertained the assembly with lively music, the time being kept by an old man who held an iron triangle aloft, striking it with a metal bar. A few couples, caught up in the rhythm, danced in the center of the deck.

One of the last to arrive was Chaoui. When he saw Delta lowering a basket of live crawfish into the kettle, Chaoui beamed. "Phew, I got here just in time, Yeah!"

After struggling onto the deck, Chaoui hobbled between whirling dancers, threading his way over to Jake. The two men stood before each other, silently communicating via eye contact.

"Where is she?" Jake whispered to Chaoui.

"She?"

"You know exactly who I mean. Sara—"

"Jake, you know why we like it so much, here, over the water?"

"Chaoui—"

"Listen to this. I read this in the paper. We're made out of ninety percent salty water just like the ocean. That's why the sea calls to us. It's too bad that hardly any of us are smart enough to listen."

"Chaoui." Tension edged Jake's voice.

"Jake." Chaoui dropped his walking stick and grabbed Jake by his shoulders. "Jake, stay here over the water. You'll be safe here. This is where the magic is. Don't you hear it calling?"

"Please," Jake said.

"No, Jake. Tell that hard head of yours to listen to me. This is where you belong right now—south of I-10."

Delta pushed a plate of steaming, red crawfish into Jake's hands.

"C'mon, I'm gonna teach you how to eat, just like your mama did." Delta led Jake to the edge of the deck and they sat down, cross-legged.

At the end of Delta's lesson on how to disassemble a crawfish, Jake took his first taste of white, curled tail meat. Before he could comment on his lack of affection for crawfish, Delta was swept off to dance by a woman with mischief in her eyes.

Jake turned his back on the party. Facing the water, he looked down at the green, floating plant life, wishing he had the courage to drop his legs over the side, to dangle them into the cool water. As hot as he was, he decided he would rather sweat to death than dare cross the green barrier.

Green. Jake thought of green eyes. To break the spell, he lifted his gaze to the sky. The furnace-red ball-of-fire sun had tumbled from the sky, to roll along the horizon. It created a sky scene—perfect, pristine, beauty that could out-do any *Hudson River School* painting. Clouds edged with red-gold suspended from long, serpentine fingers of scarlet, molten lava. Red fingers. Red snakes' tongues. Red tendrils of hair. In the sky, Jake saw Sara's hair. His hunger for her chewed at his stomach, at his heart, at his soul. He had to find her.

Scattering crawfish shells as he rose, Jake strode across the deck and jumped down into the nearest boat. He tossed off the rope that held the boat prisoner, started the motor and edged away from his floating house.

"Jake! No!" Chaoui yelled as he hobbled across the deck toward Jake. "Wha'd I tell you about pushing!"

Jake did not turn around. He headed the boat west, straight into the ruby sunset—straight toward Lafayette.

* * *

After crashing over every floating object in his path, Jake, underestimating his speed, flopped the boat ashore. He fell forward with the impact. He scrambled to his feet, leapt onshore, and searched every vehicle parked on the gravel lot until he found one with a set of keys dangling from the ignition. Flinging gravel in his wake, Jake sped up the incline that led to the top of the levee. He hesitated for a moment, once he reached the top. There stood one of the signs he had been warned about. *Private property—keep off the levee.* He remembered the warning of the man on the bridge; *Don't go on top the levee. They got some signs.*

"Bull shit!" Jake yelled at the sign. It was time for breaking rules. He followed the ruts left by other rule-breakers who had also dared to take the high road. Spitting gravel and rocks in his path, he sped and spun his way to the road that led to the interstate.

Once on I-10 the path was clean and straight, straight west into the setting sun. Jake flew past an oil well pump so quickly it barely had time for two thrusts before he left it behind. Signs topped with giant crawfish or alligator, speed warnings, stranded vehicles, none of them registered. Jake flew past them all, seeing only scarlet tresses strewn before him.

* * *

It was almost dark. Careful not to sound a warning, Jake parked down the path, far from the grey, once-whitewashed house. Cautiously, he crept over to the house, pursued by cicada screams that pierced his ears and clawed at his brain. Sweat dripped down his forehead, stinging his eyes as he trampled dry weeds on his way to the sagging house.

Before climbing onto the porch, he listened for signs of life, but the screams of cicadas deafened him. Angry at their interference, he swore silently, then crept across the porch and tried to open the window-door that had once led him to Sara. It was locked. He rattled it, but it refused to open. Anger and frustration grew inside Jake. When the twin passions had filled him completely, they burst out with knotted fists that bashed at the shutters, with feet that kicked, with shoulders that smashed through the window.

Grey, sun-bleached shutter slats spun in the air. Glass shattered and tinkled to the floor. Through a flurry of slats and glass whirling around him like a storm, Jake burst into the house, dragging with him a trail of torn, lace curtains.

Jake's explosive entry went unnoticed. The house was empty. He searched frantically, but found no signs of occupation. All appeared unchanged since his last visit. No new signs of Sara.

Kicking slats and glass out of his path, he shuffled over to the bed that had also gone unoccupied since his night with Sara. He lowered himself to the floor and grabbed a corner of the sheet. Glass jangled to the floor as he pulled the sheet over to hold it against his face.

* * *

Jake heard footsteps on the porch. His heart raced.

"Sara," he whispered into the grey, evening air as he focused on the door.

The door banged open. Through the portal walked Joey and Chaoui.

"Jaaaaake. I told you not to do this. It's not safe here. You been running into the wind so long you don't know which way it's going any more. You gotta stay out over the basin." Chaoui pleaded with his eyes.

Jake could not speak. He had no answer. All he felt was numb. Joey took Jake's arm and gently pulled him to his feet.

"C'mon. Let's go home, partner," Chaoui said.

"Home." Jake mumbled.

As they headed for the door, Joey jerked Jake back and held a finger to his lips. The trio became silent as sounds of life crunched through the weeds. Jake's eyes widened with excitement.

Chaoui whispered, "Joey, you stick with Jake. I'm gonna go see what's coming through them bushes." He left the house without making a sound.

The next minutes passed as though they also were made listless by the heat. Jake's heart beat with anticipation. "Sara," he whispered and closed his eyes. Jake snapped to attention when Joey shoved him into the next room and left him there. He started to follow Joey back into the bedroom, but was warned off by a hand gesture. Peering around the corner, Jake watched Joey position himself next to the entrance to the bedroom. He stood listening with his back to the wall. When the sounds of footsteps

261

creaked across the porch, Joey pressed closer to the wall and pulled a knife out from under his shirt.

Jake shivered. What if it was Sara who approached? He poised to run at Joey, when a form filled the window. Instead of a small, female form, Sheriff Orgeron filled the window. He spotted Jake instantly and passed through the doorway.

With one whiplash move, Joey slipped behind the sheriff, grabbed him by his hair, and pulling his head back, held his knife blade against Orgeron's throat. The Sheriff froze in place. When he swallowed hard, his Adam's apple leapt out from under the blade, causing a single stream of blood to trickle down into his shirt.

"Joey! No!" Jake startled himself with the authority registered in his voice.

Without questioning Jake for an instant, Joey followed orders. He released the Sheriff and slipped outside to disappear into the night. Orgeron, coughed, held his throat, and slid to the ground. Jake rushed to his side and knelt before him.

"Jake," Sheriff Orgeron said. "I guess it's time for me to read you your rights."

"Guess so."

As the sheriff recited the invocation according to Miranda, all Jake could hear was the wild, frenzied screams of a thousand cicadas.

Chapter 44

STRIPPED OF ALL HIS PERSONAL POSSESSIONS, dressed in pink pants and shirt—an outfit that signified he was a potential candidate for escape—Jake was ushered down a long, dark hall lined with tiny cells on each side shrouded in darkness like the antechambers of a pharaoh's tomb. The sound of soul-twisted weeping came from one of the dark cubicles. For a heartbeat, Jake was afraid it was the sound of his own voice choking on tears. The guard, who followed behind Jake, poked him with a nightstick, kept him moving down the hall, kept the rabbit sliding down another snake's black throat. The guard shoved Jake into a cell. The bars rang with anger as the guard slammed together behind Jake. Someone laughed uncontrollably. Jake's stomach twisted. As soon as the guard left, Jake examined his new living quarters.

Jake's cell housed two cots, one on each side of the cell, minimal personal facilities, and against the back wall, a tiny desk with a short goose-neck reading lamp. When Jake reached out and flicked on the lamp, it sprayed a circle of light on the desk. Grabbing the not-yet-hot head of the lamp, Jake bent it so the halo of light could crawl out into the dark hallway. The yellow-white glob purified a spot in the darkness that loomed outside Jake's cell, creating a celestial, safe area. Jake stood contemplating the glow, wishing it were a silver sun rising over the basin. And the sink dripped an even, metered beat, like the feeble heart of a dying bird.

To a symphony of dripping, weeping, laughing, and mumbled prayers, Jake curled on his cot, agonizing over why, when he had called Alligator Landing for help, why did Delta tell the sheriff he never heard of Jake. As sleep threatened to take him, Jake

263

shivered to a lamentation of low, sorrowful howlings that echoed down the hall and continued all through the night.

* * *

The next morning, with handcuffs strangling his wrists behind his back, Jake sat across from the Sheriff, watching him dial the number to Alligator Landing. Jake squeezed his eyes shut as he listened to the conversation.

"Hello, this is Sheriff Orgeron, can I speak to?" He looked to Jake for a name.

"Marie," Jake said.

"Miss Marie," Sheriff Orgeron said. He watched Jake curiously as he waited for Marie to come to the phone. "Miss Marie, I have a gentleman by the name of Jacoby Preston here. He says you know him, that you will be willing to—you do not know him? Are you sure? He seems to—Okay. Thank you, Miss Marie. I'm sorry I bothered you." He hung up the phone, then shrugged his shoulders. "I don't know what to say."

"Neither do I."

"Jake, how did you get yourself into this mess? I would have bet you were—that you were a decent guy."

"I am. I don't know how it happened, either." Jake felt the lie burning his face. The giant hand that had once squeezed the breath out of him in Rosselli's office returned, stronger than before. He remembered Rachel on the floor of his red-and-white bathroom, and acid tears etched bloodguilt paths down his face.

"You all right, Jake?" Sheriff Orgeron spoke gently. "I have to take you to New Orleans tomorrow. I don't have a choice. There's a warrant. They want you bad. It seems the girl's parents have money. They're pushing hard. Besides, I have to clear this up before Mardi Gras. I have a feeling it is going to be one hell of a day. I wish I knew what the devil's been going on around here for the last few days." He looked out the window and rubbed his forehead, "It's like the whole place is going nuts. I never saw anything like it before. Not even on Mardi Gras. Not even in New Orleans. It's like one of those stupid, scary movies on television. You know, the kind you don't let kids watch. This jail is filled with people I used to know. I hardly recognize them now. I went to church with them last week, and I don't know them today." His body vibrated as a frisson shook off his thoughts. "Jake, is there anyone else you want to call?"

Snapshots of everyone Jake had ever trusted flashed through his mind. Ellen, Doctor Higgins, Fred. He could not tell any of them about his predicament. They could not help anyway.

"Chaoui," Jake whispered as he leaned forward, pressing himself against the sheriff's desk. "Chaoui wouldn't let me down. Can I call him? He goes to the landing every night. I know he'll be there tonight. Can we call him later?"

"Sure. I'll get you back in here tonight and we'll try again."

"Thanks."

"Is there anything I can do, short of letting you out?"

Jake's expression brightened. His heart beat wildly. "The hair. Can I have the stuff from my pockets. It's only hair."

"Sorry, Jake. Could be evidence."

Jake slumped. If only he could cover his eyes with his hands.

* * *

Later that evening with a phone on speaker, the sheriff dialed the Landing and spoke with Chaoui. With Jake listening, Chaoui said he did not know anyone named Jake. He also said he had never known anyone from New York. Jake turned his back on Sheriff Orgeron's questioning gaze and staggered back to his cell, feeling as though he had been punched in the stomach.

* * *

Jake sat at the desk in his cell. For hours, he had been trying to write a letter to Dr. Higgins. The only marks on his yellow legal pad were meaningless scribbles.

"Hey, Mister New York." The guard laughed as he spoke. "We got you a roommate." The guard snickered. "Meet Zeke."

Jake jerked his head around. Zeke leered at Jake. The pen dropped from Jake's fingers and rolled across the floor. Zeke wore a green outfit. Out from underneath the dysentery-colored suit dangled long, skinny arms covered with a brown, weathered excuse for skin. Deep, straight, precisely placed crevices ran up and down and across his arms and face, giving him a frighteningly realistic alligator appearance. As he stood just outside the glow of Jake's lamp, Zeke grinned. Something glistened in the shadows. Gold teeth?

"Well"? The guard teased.

Jake shivered.

"Sweet dreams." The guard slammed the door shut behind the alligator man. The bars rattled like out of tune, metal chimes. Slowly, Zeke crept out of the shadows. Jake pressed himself back against the desk and waited for Zeke to make the next move.

"Hi, what you in for? This time, I'm in for...I can't remember. But whatever it is, I didn't do it. I know cause I'm not a menace to society. The shrink said so. I'm a good guy. See?" Zeke pinched some of the khaki fabric of his shirt, pulling it away from his body. "See? Trustee green. Hey I donate plasma, yeah. Every," he looked up at the ceiling for an answer, "twice a week. Thirty bucks, yeah. Oh shit! Hey, what day is it? I'm due to donate tomorrow. And they confiscated my bag of cans. Man. Bet they don't give them back. What do you think? Can I sue for restraint of trade? What do ya think? Can I sue? Them cans was worth big bucks, yeah. Took my flask, too. That's worth something, too." He stopped to pick at the skin on the inside of his elbow, then sucked up a deep breath, his chest rattling like a window pane battling to repel a force of hurricane winds. "So, what you in for?"

"Murder."

Zeke swallowed hard.

"I didn't do it, either."

Zeke's Adam's apple leapt up then dropped back down like the iron weight that rings the bell on the strong man's booth at a fair.

Jake slammed his sledgehammer again.

"They said I tied a girl to my bed and cut her up; I don't remember doing it."

Zeke's Adam's apple leapt up again. In lieu of a bell sound, his eyes popped open. With irises such a light grey-blue they appeared white, floating in the center of whites that were a jaundiced yellow, his eyes gave off a reverse, fried egg look. Zeke pulled a trembling grin across his leather face, revealing rotten, crooked teeth, none of them gold, with dark gaps between them like windows of a deserted house. His voice hollow, nervous, Zeke said, "I think I just got real tired." In lieu of a goodnight, he fluttered the fingertips of a gnarled hand at Jake, and in one ungainly move, he flopped back on his bunk. "Lights out." He slammed his lids down and folded his arms over his chest. "Lights out."

Zeke rested stiffly on his back, his hands folded over his chest as though he had once been carefully mummified and laid out by the priests of Hermes, only to be unceremoniously dragged into the sunlight by sacrilegious tomb robbers. His breath came shallow and even. He appeared to be asleep.

After waiting long enough to assure himself of his relative safety, with eyes trained on the alligator man, Jake leaned over the tiny desk. He flicked off the light, then shuffled across the cramped cell to lean his forehead against the bars that held him captive. Tiny bulbs that glowed in other cells pushed circular globs of light out onto the night-black hallway floor. Jake counted the row of halos, half expecting Jimmy Durante to traipse down the hall, hat in hand, waving goodbye to Mrs. Calabash.

From somewhere down the Appaloosa hallway, came a baritone, pain-filled ululation, sounding like the call of a distant foghorn, "Liiiiights oooouuuut."

Someone wept, then blew his nose. The sink kept dripping minutes down the drain, one-by-one. The night guard slammed his stick against the bars of the cell nearest the end of the row, against the chords at the end of the black snake-creature's throat. The bars rang a dull, low, hollow chime. He continued down the path toward Jake, banging the bars, clanging the warning. One-by-one, the light globs disappeared. Cot springs creaked and groaned. The laugher cackled. The howler howled. Nobody said goodnight to Mrs. Calabash.

Jake moved to the back of his cell. The guard roamed up and down the length of the hall, flashlight in hand, its yellow beam searching into the dark caverns. Afraid the wandering beam would fall across his face and, perhaps, suck away his breath, Jake crawled onto his bunk.

And with precise timing, the sink dripped minutes down the drain.

Jake shivered in the darkness of each blackout period between flashlight invasions, propped up on one elbow, using the drips to time the officer's arrival, holding his breath every time the guard passed by, every time the beam searched his cell. His body motionless, Jake concentrated his attention on the bunk next to his, squinting into the darkness, waiting for the beam to fall across Zeke, waiting to assure himself that the alligator man was still asleep. There he was, like a dry, near-crumbling Egyptian pharaoh left on display in a museum, but without viewers to stand around him and wonder what sort of spirit had filled the body, eons ago.

With every pass of the light beam, Jake scrutinized Zeke's prostrate form. It was still. Yes—he was sleeping. Jake rolled back on his bunk, banging his elbow against a metal rail that encircled his bed. Excruciating pain to ran up and down his arm. Wincing, he clutched his vibrating arm and waited for the next passing of the counterfeit sun. Somewhere between brief visits of the light, Jake let sleep tear him away from his duty.

* * *

In time with the passing of the guard's light, Jake dreamed a stop-action video of Zeke, in super-slow-motion, his alligator flesh drifting across the floor toward Jake's side of the cell. The alligator man was no longer wearing his khaki trustee's costume. His sun-baked skin, cracked like a lakebed after a hundred-year drought, looked like a full-body, reptile costume.

Blackout.

Zeke with yellow, glowing, alligator eyes—open.

Blackout.

Zeke sitting up, stretching, then rubbing his chest with the flats of his hands, his yellow fingernails curled under crooked fingers.

Blackout.

Zeke squatting on the floor.

Blackout.

Zeke on all fours.

Blackout.

Zeke slithering closer, his back snaking with each step.

Blackout.

Zeke crouched beside Jake, eyes glistening.

Blackout.

Zeke sniffing Jake's arm and bellowing a reptilian cry of love.

Black, black, black, black.

Jake's eyes flashed open. The dream was over. But next to him—on his bunk—Jake felt a quiet breathing.

The light passed. Jake eyed Zeke's bunk. Empty! Next to Jake a quiet breathing hissed in and out. The light passed. Lying next to Jake was the alligator man. Jake froze in the darkness, praying Zeke was asleep. Sweating profusely, Jake shivered and waited.

Footsteps came down the hall, closer, closer. Jake's inner self spoke to him, "You think he's asleep? Just look at his eyes. I dare you."

This time, when the light crawled across Jake's silent bed-mate, the alligator man's eyes were open, glowing yellow, staring straight up at the ceiling.

Jake backed against the wall.

Blackout.

As Jake waited for the next flashlight sunrise, he felt move-ment. His springs under his cot squealed, and the mattress sank under him.

The imposter sun rose again.

Zeke hovered over Jake, one arm stretched across the bunk, the palm of his hand flat against the wall, forming a scaly canopy over his bedmate. Jake shrank back, loath to feel the touch of alligator hide.

Blackout.

From the quivering darkness above Jake, came the hoarse, whispered request. "Jaaaaaake. Be my briiiiiiiide. Jaaaaaake. Sit by my side. Jaaaaaake. Rule the darkness with me. Together, we can blot out the sun forever."

From somewhere buried deep in the darkness, the laugher screeched. The howler wailed. The weeper sobbed.

"It is only I who loves you. It is me you have yearned for all those ugly, barren years. All else was only a dream. False prophets to tempt you, turn you aside. Only I am real. Only I can answer all your prayers. Be my briiiiiiiide." Alligator man sucked in a ragged breath like an over-excited lover. "Jaaaaaake. Fleeeeeesh is fleeeeeeesh."

The alligator man leaned down through the darkness and placed a wet kiss on Jake's bloodless lips. With the flash-bulb velocity of a striking serpent, Jake screamed and pushed Zeke away, sending him crashing to the floor.

Zeke bawled, "Guard! Get me out of here. This guy is crazy. He hit me. Look! I'm bleeding. I'm all banged up. And I gotta give blood tomorrow."

Afraid to look down, half expecting to see a crumbled pile of sand, Jake covered his eyes and cried out, "Sara!...Sara, bring me home!"

The laugher laughed.

The howler howled.

Somebody mumbled a prayer.

The lights flashed on.

Chapter 45

*J*AKE WOKE, SICK TO HIS STOMACH. He wiped his mouth, afraid one runaway cell shed by the alligator man might still cling to his lips. He swung his legs around and planted his feet on the floor. Then he bent over and placed his face against his knees.

"Preston," the booming voice of the morning-shift guard echoed. "Someone to see you. Your lawyer."

Jake leapt up and rushed over to the open door of his cell, vertigo doggedly following, clinging to him like a mantle.

As the guard led him between rows of iron bars, Jake remembered the sound of ragged baseball cards flapping against bicycle spokes, the dull slapping sound his fingers made as they tumbled along the row of iron bars that surrounded his cemetery. Remembering the pain, he curled his fingers and twisted his wrists against their constraints. Instead of majestic stone angels, or merciful cypress trees, the bars walled him away from contorted faces with twisted smiles, cowering in shadows, watching him shuffle by, flashing eye-whites lit with the glow of madness. Muffled howlings crept along the floor, following him like the swirling fog that hovered over the basin.

Elation—Nothing could dampen his excitement. Who could it be? Delta? Chaoui? Who had decided to come for him?

He could hear his prison mates' twisted thoughts calling to him, daring him to run his fingers along their row of black, iron ribs. "C'mon, Jake go for it—we dare you. Yum." Thankful that his hands were shackled safely behind him, Jake shuddered at the thought of reaching out into the shadows.

In Jake's mind, fast-forward dramas of his rescuers played in various versions, Delta, maybe Chaoui. It could not be Joey.

He would never come that close to authority. Marie? He wrestled his wrists against the metal bracelets that held him captive as his imagination ran wild. At the end of the gauntlet, Jake felt the shackles cut into his wrists as he stood waiting for his guide to turn a key in the lock of the shadow-black metal door. With one push of the guard's outstretched fingers, the door opened, yawning a slice of white light into the dark hall.

Jake took a step forward and looked through the door. His stomach knotted itself into a tight fist when he saw Camille lolling over a table like a Caesar at a feast, his head resting on his opened hand, his elbow propped before him on the table, the fingers of his other hand tapping an un-restrained rhythm on the glossy, black surface. A smile tugged at one corner of Camille's mouth. He yawned, covering his mouth with the hand that had formerly tapped the wild rhythm. Like an amateur actor overstating his case, Camille pretended to be surprised by Jake's entrance. He jerked onto his feet with fluttering eyelashes.

"Oh, Jake. What have they done to you?" He placed a hand over his heart.

Jake turned away from Camille and examined the woman who glimmered next to him. She sat motionless. Flawless, translucent skin shimmered with alabaster secrets like a canopic jar holding the organs of a pharaoh or saint. Silver-blond hair, needle-straight, slithered down over her shoulders, almost reaching the table. She was dressed in white silk. Violet-blue eyes gazed at Jake through a white veil that draped across her face. The white, flower-topped hat that supported the veil, cast a slight shadow across her perfect face. Pink lips neither smiled nor frowned. Before her on the table were a transcription pad and a pen. Like a department store manikin, she struck a cunning pose.

"So, Jake. Am I to take your interest as a good sign? Do you like it?"

Jake's attention snapped back toward Camille.

"It's yours if your want. Isn't it fine?" Camille ran a finger along the angel's arm. She squirmed at his touch. Piles of silver bracelets jingled on her wrists, windless chimes. "Isn't it perfect? So perfect that while you wear it, everybody will love you. C'mon. Let's play."

"So what's this lawyer shit?"

"Well, somebody had to come to your rescue. Who better than I?" Camille leaned intimately across the table. "Jake, you don't have anybody else. I'm all you have."

"Bull shit."

"Then who?" Camille leaned back and crossed his arms, his eyes daring Jake to answer.

"I have friends."

"Really. It seems to me that every time you try to make contact with your friends, your calls of help are refused. You might say—that you have been thrice denied by your so-called friends. Jake," Camille cooed. "And you didn't even get kissed. You can trust me. *I would* kiss you. C'mon, tell me. Where are they? Why aren't they here?" Black-brown eyes insisted on an answer.

"I don't know."

Jangling rattled Jake's concentration. He fought the urge to turn toward the silver lady. Instead, keeping his eyes coupled with Camille's, Jake fought the urge to retch.

"Yes you do. C'mon—admit it. You were nothing to them. They sacrificed you to the police. They let you lure the cops away from them as a mother bird lures the owl away from her nest. They only cared about saving their own skins."

"That's not true." Jake twisted his wrists against shackles and dropped his gaze to the distorted, upside-down reflections of his visitors, wavering on the surface of the glistening table.

The silver angel giggled. Jake looked up just in time to see her put the finishing touches of blood-red paint on her lips. She pursed the scarlet slashes together, then slowly ran a pointed tongue along them and slid one translucent lid down over a violet eye, winking at Jake.

"It's yours if you want it." Camille taunted Jake as he gestured toward the angel. "C'mon, take it out for a test drive. Take it out to my limo and slide in. We can be in New Orleans in no time. You can wear it to my Mardi Gras ball. You are still invited. You have to attend; after all, you *are* the guest of honor." Camille leaned forward and his voice fell to a hoarse whisper. "I'm the one who loves you, Jake. I worship you. I kissed you. C'mon, give it up. Trade up. Be my bride."

Jake remembered the reptilian kiss and wiped his mouth again.

"So, you think it's just that easy?"

"No, I *know* it is. I am an expert. You might even call me—a flesh addict. I have changed models so many times I do not know what I look like anymore. Besides, it does not matter. It is not the form that matters. Flesh is flesh. It is *all* that matters. It is everything. It is why we are here. You know that as well as anyone. You chose flesh too." He pointed at Jake. "Remember. You chose flesh too."

"I don't know any such thing. I never—"

"Yes you did, think back a long, long way."

Jake's stomach twisted tighter.

"C'mon, Jake—think back to a time when we were one."

Jake fixed his gaze on the scrambled reflections dancing across the table as vertigo swirled the flickering images into a blur of oil-slick colors.

"Shut up!"

"Remember. Jake. Remember me."

"Shut up!" Jake leapt from his chair, throwing himself across the table, straining wrists against metal boundaries, drawing blood. Camille calmly slid his chair back, deftly avoiding Jake's spastic attack.

In a flurry of silver wrist chimes, the angel scrambled to a corner of the small room, knocking her chair over as she fled.

The guard, who had been watching from the other side of an invisible boundary of glass, re-entered the visiting room. He grabbed Jake by the back of his collar and began to drag him out of the room.

"Stop!" Camille ordered. "I'm not through with him yet."

Like a puppeteer, the guard, still holding Jake by his collar, led Jake back to his chair and slammed him into it.

"You can go now." Camille reached down and set the fallen chair upright then tapped the seat with his fingertips.

Jingling, her hat askew, the lady of silver chimes haughtily returned to her place next to Camille. As she reached up to adjust the set of her hat, the repeating rings of silver that encircled her wrists tumbled back, clanging against each other, one by one, jingle jangle, revealing angry, black and blue circlets etched into the delicate flesh on her slender wrists, as if she'd been tied up. When she made eye contact with Jake, she stuck her tongue out at him and screwed her perfect face into the mask of a petulant child.

"Nina, be nice," Camille said. Nina let out a harumph, then fished into her satchel, withdrawing a small, round, silver-framed mirror. She searched the glass for her reflection, then seeing it, smiled in admiration. The vertigo, Jake had so recently shaken off, returned to whirl around inside him like a tornado. Nina. Nina dead on his bed. Nina here. Nina in New York?

Instead of the reality that glowed before him, Jake saw an image of Nina smiling into his New York City bathroom mirror. At her feet, he saw Rachel curled on a red and white floor. Visions of Nina's body, her last body, lying on Jake's bed, cut to ribbons, clawed into Jake's brain, crawling over his picture of Rachel. His senses reeled at the stench of slaughterhouse—to the fear, to the horror remembered—

"Okay, Jake, it is time to cut to the chase. It is about time you began to catch on. Haven't you had enough yet?"

"Catch on? Enough what?"

"Jake, cut the shit. If you want to play games," his voice fell to a whisper, "let's play for real." He leaned over and licked the alabaster arm that rested near his. Rows of silver bracelets jingled against each other; they jangled against the shiny black tabletop that reflected the world above, like ebony swamp water.

"I'm offering you the only way out. You have a choice to make here. What will it be? Prison forever—or me?" He placed his fingertips on his chest, his hands looking about to crawl away, like two matching crabs, one on each side. "Jake, I am the one. I am everything you ever wanted. I can answer all your prayers. Choose me. I am chaos. Choose the chaos of flesh. Deny spirit. Choose the chaos of blood and sensation. That is why I love this place, Louisiana. It is always on the edge. Always choosing between land and water, constantly reinventing itself, like me, always in chaos, always Becoming. Never ever Being. It is the chaos that gives me power. Join with me. Together we can rule.

Jake, pick a side. Are you with me or against me? C'mon Jake—make a choice—choose flesh—again."

Jake remained silent, afraid to open his mouth, afraid his lips would betray him.

"C'mon, Jake. I am tired of playing games. I did not go through all these machinations to take no for an answer. The sacrifice of moving to upstate New York—for months. Ugh! Just to get to you."

Something at the back of Jake's mind clicked. His eyes snapped open as if he had been whacked on the back of his head.

"What machinations? Upstate New York?"

"Jake, join us. You can't beat me."

"What machinations?" The tornado of vertigo returned. "You were behind everything," Jake said.

Camille grinned with pride. "You don't think it was an accident that we moved to Utica, of all places. And that tree-hugger bull shit I gave you out on the swamp. Pleeeease."

"This whole thing has been a setup from the start, Keith, Rachel, everything," Jake said.

"You don't *know* it wasn't an accident that Rachel's brother gave up his ghost." Camille placed one finger into his mouth and sucked it like a lollipop.

Knowledge flooded through Jake's veins like hot acid, knowledge he struggled to deny. It was not my fault. None of it was my fault. Rachel was not my fault—we were all just a list of victims. Nothing I could have done would have changed anything.

Buoyed by his release from bloodguilt, Jake rose to a stand straight and tall. "Guard, I think there has been some kind of mistake here. This isn't my lawyer."

"Jake, you don't know what you're doing." Camille whimpered. "You'll go to prison, forever."

Jake gazed at Camille, then Nina, and back to Camille.

"No. They can only keep me as long as this skin-suit I am wearing lasts. That's what it's all really about, isn't it? Flesh, it's a prison, nothing but a warm, sensate prison. Solitary confinement. That's what I remember—and there is more. Much more. I know that now. Why aren't you telling me about the rest? Why don't you want me to remember everything? C'mon. Tell me. I dare you."

"Jake this might be your last chance. Choose flesh. Choose chaos. Choose me. Flesh is flesh."

"No it's not. I own mine. I got it legal. I'm not afraid to be alone anymore, because that's all there is. Alone. Guard! Take me back to my cell!"

As Jake turned his back on Camille, a haunting vision of hatred echoed in his mind, the vision of the mask of evil and deception painted on Camille's borrowed face.

"Jake," Camille hissed, "don't go to sleep." Camille laughed long and hard, then started to hum a tune. Because the guard left the door open, Jake could hear Camille's music all the way down the throat-black gauntlet that led to his cell. Even though he knew the song was a classic, Jake could not quite place it or remember the words. As he rested on his cot, face down, with a pillow over his head, the melody played over and over in his mind.

Chapter 46

*J*AKE WAS READY when sheriff Orgeron came to get him. It was easy. All he had to do was wash his face, plaster his curls down, and tuck his pink shirt into his pink pants. He did not really care how he looked—he just needed to feel he had some small amount of control over himself.

Dreading the cutting edge of the handcuffs, Jake the rubbed bruises and angry red lacerations that encircled his wrists like bracelets. When the cell bars slid open, Jake stood and turned with his hands held behind his back. Cuffs clicked into place over his tender wrists, and he thought of the silver lady.

Jake shuffled after the officer, not looking right or left, ignoring the jeers, laughter, and tears that pricked at him from each side of the hallway. Only the lone howler managed to punch his way past Jake's perceptual screens to reverberate and imprint into his memory.

* * *

Even though the sun would soon set, it was hotter than ever outside. Jake's pink suit was soaked with perspiration before he got into the sheriff's car. Safely locked in the back seat, separated from the sheriff and his assistant by a vision-disrupting, grid-work of metal, Jake sat back, shivering in the frigid air conditioning as his wet suit transformed itself into an icy shroud. He squinted through the metal barrier—each square, part of a collage of tiny visions as if seen through the viewfinders of a hundred cameras.

Squawking phrases splashing out of the two-way radio uttered the only conversation as the car hummed along I-10, east toward New Orleans. Numb from the cold, from the lack of sleep, the lack of support—Jake agonized over why he had been denied?

He turned away from the grid-work view of his captors and slid over to the right side of the car, to lean against the cold window glass, to look south of I-10, south to where he had once found the solace of friends, family, the safety of the cypress trees, the magic, and—Sara—Sara who could bring home to him with her touch.

Images of Lafayette whizzed by. Jake tried to memorize them, to lock them in his mind like photographs so he could press rewind and play them back at some future, solitary, soul-hungry time. However, the blurred, quicksilver images trickled away like water from between clenched fingers.

The oil well still pumped in time with Jake's heart.

Click!

A farmer turned up soil, leaving clouds of dust circling around his blurred form.

Click!

Cattle grazed alongside egrets.

Click!

And behind him, the furnace sun reclined on the horizon, a red-orange ball of fire exuding a flaming halo.

Waxing and waning, Jake's breath left a patch of fog on the glass that locked him away from Lafayette. When he could feel he was nearing the basin, Jake stopped breathing, allowing the fog to clear long enough for him to see the sign designating the Henderson/Cecilia exit.

There it was. He pressed closer to the glass, wishing he could plunge through it as if it were a crystal lace curtain, white lace, green lace, any lace. The road rumbled under him, mumbling secrets not quite clear enough to hear. When the car drew near to the bridge that would lift it up over the Atchafalaya basin, traffic began to slow on the eastbound lane. Traffic on the westbound lane continued to whizz by like blood cells pumping through the arteries of an excited giant.

Once they were well out over the water, eastbound traffic slowed to a painful crawl, then froze, like the cells in the arteries of a heart in cardiac arrest.

"Shit!" The driver said. "We really need this now." He patted his shirt pocket, then pulled out a pack of cigarettes and lit one up. Smoke swirled around his head, then filtered through the screen barrier and crept over to tickle Jake's thoughts. Jake's hair stood on end. He coughed, nauseated by the image of blue smoke leaving lungs.

Time dripped away. The engine of the police car rumbled an uneven beat then threatened to stall. The smoking officer gave it some gas and it hummed efficiently again. When the sun's red glow began to spread across the water and seep into the car, the air conditioner finally lost its battle with the heat. Other stranded travelers crawled out of their cars, sweating and cursing. Just on the other side of the ledge that marked the edge of the lane, separating it from the floating forest of trees, a lone tree rose out of the water. On it perched hundreds of white egrets, giving it the appearance of a giant cotton ball blossom. Tension crowded into the car. Jake swallowed hard and filled his stomach with it. The engine fibrillated again, then threatened to die.

"We better turn it off and get out." The sheriff groaned as he opened his door.

"I don't know about that," the driver said.

The engine fibrillated again.

"I don't think we have a choice," Orgeron said. "Where's he gonna go, anyway?"

"Yeah, right." The driver shoved his cigarette into the ashtray and turned the ignition key.

The engine sputtered out.

The driver swore.

Jake coughed.

After the pair in the front seat exited, the sheriff put his hand on the door next to Jake and opened it, then helped Jake keep his balance as he climbed out onto the bridge, his hands still cuffed behind him. Jake stretched and twisted off the stiffness of the journey, but could not eradicate the foreboding that squirmed in his stomach along with the tension that still swirled inside the car.

When the sheriff slammed the door behind Jake, the cottonball cypress exploded into a million splinters of white feathers and beaks. The egrets fluttered away—in unison—scattering in all directions. Their haphazard, explosive departure sent shivers along Jake's spine. His hair stood on end. His skin tingled.

Something was going to happen—He could feel it. Bird-by-bird, the fluttering splinters of white came together, reunited, and whirled around the sky, swarming like a horde of ghostly bees.

Was Camille up to something, or—?

Dread and excitement fought for control of Jake's senses. The driver finished another cigarette and flicked it over the edge of the bridge. It sailed out over the water, then dove in.

Sheriff Orgeron broke the silence. "Jimmy, go see what the hell is this holdup."

Camille's music seeped into Jake's memory. This time, it played with the words included. Jake sang along, "I'll see you in my dreams."

The driver tilted his head toward Jake and nodded. "Are you sure?"

"Git," Orgeron said.

Jake watched the ornery driver as he slowly disappeared among stalled cars and stranded motorists. The sun glowed red against his back, and the whispers returned. Jake recognized the voice. He had heard it before, in Lafayette, when it had led him to Sara. Suddenly, he realized it was his own inner voice. Recognition led him to trust the whispers. Finally—a voice he could trust.

"Jake. Pick a side. Any side. But pick a side."

The sheriff flinched as Jake strolled across the road to peer over the north side of the lane. Black water peeked out through gaps between the patterns of scattered, green lace. Jake turned and moved to the south side of the bridge. Leaning over the ledge, he saw the same view—green lace floating on thick black water.

The voice whispered, again. *Pick a side, Jake. Choose a religion.*

The sheriff, who had been leaning against the car in a relaxed posture, stood up and fixed his gaze on Jake.

"Jake, you okay?"

The sheriff's words reached Jake's ears in a scrambled cipher. He tingled as though he had been out in the cold too long, ice-skating until frostbite nipped at his flesh. Images of the scattered egrets reverberated in his mind. The tree exploded in his memory, repeatedly, like the grand finale of a fireworks show.

When the driver returned, Orgeron said, "What's up?"

"It's a damned truck turned over. Full of pigs. And they're shitting all over the road. Shitting everywhere. Oh, God! I never saw anything like it. The driver is some skinny, stupid-looking jerk, babbling in French. He wasn't even trying to catch those damn pigs. He's just standing there, drinking a pop and watching the pigs shit. I couldn't understand anything he said except for, 'Damn, I wish this was a J.D.' He kept saying it, every time he took a swig. Awwwww, I never saw so much shit!" He bent down and examined the bottoms of his shoes.

Jake's flesh hummed—it sang to him—He became a furnace. The sun set into his heart and glowed out of his pores. The tornado of swarming egrets whirled back toward the bridge.

The smile melted from Jake's face.

The sheriff froze.

"Jake?"

Jake locked eyes with the sheriff.

"Jake, don't."

Jake smiled, again. With the grace of a ballet dancer, he stepped onto the ledge on the south side of the bridge.

The driver pulled his gun and snapped aim on Jake.

"No!" The sheriff grabbed his partner's wrist and pulled the gun away from him. "Don't do it, Jake. The water's not as—"

Jake turned away and tuned out the warning. Still glowing, he tipped his weight off the concrete ledge. Visions of burning red sunlight and white, exploding trees flashed before his wide-open eyes, caressing him as he turned and tumbled in the air. The swarm of flapping egrets whirled around Jake as if to break his fall with the fluttering tips of their alabaster wings. Jake smiled as he crashed through the green lace curtain and joined the world on the other side, no longer afraid of what he might find there.

The cold water extinguished the fire in Jake's heart. As his feet slammed against the mushy floor of the basin, Jake's body crumpled. Vines and wiggles of life wound around him as he tumbled along the slippery bottom. With the force of his contact with the basin floor, he gasped in black water. He swallowed a throat-full of slime. Without benefit of arms to splash him to the surface, Jake struggled to right himself, to kick and wiggle his way to the surface, like a snake. The undergrowth of plant life pulled him down. Something grabbed his hair and pulled at him from above. The battle for the possession of Jake continued until he was almost unconscious.

The hair puller finally won the battle.

Jake gasped to the surface and Joey completed the rescue efforts by yanking him into his boat as it hovered under the bridge that protected it from the view of those overhead. As Joey silently sculled his boat along the shadow running between the pillars supporting the roadway, Jake bent over and coughed black water from his lungs, then rolled onto his side and sputtered, "Man, I wish that was a J.D."

Chapter 47

JAKE COULD NOT TELL if the night air was cloaked by fog or if his eyes were blurred with sleep. He blinked, trying to erase the smudges obscuring his view. Someone, or something, lumbered toward him. The sound of ungainly hooves, clopping on pavement, echoed an inappropriate duet with discordant, jingle-jangle bell sounds. The apparition mutated, wavered in and out of focus, scattering confetti colors in its wake. When it screamed the scream of horses thrown overboard mid-sea, Jake woke, sweating.

Still half asleep, Jake struggled to draw breath in the oppressive heat. He pushed at the weight that crushed him down into the thin mattress. When the weight clung to him, Jake gasped, totally awake. Sara moaned and drew closer.

Fingers of sun, edging between the blinds, ricocheted off Sara's hair, setting it ablaze with the lights of fire and Louisiana sunsets. Jake wrapped his arms around her and pressed her close. Afraid he was dreaming, he blinked until his eyes cleared, then examined his surroundings. He was back on Delta's houseboat, crowded on the narrow cot with Sara.

How he got there was inconsequential. Only one thing mattered. Sara was for real, and he was awake. Sara wriggled against Jake's embrace as she woke, smiling. He kissed her and it was if beams of light traveled from their inner cores, and at their lips, met, binding them together with a laser cord of pure energy.

Sara pushed Jake away and leapt from the bunk. He grabbed her hand and tried to pull her back.

"No!" Sara said, in between ragged breaths.

"Why?"

"I can't let my guard down, again. It's too dangerous. Please, don't tempt me."

"Dangerous?" Jake sat up and started to rise. Sara kept him at bay with a hand gesture. "Dangerous? What's going on? Sara, where have you been?"

"I've been in New Orleans, watching Camille and his adherents."

"Adherents? Watching them what? What do you mean dangerous?"

"The interpersonal resonance between us is too powerful. Camille might sense it. He might find you through me, or me through you. I have to protect you. That's why I'm here. The *only* reason I'm here."

"Wait a minute. I don't need anybody to protect me. And I'm not afraid of Camille."

"You should be." Her voice lowered. "You should be very afraid. He is an extremely dangerous—entity, and he's here to stop you any way he can. To destroy you or worse, to turn you aside."

"Me? Why me? I'm nobody."

Sara exhaled deeply. "There is no such thing as a nobody. We're all a splinter of the divine, here for a purpose, to play our part, to—"

"Stop! You're starting to sound like Miss Marie. The next thing I know, you'll be raving about runaway cats."

"Marie is a very wise woman. You should've listened to her. You should've stayed here instead of running off looking for me, chasing after the impossible. You put us all in jeopardy. You could have ruined all our plans."

"Plans? What plans?" Jake moved toward Sara. She whirled around and ran out onto the deck, slamming the screen door. Jake stood inside, watching her through the tiny viewfinders formed by the metal wires of the door screen fabric. After standing at the edge of the deck, looking out over the water, she sat down and dropped her legs into the water. Jake slipped through the door and sat next to her. He lowered his own bare legs into the cool water. A billion miniature suns flickered across the water, kissing their flesh like tiny, silver fish. Jake swung his legs against the shimmering reflections.

An imperceptible current dragged a beer can and a blue heron feather within his reach. "Pigs everywhere. Everywhere you go, human pigs." Jake retrieved the can and tossed it into a garbage can then rescued the feather. "Sara, you need to tell me. What plans can I ruin?"

"It's nothing you need to worry about. You have concerns that are more important. Just stay where we put you until it's over, and everything will be okay."

"You should know by now that I'm not about to stay put, anywhere. Besides, how can anything ever be okay again? The cops think I killed someone."

"Don't worry about that. There will be a confession, very soon. You'll be off the hook."

"How do you know?"

"It's already arranged."

"Arranged? I don't want some innocent person taking heat for me."

"It's *not* someone innocent—and it *is* someone who has nothing to lose."

Sara rose, padded to the opposite side of the deck, and stood leaning against a pole, shielding her eyes with her hand, gazing across the water.

* * *

Jake felt the shards of colored light crawling across his back, dancing like nimble flies on sticky feet. When he turned, they swarmed across his bare chest, buzzing gently, reminding him that he had, days ago, left Rachel's prism hanging over the deck. His eyes snapped to the beam. The prism was still there, motionless, pure, waiting for his touch to transform it. When he returned it to its rightful place, hanging from his neck, the crystal spear felt cold as lifeless flesh. He covered it with his hand until it warmed to match the crimson heat of his blood. Jake's heart raced. Sounding like the hooves of a galloping horse, his pulse pounded against his eardrums. He closed his eyes and, through dark inner night and the lightning sparking under his eyelids, the multicolor image he had dreamt, returned, moving closer. But the motor of an oncoming boat drowned out the sound of the horse's screams. When the boat rammed the side of the deck, Jake blinked himself back into the blazing afternoon.

Michael Limon crawled out of the wobbling, aluminum boat and slid on deck. It looked like his greasy, black hair had not been washed since he had first seen him in New Orleans. Jake's hands moved to his own hair. Feeling his curls taking charge, Jake knelt, dipped his hands in the water, and plastered down his unruly locks, all the time watching the greasy man as if he were a mirror.

Following the trail of the greasy man, a boat full of motley characters climbed onto the deck and found places of shelter from the blazing sunlight. Sitting with his back against the door to the house, Limon retrieved a knife from inside his pant leg, then polished it on his jeans. Over and over, he repeated the ritual—he looked into the shiny metal, breathed fog onto the silver surface, then polished it on his thigh. Two more boats ripped the surface of the water as they sped to the houseboat, leaving beads of water to fan into the air. Jake moved to Sara's side.

"Sara, who are these—people?"

Placing a finger on Jake's lips, Sara shushed his questions. "This is not your concern."

"Wait a minute. I'm some kind of part of what's going on here, I think."

"But that's the point. You're not supposed to think. You're supposed to learn to follow your heart and let the knowledge find you."

"What?"

Sara dismissed his protests with her back.

"Okay." Sara spoke to the rag-tag assembly sitting in a semi-circle before her. "Insiders. Anything to report?"

A man wearing a flouncy blouse and spandex leopard skin pants spoke. "No changes in party plans. He's already fixing up the Bete Noire. You should see his costume."

Sara interrupted. "What color?"

"Silver. Sparkly. All silver and rhinestones and beads. Silver beads. Sort of a Louis of France shtick. You know. Tights. Prissy jacket and a crown. And what a crown it is."

"A mask?"

"But of course. A silver Zorro mask with a peek-a-boo veil to cover his mouth and chin. He told all the rest of us to dress like lords and ladies. Very she-she."

"The time?"

"As soon as the sun goes down, we'll start."

"Invitations?"

"Gott'm."

"You're wonderful."

The flouncy man smiled and crossed his arms.

"And costumes that will blend in?" Sara said.

"Please. How could you even ask?"

"Justine, we know you would never let us down." Sara smiled at the pouting man. "Just after sunset, we'll arrive. One-by-one, except for Justine. Camille will be expecting him to bring a boy-friend." Sara nodded to a slender young man with blond hair. "You get to play Justine's date." The blond boy rolled his eyes.

"Now remember, as long as we remain undetected, it's best to hold out until the last minute to make our move. We'll wait until the chaos is at its peak of frenzy before we do it. And the first move is—I take Camille. Then you all follow suit. Hit your marks. You know who they are. The only alternative plan concerns the possibility that Camille, or one of them, will sniff us out. If that happens, the only rule is we all go for Camille, and maybe, one of us will get lucky." Sara's voice cracked when she spoke again. "Is anyone starting to fail?"

Two grey-faced men raised their hands, reluctantly.

"Today is Sunday. Can you make it? Can you hold out until Tuesday night Mardi Gras night?"

One grey-faced man nodded. The other closed his eyes and shrugged.

Her voice soft, Sara said, "I know how you feel. I'm starting to fade too. Nevertheless, do your best. It's only a little longer. Marty, how is the street atmosphere in New Orleans?"

A skinhead splattered with tattoos, decorated with countless earrings, said, "Hot! Nuts! Crazies everywhere! People blowing each other away! And the cemeteries—nuts! The heat barrier still won't let any spirits find the light. It's so pathetic. They don't know what to do. They're trying to push the earth bounders aside, to move in on their flesh. Schizos everywhere. Some of the lost just wander in a frenzy, helpless, craving flesh. And Camille loves it. A whole city, no, a whole region under his control, dancing to his tune. He'll shit when he finds out we got through before he raised the temperature. He'll shit! I can't wait to see his face!"

Jake remembered once saying the very same words and shivered. Then he noticed that even though Sara's cohorts looked ill, grey, they had a certain glow about them, an aura of sorts.

"Marty," Sara said, "you know better than to act like that. Mind the shadow. Do not let it bend you. Mind the shadow."

Marty lowered his head.

"Okay," Sara said, "except for Justine, we all stay out of New Orleans. Until last minute. Until party time. That minimizes our chances of being unmasked. I know the chaos would probably cover us, but we can't take any chances." She shook her head and paused for a moment. "It will be good to have done with this. It will be good to get back."

Sara's prayer was echoed by murmurs and nods. She tilted her head as if to position herself for listening. Then her hand flashed up in a silent warning. The group snapped to attention, and each of them reached for weapons concealed under their clothes. They remained poised. Listening. Waiting. A boat raced toward them, its wake leaving a rooster tail of silver beads spraying up into the air. Joey was driving, and Chaoui sat next to him.

"Haul ass!" Chaoui shouted. "Police boats everywhere!"

The assembly broke and scrambled to their boats. Sara grabbed Jake's hand and pulled him to Joey's boat. Within seconds, the houseboat was deserted. All signs of life were gone before the water settled back into its reflective disguise.

Chapter 48

HE SUN FINALIZED ITS DAILY FAREWELL PERFORMANCE. Red and gold had fought for possession of blue, and once again lost the battle to a wash of star-sequined navy. Joey guided the boat to a gentle stop, still far from shore.

"You guys gotta get out now," said Chaoui.

"Here?" Jake said.

"You just follow Joey and everything will be okay. I'm gonna put on the lights and lure the cops away, just like a mama bird does."

Teeth clenched, Jake lowered himself over the side of the boat. It tilted with his weight and rocked as he released it. Grateful the water only rose to the level of his heart, Jake held his arms up to aid Sara as she followed him into the water. In the starlight, Jake could see panic in Sara's eyes as she realized the water was too deep for her. She slipped her arms around Jake's neck as he held her tightly against his side, safe above the surface. As Jake followed Joey into a tangled, overgrown section of the basin, Chaoui skillfully edged the boat back into the open, started the engine, and raced away.

The swamp was alive with night-cloaked activity. Fish leapt into the air and splashed back down, rewarded with bellies full of insects. Underwater life snaked by, gently brushing against Jake's legs. Eyes of red and gold peered calmly, then disappeared beneath the surface. The air was filled with the hooting of owls, the squawking of frogs, the screeching of night birds.

Surface debris clinging to him and trailing behind like a host of followers, Jake sloshed after Joey, through mud, past floating logs, around cypress, past alligators and snakes, all the while holding Sara close, preventing her from slipping beneath the

290

surface when they passed over places where the floor of the basin eluded their weary feet. When Jake's arms began to tremble, threatening to admit defeat, a grey shack perched well above the water on cypress poles slipped into view.

Joey climbed the slippery ladder that led up to the tattered door, then reached down and grabbed Sara's arms to help her dripping form into the ramshackle sanctuary. Next Jake stumbled through the dark rectangle. Blinking against the gloom, he backed against a wall and slid to the floor, darkness eclipsing the murky puddle that spread on the floor underneath him.

Joey lit an oil lamp and the one-room hunting camp glowed with golden, flickering light that drew memories of another lamp-lit night in Lafayette. Sara put her hand on Jake's shoulder, and he knew she had felt his thoughts touching her.

With a jerky movement, Joey slapped his breast pocket, then fished out a soaked pack of cigarettes. He groaned, then snapped his fingers, rushed to a dark corner of the room, and rummaged through a wooden chest. A smile flickering across his face, he extracted a plastic bag filled with emergency supplies: candles, matches, and cigarettes. Joey clutched his treasure in one hand, stood on his toes, reached up over a ceiling beam, and retrieved a rifle. He checked to see that it was loaded and he left Sara and Jake alone in the cabin.

* * *

Jake pulled Sara toward him, but she tore herself away.

"No."

"Sara. I didn't mean anything. I just—"

"No! I told you earlier! No! Flesh confuses purpose. One touch is enough to call up a shadow. One touch is enough to transform spirit into flesh. And I chose spirit. I still choose spirit."

"But in Lafayette—"

"That was then. I let my aching hunger for your soul bend me. I could not resist your pull, but now, I have to be strong. I cannot take any more chances. *We* can't take any more chances."

"Sara, I don't get any of this." Jake paced back and forth before the row of screened-in windows that lined the front of the cabin. Screeches and howls wavered through the darkened air as heat lightning snaked its way among the cypress. "What's going on? How did I get here? Look at me. One day I'm a pretty-damn-good photographer in New York City. Then, click, I'm in a shack out in God-only-knows-where, soaking wet, covered with slime." When he caught a whiff of cigarette smoke, Jake groaned, then unbuttoned his soaked shirt and threw it to the floor. It landed with a splat. "I have police after me. I feel like I'm being flushed down river rapids. Don't I even have a right to know which river I'm on? And for that matter, what are you planning in New Orleans?"

"The kind of answers you need, I can't give. You have to see them for yourself. Just be patient. It won't be long."

"The way things are going, I may not live much longer." In one deft movement, Jake was by Sara's side. He grabbed a fistful of her hair, and covered her lips with his.

Sara pushed Jake away. "Stop. No more."

"But—"

"Okay, you want to know, fine. It won't do you any good."

"I don't care. Tell me anyway." He moved toward her again.

Sara jerked herself away from Jake, then stepped back and pointed at him. "You chose this." Wagging her finger, she repeated, "You chose this. So did Camille. We were all together, once. Once we were all together, three splinters of the divine, together, all a part of the one soul. However, it was not good enough for him or you. Camille craved flesh. So he broke away, broke the rules. He bypassed the bargain of forgetfulness and took on flesh. No, he stole flesh."

"What, are you comparing me to Camille here?"

"No. That's not what I'm saying. The only similarity between you and Camille is the fact that neither of you were evolved enough to have been totally purified from sensuality, to be freed from the cycle of births, to enter into a divine state. But that was all right. We each start out that way. With every cycle of birth and death, a soul evolves, learns, becomes closer to the journey's end. Becoming was easy for me. And you were almost there. One more exile was all you needed.

"But Camille—when the shadow touched him—he was lost. He was too weak to resist; so the shadow dragged him into a lightless cave. Now we have to stop him. He has been causing an unbelievable disruption to the cosmos. Stolen bodies do not last long. So he has to keep switching. And with every switch, he releases a soul before its time, before it has had a chance to reach its potential. Then the heat. He knew we would be coming for him, so he built the heat barrier, the humidity, thinking he could stop us while he makes everything alive here crazy. The air is so heavy and the downward pressure so strong that sparks released from this area cannot reach the light. He thrives on the chaos. They all do."

"Ralph." Jake whispered. "The bartender from Bourbon Street and his mother-in-law."

"What?"

"Nothing. Wait a minute. Where did you get this?" Jake ran a finger down Sara's arm.

She shivered. "It's not stolen. It was...donated."

"Donated?"

"Donated. We were not desperate, and we were not particular about the form, so we could afford to take our time. We collected volunteers, so to speak. They all agreed to the trade off. We found them in back alleys, in prisons, in emergency rooms. We traded places with souls that had given up, no longer had the strength to go on. Murder victims—the executed—suicides."

The word suicide rang in Jake's ears as he remembered Heather's concerns for Sara. His stomach turned as he said, "Then the real Sara—"

"Gone."

"And all these people, Miss Marie, Chaoui, Delta?"

"No. They are earth bounders. Normal and, for the most part, unaware of what's going on."

"Wait a minute. I've seen things that have convinced me that just about anything you tell me could be true, but how did you explain this to them?"

"We didn't. The people here have an uncanny ability to sense whom they can trust. And they have a deep, if unconscious, appreciation for the magic that's all around them, magic that others refuse to see. And they know how to follow their hearts without question. They do not explain themselves and did not expect us to either. They simply believed in us and agreed to help.

It's as simple as that." The snap of a match being struck crackled in the air. "And Joey?"

"Well—he's an exception. There is a wildness in him. He walks a thin line between their world and ours. He's a part of the wildness that is one of the few remnants left of the past, other than customs that outsiders are so wont to leer at. Joey is a part of the silent secret that outsiders never get to see."

The bellowing of an alligator echoed across the water. Jake looked out into the darkness for a glimpse of glowing eyes. The air hummed and static electricity snapped at Jake when he put his hand on the window screen. Off in the distance, phosphorescent light waves flickered in the sky, just over the tops of the cypress trees.

Sara laughed. "Camille is so consumed by lust that he never counted on this." She pointed at the sky. "The basin is the ultimate representation of the choices we have to make. Opposites. Solid versus liquid. Positive versus negative. Flesh versus spirit. The basin is constantly reinventing itself. Always Becoming. Never Being. Always being divided and bent by man and his greed. Camille loves that part. However, he never expected—that all those pathetic, frenzied, homeless sparks of intellect that he freed, little by little, have been finding their way here, adding up, like stored energy in a giant battery. The basin has become an immense power source. If all goes well, he will be in for a big surprise, partly of his own making. I believe we will be successful in stopping him."

"Stopping him from what."

"Stopping him from having you."

"Me? Why me?"

"To bend you, divert you from your purpose, or worse—to steal your spark. We are not sure. But stop him, we will."

"How?"

"Release him suddenly, leaving him with no sanctuary. Like you did to Devereux. He'll be forced to return to the source to face his maker."

Jake closed his eyes and willed away memories of his last days in upstate New York. "I need to go with you to New Orleans. I need to face Camille."

"No! Absolutely not! You cannot be a part of that. It is too dangerous. You are not ready. You are too important. *Your purpose* is too important."

"Purpose? What Purpose?"

Sara touched Jake's face with gentle fingers. "Jake, you look so tired."

"No. I'm okay. I'm fine. Don't try to change the subject."

"Shhhhh." Sara placed fingertips on each of Jake's temples. "Shhhhh. You need to get some sleep."

"No. I want to—"

"Shhhhh."

Jake's eyelids flickered against a weight that pulled them down. He groaned as he lowered himself to the rough planks. Sara guided his descent, gently, then cradled him in her arms, rocking him, smoothing his hair, smiling as his curls wrapped around her fingers and clung to them with the rose petal strength of a tiny baby's grasp. Somewhere in the darkness, silver fish leapt up over the surface of the water to capture unsuspecting insects and splash back down into the depths of the basin.

In the darkest hollow of the night, Sara bent down and whispered in Jake's ear, "Remember, my love. Everything is a union of opposites. As flesh casts a dark veil over spirit, so spirit enters flesh as a spark of light. And as destruction comes of chaos, so does creation." She kissed him, then gently slipped away while he slept.

Chapter 49

*J*INGLE JANGLE. JINGLE JANGLE. The jingle-jangle rider rang in the air, each note a bit of colored light swarming around him as he and his grinding, screaming mount stumbled closer. Jake peered through the blurred colors, struggling to see who rode toward him.

"Wake up, Jake," said Delta. "We gotta keep moving. Can't stay in one place too long. Don't want the cops to catch up with you."

Jake's eyes snapped open, and at the other end of a black cave, he saw blinding gold and silver sparks swarming, dancing. Jake lifted his face off the floor and pulled his view away from the knothole that crossed the boundary through the roughly hewn floorboard.

Jake sat up and brushed dead leaves and wood splinters off his bare chest. The debris fluttered down, returning to the floor. Delta tossed Jake the damp shirt he had discarded the night before. Jake rose from the floor and fumbled with his shirt buttons. "Where's Sara?"

"Jake, you gotta put that out of your mind now."

Jake finished buttoning his shirt as he walked over to a mirror that hung, lopsided, against a back wall. A face he was not sure he knew looked back at him. Red-rimmed eyes peered through a filthy face. Snakes of black hair curled into a serpentine crown.

"Where is Sara?"

"Gone, Jake. Gone."

From the red-rimmed eyes that stared at Jake in the glass, silver sparks fell. Deep inside Jake's soul, a roar of pain quickened and grew until it burst out through his lips. When the roar had finished echoing against the cypress walls that surrounded him, Jake smashed his face against the mirror. It sprang to life as it shattered, turning into a hail of silver shards that shivered to the floor, leaving a veil of sparkling bits across Jake's chest and shoulders. As he followed Delta to his boat, Jake glistened in the sun and crimson tears dripped from his broken nose.

Jake found a place at the back of Delta's boat. He watched the tattered cabin shrink from view as they followed the channel that led toward Henderson. As they passed under the limbs of a tree that stretched out over the water, Jake broke off a straight, thin branch. Like Hansel, as he wound his way through the dark woods Jake dragged the tip of the branch in the water, trying to leave a trail in the duck weed veil, but the duckweed defied him by healing upon his passing.

* * *

Jake sat on Marie's rocker. The view from the Alligator Landing porch was a slightly warped, mirror image of what had come before. The ducks bobbed on the water as usual, squabbling with each other. Instead of harmless disagreements, they engaged in true battles. Blood-spattered feathers spun in the air and floated on the waves. Delta's hounds bayed and paced their enclosure, mindless, around and around, nipping each other after each collision.

Jake rocked and tapped the porch rail with his soggy stick. The sun was high, blazing. It seared the ground, burning the last few blades of grass still clinging to life. The blades wilted before Jake' eyes, in fast forward.

Jake tried to breath evenly, to lower the tension building in his chest. Ignoring his wishes, his lungs sucked in breath at their own uneven, gasping gait. His heart tagged along, frantically.

At the corner of his field of view, a pickup hauling a horse trailer along the top of the levee left a long, swirling trail of dust in its wake. Leaving the grey snake of dust to roll itself to death, the truck turned and slowly crept down the side of the levee and came to rest beside Alligator Landing. Chaoui slammed the pickup door.

"Jake. C'mon down and look at these horses. Boy, did I get a good bunch. Come see." Chaoui grinned wall-to-wall.

Using his stick, Jake tapped over to the truck to stand next to Chaoui. He peered between the horizontal slats that lined the side of the horse trailer. Packed two-by-two, six horses of various colors breathed anxiously in the close quarters: reds, browns, one buckskin, and a pale dapple-grey that whinnied at Jake. The restaurant door slammed after Delta as he raced down to the trailer to have a see.

"Chaoui," Delta said. Then he whistled. "These are some pretty horses. How much is the rent gonna cost me?"

"Well," Chaoui said. "The guy has this daughter that needs a place for her wedding."

"Oh, no. Not that again. You gotta stop giving my restaurant away."

"Don't worry. They promised it would be a real small thing."

Delta shook his head and Chaoui beamed with pride. As he circled the truck to get a look from the other side, Delta passed the windshield and said, "Phew. How did you see through them dead bugs? Shit! You gotta be crazy to drive like that."

Jake moved to stand beside Delta. Ogling the almost solid layer of dead insect carcasses, Delta said, "You better get'm off before they turn to cement."

Chaoui nodded.

"C'mon," Delta said. "Let's get out of this sun. We gotta have a meeting, get our plans together." Seeing that Jake had ignored his words, to stand and stare at the wall of insect stains, Delta said, "C'mon, Jake, we gotta fix that nose." When Jake ignored him, again, Delta shook his head and headed back the restaurant, calling out to Jake, "Don't get any ideas. Don't even think you can even reach the levee without us catching you."

Jake lifted his stick and used the tip to etch a squiggly line through the patch of dead insects spread across the windshield. As he circled the truck, his toe hit a barrier, almost causing him to trip. Next to the truck, protruding from the ground, was an ant pile swarming with scarlet life. Smiling crookedly, Jake pushed his stick into the pile and watched as a line of ants began to march up along the stick that had disturbed their sanctuary. Before the tiny army could reach his fingers, Jake leaned the stick up against the truck and let go. Within moments, the windshield of carcasses was covered with a red, crawling mass. Jake left the truck under the flood of hungry fire ants.

* * *

"What?" Jake said.

"I said close your eyes and hold still."

Jake closed his eyes. He felt a hand at the back of his head then screamed when somebody grabbed his nose.

"See," Delta said. "That wasn't so bad. Been doing it all my life. We guys get a broke nose couple times a year, and we still look like models. He grinned and posed."

When stars stopped flashing before his eyes, Jake considered searching out a mirror.

"So," Jake said to Delta. "What's this big meeting about?"

"Mardi Gras—what else?"

"Mardi Gras? The whole world is turning upside down, and you're worried about Mardi Gras? What the—"

The small gathering fell silent. Looks of disbelief passed over their faces.

"Mardi Gras doesn't wait for us to be in the mood. It's something that has to happen in its own time. And tomorrow is that time. Mardi Gras is something we *have* to do."

"Why?"

"We don't know. We just do it."

"Okay," Jake said. "So, do we ride on floats and throw beads, or do we stand on the street and catch them?"

"Beads?" Delta's face registered disgust. "We don't catch beads—we chase chickens."

"Chickens?" Jake said. "This is a joke, right?"

"Hell, no. Chickens. You can't make any kind of gumbo out of beads."

"Chickens?"

"Jake, we gotta get something straight here. We ain't doing Mardi Gras in New Orleans. We're going to Mamou. In New Orleans, Mardi Gras is this sissy, dress-up thing. You got these rich people making believe they're royalty, making believe they know what Mardi Gras is about. All those bead parades are bullshit. And at the end of Mardi Gras in New Orleans, you got these two Krewes, the Krewes of Rex and Comus. Rex, his

299

identity is a super secret. Rex and Comus get together and do this wife-swapping thing. It's disgusting."

"Yeah," Chaoui chimed in, shaking his head.

"Wife Swapping?" Jake said.

"Yeah," Chaoui repeated.

"There's this guy, Comus," Delta continued, "he's dressed in silver and he's supposed to be the god of mirth."

Chaoui chimed in, "Can you believe?"   .

Delta continued. "Well, this guy, Comus, dresses in gold and has a big ball, the dancin' kind. You know. Anyway, Rex leaves his ball and goes to the one Comus is having, then the two guys swap wives and they do this grand march around the ballroom with some opera music playing. Then after they do a toast, Mardi Gras is officially over. How's that for dumb?"

"Okay. So you catch chickens. That makes sense?"

"No, partner," Delta put his hand on Jake's shoulder. "We don't catch chickens, we chase chickens. Then we eat them."

"We?"

Delta nodded. "That's the tradition. Now that you're one of us, you gotta chase chickens too. We put on our costumes, chase chickens, and then we take the chickens back to town for a big gumbo. Enough for everybody. Now that's how to end Mardi Gras—with gumbo."

"Why?"

"We don't know. We just do it."

"Chaoui, do you chase chickens too?"

"No. I got this bum leg. I stay here and hold down the fort. Somebody's got to be ready to make bail for these guys."

The slamming of the screen door punctuated the end of Chaoui's statement. After storming through the door, Marie stomped straight over to Jake and plopped an unevenly stuffed plastic garbage bag on the table in front of Jake.

"Cher. Here's a costume—for tomorrow." She stood, hands on hips, her chin jutting out, waiting for Jake to unveil the offering. He slipped one hand inside the bag and felt the cool hand of satin. He pulled out what his fingers touched—the top half of a gold satin costume—a shirt of gold satin. Across the front, shivered four embroidered scenes: a red rooster crowing, a begging man, a costumed man dancing on his horse's back, and a line of horsemen disappearing into the distance. Jake shuddered as he ran his fingers over stitched-up tears, scars of many a Mardi Gras past. Rows of glistening, golden fringe ran all over the shirt, like the row of flames that encircle the sun. Next, he pulled out golden-fringed trousers to match. Intrigued by the elongated hump that nestled far back in the bag, Jake reached in one more time and slid out what turned out to be a long, conical hat of gold with fringe swirling barber-pole-fashion up to the peak, and a short cape that fell around the sides and back, like a curtain.

"A dunce cap?"

"No. It's a capuchon." Marie's lips trembled, and her chin moved a notch higher. "That was my husband's costume."

Jake swallowed hard. "I'm sorry, Marie. Really. It's a fine costume. Am I supposed to wear it?"

"Of course. That's the tradition. And you're one of us now, remember?"

"Right. I remember," Jake whispered as he ran a finger along the gold sequins that ran in a spiral, up along the cap, criss-crossed with the fringe. Marie's toe tapped the ground restlessly. The thumping pulled Jake's attention to Marie's feet. Then he looked up at her face and followed the direction of her gaze back to the black plastic bag. One more small lump disrupted the otherwise flat surface.

Marie nodded.

Jake reached in, located, and extracted the final item.

A mask.

Jake's heart clashed against his ribs when the visage appeared from under the shiny black envelope. The mask had been fabricated of black-wire window-screen mesh. Its eyes were buttons, its nose, long, pointed, phallic, and graced at the tip, with a safety pin that sported a round, golden jingle bell on each end. Its mouth was a reverse scarlet splash of a smile. Its long handlebar mustache and full beard were made of crimson hair, stolen from the mane or tail of a horse. Jake ran trembling fingers through the fall of scarlet hair. He fought to resist the urge to raise the silken strands to his lips. And the button eyes stared at him, soulless.

"It was my husband's costume," Marie said. "I had to fix it up for you." She beamed and waited for a response.

"It's a real fine costume," Jake said. "The best I ever saw. I'll be real proud to wear it." He lifted the mask to his face. The mesh screen made the view of Jake's surroundings appear to have been painted on a roughly woven canvas.

"Just like looking through a curtain, yeah. A lace curtain," Marie said. She nodded and headed for the door. Jake rushed after her and caught her before she left, just in time to surround her in a bear hug.

Jake returned to the table. When he looked down at the mask, his heart threatened to burst from his chest. He placed his hand over his breast pocket to hold down his racing heart. Doing so, he felt something sharp jabbing into his flesh. He reached into his pocket and discovered two jagged shards that had fallen from the mirror, earlier that day. As Jake held the shards in his trembling palm, they shot sparks of reflected light at him.

"Delta. Do you have any glue? Real good stuff?"

"Sure." Delta went into his office then returned with a tube in his hand.

Jake took the tube without comment. Slowly, so as not to damage the aged window-screen fabric, he twisted one of the button eyes until the threads holding it on snapped. He repeated the procedure with the other button. In the places once held by each button, Jake glued a shard of mirror. He picked the mask up and examined his handiwork. And looking into the mirror eyes, he saw his own reflected back at him. Jake raised the mask to his face, once again, and looked up at Delta. Seeing his own blue eyes looking back at him, Delta crossed himself, then said, "We gotta get our horses to Mamou before dark."

* * *

Sitting next to Delta in the front seat of the pickup, Jake marveled at the untainted windshield.

Chapter 50

HE SUN THREATENED TO SET as Delta's truck rumbled over sun-baked tractor ruts that criss-crossed the drive leading to Hotel Mamou, a ramshackle horse barn that had weathered many a Mardi Gras. Lights burning within cast golden fans out through gaps between shrunken boards into the half-light of dusk.

"We're here," Delta sang, his voice mimicking the light in his eyes. "We stay at this place every year. It's tradition. It's great to have a place where you can puke and not have to worry about pissing somebody off or gettin' a clean-up bill. C'mon, let's get the horses out and set up camp."

As Delta led the first horse out of the trailer, he stopped dead and said, "By the way, city boy, do you know how to ride horse?"

"Remember?" Jake said. "I'm one of you guys now."

Delta scrunched up one eyebrow and stared at Jake.

"Yeah," Jake continued. "I rode a horse, once."

"Once?"

"Yeah. Some of my friends and I got real drunk once and stole this cop's horse in Central Park. We took turns riding him, the horse that is, till we heard sirens. Then we had to let him go. Damn thing tried to follow us home."

"Oh boy. That's a real cowboy, him"

"Hey," Jake said. "You asked."

* * *

The rest of Delta's friends arrived with more horses, coolers packed with beer, and costumes in bags and boxes. The crew of revelers staked out landing strips by rolling sleeping bags onto freshly strewn hay. Jake chose a spot away from the rest, close to the door. As he rolled out his makeshift bed, the sound of crickets trickled through the door, gently at first. Then the crickets jacked up their song into a torrent of soprano bell sounds. Jake shook his head to be sure his ears were not ringing, to be sure the sound was actually coming from outside. Joey, who was sitting by the door, fondling an unlit cigarette, laughed at Jake's city-boy naïveté.

* * *

"Hey! That's my tit!"

Jake whirled to face the source of the exclamation.

"No it's not!" said the red-bearded man who had once stood next to Chaoui at the Alligator Landing bar.

"The hell it ain't," yelled a gap-toothed man wearing a huge bra over his hairy chest. One cup was filled and the other hung limp. "I know my own tit when I see it." He dropped his dress.

"Bullshit," said red-beard. "I cut these out of my own couch cushions, just last night. The wife chewed my ass for it. Ask her." He held two, matching, unevenly carved foam cones. "See?"

"Well, what am I gonna do like this?" Gap-tooth gestured toward the empty side of his bra.

Red-beard picked up a handful of horse droppings and tossed them at his competitor. "Stuff the other side with that."

"You ass hole!" screamed gap-tooth. He reached down and raked up a heap of yellow straw with splayed fingers. After meticulously stuffing the empty cup he said, "Now I can be the man with the golden tit."

Laughing, Delta slapped Jake on his back and said, "Le coquin vole aun autre, le diable en ris."

Jake froze.

"Delta," Jake mouthed the words twice before they would leave his lips, "what does that mean?"

"Mean? Uh. Let me think in English. Okay, it means, *when one thief steals from another, the devil laughs.*"

Jake leaned back against the side of the barn. A protruding nail jabbed his back, jerking his weight back onto unsteady legs. Perspiration leapt out of his pores. He smeared the beads of sweat across his face with a trembling hand."

"Jake. You okay?"

"Yeah. Sure," Jake mumbled.

"C'mon, bro. Time to get your costume on," Delta said.

"Costume? Tonight? No, tomorrow is Mardi Gras."

"I know that. But this is Lundi Gras, Mardi Gras Eve. We're gonna go to town in costume so the cops can't spot you."

"Town?"

"Yeah. Lafayette. We gotta go to the dance hall. It's—"

"I know," Jake said, "it's tradition."

"Riiiiiiiiight. We used to go to the street party in Mamou, but it's way too crazy there. Half the time we would end up spending Mardi Gras knocked out, face down in the street under a foot of empty beer cans. Or worse, we would end up in jail. Missed the whole Mardi Gras, just about every time. Them Mamou guys are crazy. They love to fight, them. Anyway, now we do Lundi Gras in Lafayette just to keep out of trouble. It's a pain in the ass, but worth it."

"I can stay here. I don't feel like—"

"No way," Delta said, "you don't think we're gonna take our eyes off you for one minute, do you?"

"But—"

"But, nothing. You're going with us. That's just the way it is. Here's your costume." Delta tossed a wad of checkered satin toward Jake.

"But that's not my costume."

"For tonight it is. My pop's costume only rides on Mardi Gras. This one will work for tonight."

* * *

As they passed through the door out into the fading evening, Jake said, "What about Joey. Why isn't he wearing his costume?"

"Oh, you know Joey. He has to do things his own way."

Amid a group that included a scholar with an over-sized mortar board hat, a nun, two hairy-chested women, and assorted medieval gnomes with conical hats, Jake strode toward the trucks, wearing a checkered jester costume, carrying a plastic mask in one hand and, in the other, a hat with three curved points ending in jingle bells.

"Okay now," Delta addressed the crew. "We're going in these two trucks; so first let's count heads. One, two—twelve. Okay," he yelled over the shrilling of the crickets, "six in each truck."

Like children on a sporting field trip, fighting over which team they would play on, the costumed men pushed each other as they scrambled into the trucks, some in the cabs, and the rest out back in the beds.

"Hey, Tits," Delta yelled to red-beard. "Can you drive for me? I think I had one too many beers, already."

"Okay."

Delta leapt out of his place next to Jake. Red-beard tried to stuff himself into the space behind the wheel.

"I can't fit. My tits are in the way."

Delta examined the situation and tried to stuff the foam mounds behind the wheel.

"No way. It won't work," said red-beard. "I'll be all lop-sided." He popped out of the truck and loped over to the other, then crawled over the tailgate. Delta slipped back into his original place, crossed himself, and started the truck.

As they headed south, toward I-10, the setting sun splashed a mask of red across the right side of Jake's face. When they met I-10 and turned east toward Lafayette, the red glow crawled around behind Jake and sat on the back of his neck until the sun dropped below the horizon, pulling its glow along with it, leaving a creeping darkness behind.

* * *

Darting silhouettes streaked across the distorted streets of Lafayette. They moved with such erratic speed, a poorly timed blink could mask their passing. Police cars screeched after the frantic shadows, sirens wailing, whirling lights flailing the darkness with streaks of red and blue. Screams echoed around corners. Hysterical laughter knifed through the heavy air.

Up ahead, the road split not into divergent directions, left and right, but into two ways to reach the same end, one up and over railroad tracks that crossed the road, and the other, tunneling below the tracks.

The wail of a train whistle grew louder and louder as an unseen train approached, heading for the intersection with the road. Delta pushed his foot down on the gas pedal, causing the dial on the speedometer to lean to the right. The truck and train, coming from directions perpendicular to each other, raced for the crossroads. Jake's breath caught in his throat as he participated in the deadly game of chicken, sitting frozen in the dunce seat.

Just as the street split in two, Delta chose the lower path. The road dropped down, sucking the truck and its whooping captives deep down under the train tracks, then, with a stomach-turning dip, whipped them back up to ground level. When the streets were again visible, the force of speed lifted the truck into the air, then dropped it back onto the street. The riders squealed like giddy children stuck at the top of a Ferris Wheel, holding their arms up in a "look, mom, no hands" posture. Delta whisked the truck around a sharp right corner and the riders were pulled over the side by centrifugal force, some losing their grip on half-empty beer cans.

* * *

Delta jammed the pickup into a narrow space between two other trucks. The riders spilled over the tail gate, adjusting their costumes as they headed for the dance hall.

"Here," Delta said. "Don't forget your mask. Can't have cops messing up Mardi Gras."

Jake took the opaque plastic mask and slipped it over his face. In an instant, the narrow space between his flesh and the molded shield filled with the steam of his breath.

* * *

The dance hall was packed with revelers, belly to belly whether they knew each other or not. Whether lovers or strangers—it mattered not—flesh met flesh with only a barrier of perspiration-soaked fabric to separate the members of the crowd from each other.

As Jake sucked down beer after beer, he scanned the crowd for a glimpse of Sara, all the while knowing with every cell of his body that she was very far away, preparing to dance with the devil.

Blackout!

Every light in the dance hall snapped off in unison, leaving behind a steamy, black void. Jake's senses strained to defend him from what the darkness hid from his eyes. The acrid scent of something burning assailed his nostrils. He coughed. Feather-tip fingers touched his glistening face. The crowd roiled like storm clouds, whirling him away from his place next to Delta and Joey. Jake gasped for breath as he once did while tumbling underneath the green lace barrier that hovered over the basin. As the current of flesh carried him further from his safe harbor of comrades, Jake prayed Sara would come to bring home to him.

A glow of blue light appeared over the stage area, illuminating clouds of sapphire-tinted smoke that rolled and swirled like the crowd. As the current carried Jake closer to the stage, the blue smoke touched his face, sticky like flypaper. He tried to break loose, to swim back to safety, but was helpless against the pull of the undertow.

From the back of the stage, a fantastic mask whispered into view. As the mask of purple and gold satin moved closer, the crowd pushed Jake toward it until he was crushed up against the edge of the stage.

His own mask threatening to smother him, Jake gasped for air in the clouds of swirling, suffocating smoke. On stage, the purple and gold mask moved closer, haloed by a mane of satin fringe. The spotlight widened its target area and the rest of the costumed man, who seemed to float across the stage, edged into view, still partly hidden by the embrace of the fog. The witch-doctor form slipped closer and closer, surrounded by a cloak of purple satin. He carried a long, twisted, wooden staff. A serpent coiled around it, its carved head forming a crown for the staff.

Bang! Bang! Bang!

The witch doctor slammed his staff down three times. The wooden planks of the stage echoed with each attack. Then he began to sing in a striking, plaintive voice, a cappella, in a minor key, his French words mumbo-jumbo to Jake. As the witch doctor sang and whirled, his purple cloak spinning around him, Jake shivered. He ran his hand down his chest, wishing he was wearing his golden Mardi Gras costume embroidered with sacred tattoos, sacred armor. Every now and then, the witch doctor would interrupt his song of mystery to pounce forward, to lunge at the crowd and hold his staff over their heads as if in benediction. And Jake thought he heard the jingle-jangle rider ringing in his ears like a million crickets.

The witch doctor lunged toward Jake and shook his mane of satin ribbons as if to shake the jingle-jangle sound out of his ears. Then he went on with his song, wailing, almost crying until his mysterious message was complete. When the song was over, he spoke.

"Life is a masquerade." The witch doctor inhaled deeply making a snake-like hissing sound. "And Mardi Gras is a carnival of truth. On Mardi Gras, you get to wear the mask of truth, the mask of who you really are, which is always opposite to the one you wear each and every day of the year." He surveyed the crowd as if waiting for a response. "And on Mardi Gras, Hermes, the master of boundaries rules." He banged his staff on the ground three more times.

"At midnight, Mardi Gras officially begins and all boundaries dissolve so that the dead can walk among us. Masked. Look around you. See anybody who might be one of them? You know how the joke goes. If you don't see one around you, then maybe—" He held up his staff and whirled around like a compass held too near a magnet, his head thrown back, his cape and mane floating in the blue smoke. "Then maybe it's yooooouuuuuuu!" When he stopped whirling, he was looking at Jake, his staff held out before himself. His eyes locked with Jake's, the witch doctor reverently tapped Jake on each shoulder, as if knighting him.

Jake's flesh buzzed. He heard the jingle-jangle rider approaching and stared at the witch doctor, waiting for him to unmask, to prove he was not the rider.

* * *

The blue fog began to dissipate as if inhaled and purified by the lungs of the crowd. Suitably costumed musicians joined the witch doctor on stage. When his court was in place, the witch doctor, with his back turned to the crowd, slid the mask off his lowered head. Then he untied the cord that held his robe tight around his neck, letting the purple satin slither to the floor and puddle around his feet.

His back still to the crowd, clad in a lavender satin suit, the witch doctor continued. "The day after Mardi Gras, lent begins. It's a time of the spirit. That's why some people say that Mardi Gras represents a casting off of the flesh." He turned and paced

309

over to the edge of the stage, then looked up with black-brown eyes, crowned by a cap of raven-dark curls. "I don't know about you, but—"

He put one finger in his mouth, slowly pulled it out, then touched it to his right hip. "Sssssssss." He imitated the sound of steam and yanked back his finger as if it had been burned. "But I think I'll keep mine."

He grabbed a whistle that hung from his neck and blew out a shrill, metallic scream. The band tore into action, pumping out hot rock'n'roll. The witch doctor transformed into a rocker. He gyrated, danced, and gestured, whipping the crowd into a frenzy. Items of women's clothing flew over the stage, fluttering down onto the planks. Partially clothed dancers slithered against one another. Beers splashed to the floor, making it as slippery as the bottom of the basin. Some dancers slipped and fell. Others, tripping over their comrades, joined them on the floor. Jake, still vibrating from the touch of the witch doctor's staff, barely felt someone grab his arm. He followed in a daze as Joey led him to the pickup.

* * *

"I'm too drunk to drive. Delta waited for the others, slumped over the hood of his truck. Tits, you gotta take my place. I'm not gonna make it."

"Okay, I'll try." The hairy man in the over-stuffed gingham dress pressed himself behind the wheel of Delta's truck as the rest of the gang piled over tailgates for the return trip to Mamou. Tits started the truck. "So far, so good," he said as he groaned the truck out of its tight parking spot. Once out on the open road, Tits yelled, "Yahooooo! Look. I've got, not one, but two designated drivers." He raised his arms and turned the wheel with his mammoth breasts. The truck careened toward the side of the road. Jake grabbed the wheel and steadied the truck until Tits calmed down and took the wheel with his hands. Joey sat next to Jake, unruffled, soberly chain smoking.

* * *

When they pulled into the yard of Hotel Mamou, Jake leapt out of the truck, overjoyed to have arrived in one piece. "You guys are fucking nuts, a bunch of clowns," Jake yelled.

"C'mon, don't be like that," Delta said. "Okay, let's count heads. Gotta be sure we all made it back. Thirteen. Okay. We're all here."

"Wait a minute," said a nun. "What's this?"

Jake looked over the side of the truck and said, "It looks like a dead elf." Delta grabbed the Elf's legs and began to help the nun drag him toward the barn.

"I won't sleep in the same barn with this guy," Jake said. "He could be a serial killer, for all we know."

"Awe, don't be like that," Delta whined. "We can't leave him out in the yard. The big betaille will get him." Delta grabbed the legs Jake had dropped and helped the nun get the unconscious Elf into the barn. "Let's leave him by the door, just in case. He don't look too good."

"No. I'm sleeping by the door," Jake protested.

* * *

As if victims of a massacre, the costumed men dropped to the ground and begin to snore almost immediately. Half drunk, Jake flopped back on his sleeping bag and, with his arm over his eyes, tried to sleep surrounded by men who snored louder than the horses.

* * *

The jingle-jangle rider came closer. Jake heard the horse's joints grinding. The rider came so close, Jake could feel the horse's breath on his face, hot, foul. When the rider raised a hand to his mask, as if to remove it, Jake panicked. He strained to wake. He screamed to himself, make a noise, move, anything, just wake up. Just as the mask began to slide off the rider's face, Jake was shaken into the conscious world. The Elf had rolled over, slamming his arm over Jake's chest. Jake pushed the arm off him, then rose and sat on the chair by the door. With his eyes wide open, he silently waited for dawn.

Chapter 51

*J*AKE LUMBERED OUT OF THE BARN, hung over, his ears
pained by the piercing song of a million tree frogs. He
picked straw from his hair, stretched and thrust himself into the blizzard of fog that waited outside. He saw nothing
but white, nothing but for a tiny, red glow that flickered amidst
the storm of suspended water particles. The tiny beacon moved
closer. Somewhere in the fog-shrouded distance, a locomotive
howled as it rushed along its solitary path, unseen. Jake walked
toward the red glow and met Joey, head-on.

Exuding smoke from his nostrils as he spoke, Joey said, "It
really sucks to be a train."

"What?" Jake strained to hear Joey speak again.

"Being a train. It sucks...Always stuck on a track with only
one way to go. And there's only room for one on a track. That's
the worst part. Howling your guts out, saying the same thing,
over and over, nobody ever answering back." Joey pulled fog
through his cigarette again, then exhaled and gazed out into the
whiteness. "Sucks."

Joey headed toward the trucks. Jake grabbed his shoulder.
"Saying what? What do trains say?"

"You know," Joey said. He flicked his cigarette to the ground
and stomped out its feeble glow. He lit another, and blowing blue
breath into the fog, walked away.

"Jake!" Delta's voice echoed from somewhere in the dark
recesses of the barn. "Time to suit up."

* * *

Wearing his golden suit of tattoos, hiding behind his second
skin of psychic armor, Jake sat next to Delta on the front seat of
the rumbling, hay-packed pickup. A fully loaded horse trailer

312

creaked behind. The screen mask with mirror eyes rested on his lap. He fondled the red horsehair mustache that spilled from it.

Veiled by fog, the road ahead was visible for only a few yards. Occasionally, pairs of golden headlights rushed at the pickup like rabid fireflies. A chocolate waterway snaked alongside the road, racing with the headlights of Delta's truck. The morning was black and white and inky blues; a stark watercolor. Hints of black, dry-brush trees reached up out of the ground like hands of glory, their bony fingertips fading into the churning fog. Fields, flooded with silver-grey water, separated by fingers of land, were pockmarked with hundreds of conical crawfish traps.

The pickup rumbled over the planks of a wooden bridge as the road crossed paths with the bayou. On both sides of the waterway, trees reached out to each other, touching in poignant, fingertip unions, like parting lovers.

Delta stopped at a crossroad.

"Good your side? Hey! You gotta help me drive, you."

Jake pulled his attention away from the bayou and peered into the fog, searching for oncoming traffic. "Looks okay over here, I guess."

Delta eased down on the gas pedal, and they crossed the intersection. Confident because they appeared to be alone, Delta increased their speed.

Out of the fog, burst the feathery image of a man staggering towards the pickup, straight in its path.

"Oh shit!"

Delta pressed the brakes. As the truck slowed, the horse trailer began to fishtail. Jake grabbed the armrest on his door and braced himself. The staggering man loomed ahead in the protracted moments that stood between the truck and disaster. He cradled a silver foil twelve-pack of beer under one arm and held a brown paper wrapped bottle in his right hand. Just before impact, he raised the bottle to his lips, cranked his head back for a long gulp, lost his balance, and tumbled into a gully, just at the decisive moment. Delta slid his foot off the brake, recovering control of the vehicle, and avoiding certain disaster.

"Holy shit!" Delta said. Jake kept his focus on the road ahead.

* * *

The image of Mamou crept out of the fog like a deserted ghost town, its main street littered with debris—plastic cups, aluminum cans, shreds of discarded clothing. The silent avenue echoed with an occasional whoop or the scream of a distant horse.

Delta parked his truck alongside the American Legion and turned to Jake. "Jake, you gotta put your mask on now. And you can't take it off all day. Remember, that's the rule."

Jake looked down at the mask waiting on his lap. Daylight had crept over the horizon, breathing morning onto the mirror eyes. They gazed up at him—silver—they gazed up at him with his own eyes until he grasped the mask and turned it away. He placed it over his face and stretched the elastic band around his head, then looked up to view the world through the wire curtain. His gaze fell on the road that led back to I-10.

"Remember," Delta warned, "Joey will have the keys, and he'll be watching you. So don't get any ideas about getting away."

Jake stepped out of the truck and tied on his capuchon. An infinitely fine, almost imperceptible mist fell as they helped Joey lead the horses out of the trailer. The beasts, as if sensing anticipation suspended in the air, came crashing out of the trailer, blowing fog through their nostrils, whinnying, tossing their heads, their clip-clop steps sounding like palpitating hearts.

A clown clutching a constellation of helium balloons passed as Joey and Delta saddled the horses. A dapple grey wearing a feathered Indian headdress and fluttering foil Mardi Gras socks clopped by, carrying on his back Mr. Death, a tall, thin man wearing a black top-hat, a tie, and tails, his face painted like a skull.

The pickup loaded with the rest of Delta's friends arrived. Tits and the rest of the gang piled out, carrying the dead Elf with them. The Elf, finally semi-conscious, smiled and waved to the crowd as they heaped him onto a horse. He leaned forward and wrapped his arms around his horse's neck as if to find a cozy spot to sleep.

The silver-grey horse with a black mane pulled loose from David and threaded its head under Jake's arm.

"Looks like this one is in love with you, Jake. Take him."

Jake took the reins and hoisted himself onto the silver horse's saddle. Somehow, he felt at home there.

"C'mon, Jake, let's get under the trees while there's still room. Joey will meet us there after he gets his costume on."

In front of the American Legion gathered a stand of live oak trees. Their branches reached out horizontally, resting on each others' shoulders like a group of football players in a huddle. Their intricately interwoven limbs formed a canopy that stretched over the lawn. Underneath loomed a dark, silent haven. Protected from the mist, Jake and Delta led the horses to the center of the yard and stood alone, the first arrivals.

"When do ya think the others will get here?" Jake whispered, afraid to disturb the gravid silence that hovered under the canopy.

Delta shrugged.

"Caw! Caw! Caw!" The rending screams of a crow shattered the silence.

Jake whipped around to look toward the source of the disruption. Invisible until he moved, like a walking stick or a lizard, a man camouflaged in a patchwork of fabrics representing every earth color sat perched on his buckskin horse with only a torn blanket for a saddle. Browns, moss greens, blacks all peppered with gilt bells and dusky roses vined up his arm and climbed in a spiral to the point of his conical hat. Frightened by the sounds that ripped out of its rider, the buckskin horse whirled around. The Green Man swigged lustily out of a beer can. Struggling to control his horse as it whirled, the Green Man's Lady Godiva-like cascades of Spanish moss hair that poured out from under his hat, rose into the air and swirled around him like the garlands on a maypole.

Jake locked his gaze on the Green Man and examined him for signs of humanity. A screen mask painted blue on one side and red on the other expunged his features. A crooked, purple, pointy nose protruded from the line of demarcation that marked the meeting place between opposing colors. Black horsehair formed a beard that dripped from his chin. Layers of tattered rags hung from him like the seven veils of a belly dancer. High-water pants, each leg a different color, did not quite meet the tops of black, scuffed, cowboy boots, exposing an expanse of human flesh. The Green Man froze. His mottled form dissipated, and again became one with the background of bushes and trees.

A man with a death face and a black funeral suit split up the back staggered by Jake, then passed out, face down on the grass. Other horsemen clad in medieval costumes with pointed hats and multi-color fringes moved under the trees, dragging in tow horses decorated with rows of Mardi Gras beads and feathers. Sightseers, oppressed by the weight of cameras, pushed through the conglomeration of costumed men and horses. A small boy laughed past Mr. Death, but screamed in terror when he spotted the Green Man. The boy's mother turned the child's face to her shoulder and rushed away, crooning, "Don't look, baby."

A large covered trailer loaded with musicians pulled up and parked near the Legion hall. Silent, their instruments mute, they stared at the American Legion.

A flatbed trailer, dragged by a small, green tractor, followed next in line. Jesters, medieval clowns, monsters, gnomes, nuns, priests, scholars, Indians, pirates, and bearded women, each carrying at least one can of beer, queued in a shoulder-to-shoulder mass outside the Legion hall.

When the Capitaine arrived, all horsemen dismounted and the crowd parted in silence. Unmasked, dressed in jeans, spurs, a cowboy hat, and a long, purple satin cape, the Capitaine unlocked the doors to the Legion and led his runners into the empty hall. The runners filed in solemnly and lined up in rows facing a makeshift stage. Jake stayed close to Delta. When they all found places and became silent, the Capitaine spoke from an elevated position on the stage. The runners stood, enthralled, their only movements, arms passing beer cans to hungry lips.

"Okay, men. Listen up. I'm only gonna tell you the rules once. First of all, men only on the run. We'll be checking you on that. No weapons. You will be searched. No fighting. Everyone is required to be fully masked at all times. Disobeying the orders of any captain will result in your being ejected from the ride. No profanity or indecent exposure. Most important, you must stay on the public roads until the landowner gives me the go-ahead for you to enter onto his private property. Remember, this is about tradition."

As the Capitaine spoke, middle captains searched the riders, row-by-row. The Capitaine paused until the search was over then said, "Okay men, let's have a safe ride."

* * *

The congregation burst out of the hall, whooping, screaming, yelling, "Marrrrrdi Grrrrrras! Marrrrrdi Grrrrrras!" Jake was carried along by the throng.

Horses whirled, pawed the ground, and leapt with excitement, fog pouring from their nostrils as their riders mounted. The crew of horseless chicken chasers swarmed over a flatbed trailer, jumping up and down in unison, causing such a quake that the driver of the green tractor was almost dismounted. He clutched the steering wheel with one hand and his hat with the other as he hung, sideways, off his seat. The band tuned up as the riders led their horses onto the street.

"Remember, men, two-by-two." The Capitaine shouted his command from atop his golden-brown mount. The shaggy stallion, eyes fogged by age, pawed the ground, as if to impress the crowd with his rank. The Capitaine reached down and slid a flag from under his belt.

He unrolled the white square of fabric, raised the banner up over his head, and held it there until he had the full attention of the crowd, until everyone was breathless, suspended in time, silent...Then, he waved the flag and the multitude screamed and whooped. The band ripped into the Mardi Gras Song, and two-by-two, the procession marched down the street toward the edge of town.

Onlookers lined the street, waving flags, taking pictures, honoring the departing warriors as they marched off on their quest. The procession turned to pour itself onto the black-ribbon highway. The line of horseman, their colors muted by the fog, looked like a string of Christmas lights someone had forgotten to plug in. The long procession trickled into the fog, as if disappearing into another dimension. Jake watched from his position at the end of the line and remembered the parking lot mural in Lafayette. The colors whirled in his head. The sound of the parade echoed off in the distance, as if another duplicate procession was marching just

317

outside his field of view. Jake watched from his position at the end of the line.

* * *

When they reached the first farm on their list of targets, the revelers gathered at the front gate and waited for the Capitaine to ride ahead and negotiate with the landowner. "Mardi Gras— Mardi Gras," the runners chanted. A few anxious clowns and gnomes slipped through the gate, unable to contain their excitement any longer, unable to resist the lure of a mud pit. Some dove, some slid, and some rolled, but they all ended up flopping around in the waist-deep muck like drunken seals.

A middle captain rode over to the pit and pulled a flapping bird out from under his cape. "Practice chicken," he yelled over the din. He threw the chicken into the mud pit. The uniformly brown pit dancers dove after the hapless bird, followed by another wave of revelers who jumped the fence and piled on top of them. When the squirming heap finally unraveled itself, a slippery, brown nun rose from the mire with a mud-plastered chicken flapping wildly in his hand. The runners whooped and howled at their first taste of victory.

The Capitaine rode over to the gate and disturbed the victory celebration. "If you want to catch a chicken you have to dance for the man."

The band cranked out the Mardi Gras song and the mob rushed through the fence and danced, in mud, on dirt, on grass, and some, standing on the backs of their horses.

"I'll hold the horses while you guys run," Jake said to Delta.

"Awe, don't be like that," Delta whined.

The band stopped playing, mid phrase, and all heads turned toward the captains. Delta relented and ran off to join the foray. With a splattering of soil clots kicked up by his horse, one of the captains rode off into the field, a hundred chicken chasers in frantic, tumbling pursuit. Well out ahead of the pack, the captain whirled to face his pursuers and taunted them with a display of empty hands.

"It's a fake," runners yelled in unison. The crowd scrambled for a new direction, bumping heads, tripping over each other. Another captain, on the far side of the field, blew a whistle and

318

waved a chicken over his head. The runners raced off after the mounted man, tumbling over ruts and each other. The Capitaine spurred his horse into a full gallop. He waved the chicken over his head and tossed it into the air. It flapped to the ground and scurried off in a zigzag direction. The runners chased after it, whooping and howling, crashing through bramble bushes, around sheds, over woodpiles, until the chicken slipped through a wire fence. Catching their clothes on barbs, the runners flopped over the fence, only to have the chicken change sides again, and again. One of the runners fell on the chicken and the chase was over. The victor leapt to his feet, and like a football player who had just made a touchdown, he danced with the flattened chicken held high. A whistle blew and the crowd raced after another captain, and then another, until twelve more chickens were captured.

One-by-one, the victorious chicken chasers turned their prizes over to the Capitaine who then handed them to the man in charge of tallying up the results of the chase. Each chaser's name was carefully recorded as his chicken was tossed into a crate in the back of a pickup. A pirate marched over to the Capitaine, his eyes glowing, his chest filled with pride, a chicken held high. Before he relinquished his trophy to the Capitaine, he yanked a fistful of feathers from his prize and stuck them in his hair.

From his place just outside the limits of the farm, Jake watched, apart, and not a part.

* * *

Delta ran to Jake, his costume torn, the point of his hat bent over. "Jake. Man, you look too sober. It's time for a beer." He handed Jake two sweating cans. The sun threatened to burst through the thinning veil of fog. It waited, patiently, showing itself only as a circular specter that glowed through the center of a heavy, white cloud.

The horse that carried the Elf sauntered up to Jake. When it came to a stop, the Elf slowly slid off his saddle and tumbled to the ground. Jake handed his beers back to Delta. "We can't leave him here, can we," Jake said.

"Nope."

Jake leaned down, pulled the Elf to his feet, and tried to stand him against his horse. He slumped to the ground. Jake draped him over his shoulder, carried him to the chicken truck, and deposited him next to the coop. The chicken counter shrugged his shoulders and shook his head as he positioned the Elf so he would not interfere with his ability to close the tailgate.

Jake returned to his place next to Delta and retrieved his beers. He drank one beer straight down, and started the other as soon as he was back on his horse.

"I know who you are!" Pointing up at Jake was a grotesque clown with an orange nose twisted like a wilted carrot. "Ha-ha-ha-ha-ha-ha! I know who you are!" The carrot-nosed clown danced and sang in a screeching falsetto voice, like a bratty child, "I know who you are! I know who you are!"

The Capitaine blew his whistle and the throng haphazardly recovered its two-by-two form and followed him toward its next appointment. Jake, his heart beating erratically, turned away from the mocking clown and rode away without looking back. However, the song echoed in his mind. "I know who you are." And Jake thought, for just a moment, he could hear the jingle-jangle sound of his dream rider approaching.

Holding his position at the end of the line, Jake watched the procession turn another corner. This time, as the line of horsemen stretched across the horizon, the veri-tone grey cloud cover slid back like a lazy eyelid, changing the watercolor sky painting of grays and blacks to a *Hudson River School*, full-color sky. The golden sun flamed down at Jake, forcing him to drop his gaze to the ground where a breeze blew swirls of maple seeds in circular patterns. Their tan surfaces blazed golden in the sunlight as they spun on the ground like hundreds of sparkling-eyed fish. Jake gathered up enough courage to look back up at the horizon, his breath caught in his throat.

Someone had plugged in the string of Christmas lights, and the procession of satin and beads and sequins glistened in the sunlight like a river of molten gems, each spark of color, a star fallen from the sky. And as Jake passed under the maple tree, a rain of spinning helicopter seeds spiraled down on him, like a shower of golden-eyed fish.

* * *

A half hour and a good number of beers later, the procession neared the next stop—a small house at a crossroads.

As they tied their horses to the fence that circled the property, Delta said, "Partner, this is a real fun stop. This guy throws chickens, and if we beg real good, he gives money too. C'mon. It's for a good cause, remember?"

Jake uttered scoffing sounds as his alcohol numbed fingers fumbled at their task.

Delta grabbed the reins from Jake and tied his horse to the fence. "Couillon! I gotta take care of you just like a little kid. Now c'mon; let's do it." Delta gave Jake a second to respond, then left him with the horses.

A jagged-edged shadow fell over Jake. He turned and faced the Green Man. The Green Man tethered his horse next to Jake, nodded, and leapt over the fence, his veils flapping in the wind like the wings of a great bird

A glistening waterfall of revelers toppled over the fence and gleefully flopped to the ground taking advantage of the fact that the homestead was set lower than the road. They rolled down the steep expanse of grass that led to the house, then leapt to their feet, dizzy, bumping into each other, some falling to their knees, begging. A rider, dressed like the bride of Hitler, pulled the landowner's wife off a porch swing and forced her to dance with him. Davy Crockett, in orange satin, yanked the woman's child off the porch and pretended to kidnap the boy who kicked and screamed all the way to the beer truck.

"I know who you are! I know who you are!"

Jake whipped around just in time to see the carrot-nosed clown, with an theatrical gesture, drop to one knee, put an invisible camera to his face, and scream, "Cliiiiiiiick!" Then he laughed through his screen mask decorated with jumbled, oversized teeth. "I know who you are! I know who you are!" The clown danced around Jake.

Jake shuddered, then spun around, and scrambled over the fence. His costume caught on a nail. Trying to unhook his pants while half over the fence, his mind addled with alcohol, was more than Jake could handle. He lost his hold on the whitewashed plank, flopped to the ground, and racing with his heart, he tumbled down the hill, crashing into the heap of revelers.

"This man's got money for us," the Capitaine yelled. "If you want it, you have to dance."

All around Jake, the heap of riders untangled itself and rose into a dancing mass. A bishop grabbed Jake's arm and pulled him to his feet. Jostled by the drunken crowd, Jake searched for a way out of the mass. He spotted the carrot-nosed clown dancing toward him and panicked. Jake danced back into the crowd and melted into the rainbow. When the riders fell to their knees to beg, Jake followed suit, glad to be close to the earth. Just like the rest, he crawled on his knees, pointing to his open palm, begging. When a vision of a quarter hitting a New Orleans sidewalk whisked past his mind, he shivered and huddled on the ground.

He was begging in public, something he swore he would never do.

Planes buzzed overhead as they circled the celebration. A rope hanging from a tree was adorned by a half dozen red-green-gold-purple-orange-blue men who swung from it like a bunch of screaming, wild fruit. A cowman stood on his head, on his saddle, and danced upside down with his rubber udders falling over his face. Groups of riders danced, standing on their horses, switching mounts in time with the music. Another group laid claim to a small mud puddle, only a few inches deep. They danced on their horses, then leapt into the air, turned back flips, and belly-whopped into the mud.

The music hushed. All eyes turned to the Capitaine who pointed his flag to the roof of the house.

There on the roof, sat the landowner and his sons, guarding a coop full of chickens. The first chicken flung into the air sailed off toward the road. The crowd scrambled after it, drawing Jake along. He tried to break away from the throng, but at every turn, it reformed around him like the egrets over the basin. The next chicken sailed toward the back yard. The crew swarmed around the house like a mass of ants after sugar. One of the runners ran into a protruding air-conditioner. His head smacked it with a bong. He staggered back and fell flat on his back. A singing crowd danced around him and poured beer into his mouth. When he was revived and staggered to his feet with gestures of rebirth, they cheered.

One chicken sailed after another.

Jake spotted the green man on the roof, creeping up behind the landowner, poised to steal the last chicken. The farmer tossed the final prize before the Green Man could reach his goal, so he dove off the roof after it.

The Capitaine's whistle turned the horde back toward the horses. A beer clasped under one arm, and another in his hand, Jake remounted his horse and rode toward the head of the line with Delta following on his trail.

The bride of Hitler rode past, wig askew, his skirt hiked up to his hips, hefty legs scratched and bleeding. A nun drinking amber beer from a plastic hospital urinal, yelled, "Hey sweet thing." He added a wolf whistle. The cowman mooed and wailed, "Where ya going, doll?" Then he fell off his horse.

The flatbed piled deep with horseless chicken chasers bounced like it was being rocked by an earthquake. As the procession sparkled toward the next stop, music swirled in the air, circling around them like a tornado.

Jake heard the jingle-jangle rider on his grinding, machine-noise horse. A chill ran down Jake's sweating body. And "I know who you are" echoed in his ears as he rode with the crowd. And a chill ran down Jake's sweating body as

Jake was a part, but still apart.

* * *

The next farmstead crouched, trembling, far out in the middle of a field like a family of frightened, brown toads, camouflaged by matching grass. A weathered barn and a few out buildings huddled around the tilted farmhouse. A moat composed of hundreds of egrets encircled the farm. They grazed on acres of brown, brittle grass that had been mowed and crushed into even rows. Breathless, the riders stood poised like steeplechase riders waiting for the starting gun.

The band was silent.

Sweat dripped from flesh and aluminum cans.

The Capitaine's horse pawed the soil, raising a cloud of dust as his master held his flag high over his head, the white cloth slowly waving in the breeze like an egret's wing...Then he whipped the flag down.

Screams and whoops almost drowned the sound of horses' hooves pounding across the earth. Clots of soil and stones flung up by flailing hooves bounced off faces and arms, stinging bare flesh. The ground rumbled with the fury of the charge. A reverse blizzard of a thousand egrets rose into the air, flapping to escape the onslaught of charging horses and wailing riders. A transitory cloud of white feathers blotted out the sun for a tremulous moment. Jake clutched his saddle horn with one hand and struggled to keep his seat. Two riders fell just ahead of him. Jake's horse stumbled over the fallen clowns, but managed to keep its footing and raced with the pack of electric fireflies.

Within moments, the farmyard blossomed with colors and hysteria. Music of accordion, fiddle, and French lyrics continued, non-stop. A few riders discovered a tiny mud puddle and back-flipped through the air, splatting into it from their weary horses. Chickens sailed from the top of the barn. The balloon clown lost his grip on his multi-colored bundle under an oak tree. The colored orbs floated up and lodged in barren branches. A clown danced on his horse, a rooster's head crowing from the opening of his un-zipped pants.

A guinea hen, tossed from the barn roof, landed in the oak tree. In an instant, the tree was filled with squirming satin, sequins, fringe, beads, and feathers. Runners swarmed over the tree like variegated fruit as they clambered after the trembling hen. Dislodged by the climbers' machinations, balloons shook loose from tree branches and rose into the air, one-by-one, sailing off, out of reach of flailing arms and grasping fingers. And the bells on every costume pulsated in a heartbeat rhythm like cicadas. Accordion notes rang in competition with metal chimes that hung from the farmhouse porch. And a group of wild fiddles sang with exquisite madness, like a swarm of giant mosquitoes frantic with blood lust.

Jake danced in the middle of an explosion in a confetti factory. Every color ever created reverberated in slow motion, throbbing as a mass driven by a single heart, echoing the voiceless music of the spheres. A man in a red costume embroidered with the two theater masks knelt before the Capitaine, holding by their legs two shrieking roosters that clutched each other's throats in a death grip. Another hero danced on his horse with a rooster's neck clenched in his mouth. When he tried to rip the rooster's head off with his teeth, the rider lost his footing, toppled over backward and hit the ground, never letting go of his prize. Men danced, arm-in-arm, hugging and kissing. Giggling children threw bags full of confetti from the loft of the barn. The paper bits fluttered to the ground like millions of newborn butterflies. The landowner's wife handed out hard-boiled eggs. Jake slipped his egg out of its shell and popped it into his mouth, whole. Accordion notes rang like delirious wind chimes. And the cicadas woke from their silence and added their ululations to the cacophony. And confetti swirled in the air.

Jake reached out, opened his hand, and swept the air. He clenched his fist and held it against his chest. Then he looked down and opened his hand to see it painted with color. He felt a smile spread across his face and warmth grow in his heart, a warmth that spread throughout his body. He tossed the colors into the air and they fluttered away like newborn butterflies.

Sweat stung his eyes and soaked his armor of golden tattoos. Dizzy, he looked up at the sun. It glowed golden, encircled with a halo fringe of flames. Slowly, it began to spin in place and gathered speed until, gradually, it transformed into a gilded mandala. Across the yard, just below the sun, four middle captains stood motionless on their horses, their purple satin capes undulating in the wind, like the wings of divine butterflies dancing in the sunlight.

And Jake felt it—finally—the knowledge quickening inside him.

He knew that the revelers were no longer clowns. Never were. They were manifestations of the spirits of wizards from the past whose magic was so strong that they could slip through time to dance victory jigs on the backs of the dumb beasts of today, to assert their unchallengeable domain over the future. The wizards danced to be sure visions of the past would pass unconscious knowledge to the present, into the future. Tradition. Wild fiddlers kicked up the speed of their ravings. Jake's will offered his self to the rapture.

Thunder rumbled in the distance.

A red rooster was flung off the barn roof. Jake ran across the yard, never taking his eyes off the bird. He stumbled over bodies and beer cans as he ran, never taking his eyes off the talisman. Pushing through the mob, no longer tired, no longer dizzy, Jake raised his arms to the sky. Wings outstretched to resist the pull of the earth, Jake's pull, the rooster hovered as long as possible, then lost its grip on the air and fell into Jake's hands. Jake felt a frantic heartbeat pulsing through flesh and feathers, the jingle-jangle bells and machine sounds played in his ears—discordant music. He knew who he was—and he knew his name. When the unknown was named, Jake knew he had nothing left to fear. All evil creatures that had ever breathed in the darkness were slain. He was no longer afraid of the carrot-nosed clown.

The thunder rumbled again, calling to Jake.

Slowly, with a vision of four sparkling captains wavering before him, Jake moved toward his horse, the rooster's throat clutched in his fist and the noise of the jingle-jangle rider following him. The sun whirled and spit flames and a waterfall of sparks as Jake climbed onto his hors, then effortlessly stood on the saddle. And with the lightness of the chosen, he danced with the crimson rooster's throat clutched in his left hand. The animated tattoos on his costume rippled over his flesh, dancing with him as he grabbed Rachel's crystal with his right hand. Jake held the prism up to the sky, gathering the sun's rays to himself, and splitting them into a rainbow of sparks that hailed down over the yard. They swirled spasmodically, each quickening independently, then gathered together to form a vision of the jingle-jangle rider.

There he was, dancing on his horse, in front of Jake, a mirror image, mimicking Jake's movements. For the first time, Jake could see with perfect clarity that the horse was not of flesh and hair. It was a chimera formed of the shadows of modern man. Its eyes were rolling dice—its tongue, a lolling one-hundred dollar bill—its penis, a hypodermic syringe—its hindquarters, a politician's face—its body, a one-armed bandit spewing coins—its legs, creaking, grinding, rusted oil derricks—its hooves, circular saw blades—its sweat, blood—its fleas, squirming denizens of hell.

Jake and the Jingle-Jangle rider danced before each other. They moved closer until, beat-by-beat, they became one.

Jake knew he had been chosen, knew his purpose, knew he was to be a revealer.

Jake danced until, little-by-little, beat-by-beat; the chimera horse fell to its knees and crumbled into the earth, screaming in pain. The vision was gone.

Jake dropped himself down to a sitting position on his horse. The carrot-nosed clown stood silently pointing at him, motionless. Then the Green Man rode up to Jake and reached out his hand. When he unfurled his fingers, Jake saw what was offered to him—the keys to Delta's truck. Teeth clenched, Jake released the rooster, whirled his horse around and raced toward Mamou, toward the sound of thunder.

Chapter 52

A PROCESSION OF OVERHEATED METAL and frustrated drivers flooded I-10. Jake followed the flow, east toward New Orleans, heeding only the counsel of thunder rolling across the horizon. The traffic picked up speed just before Henderson. Jake's heart followed suit. His heaving lungs flooded his brain with oxygen, making it drunk with energy. He heard the music of frenzied fiddles, coursing him like a swarm of rabid mosquitoes lusting after the smell of overheated blood. And the lazy eyelid in the sky slid closed, transforming the Hudson River sky scene back to black and white, leaving the sun to cower just above the horizon.

Jake knew he was approaching the Henderson/Cecilia exit when he felt a tingling like insect feet on his flesh. The smell of dank wood and ozone assailed his nostrils, and the sound of screechings and bubblings overpowered the fiddle song as Jake's truck carried him out over the basin. Off to the right, south of I-10, an aurora borealis glow throbbed, whirled—a phosphorescent cyclone of light, connecting the earth and sky like an undulating umbilical cord.

The sun retreated.

Jake continued toward New Orleans, escorted by a vertical cloud of light that thundered along side or just ahead of him, sometimes crossing in front of him to whirl north of I-10. As if bored with Jake's slow pace, the cloud raced far ahead, anxious to arrive at its destination.

With every rumble of thunder, a spiraling stream of scarlet lightning flashed, electrifying the cloud with a red glow, threatening to explode it with energy. Jake remembered the red bulb that hung over the altar of the tiny church he had attended as a child.

Jake no longer followed the flow of traffic; he followed the storm. Like a hound searching for a scent trail, the scarlet lightning whirled inside the cloud, and continued switching sides of the road. And with every flash, the cloud glowed red.

* * *

Once in New Orleans, Jake headed towards the Bete Noir. Like arteries hopelessly corroded with plaque, the streets of New Orleans soon became impassible. Jake found himself mired in a stone-still gridlock, so he parked his truck in the center of an intersection and began to walk.

"Hey!" A police officer yelled. "Get your ass back in that truck and move it."

The police officer stepped in front of Jake to face him down. He froze when he saw his own eyes in the silver shards of Jake's mask. Jake walked around the stunned officer and thrust himself into the crowd that jammed the street. Not a single inch of pavement was visible. Jake was just another cell channeled the by the whim of the crowd, by the living current. Hot, sweaty flesh crushed him from all sides. He strained to suck in oxygen through the stifling heat, and he strained against the bodies pressed against his chest. The current carried him around a corner, faster, tighter, lifting his feet off the ground. Block after block, Jake was swept downstream, unable to touch bottom.

New Orleans had bloomed again. The barren stick trees that lined avenues blossomed with uncountable strings of weird fruit. Beads of every imaginable design hung from each branch. Bead serpents infested wrought iron porches. They twined around throats, arms, and legs, like sparkling constrictors. Naked bodies danced on balconies and reached out for more beads thrown from the ground level. Like lifeguards, parade watchers huddled on homemade, wooden platforms that raised them high above the waves of humanity.

Jake washed past them all.

The thunder rumbled. Jake looked up into the air to search for his hound—his scarlet lasso of lightning. The sky was black. Straining, he managed to free one arm, to raise it to the sky like a drowning man reaching up from a ravenous sea.

However, Jake was not drowning, he reveled in the knowledge that there was no chaos—that all is design. His raised limb was not a gesture of futility; it was a call to arms. His gesture summoned the universe to him, called the stars and light and colors and flesh to gather around him. All answered. And off in the distant sky, Jake caught a glimpse of scarlet.

Twisting in the hurricane of flesh and color, Jake washed downstream, around corners, down confetti-flooded streets, until the river of humanity carried him to the gate that led to the Bete Noir. He grabbed the black iron bars and pulled himself ashore. Struggling against the tide, Jake slid his battered frame behind the gate. As he leaned against it, heaving with exhaustion, Jake heard a trumpeter calling from the crowded street.

The alley was black, as always. Alive, as always. Jake traveled its length, time collapsing into itself, his entire life playing before his eyes in fast forward. When he reached the end, Jake kicked the door; it flew open. Camille whipped his head around to face the black rectangle. Jake stood concealed in the darkness of the cave.

"Jake. Is that you? Of course it is." Camille shifted nervously on his throne. He sat on a platform that raised him above the crowd, surrounded by hundreds of flickering candles and his krewe of sparkling courtiers. Instead of a frenzied party, the Bete Noir was a tableau of royal opulence. The crowd parted, leaving an unobstructed channel flowing from Camille to the door.

"Come closer, my dear. Let me see you. Take off your mask and have a toast with me. It's time to end the masquerade."

Jake remained in the shadow.

Camille squirmed, then leapt to his feet. "What's the matter? Cat got your tongue?" Camille's voice lowered to a growl, "Or was it that shitty little dog?" He ripped off his mask and threw it to the floor.

Jake swallowed hard and searched the room for a sign of Sara. He reached up to his heart and placed his hand over Rachel's crystal. It throbbed with his pulse. He drew his other hand over the embroidered tattoos, his physic armor, to be sure they were still there.

"Ass hole!" Camille screamed into the darkness of the cave. Then he turned and shouted, "Show him the catch!"

The silver lady dragged a struggling form onto the platform. Even though she was surrounded by yards of red lace and satin, masked, Jake knew it was Sara. Securely imprisoned in the arms of the silver lady, Sara stood motionless, gazing straight towards Jake, her eyes begging him to turn and run.

"Jaaaaake," Camille whined, "can you believe they thought they could outsmart...*me*. Actually, they almost did. But, as you can see, I'm in control, as always."

Sara made a move toward Camille. He leapt away from her touch and vibrated with a violent frisson. "Well, Jake. Am I right to assume that you are ready to make your decision? Are you ready to make your choice, ready to choose a side?" Camille tilted his head and waited for Jake's answer. "So, what's it to be? Spirit?" Camille aimed a sneer at Sara. "Or flesh?" Camille placed his fingertips against his chest and winked. "C'mon, Jake. It's time to choose." Camille's voice lowered to a growl, "Let me see you."

"I don't have to choose anything." Jake's voice was hoarse. "You see, some of us...can have it all."

"C'mon, Jake. Quit kidding yourself. Choose me. Choose unlimited passion. Choose flesh. Choose instinct. Choose chaos. Choose me. I have everything you could ever want, every pleasure, every excess, every—"

"No," Jake said. "*I* have everything *you* could ever want. Flesh *and* spirit. Flesh *and* the knowledge. Flesh *and* the spark. The assimilation of opposites."

Camille vibrated. He breathed in uneven gasps. "Show yourself to me. Let me see you."

"No!...See yourself."

Jake moved into the light, his mirror eyes flashing.

Camille gasped.

"Don't come any closer," Camille hissed. "If you come any closer, I'll kill her."

"No you won't," Jake said. You can't. You can't kill spirit. It lives on forever.

Camille's hands formed fists. He pounded them against his hips, repeatedly. He paced, stomping his feet with each step.

Then he stopped and pressed his fists against his temples, his face contorted into a mask of pain.

"Jake. Okay." Camille dropped to his knees. "It's you. It's not me. It's you. Come," Camille moved aside and pointed to the throne. "Take the throne. It's yours. It was yours all the time. Please, forgive me. Let me share your light. Let *us* share your light." He made a grand gesture toward the crowd. "We need you to feel alive. We are nothing without you. Rescue us from this...cave."

Thunder shook the courtyard. A red glow lit the night. Camille looked up at the sky then back down to Jake who had moved one step closer. Camille slid back against the throne.

Jake moved another step closer. Camille shrank back, his eyes fixed on the silver shards that lit the courtyard.

Jake moved closer, again, lifting his arm, offering a hand to Camille.

Thunder crashed. Camille started, but kept his gaze fixed on the sparks emanating from Jake's mirrors. Camille's lips trembled, mouthing silent words.

Jake moved closer.

With a flash of orange hair, Simone dashed from the crowd and leapt on Jake. Jake shoved Simone aside and slammed him to the floor. Simone's orange pate hit the tiles with a cracking sound, then he lay motionless. Camille gasped audibly and raised a hand to his mouth, biting his fingertips as he cowered against his throne.

Jake looked down to see a small knife protruding from his chest, just above his heart. He felt no pain. A narrow stream of blood trickled down over his satin tattoos. Jake pulled the blade from his flesh, then dropped it to the floor.

Camille whimpered.

Thunder rolled again, and the sky flashed red, lighting the courtyard with a crimson glow.

Jake moved toward Camille, his mirror eyes projecting silver beams that pinned the cowering man like the weight of sin. Jake stood in front of the throne and held out his hand, offering it to Camille.

Camille, his gaze still locked onto the mirrored shards, shivered and reached trembling fingers up to Jake and hesitated.

"Jacoby," Jake called to him.

"You know." Camille shivered, then took Jake's hand.

At their touch, the sky unleashed savage thunder. Camille's eyes rolled back in ecstasy, his lids flickering. Then, Jake reached out with his other hand and grasped Sara's fingers.

"I now open the gate," Jake said.

A torrent of rain fell on them.

Camille gasped. His mouth opened wide as he exhaled a scream, a scream loud enough to drown the next crash of thunder. Lightning flashed crimson, turning the whites of Camille's eyes red. He screamed again and again.

The courtyard transformed into a battleground of opposing forces, a Bosch vision of hell.

The silver lady tried to drag Sara off. Sara wrestled away from her, never losing her grip on Jake's hand. Limone leapt to the stage and with one deft movement, cut Nina's throat. The red cloud hovered over the courtyard, and the scarlet lasso flashed and searched.

Camille scrambled to escape, but Jake kept his hand firmly clenched in his fist. Their battle knocked the throne off the platform. It split in two as it crashed to the tiles. And the scarlet spiral of lightning searched.

With a frenzied move, Camille tore his hand from Jake's grip, inadvertently ripping Rachel's crystal from its wire. The prism clattered to the platform and rolled over to Camille. Cat-like, he whisked it up and held it in his trembling fist, point down.

"See what you get, Jake!" Camille screamed. "See what you get for trying to be a hero! See what you get!" Using both hands, he jammed the pointed glass into his own chest. Thunder rolled, end-on-end. The scarlet lasso of lightning whirled, spiraled, then sniffed out its mark. When it made contact with the prism, the sky flashed red, and looking up at the sky, Camille screamed one last time as his essence was sucked up through the scarlet cord. His flesh suit dropped to the floor of the stage.

Letting go of Sara's hand, Jake dropped to his knees to be sure Camille's body was no longer occupied. Then he dropped his mask and took Camille into his arms to embrace his empty shell.

"Where are you now, Jacoby?" Jake whispered.

Rain continued its attack on the courtyard, washing paint from faces, destroying feathered headdresses, flattening starched gowns, spreading a flood of red across the tiles. With each ending, a phosphorescent glow wavered from a stilled body, to rise up and follow the lightning.

And somewhere else in New Orleans, the Krewes of Comus and Rex met and paraded around a ballroom.

And somewhere in Mamou, one by one, the runners removed their masks.

Chapter 53

MUSCLE SPASM TWITCHED Jake's body off balance. He woke when he felt his body fall from the stage and hit the slippery tiles. No candle flames flickered in the courtyard. The night sky reigned over New Orleans. Only the barest hint of moonlight dared enter the sordid courtyard. Like a low range of gently rolling mountains, bodies lay haphazardly strewn across the Bete Noire landscape. Jake pushed himself into a sitting position. Trembling, he whispered, "Sara." He knew she would not answer. He knew she was not there. And he knew where to find her.

Jake stumbled over the obstacle course, toward the wooden door. Strings of beads hobbled his feet and dropped from above to snake around his neck. Twisted, torn fabric, remnants of shredded garments tripped him, slowed his step. Broken glass and carelessly outstretched fingers crunched under his feet. Pushing the door open, only long enough to slip through, Jake left the Bete Noire.

Rain fell in heavy sheets as Jake felt his way along the passage leading to the street. The cool drops plastered his hair, soaked his costume, and began to wash away the crimson stains. When Jake reached the street, the display before him knocked him back a step. The Mardi Gras bacchanal had been transformed into a tableau of the day of reckoning, an apocalyptic vision of post-nuclear holocaust destruction. Dazed Mardi Gras survivors with wild, unseeing eyes wandered aimlessly. Looking like runaways from a Bosch triptych, some only partially clothed, some dressed like clowns, some battered and maimed, they leaned on each other as they rambled through an ocean of broken bottles, aluminum cans, and plastic cups. The sea of debris crackled and crunched under their feet.

Broken glass jangled in their wakes, like earthbound wind chimes. Shop windows not boarded over had been smashed out. Lying on its backs like a dead roach, an overturned police cruiser blocked the road. Living gargoyles leaned motionless against buildings as rainwater spilled from overhead gutters, splashing down on them, rushing in torrents over their heads and shoulders.

A hand gripped Jake's shoulder from behind. He whirled around to face an attacker. When the police officer saw Jake's face, he froze, one hand on the butt of his pistol and the other still clutching Jake. His eyes held fast by Jake's gaze, the officer backed away, his arms raised to display his open palms. Jake dismissed him by turning away.

Jake continued around a corner that led onto Bourbon Street. Like snakes dropping from trees, strings of beads shivered off overhead porches, slithering in Jake's path, circling his ankles with glistening shackles. The pace of the crowd increased as they stumbled down Bourbon Street, all wobbling in the same direction like a school of drunken fish. Laser-like beams of red and blue searchlights whipped the crowd, causing them to bow their heads, to cover their eyes like Adam and Eve cast from the garden in shame.

A voice blared through a bullhorn, "This Mardi Gras is officially over. Please clear the streets." Shielding his eyes from the lights spinning atop a pair of matched police cars, Jake squinted past the hysterical colors to see a wall of thirteen black horses, rain glistening over them like iridescent gems that tumbled into the ocean of debris.

The equine wall moved steadily closer. Steam hissed from dilated nostrils as their breath warmed the cool night air. Instead of wizards from the past, this line of horses carried police officers who hid behind blue costumes, bulletproof vests, and round, white helmets.

Jake backed into a doorway and cloaked himself with night ink. The police line marched past, hooves marking a rhythmic beat, leaving behind a wake of confetti-colored garbage and the words blasted from the bullhorn, "This Mardi Gras is officially over. Please clear the streets."

* * *

In the golden light that fell from the street lamp glowing across from Sara's apartment, Jake could see that the full-length windows leading onto her iron-railed balcony were open. A veil of lace curtains blocked his view of the interior, but he knew Sara stood just on the other side.

Jake crossed the street and passed through the tattered screen door. Slowly, he climbed the stairs to the second floor, to Sara's apartment. As he reached the landing, Jake could see Sara through the wide-open door to her apartment. She stood before the window, looking out into the night. Barely perceptible strains of music from a faraway source managed to make themselves heard beneath the hammering of rain on the roof. Jake moved to stand behind Sara. She leaned back against him.

"I was afraid you might not get here on time," Sara whispered. She turned her head so she could caress Jake with the side of her face.

Jake put his arms around her and brushed her cheek with gentle fingertips.

Sara moaned at his touch and said, "I have to leave now."

"You're not going anywhere. I won't let you," Jake said as he pressed her closer.

"Jake, it has to be this way. It's the only way."

"No! What are you talking about?" He whirled her around to face him. "I've been searching for you all my life. I won't let you go now that I finally found you."

"Jake. It is not me you were searching for. You must know that now. Besides, you have no choice. This flesh is too tired to carry me any longer." She looked down at her outstretched arms, then caressed one with the other.

"It doesn't matter," Jake said. "You can get more the same way you got this. Switch again. Like before. You don't need to be Sara. Not for me. I don't care what you look like." He grabbed her shoulders and shook her gently. "It doesn't matter. Please. Stay. It doesn't matter. Flesh is flesh. It's not the form, it's what's inside that matters. I know that now. Please. Please. Please. Stay. Take another form, any form, but stay. A bum, a crone . . . an alligator man. I don't care. Just stay. I need your soul to nourish me. I need to feel your warmth, to hear a heart beat next to mine. I need to look into any eyes, knowing you're on the other side of them."

"No, Jake. I have gone far beyond that point. My spirit has been purified from sensuality, from the need for flesh. I do not belong here. I have the knowledge, and once you know, really know, you are different and can never go back. You chose this exile—I did not. You chose to take on flesh one more time, for a very important purpose. The universe is counting on you to fulfill that purpose. You cannot fail. Reveal to them the beauty, the good. I yearn only for union with the world soul. Pure spirit cannot exist on this plane of evil. When your task here is complete, we can be together, once again, forever. I will wait there for you. You know that."

"No. It's too long. I cannot survive without you. Life is too long. It hurts too much."

"No." Sara placed one finger over Jake's lips, then whispered. "A lifetime is only one kiss among a trillion stars. You have mastered chaos, learned how to turn it into a creative force. This is your last lifetime. Enjoy it. Flesh is not only a tool, a prison, a temptation—it is a sacred reward. Savor it. Savor every touch, every breath, every vision—Hold me."

"But—"

"Shhhhhh." Sara shivered. "Dance with me one more time. Let me pass through you on my way home."

"No. Please. I cannot go on without you. Sleep with me under the cypress trees, just one more time. Please—"

"Shhhhhh. Jake, there is a bond that transcends any distance no matter how far, a bond that transcends the loss of flesh . . . death. Listen carefully, and no matter where you are, you will hear a heart beating next to yours. In the coldest winter, feel my warmth. In the blackest night, look up into the sky, and see my eyes. I will always be with you. I *am* you."

"No."

"Jake, dance with me one more time. That's all I ask."

Jake grabbed a handful of Sara's hair and held it against his face. Sara kissed the hand that held her hair. They touched faces, lips. They kissed hands, fingertips, foreheads, trembling lips, frantically trying to fit a lifetime of touching into a precious, few moments. From the dark street came strains of distant, twin, Cajun fiddles, weeping with a song of the exquisite pain only parting lovers understand.

Sara shivered, again. "It's time, Jake. Please. Do not keep me here any longer. It hurts too much."

With a groan of despair, Jake held Sara in his arms and led her through the waltz of intermingled fiddles. Jake pressed his eyes closed as tightly as he could, but tears managed to creep out from between the trembling barriers. Together, Jake and Sara whirled around the room with only stars to note their grace, with only rain on the roof for company, with only lace curtains waving in the breeze to mark their passing.

When the fiddles ceased their plaintive cries, Sara's knees buckled and she began to sink to the floor. Jake held her tighter, trying to keep her in a standing position. Sara's form fell limp, but Jake continued to mark the tempo of the nonexistent waltz. He held Sara closer as if to squeeze one more breath from her lungs. As he felt her spirit begin to enter him, electric, like the glimmering of a thousand tiny, silver fish kissing his flesh, Jake stopped dancing. For one, infinitely rapturous moment, they were one as they had been before and would be again. When her presence filtered away, leaving him alone, Jake sank to the floor, letting Sara's form fall with him.

Pressing her face against his chest, Jake howled the howl of the lone locomotive passing in the night..."I love you."

Nobody answered.

* * *

Jake shook Sara's form. He rubbed her arms. Then he reached over to the daybed next to the window. He pulled the blanket off the bed and frantically wrapped it around her, pressing her tightly wrapped body against his.

"Stay warm. Stay with me." Rocking back and forth, Jake howled again, "I love you."

Nobody answered.

* * *

When Jake could feel no more warmth emanating from the flesh Sara had lent to his other half, he carried her to her bedroom. He pulled the bedding back and reverently laid her on the sheets, then covered her with the blankets. After looking into her eyes one more time, he closed them forever. Kneeling next to the bed, he held Sara's hand against his face until the sun began to slip its golden fingers down the streets and alleys of New Orleans.

Chapter 54

Y THE TIME JAKE FOUND HIMSELF back on Bourbon Street, the sun had dried his costume and New Orleans was recovering from Mardi Gras. The sea of debris had been swept away, leaving streets open for business, once again. Horse-drawn carriages carried tourists on leisurely voyages through the French Quarter. Flabby, used car salesmen from Peoria laughed and pointed at Jake as they passed. As they snapped pictures of him, Jake realized he had become just another attraction for jaded tourists to gawk at. He remembered Delta's words, "You're one of us now," and he understood.

The knife wound sent shocks of pain down along Jake's arm, so he crossed the street to rest in the shade. Sitting on a stoop was a black man of about seventy, dressed in a tattered, brown suit. The cuffs of his too-short trousers rode well up over unmatched socks. On his lap rested a gilded accordion, not a Cajun accordion, but the full-sized, *Lady of Spain* type. Hundreds of tiny, gold-backed mirrors encrusted the surface of the instrument.

Gold teeth winked at Jake when the accordion-man spoke. "Ooooooooeeeeee. You sure look like you did some Mardi Gras." He cackled. "You better get yourself to Charity right soon else you gonna bleed out."

"Sure. I'll do that." When he spoke to the man, Jake noticed the fractured cigarette tucked behind the band of his black fedora. It was a Camel. Jake just knew it.

He turned away and watched workmen repairing a broken window across the street. He tapped his foot nervously. Then turned back to the accordion-man. "Hey. Is that a Camel?"

"Huh?" The accordion-man rolled his bloodshot eyes upward. "Oh, yeah. Yeah."

Jake turned away and tried to focus on the progress of the repair team as they labored in the heat. His reflection wavering in a nearby window caught his eye. Over-long greasy hair coiled into ringlets plastered to his head. His face was dirty, his eyes bloodshot and ringed with red. His nose was crooked. "Huh," Jake mumbled to his reflection. He shook his curls free then he smiled at his mirrored image.

"You wouldn't have another, would you?" Jake said to the accordion-man, gesturing toward the Camel.

"Nope. My last one...Could be the last one in New Orleans."

"Is it for sale?"

"Could be."

Jake slipped his hand under his costume and searched the pockets of his jeans until he located a damp, crumpled bill. He fished the bill out and tossed it into the air. The accordion-man caught the bill and flipped a pack of matches back to Jake. Then he handed Jake the distorted cigarette.

"Hey boss," said the accordion man. "Them things can kill you."

"I know. Can't let that happen. I have a big job to do." Jake licked the cigarette and held it straight as if saliva could heal the fracture. Then he said to the accordion man, "They call that spit art."

"Yes, sir. Whatever you say."

Jake lit the Camel and filled his lungs with smoke. Exhaling, he watched the blue cloud leave him and rise into the violet, morning sky as the still-visible moon smiled down on him. He dragged one more pull of smoke into his lungs and marveled, without fear, at the sight of the cloud that left his body and rose to the sky. When the cloud dissipated, he tossed the cigarette to the street and stomped it out.

The accordion man let out a whoop of joy when he unraveled the wadded bill and saw it was a twenty. He shoved it into his pocket and ripped into a lively, staccato tune. His nimble movements shifted the accordion and its mirrors, sending a hail of golden, mock suns swarming over the street.

Jake began to tap his feet in time with the music. He nodded to the accordion man and said, "The universe belongs to the dancer." The accordion man nodded agreement.

Smiling, Jake stepped out into the street and placed himself where the gilt sparks could clamber over him, kissing him like tiny, golden-eyed fish. He bathed in them, a shower of gold. Then he adjusted the beads snaking around his neck and began to dance, the dance of the lone pine, the only tree in the forest of shrubs, the only tree tall enough to catch whispers in the wind. He danced the dance of the lone pine, the dance of creation, twisting and turning in the sunlight, taking nourishment from the golden shards, keeping rhythm only with the beat of his own heart. And Jake's shadow danced alongside him, never missing a step.